THE BLUE DANUBE AFFAIR

THE BLUE DANUBE AFFAIR

C. M. Jonnard

iUniverse, Inc.
New York Lincoln Shanghai

THE BLUE DANUBE AFFAIR

iUniverse, Inc.

For information address:
iUniverse, Inc.
2021 Pine Lake Road, Suite 100
Lincoln, NE 68512
www.iuniverse.com

ISBN: 0-595-30471-0

Printed in the United States of America

To my family and friends,

whose support, patience and understanding

made writing this book possible.

Contents

I
PARIS

1

The Blue Danube Diamond

The FBI special agent showed up at the house overlooking the Caribbean where Janine Gordon, Tom Lyons, Stanley Short and Jake Santana, were holding a vigil around a table on the veranda near the dock where they could watch the baby blue waters of the lagoon and the sea beyond the breakwater through the wind swept palm trees. Birds swept down from the sky to the manicured lawn by the pool nearby to grab the crumbs left over from breakfast.

The young man studied the forlorn faces in front of him and followed their eyes fixed on the horizon way over the breakwater.

He ventured to ask in a timidly low voice.

"Anything turn up?"

A shrill voice from inside called out.

"Tell him to go away. He will bring us bad luck."

"Who's that?"

"Nicole Colbert," replied Janine. "She and her cousin, Christine, live here. You must forgive her.

She's very upset. Max, her boyfriend, is out there, and so is Pierre La Salle, Christine's fiancée."

"I don't blame her," the FBI agent noted sympathetically. "I would feel the same way about someone I loved."

Janine broke down and began to cry.

"I can't believe this could have happened to my father," she moaned. "This is such a nightmare."

The agent nodded.

"I'm sure. It was a terrible accident. The air traffic control people tell me the Lear jet crashed into the sea on its descent to the airport. It might have been pilot error. Was the pilot George Lerman?

Jake Santana and Tom Lyons glanced at each other.

"Yes," answered Jake after a few moments.

"Well, there's an open warrant for his arrest in connection with a killing in New Jersey. But I suppose that may be a moot issue by now. Has the search turned anything up?"

Tom Lyons sighed.

"The plane is out there, but no bodies were found yet, if that's what you mean."

"That's odd, don't you think? Bodies must be out there."

"Max Gordon's tape recorder was recovered yesterday," Jake Santana volunteered, and he pulled a small black box out of his pocket and placed it on the table.

"It was in a watertight container. We listened to it last night," said Stan Short.

"A tape recorder. Is that's all? How about diamonds, the Blue Danube diamond, specifically? Did they find anything like that? We received a report that contraband diamonds might have been on board?"

Stan smiled and patted the recorder on the table.

"That's where this comes in. Not that we know. But if you want to learn about the Blue Danube and about diamonds in general, you need to listen to Max Gordon's story. He must have recorded it between here and Paris. It's quite interesting, a little confusing at first because he starts near the end. But it's fascinating all the same. In fact, it's almost autobiographical. Perhaps, you'd like to listen to the tape. I had the battery charged."

The FBI agent shrugged his shoulders.

"I might as well," he muttered. "Nothing else is going on here."

*   *   *

This has the makings of a bad news flight. Our flight from Paris to Brussels on the chartered Lear with George at the controls was uneventful enough. Pierre La Salle wanted to make a pit stop there to retrieve the conflict diamonds. That part was uneventful. But engine trouble developed soon after and we had to make an unscheduled landing in the Canaries. That held us up a week. Now up in the sky again and bound for the West Indies, George Lerman is experiencing more problems and I'm now having doubts about our getting through this experience alive.

Fortunately, I found this pocket recorder on board, and this affords me an opportunity to at least leave an oral report of what has been to date a strange but wonderful adventure in the event we never reach our final destination alive. My memory is hazy at times, and so I start near the end of my story, which for me was in prison, instead of at the beginning. My hope is that as I speak, I will begin to remember the events in the sequence in which they occurred.

And so, my story begins with a loud bang and a voice.

"Welcome to prison, Max. Enjoy your final days."

The blindfold was removed but there was nothing to see.

"Raise your arms, Max."

I complied.

"Higher, Max!"

Rough hands grabbed my armpits and tossed me like a sack of potatoes to the ground. Sight returned briefly and I found myself face down on the cold slimy surface of a stone floor. A door slammed shut and the jarring rattle of a bolt seared my mind. A headache brought water to my eyes and I cradled my head in my arms.

The pain was unremitting and my upper arm stung from the needle shot. It was over, I decided. I sighed, smiled, closed my eyes and consigned my soul to its unknown destiny. Somewhere, from far away, I heard the faint sound of what could have been a compressor or respirator, or so I thought. The prison was old. The sound undoubtedly came from the trembling bellows of a pump pushing air through ancient ventilator ducts. Blackness returned, but through it I could hear Pierre La Salle's voice, and that of his very long time assistant, Simon Perez, agreeing in the background.

"You know, Max," the Interpol director was saying. "There is nothing here for us. We should really consider relocating to the islands. I hear the climate is wonderful, the women are glorious and the cuisine is superb."

"Yes," echoed the voice of Simon Perez. "We should all retire to the islands and leave the cold forever."

What a crazy idea it was. Or was it…?

I have a theory about life and death. Everyone in the twilight between life and death, has a dream to soften the journey to eternity. If one wakes up, all is well. If not, then that's that. Brian Donovan put it this way.

"Don't fall asleep," the bartender at Colin Adair's Bernardsville Club hotel said. "And don't dream. Just keep drinking."

Poor Brian. He was dead. I wonder if he had a dream before packing it in.

Mike Surrey, who was with us that day, had raised his glass.

"I'll drink to that," he said.

Poor Mike. He too was dead.

But how about me? Was I dead or was it merely the next day?

"Monsieur Max Gordon?"

Three hard knocks at the cell door.

I was lying face up on a stone platform that extended from the wall and served as a bed. My body was stiff and numb and I could barely budge. More knocks. The voice was insistent.

"Max Gordon. You have a visitor."

I heard the door creak. It opened just wide enough to admit someone who who looked like a priest. Can you believe it? A priest coming to see me?

The door slammed shut behind him and I was too tired to ask him to leave.

Anyway, It was early in the morning and I should have been happy to have someone visit me so early in the morning. I could tell it was early from an amber ray that burst through the bars of a small window near the ceiling and brightened a spot on the floor.

I wrenched myself up into a sitting position with my legs and feet dangling over the edge of the platform and rubbed my eyes. I was awake.

My sore head and aching body were real. The priest clutching a bible and standing nervously in front of me was real. The cell was real. I was not dead. I was alive, thank goodness. I was alive. Alive!

It was good to be alive, and I began thinking of the story I was going to tell my friends when I got back. "Where am I?"

"La Petite Conciergerie," the priest replied in French. "Have you lost your bearings? This is Paris."

Memory returned.

Ah, yes. La Conciergerie. It was a prison for the condemned on a small island in the middle of the Seine during the French Revolution. It shared the island with the Notre Dame cathedral. La Petite Conciergerie was the annex in the rear of the justice ministry on the right bank of the Seine and was used for the prisoner overflow from the main prison who awaited their turns at the guillotine.

The ministry itself occupied a vast complex of three story Mansard style buildings between a large plaza named Place Vendome and Rue Cambon, a dark, narrow street. Was this where I was being held?

Access to the justice ministry from the plaza, at the center of which stood an imposing column commemorating one of Napoleon Bonaparte's victories, was through gilded iron gates that led to a courtyard surrounded by offices with breezy floor to ceiling windows. A heavy wooden gate between a low row of buildings at the courtyard's far end lead to still another compound enclosed by a stone wall that served as a fortification of sorts. The prison cells were inside the walls and those on the Rue Cambon were windowless and dark. Those fronting on the compound had tiny window slits that afforded a view of a stone hut standing near a serious looking guillotine silhouetted against the sky. I was lucky. My cell faced the guillotine and had light.

I wasn't sure but I think I was the prison's only occupant. The story I heard was that it was to have been turned into a museum but the idea was squelched for budgetary reasons, and of course its existence was never noted in tourist guide books.

Despite the light and a worm's eye view of the gray cobblestone compound and the guillotine, my cell still trapped the cold, the dampness and the smell of centuries of human waste and despair left by the condemned who counted their final hours before being carted away for torture and execution. Now as then there was little else to do but to watch the cockroaches and rats slither across the floor by day and wonder what strange creatures crawled about at night.

In all respects, The elegance of the justice ministry and its environs totally eclipsed the very existence of the grim prison. The ministry's facade meshed seamlessly with the post Renaissance architecture around the Place Vendome that embraced chic hotels like the Ritz and fancy boutiques like Cartier.

Something was wrong. Clearly, Jouvet wanted to have me killed. Then why would he have allowed a priest to visit me, thereby creating a witness to an otherwise anonymous murder?

It was best to go along with the pretense.

The priest was young, about the same age as Janine, my daughter. He was sandy haired and fair faced. I guess that's how all clergy started out, young and innocent. How old and worn I must have seemed to him by comparison. How dirty and unshaven. Could he smell my foul breath? I could.

And I didn't catch the name. Perhaps it was indifference or maybe it was a combination of anger, regret, aggravation and ultimate resignation.

The voice seemed timid but it brought me back to my senses.

"Max Gordon?"

"Yes?"

The priest hesitated briefly before sitting down next to me. He sat there, at a loss for words, leaving it to me to start the conversation.

I obliged.

"What brings you here, Father, at this ungodly hour?"

"My mission is to comfort the sick, the dying and the condemned."

His English was halting. He could have spoken to me in French, but he was probably unaware I was bi-lingual.

I tried to put him at ease.

"You do your stuff," I urged in French to ease his chore. "I have no idea what it is, but I have time, until dawn tomorrow, I was told."

This was indeed a strange script.

"You seem to take your fate in stride," the priest observed. "Are you not nervous, a bit apprehensive, perhaps?"

I laughed.

"It's not the shortness of life but its uncertainty that torments. But since my fate is set, I'm relaxed if not comfortable."

"Have you given thought to escaping from here?"

"Naturally."

"And if you escaped, what would you do?"

"I would get married and go back home."

"To whom and go home to where?"

"A woman I met here in Paris. And home is in New Jersey."

"And if she refuses?"

"I would cope and recover. But about your question about escaping, It is worth trying. Outside the door on the floor is a rusty grating over a hole that drops into subterranean passages leading to sewers and tunnels where one can travel across Paris, even under the Seine, without coming up for air."

"They should be tourist attractions."

"Some are. But below us the only tourists are rats and roaches who visit and share my food."

"You seem to know a lot about this city."

I nodded.

"I was born in this country. I should tell you a story, Father."

The young man smiled, leaned against the wall, looked at his watch and folded his arms.

"We have time," he noted. "What kind of story do you wish to tell?"

"It's a story about the Blue Danube, Father. Have you ever been on the Blue Danube?"

"The river? No, I haven't."

"Well, it runs a long zig zag course from Central Europe to the Black Sea. This story is also about zigs and zags."

"Like life?"

"Like life."

The priest smiled faintly.

"Life is a stream that grows into a river," he said. "It flows until it reaches a sea beyond the setting sun and we are tiny organisms in this essence of life that runs forever. Sometimes we make it to the sea and sometimes we are stopped along the way."

"Did you learn that at a seminary?"

The priest shook his head.

"No," he replied. "I visited the National Gallery of Art in your capital once. Four paintings by the American artist, Thomas Cole caught my eye. Each one depicts a stage in the life of a man. The first is an infant adrift in a small boat floating down a stream from a cavern into the sunlight. The second is a youth guiding his vessel under a midday sun, unaware of the pitfalls lying ahead. In the third, the youth is now a mature man struggling to keep his boat afloat in stormy waters of life in the late afternoon. In the fourth and final frame, we see an old man, his boat battered but afloat, finally reach the sea. Where are you in this river of life?"

I could not think of an answer.

"I don't know," I said finally. "I need my own panel between the third and fourth frames."

The priest laughed lightly.

"No. There are only four frames. But let's get back to your story about the Blue Danube. I assume you mean the river."

"No," I answered. "I'm talking about a diamond called the Blue Danube."

The Blue Danube was a large diamond, a legendary diamond, I explained. It was over 140 carats of blue brilliance. It had a perfect cut and was thus extremely rare. Its unique history surrounded it with an air of mystery.

"Like Paris?"

"Yes. Like Paris."

I had a soft spot for the city. It sparkled. It was a city that changed with the mood of the seasons. Its brilliance radiated life and warmed the soul. It was occupied many times but never conquered.

"A more perfect diamond could not be cut by human hands," a friend of mine once observed. The friend, or former friend I should say, was Otto Katz, a diamond cutter and appraiser.

I was biased, of course. But Paris was not home. Home was a small town in Morris County, New Jersey, suburban, stable and predictable. Paris was the mistress, tempting and dangerous.

I always thought a society's personality was revealed by the layout of its city streets. For example, New York's streets were laid out in columns and rows in an easy-to-remember sequence of numbers and names. One could be blind and never get lost in New York. It had a logical, practical layout.

Paris streets were more eclectic. Its avenues, boulevards, and streets were shorter and names along the same thoroughfare tended to change every few blocks. For example, a north-south avenue ran from the Opera Garnier to the Rue de Rivoli and Tuileries Gardens near the Louvre. It started as the Rue de la Paix at the opera and ran two blocks to Place Vendome where, at the Rue Saint Honore, it became Avenue De Castiglione for two more blocks until it ended at the Rue de Rivoli.

It was easy to walk one small block away from the main avenues and get lost in a maze of narrow winding streets and alleys that curved, twisted and turned and frequently lead to dead ends.

It was ironic that I should be trapped in such a tony neighborhood. The justice ministry shared the street with the Ritz hotel on Vendome's west quadrant. All around the square were five star hotels, high profile business offices and private residences, pricey restaurants, boutiques and many of the world's premier jewelers. Did anyone besides the priest know I was here?

Cartier was perhaps one hundred yards away, although another Cartier store graced the Rue De La Paix near the Westphalia hotel a block north and a short stroll from the Garnier Opera. There were probably more Cartier stores in Paris than there were discount stores back home. Opposite the justice ministry on Vendome, like bastions of wealth, stood Mauboussin, Boucherons, Harry Winston, Bulgari, Chaumet, Georg Jensen, Buccelatti, Van Cleef & Arpels, Maison Dore, and Kumari, who shared its street floor with Maison Dore whose main office was on the Rue de la Paix directly across from the Westphalia. Space not occupied by boutiques, restaurants and hotels was taken up by investment banks, their blinds drawn to protect the privacy of clients.

The structures all around facing Vendome, like the Palace of Justice, as the justice ministry was formally known, had eighty foot high identical facades making it difficult to distinguish the Ritz and the Justice ministry from each other and from all the other structures. To the purist, Place Vendome was a study of extreme architectural splendor in the style of "La Grande Epoch" as some people called it. Buildings rose no higher than three or four stories with floor to ceiling curtained windows to allow for maximum light and air flow. It was all very exquisitely beautiful and very expensively elegant.

I had a friend, Otto Katz, who worked for Kumari. He was the one who took me under his wing years ago and taught me about diamonds. He said he was a Dutchman, although some people thought he was German. A big bear of a man with a Santa Claus beard and twinkling eyes, he favored olive drab corduroy suits over shirts with open collars and no ties. He started out as a diamond cutter, became a Kumari appraiser and eventually joined Rajeesh Kumari's management team. He had a different take on Paris.

"Paris is a black widow spider in a white bridal gown. You will fall in love with her and in the end she will kill you."

Rajeesh Kumari was a self made entrepreneur from India who had jewelry stores in the world's major cities. Short with dark sparkling eyes behind a set of old fashioned horned rimmed glasses, his face was a happy reflection of success. His personal goal was to find the Blue Danube's twin or obtain the Blue Danube itself. He liked to be called 'Raj.'

"Get me the Blue Danube, Max," he once said, the grin never leaving his face. "I will make you rich beyond your dreams."

Would I ever see Vendome and the bright lights of Paris again? In theory, if I could break out of the cell, and if the grating outside was not bolted shut, I could eventually make my way through tunnels like a rat to Napoleon's column in Vendome and then to the street through a service door. What a fantasy. It was nice to dream.

I looked at the priest. A glow from the cell window washed away the amber light of dawn to usher the start of another beautiful summer day. I heard the opening strains of the Marseillaise in the distance and figured that a band was preparing for the Bastille Day parade tomorrow.

The priest's face was oddly familiar, and I had to ask.

"Have we met before?"

"No," he replied

"Well, if you don't mind my saying, Father, you look too young to be a priest, especially one to be given this gruesome duty."

"There was no choice. This is a holiday week; all the priests are away with their families. I am a stand in for someone else. As you may have heard, we have a growing scarcity of clergy in France."

"We have the same problem in the States," I added. "But you know, what I really need is a rabbi. After all, I'm not Catholic."

The priest nodded.

"Are you being treated well?"

"No complaints. French food is good, and for the condemned it is superb. And I do get my choice of wine and champagne. And I can look outside. I can jump up and grab the window bars, lift myself up and see what's going on. Yesterday, I watched a guillotine being wheeled out and tested. Do you think it's the same one used during the French Revolution?"

"I do not know."

I tried to draw the priest out.

"Do you know Jouvet, the deputy minister?"

He shook his head.

"I was allowed in by the building security chief."

"Well, Jouvet said France has no death penalty in France. Is that so?"

"Yes. The death penalty has been abolished. Yours may be a special case."

"I suppose I should feel honored, Father. What do you think?"

"Death is a rite of passage," said the priest. "It is rarely an honor."

"I agree. But getting back to the streets of Paris...are you a Parisian?"

"No. I am from the south. I dislike big cities. I prefer the country."

"That's too bad. Paris is a special city. I'm an American citizen now, with dual citizenship. I can be executed in either country. But I can tell you a lot of trivia about this town. To me, Paris isn't the Eiffel Tower. The real Paris, its soul, its history and its secrets, lies in the darkness of its bowels under our feet, in the sewers, caves, tunnels and the old passageways that snake their way under the city's streets."

I happened to notice the priest's hands.

"A diamond pinky ring," I pointed. He turned it inward.

"I don't mind, and I won't tell," I said. "May I see it?"

He held out his hand.

"It's a beautiful round stone," I observed. "About one carat?"

"Yes. One carat. 'IF' quality with 'D' color, I was told. My mother gave it to me years ago. She said it was a perfect stone."

"Well, it looks perfect to me," I nodded . "If you ever have it tested and it bears out what you were told, the gem would have a 'dump' wholesale value of almost ten thousand dollars. In a ring, the wholesale price doubles and the retail would be from forty to fifty thousand dollars. The ring looks familiar, but don't mind me; my mind and eyes have not been sharp these days."

"Do you travel to Paris often?"

"Yes, quite often. I stay at The Westphalia, on the corner of Rue De La Paix and Rue Daunou, a short walk from here."

"Why do you stay at the Westphalia? It is expensive."

"Yes. It's expensive; it's an eighteenth century converted mansion, and its location is ideal. Cartier is one of my clients. The windows in Suite 209 that I occupy face Rue De La Paix and Maison Dore, another international jeweler and one of my clients. My clients are within walking distance. And Pierre La Salle of Interpol has an office at the justice ministry. I work with him chasing down stolen and smuggled diamonds. There are other fine hotels where one can stay. The Meurice, the Lotti and the Intercontinental. They are on the Rue De Castiglione, a stone's throw from here. But I like the Westphalia. I could stay elsewhere, but in my business, if you want to run with the best, you must stay with the best."

"What do you do for a living?"

"I'm an investigator for Sentinel Insurance in Florida. Much of my work is here. I get 10% of the insured value of all recovered gems."

The priest shook his head.

"Those you deal with cannot be real people."

"I wouldn't say that. They are real people. They just have more to spend and lose. They also lie and steal more, some even kill, and they all specialize in deception. My current trouble stems from a conspiracy surrounding the Blue Danube."

"Who owns the Blue Danube?"

"That's a good question, Father. It was part of the Adair family estate in New Jersey and kept in Dore's Morristown vault where it was insured by Sentinel."

"Who are the Adairs?"

"Who were they is more appropriate. They were multi-millionaires. The present generation consisted of twins, Colin, Henry and their sister Colleen by adoption who I married and through whom I had Janine.

"Mel Solomon, Sentinel's CEO, was an Adair family friend. In fact, we all grew up together."

Mel was a nice guy in his own way. In school, he was the schlemiel who couldn't get a date. Mel's closest friend was Sol Weinberg, the short, pudgy CEO of Centurion, Sentinel's competitor. Both Mel and Sol smoked big, fat cigars. It was a cozy arrangement. Sentinel owned half of Centurion who owned half of Sentinel. Sentinel held the policies on the Blue Danube and owned stock in the Adair family businesses and was one of its major bond holders. Centurion had the Dore and Kumari insurance accounts.

If Mel was the schlemiel, Sol was the schmegegi. They couldn't find girls for the prom and ended up going together, like Tweedledee and Tweedledum.

Except that Tweedledee was twice the size of Tweedledum.

Come to think of it. I couldn't get a date either. So I stayed home.

Sol finally married a model and Mel married a hooker. They had no kids and both divorced early. The two insurers wanted to merge their enterprises but never got around to it. Sol was personally loyal to Mel, he always stoutly insisted, and would not make any moves unless Mel gave the green light.

There was more. Sentinel was a financially troubled company. Its business and those of the Adair family were failing and had to be leveraged by debts backed by the diamond. The family was hemorrhaging cash. The funny thing was that when disaster loomed, money, usually cash, would come turn up to save the day and discharge current obligations. Often, it was Sol Weinberg's Centurion that came up with the rescue packages.

Through my work for Sentinel and my marriage to Colleen, I became the Blue Danube's watch dog at Maison Dore's branch in Morristown that was managed by Joe Kelly, one of Mike Surrey's buddies and one of my good friends. It was a do-little job that paid well and satisfied my ego and was a risk-free way of being a rich big shot.

The twins controlled the Adair holdings. Henry was childless but Colin had married Eva Barton, the daughter of German immigrants, and they had a boy and a girl, now grown. Colin and Henry Adair hated my wife because a third of the Blue Danube belonged to her and naturally Eva was not enamored of her either. They must have hated me even more because I was an interloper who dug his way to the family fortune by marriage. Family gatherings were strained at best and Colleen and I were usually ignored.

"But exactly what did you do to end up here?" The priest asked.

What did I do? It began about a year and half ago. I should have been in New Jersey for the diamond's annual inspection, but at the last minute Mel Solomon sent me to do some work for Interpol and had Otto Katz stand in for me to witness Carl Haussmann, Louis Dore's partner, re-authenticate the

Blue Danube. Once I was in Paris, Pierre La Salle shipped me off to Brussels to examine suspected conflict diamonds from Africa to raise cash for a civil war raging somewhere on the continent.

2

The Hospital

Carl Haussmann looked scrawny, pale and insignificant and barely moved on the hospital gurney. One of the best diamond cutters and appraisers in the business, his word could make or break the value of any gem stone on the market. He was the consummate expert, armed with a steady hand, a knowing eye, a quick wit and a sharp tongue. But now he seemed helpless and scared.

He never minced words and was no time waster. So when he called me in Brussels from the airport in Newark and asked me to meet him in Paris, I knew there was a problem. Fortunately, my work on the conflict diamonds was completed and I was due back in Paris to be debriefed by La Salle. So, the proposed meeting with Carl was timely.

But poor Carl suffered an in-flight heart attack and had to be hospitalized upon his arrival in Paris. My last conversation with him was at the hospital, where he lay on that stretcher in a long narrow hall with yellow walls and vinyl tile floors, waiting to be wheeled into the operating room. His partner, Louis Dore, nervous and frightened, was at his side.

I never cared for hospitals. They are torture chambers at one end and death chambers at the other end. Patients are held prisoner to beds by tubes inserted into their bodies. They stare through empty eyes as they are stripped of all command and dignity by faceless handlers as the world looks on with morbid curiosity. I'd swear that hospitals are designed by the Devil's architect and decorated by his demons.

My uncle who raised me had a fatal heart attack and had to be hospitalized, just like Carl. I remember visiting him the day he died. He seemed to know he was finished.

"The end is near," he said, "when demons from your past come dancing at your feet."

I wondered if Carl knew he was dying. His body was barely concealed by an ill fitting hospital frock and his chalk colored arm trembled as his hand reached out and grabbed the sleeve of my blazer jacket. A tingling chill from his touch radiated throughout my body.

"The Blue Danube," he gasped, looking anxiously at his partner. "I cannot talk here."

Louis Dore started to perspire. Poor Louis Dore. He was always shifty-eyed and suspicious of everyone. He must have been born with a guilty conscience.

I think he owned only one suit, a blue one. I never saw him in any other color suit. He wore it now, that plain blue suit over a plain white shirt and a plain red tie. All in all, he was about as interesting as a rain cloud, but he too knew the jewelry business and had, over the years, turned Maison Dore from a humdrum single store into an international chain.

Louis adjusted the tie under his jacket, pulled a handkerchief from the rear left pocket of his trousers and wiped the sweat off his brow. His small beady eyes followed my every move behind thick, steel rimmed glasses.

"What does Carl mean?" he asked.

It was best to ignore the question. This was not exactly where I wanted to be and my stomach was upset.

"I don't know," I replied simply.

Carl was booked on a one-way ticket. I wished him all the best and tried to avoid his eyes. A nurse finally came over, gently pried his hand loose from my jacket and lowered it back to his side on the outside of the sheet that covered the rest of his body.

Carl tried to smile through labored breathing.

"I am sorry, old friend. We will talk at a better time."

"Not a problem," I said. "Your health is more important. The Blue Danube can wait."

Carl began gasping for breath.

"Ah yes, the Blue Danube. A fantastic jewel with a fascinating history."

"What happened? What is he saying? What does he mean?"

Louis Dore leaned over his partner as if he expected to learn something of importance.

Carl smiled feebly but secretively.

"There is nothing. Nothing. Everything is as it should be. The diamond is safe. I appraised it. Mel Solomon and Otto Katz were there to witness the process."

From the year I married Colleen, Carl Haussmann performed the annual January ritual of inspecting the Blue Danube with me as his witness at Dore's spacious Morristown store. He looked it over and appraised while I recorded the ritual for Sentinel and the Adairs. Otto began showing up more often in recent years, leading me to believe that Kumari and Centurion had acquired a vested interest in the diamond. This was the first time I missed the occasion but I was comfortable with Otto being there. He was almost as sharp as Carl and not very easily fooled.

In a way, I was glad to be away on serious business instead of being stuck with busy work for the Adairs and Sentinel under the dubious claim of being a diamond expert. It was no secret that were it not for the fact that I married Colleen, I would have had to have found another line of work, maybe in sales or real estate. For me, marriage into the Adair family was an opportunity sent from heaven and I resolved to make the most of it.

Carl was suddenly seized with a coughing fit.

"My God," he cried. "Where is my life? I am dying!"

The pained expression on his face has haunted me to this day. He wanted so desperately to live. I would have done anything and everything at that instant to keep him alive. But all of the world's treasure and all of the world's genius could not turn back destiny's clock. I just knew his time was winding down. .

He lay there hopelessly and I looked on helplessly.

Louis and I exchanged glances. Carl's fate was in someone else's hands. He grabbed my arm again, but this time I felt no chill, just a heavy sadness. And then his arm let go. There was nothing more to do or say except to watch two attendants roll the stretcher through the operating room's swinging doors at the end of the corridor.

The doors swung open and the stretcher disappeared in a black void on the other side. Somewhere off in the distance I heard the sound of a compressor or generator followed by a door slam, followed by silence.

Things like that bothered me. The squeal of chalk on blackboard. A high pitch whistle or an untuned microphone. I never realized until now how much the sound of a door slamming unnerved me. But it did. A slamming door had a note of finality about it. The sharpness of its sound, like a clap of thunder, gave me a start.

I blinked hard this time and winced from a brief sharp pain on the upper left side of my chest that radiated quickly to my upper arm. The pain disappeared as quickly as it appeared. I hoped Louis did not notice.

He too must have heard the door because he looked at me.

"It must be the surgeon going in through a side door," he said.

We walked slowly down the corridor and sat down on a bench near the operating room to wait. Our voices echoed strangely in the hallway.

"What brings you to Paris?" Louis asked.

"Pierre La Salle wants to see me about my trip to Brussels and Carl called and asked me to meet him in Paris. He probably wanted to brief me on the Blue Danube's inspection."

"Undoubtedly. What's happening in Belgium?"

"You probably know more than I do. Interpol agents intercepted a cache of diamonds from Angola and Sierra Leone consigned to Kumari for you. But don't worry, Maison Dore is clean so far. La Salle wanted me to inspect the shipment but Henry Adair arrived ahead of me with paper work to show that the lot was legitimate. It was released to him yesterday. How is he involved with you and Kumari?"

"Henry is one of our commission agents. He buys and sells for us and for Kumari. He also owns stock in our company."

"Does Maison Dore still buy from Kumari?"

Louis Dore shook his head.

"We used to but that relationship is over. Diamonds from central Africa are usually stolen by terrorists to finance local wars. That's why they are so competitive. The Africans need turnover. So, we try not to get tangled up in contraband. This was a one-shot deal."

"Oh? Incidentally, I ran into Larry O'Leary . What's he doing in Europe? He should be running Colin's hotel back in New Jersey."

If Louis thought he was being baited, he didn't bite. He looked away.

"Right now, we are dealing in South African stones," he declared.

"Does Maison Dore still offer its global guarantee to clients?"

"Yes. There has been no change in policy. A client can, for example, buy a piece of jewelry at our Paris store for, say, a million Euros. The client has the right to return the piece within one year of the invoice date to any one of our stores in the world for a full refund in local currency. If it is returned to our New York or New Jersey store, the client would receive the equivalent of a million Euros in U.S. dollars at the current exchange rate. It is a very good deal for our clients and for us. We move inventory globally and legally duty free with buyers doing the smuggling if they do not pay the import tariffs."

A faint smile was on his lips.

"We do well. Most of our clients are corporate, as you can imagine. Even if they pay the import taxes, they are ahead. That is why we have stores in all countries."

Then he abruptly changed the subject.

"Are you staying at the Westphalia?"

"Yes."

Louis tried to lighten the air with small talk.

"You have been at Sentinel many years I think?"

"Yes. And I think I'll stick around. You guys will have to tolerate me a while longer. Has Henry returned from Belgium?"

"Your brother-in-law was supposed to meet Carl at the airport yesterday when the plane landed, but he never showed. Air France called me, but I was out of town. A friend of Colin who was traveling with Carl stayed with him up to the moment an ambulance arrived to take him to the hospital."

"What about Carl's belongings?"

"I heard the friend cleared them through customs and had them sent to our offices. Your Interpol friend, La Salle, showed up with several of Jouvet's special police from the justice ministry and took everything else."

"Does Colin's friend have a name?"

Louis Dore shrugged his shoulders.

"There was no time to make inquiries. The name I was given was one John Cork."

"Johnny Cork? I know Cork. We served in the same army unit. He's not in the jewelry business! He drinks for a living."

"I know of him," replied Louis. "I too thought it strange."

"Where's Henry now?"

"Oh, he should be on his way to the Bahamas to meet Colin. He will return in a few days. When are you leaving?"

"Soon. How's Henry's health these days?"

Louis took a deep breath.

"Much improved. Those treatments he is receiving in the Bahamas must be working. He has gained weight and is the spitting image of his twin. I think he is cured because Colin has been talking about retiring and selling him his interest in all the family enterprises and in the Blue Danube as well."

This was not news. Rumors of Colin's wishes to retire were at least one or two years old. The lingering question in my mind was why Colin would want his share of the Adair estate to pass to his cancer stricken brother unless, as Louis indicated, Henry was cured. A related question mark was Eva. I'm sure she was not exactly thrilled at the prospects of her husband disposing of all his assets unless she was guaranteed a security blanket. I had dated her before she married Colin and I knew her to be the original gold digger.

I frankly never cared what Colin and Henry did or agreed to. They were not my favorite people. But I was concerned about the future of the Adair family estate, for Colleen's sake while she was alive, and now for Janine's sake.

To be fair, Colin and Henry despised me as much as I disliked them. But worse, they hated Colleen, their adopted sister who was the offspring of a union between their philandering father and a cocktail waitress. They had tried their best before we were married to have the adoption set aside and to have her disinherited on the claim that their father was mentally unbalanced and had been deceived by the waitress into believing that the infant was his. The attempt failed.

Colin, more than Henry, became extremely agitated when Janine was born. He was married to Eva by then and had two children. In his view, Janine took over the heiress slot vacated by Colleen upon her death. The relationship worsened when Janine married early and had two of her own children and Colin's kids, although adults by then, were not even close to marriage. Add to the mix a measure of financial angst and it was easy to see the stress lines.

Colin and Henry, as twins, made for an odd couple. Colin lived in New Jersey and tended to the family enterprises and Henry lived alone in Paris and rarely visited the States after Janine was born. About two or three years prior to my Antwerp trip, Henry started traveling to the Bahamas for cancer treatments where he would meet up with Colin several times a year.

Carl and Louis were also strange bedfellows. They were old bachelors who were consumed by their French ancestry. Carl claimed he was a descendent of Georges Eugene Haussmann, the same Baron Haussmann who designed the broad avenues of Paris in the late nineteenth century. He was never able to make good on that claim, and that bothered him although it never blocked his success.

It was a lucky break for Louis Dore when he landed Carl as an employee and eventual partner. Before then, Maison Dore was a small, single store on a Paris side street despite the fact that Louis insisted that he was related to Paul

Gustave Dore, a painter, illustrator and sculptor who was a contemporary of Baron Haussmann.

Although Gustave Dore lived and worked n Baron Haussmann's Paris, I didn't think they ever met and I didn't think that Carl and Louis were related to them in any way.

It was nevertheless the union of Haussmann and Dore that gave the firm its stature and enabled it to move to the trendy Rue De La Paix. In Paris alone, Maison Dore had outlets on Vendome, on Castiglione and on the Rue Du Faubourg Saint Honore near the Elysee Palace. Their showrooms attracted money like flies were drawn to light.

Maison Dore's fame was guaranteed when Colin Adair made the firm its official jeweler and Blue Danube keeper and Sentinel its insurer. It was good for them and good for me. However, Sentinel underwriters would not write a covering policy for the diamond unless the Adairs agreed to lodge it outside the family home.

A compromise was reached. Maison Dore bought an old crumbly building on South Street in Morristown from Mike Surrey whose family had owned it forever. Mike was a good friend of mine. He was a master electrician turned head waiter at Colin's Bernardsville Club hotel turned full time alcoholic and therefore retired. It was a good deal for all parties concerned. Mike needed the money and the building was in a prime location for a fancy jewelry store and fairly close to the Adair residence in Bernardsville. The store had a heavy steel vault in back where the diamond was laid to rest.

Size was not the Blue Danube's claim to fame as I told Janine a few days before leaving for Belgium.

"The Blue Danube is not great," I told her. "It is spectacular! It's dazzling, blinding perfection, with the accent on perfect! One hundred thirty nine and one-half carats of sparkling blue sapphire shaped brilliance and unabashed perfection. Its frozen heat radiates beauty, desire and power. Great wealth has flowed from it like a river from the day the Adair family acquired it over a century ago. It has transformed a small time enterprise into an empire."

I wanted to tell her more, but women change subjects without warning and Janine was no different. She was in a nagging mood that day. All she wanted to do was to harp upon my eating habits, saying that I should stop eating so much so fast and start exercising.

She had a point. Not that I was an Adonis but I was clearly overweight.

My stomach knotted up as I waited with Louis. As I said, hospitals scared me. This one reminded me I was overdue for a checkup. Janine was right. I was not living right. I tried not to think of my own malaise and asked Louis about a strange name I came across on the shipping documents covering the conflict diamonds in Brussels.

"Emile Barco. Does the name strike a bell?" I asked.

Louis looked down the corridor.

"Emile is Henry's friend. A kind of silent partner. He lives in Basse Terre south of here. He maintains a low profile and keeps himself scarce. I rarely see him."

"That's a coincidence," I said. "My mother lived there before she died. I was wondering, Louis. Did Henry ever become a French citizen?"

"Yes. When he joined our firm and married Nicole Colbert."

This was a sore subject and I chose not to pursue it.

"He is much like you," Louis said. "He is an American turned Frenchman while you are a Frenchman turned American. I have always been curious about your name, Max Gordon. It must be an invented name?"

"I suppose. I was born Maksim Anjou. My mother was from Odessa. She went to France with my grandfather and married a Jai-Lai player, Armand Anjou who ran off when the war started . Her maiden name was Gorovitch but I used the name Anjou and changed it to Maxwell Gordon, an anglicized version of Gorovitch, when I turned 21. I did it for my grandfather who died with my mother during the war and for my uncle Alex, his brother, who brought me to the States when it was over."

"Where did they die, Max?"

"I don't know where my father died, but my mother died in Basse Terre."

"You have renounced France then?"

I had to think my answer over carefully.

"No. I renounced my father."

Louis smiled slightly.

"Are you strictly a ten percenter?"

"You can call it that," I replied.

"Ten percent on everything? Even the Blue Danube? If, hypothetically speaking, it disappeared?"

"Especially the Blue Danube, hypothetically speaking, of course."

"Of course."

A doctor emerged from the operating room.

"Maxwell Gordon and Louis Dore?"

We stood up.

And so Carl Haussmann died. He had no wife, no children, no successors, only a partner who was out one good diamond cutter and appraiser. He had no friends to carry his body and no family to mourn his soul.

3

The Justice Ministry

With age comes a procession of death among contemporaries that forces us to confront our mortality. Carl's passing was frightening. He was not big and fat. He was short and thin, ate and drank little and did not seem a candidate for a heart attack, least of all a fatal one. Here lay the capriciousness of life. We were here one moment and gone another. I did recall however that Carl was a diabetic.

Louis and I parted company outside the hospital. It was raining and a shiny dark gloss covered the streets under gray brown clouds that cast a ghostly haze over the neighborhood's ancient buildings.

To remain in Paris for Carl's funeral was pointless. My presence would not bring him back to life.

The weather was cleared the next morning by a cold January sun. I booked a flight home and called Pierre La Salle at his Interpol office at the justice ministry. He must have been anxious to see me because I was told to come over right away.

I held La Salle in great admiration. He was a master sleuth and a piece of work in his own right. Hailing from Lyon in east central France, his French was pure, polished and lyrical. Well groomed and always in tailored suits and highly starched french cuffed shirts, he was the quintessential high ranking Eurocrat. Not even a strand of his slick dark hair that was combed over a bald spot was out of place. He had an aristocratic nose and inquisitive eyes. He spoke slowly and clearly and rarely rambled away from the subject at hand. .

His office, like many in the complex, was filled with gold gilded furniture that could have jumped out of a glossy museum catalogue. It was in keeping with the grand epoch Parisian style of government buildings and trumpeted the importance of its occupant in the bureaucratic pecking order.

Interpol was an independent international police organization not under the French flag, but La Salle's position was a liaison post between the country's justice system and Interpol. I had heard years ago that Otto Katz and Henry Adair had vied for the job when it opened, but its titular director was always a Frenchman and La Salle was given the nod. I envied La Salle but not his job. It was a very politically sensitive position.

Much of the decor in La Salle's office was in a Renaissance era motif that caught the natural light flowing in generously from the high windows facing the monument on Place Vendome. A huge crystal chandelier hung from the ceiling over a generous bouquet of freshly cut flowers arranged on a round, gold leafed conference table. On the walls were bronze sconces, electrified for the needs of the modern day. Between them were paintings of historical figures and events.

I was admitted through a check-point under the ministry's livery portals on Vendome by several uniformed guards and passed to another, armed with an automatic rifle, who escorted me with Simon Perez, the Interpol director's personal secretary, up a flight of marble stairs to the second floor. A young man was going down the stairs as we ascended. He was wearing an attractive diamond pinky ring that caught the light when we passed one another and made momentary eye contact.

At the top of the stairs I had to stop to catch my breath.

"Are you all right, monsieur Gordon?" Simon Perez asked.

I recovered my equilibrium.

"Fine," I whispered hoarsely. "Fine."

Ushered into the director's office, La Salle greeted me at the door while the secretary stood beaming.

"I will go going to Disney World soon," he announced happily.

"That's fine Simon. Monsieur Gordon can tell you about Florida later."

The secretary nodded understandingly and departed.

"I see prosperity has not passed you by," La Salle said, shaking my hand.

"You're looking well yourself, director. But I don't know about my riches. I'm wearing the same blue blazer you have seen me in for years."

I sat down in front of his desk and exposed the threadbare underside of my jacket's sleeve.

"I'm due for a new wardrobe and can't afford it."

La Salle leaned back in his chair and laughed.

"Your problem, Max, is that your assets are all tied up in cash. But this is not about your wealth; I am admiring your girth. You have gained weight since we last met. You must be living well."

I groaned inwardly.

"The family is well, Max?"

"We manage to survive. Your wife and kids. They're fine?"

"You are a true diplomat, Max. You mean my ex-wife. We divorced a few years ago."

"I'm sorry, Pierre. I had no idea."

"Oh, there is nothing to be sorry about. We remain friends. But to answer your question, she is happy and shopping more, and the more she shops the fatter she gets. And my children are now adults who still manage to spend my money. But to tell you the truth, Max, this life is beginning to wear down my nerves and ruin my wallet. Do you recall our talk a few years ago? We talked about running off and moving to an island in the West Indies."

"Yes. Tom Lyons and Jake Santana also felt the same way."

"Ah. How are my friends?"

"Tom is fine. He is still with the Morris County sheriff's office, and Jake is now detective inspector Santana in Palm Beach County. And with that kind of fame goes the usual underpaid aggravation."

Jake Santana was part of our "good old boy" network, having been in the army with us. He was a Cuban-American raised in south Florida and with whom I had worked on many occasions on jewelry heist and fraud cases. A muscular six-footer, bald as a cue ball and sporting a pencil thin moustache over a Cheshire cat smile, he was always dapperly dressed in silk suits and lizard shoes, conveying the idea that police work was not his sole source of income. A gold tooth reflected light when he smiled as did a diamond pinky finger. He evidently did well enough to have a driver on his personal payroll who was Colin's brother-in-law, Frank Barton, Eva's brother. Besides being Jake's eyes and ears, he was his gopher and right-hand man.

"And what about George Lerman and Ed Houston? How are they?"

"They're still in the knee cracking business," I replied and elaborated. "They do collection work for Sentinel and Centurion's finance divisions, going after delinquent accounts and that sort of thing."

"Does George still fly jets?"

"Sometimes," I said. "He does charter work and special assignments."

It was remarkable how well informed Pierre managed to be.

"Any romance in your life now that you're single?" I asked.

There was a twinkle in Pierre's eyes.

"Romance is a rare occasion at my stage in life. However, I am keeping company with a woman. As a matter of fact, you know her. She is Christine, Nicole's cousin."

"Nicole Colbert, Henry's former wife?"

"Yes. And by the way, Nicole speaks of you often, Max. Her son has just left my office. He is a starving actor and wants a job with Interpol."

"I thought Otto was dating Christine."

The Interpol director shook his head.

"That is an old story. He was but she wanted marriage and he got, how do you say, cold feet?"

He then asked the obvious.

"I thought you would have taken up with Nicole after Colleen died. Why did you let Henry spoil your game?"

"I'd rather not discuss it, Pierre. Anyway, that was a long time ago."

"Agreed. Can we then talk about Brussels? What happened there?"

"I discovered that the suspect diamonds were flown into Belgium on an Air France flight under Airway Bill Number One Zero Seven."

"What is so strange about that? All airborne cargo is recorded that way."

"I also found out that the same airway bill number was assigned to earlier diamond shipments from various points of shipment in West Africa. In all cases, the routing is identical and the cargo is always the same: ten to twenty uncut diamonds, each of which would amount to a ten carat diamond when cut. The cargo is consigned to Maison Dore in care of Kumari in Antwerp. Now, that's harmless enough. However, a new customs duty agent trainee in Belgium was given busy work and did a routine check of Maison Dore's import documentation. His review indicates that only seven stones were actually declared. In other words, ten diamonds were shipped of which three disappeared."

"There have been ten consignments that I've uncovered, each using an airway bill using the same number, One Zero Seven. That means to me that a total of thirty stones have been purloined that I know of, including the last consignment that arrived a few days before I did. Number One Zero Seven is a code for a customs official on the take with Maison Dore or Kumari to open each consignment with that way bill number and remove three stones before handing the parcel to a Dore or Kumari representative. I even dug up one of the reps' name, someone named Emile Barco. At least, that's the name on the paperwork. But it was Henry Adair who appeared this last time."

La Salle grinned.

"Did you know that Larry O'Leary, Colin's manager, was in Belgium?"

"In fact, I ran into him," I replied.

"That is correct, my friend. And did you know that one month prior to that a chap named Brian Donovan paid Maison Dore a visit. I hear he works for this Larry O'Leary. Indeed, we know of at least two more fellow travelers who have periodically paid visits to Maison Dore: a Michael Surrey and a John Cork.

"Michael Surrey and John Cork?"

A twinkle appeared in Pierre's eye.

"Yes. They must love Belgian culture and cuisine, Max."

"Then you suspect that something is going on."

"Yes. They arrive a day or so before that special airway bill number turns up. They stay a few days and then return to your country. Interpol believes a connection exists between them and the missing diamonds. Unfortunately, we have no motive. No theft or loss has been reported; no insurance claim has been made. Certainly, you would have known about a claim, Max, and you would be hot on the trail or else I would not have had to borrow your services. We have thirty major uncut diamonds missing and no one seems to notice or care. I believe that many more diamonds have been stolen this way in the past several years. We are looking at a cash flow amounting to several millions of euros a year, Pierre. And then we have this person, Emile Barco."

La Salle asked, "Have you ever met Emile Barco?"

"No. Do you know him?"

"Our very wealthy invisible man. Our research indicates that he is from Alsace and that he had two brothers, a much older one who migrated to your country and a slightly older one who died during the Nazi occupation. The slightly older one acquired land in Basse Terre by marriage, 200 acres to be exact. When he died, along with his wife, the property went to Emile Barco."

"What about the oldest brother? Did her get anything?"

"We have no idea where he ended up or what he ended up with, but now we will find out. Anyway, this Emile Barco received government funding years ago to turn the property into a wild life refuge with the right to sell wild game permits during the hunting season. He used some of the money to build himself a nice spread complete with a gatehouse on the estate."

"Did you ever see the guy?"

"I met him once at a dinner party."

The Interpol director made a limp hand gesture.

"He had a goatee and wore his hair in a pony tail. I could swear it was a wig. Quite frankly, I thought he was comme ci-comme ca. He is a friend of Henry, according to Louis Dore, a most silent partner in the jewelry and import-export business, I am told, and very connected here at the justice ministry. And you know that John Cork flew to Paris with Carl Haussmann the other day," La Salle continued.

"Louis told me, but how did you find out?" I asked.

"When one of the world's best diamond cutters dies suddenly, Interpol finds out right away. We have been tracking the Dore and Adair businesses for years. Their affairs are terribly tangled, just as all the circumstances around Carl's death are extremely bizarre."

"You suspect murder?"

The dapper Frenchman scratched his head with a manicured finger and pushed his hand carved office chair away from the ornate desk.

"I suspect everything and everyone, including you, Max."

I stayed poker faced.

"What bothers me, Pierre, is that Carl's traveling companion is an old army buddy of mine. He's a drunk who scavenges for a living. I never pegged him as a world traveler. He and Carl make a lousy fit. He disappeared when Carl was taken to the hospital. Is there anything on that?"

"No. We retrieved Carl Haussmann's things from Maison Dore and found nothing, just clothes and personal effects."

Two birds arguing outside momentarily drew my attention. But the sound of sirens from a police motorcade passing through the portals into the vast inner courtyard frightened them off.

La Salle' piercing eyes and masterful nose focused on the gold watch that peeked out of the French cuff that framed his left hand.

"Marcel Jouvet, our deputy minister, has arrived," he declared. "Always on time. Old bachelors are that way. They have nothing else to do but to be on time. I have a luncheon date with him. Will you join us? He has been asking about you."

"Lunch? Here?"

"Of course not. Our cafeteria is for the employees. Lunch is at the Ritz."

"Next door? It sounds tempting."

Simon Perez entered the office through a side door and handed La Salle a note.

"From the Interpol laboratory," he said.

"And the police report?" La Salle asked pointedly.

"We have it, and also the autopsy report."

The secretary looked nervously at me and then at the director.

"Well, what does it say?"

"Heart attack induced by a diabetic seizure," the secretary replied. "The subject was a diabetic who took the wrong medication before boarding the flight. The tests are tentative but they point in that direction."

La Salle took a deep breath.

"Most interesting. You may leave us, my friend."

"Oui, monsieur le directeur."

The secretary exited.

"It seems we have a problem," I noted.

The Interpol director nodded.

"Yes. We have a murder."

Leaning forward, he added, "You and I go back many years. You must admit that this is a mind bender. We have a dead diamond cutter who flew directly from your country to Paris right after appraising the Blue Danube. We have an old army friend of yours wandering about Paris and we know that Carl called you before leaving for Paris. Finally, we have a gang of Irish thugs who work for Colin Adair and who are into diamond smuggling. Do you have a theory, Max?"

"Maybe the Adairs are supplementing their incomes?"

"Maybe, Max. Maybe. But why? I also hear that Otto Katz is kept busy on loan to Maison Dore cutting diamonds in New York. I am sure he the one who has been working on those missing diamonds. But again we have no proof."

"I'm overwhelmed," I responded.

"I thought you would be. And we have another development for you."

"And that is?"

"We discovered that ownership of all Adair businesses and assets in the United States and Bahamas are being transferred to Henry Adair by his brother. The transfer may include the Blue Danube, but I am not sure. Did Carl say anything before he died?"

"No. He wanted to talk about the diamond and I told him it could wait. But Louis mentioned something about that. That could include the rock. In view of Colin's difficulties, I wouldn't be surprised to see the Blue Danube on the market. It would also make sense to transfer everything to Henry to avoid stateside creditors."

The Interpol director stared vacantly at the ceiling.

"It would be nice if we could have a close look at that diamond, Max."

Pierre's intimate knowledge astounded me. Interpol was on to something.

"We do our homework. There's something else you should know. Have you any idea how much land costs in the Basse Terre hunt country?"

I looked at the window again. The birds were back, singing away and their differences apparently resolved. They stayed for a few seconds before flying away together.

"You see, Max," La Salle observed. "The birds made up, but there will be no chirping among any of us if these issues are not resolved. Anyway, land in Basse Terre runs up to 500,000 euros an acre today as a result of high end real estate development. If Barco has 200 acres, we are counting 100 million euros. Moreover, I hear that our scientists have reason to believe that natural gas reserves may lie under the swamps of the Sologne forest at Basse Terre. If those rumors are true, our friend Emile will be a billionaire many times over. But in either case, Emile is very wealthy."

"If that's so, Pierre, why would he want to involve himself with conflict diamonds?"

The Interpol director rubbed his hands together.

"Who knows. Perhaps contraband diamonds offer more income than the sale of hunting permits, Max. After all, maintaining 200 acres is an expensive proposition. You must agree that complex questions such as yours sometimes have simple answers."

I marveled at Pierre La Salle. This time I knew for sure why he was a super sleuth and why I was a mere insurance investigator.

"I hope so, Pierre. I take it that you've seen Henry. How does he look?"

"He was looking drawn at first, but those cancer treatments he is receiving in the Bahamas may be working," La Salle replied.

"The last time I saw him, he looked much better."

"Louis says the same thing," I noted. "He says that Henry looks like his brother again. And the Colin I know is husky and healthy."

La Salle shrugged off my comment.

"But about the Blue Danube. I'd like you to have another look at it, maybe with a neutral expert. I want to know that the diamond is safe."

"I'll have to clear this with Mel Solomon at Sentinel."

"Sentinel and Interpol have mutual interests, Max, beyond the company's coverage of the diamond and La Maison Dore."

"Oh?"

Pierre smiled.

"Those mutual interests have nothing to do with me, but I must maintain a good relationship with the justice ministry. It is Jouvet, our deputy minister for internal security. He is heavily invested in Sentinel, and through Sentinel he serves on the boards of several firms companies insured by the firm. One of them is Rhone-Fayette. I believe that your daughter's husband now works for their American division, the Fayette Corporation."

"Isn't that a conflict of interest?"

"Ah. A conflict of interest, you ask. Life is a conflict of interest."

La Salle looked at his watch.

"It is time for lunch. Lunch is such a wonderful opportunity to reflect over the past, the present and the future. I guess you have been with Sentinel for many years, Max?"

"It's funny, Pierre. Louis mentioned my career at Sentinel too."

"What I mean is that should you ever leave Sentinel you would collect a decent pension."

"I haven't thought about it, Pierre. What are you suggesting?"

"I am suggesting is that you consider a position with Interpol when you do leave Sentinel. Your pension would follow you."

"What kind of job are we talking about?"

La Salle became defensive.

"This is not my initiative, Max," he hurriedly explained. "It comes from the deputy minister. French internal security needs a specialist like you to work with Interpol. You can earn income on top of your pension. Jouvet tells me he can arrange for the income to be tax free with you working in the States."

"It's tempting, Pierre. But maybe we should start a business where we can control our own action."

La Salle rose from his chair and said, "I like your ideas, Max. Shall we? The deputy minister is waiting."

4

The Ritz

"Nicole says you are quite an expert on our city below the city."

"Yes? But in what context?"

"Oh. We were only chatting. Apparently, you spent your early years here."

"That's right."

And so, Pierre got me started.

"Did you know, for example, that Vendome was once an open field?"

"Do tell."

"Yes. Place Vendome was a grazing pasture for animals kept within the city walls. It was surrounded by the old city which was a hodgepodge of narrow garbage strewn streets and alleys. During epidemics, the field was used to incinerate the dead before their removal to the catacombs on the Left Bank. Later, the government erected many of the buildings we see today over the old slums around Vendome which were left intact under the new city. A network of underground sewers and water works was then built under the ancient streets to direct waste into the Seine at about the same time that subterranean conduits were carved out of the bedrock. Today, they connect the river's right and left banks and extend all the way out to the suburbs.

"There are three layers to Paris. We are standing on the third or top layer. The layer below us, the second tier, has the tunnels for the metro, adjacent tunnels and the city's present water and sewerage system. The first and the lowest tier is deeper still, and that's where we find the old sewers, tunnels and sealed over streets. Without much effort, we can descend from here to the city's depths and travel from one end of Paris to the other without seeing daylight. Fascinating, isn't it, Pierre?"

I noticed that La Salle was not listening.

"Yes, Max. Fascinating."

"Place Vendome, originally called Place Louis-le-Grand," I went on, choosing to ignore his deaf ear, "was designed by Jules Hardouin-Mansart during the reign of Louis XIV with a statue of the French emperor on a horse. The current square took shape in Napoleon Bonaparte's reign when he had a column to his honor built in the center. That column was destroyed in 1871. The monument we see today replaces it."

"You should have been a history professor," said La Salle. "Ah. We are at the Ritz. I hope the minister will not subject us to a long lunch."

Then, out of nowhere he asked, "By the way, Max, how's Eva? Is she and Colin still married."

What a strange question?

"So far as I know they are. You'll have to ask them or perhaps Henry when you see him."

I learned long ago that the French take lunch, "le dejeuner" they call it, and all their meals seriously. Lunch can take up to two hours. This is why many Parisians return to their offices after lunch and work until the early evening when they prepare for dinner while most of us are watching the late night news.

I had dined at the Ritz before. Lunch was a pleasant, overpriced exercise guaranteed to keep the belly flat and the liver bloated. Wine poured but the real food was meager although its presentation was a work of art. The final bill was never less than fifty dollars per person no matter how sparingly one ordered. I was glad when Pierre said lunch was on the Republic of France.

Meeting Marcel Jouvet was an experience. The deputy minister was tall and thin as a rail. Older and way beyond retirement age, he had an annoying habit of avoiding eye contact and his speech was ponderous, as if he was lecturing, delivering a church sermon or making a political speech. But it was a free lunch and besides, his offer delivered by La Salle tickled my imagination.

I could sense that this was not a social luncheon and that the minister had an agenda. La Salle wanted to discuss the business of Maison Dore and the Adairs but Jouvet stayed focused on the Blue Danube diamond.

"La Salle says you recover jewelry on commission," Jouvet said. "Does the Adair diamond fall within your bailiwick?"

"I would think so, Minister, if someone were to ask me to search for it, and assuming it was missing. And of course, it isn't. It was inspected a few days ago in New Jersey while I was in Belgium." "Of course," Jouvet repeated. Then he dove into the meat of the subject.

"We have followed the Blue Danube's path for generations. It is part of the history of France," he declared with finality after his second glass of wine.

I could see where Jouvet was going.

"It was one of Haussmann's ancestors, also a diamond cutter, who was invited to India by a sultan named Kumari to cut and shape a 279 carat light blue diamond called the Great Mogul into two fine sapphire shaped gems. Rajeesh Kumari, who as you know owns a chain of fine jewelry and china boutiques, is one of the sultan's descendants.

"Anyway, what resulted was a gem of the most unparalleled beauty and perfection. The sultan had once been to Europe and visited the Blue Danube river. That is how the diamond earned its name."

La Salle grinned approvingly.

"You see, Max. Like you, The minister knows his history."

Jouvet's face was expressionless and he spoke in a monotone.

"The sultan's domain was in southern India which in the eighteenth century was under our control. The French governor, to keep the sultan subservient, kidnapped his sons. A few years later, when the English were about to expel the French from India, the governor traded the boys back to the sultan for the Blue Danube. It made its way back to Paris where it became the property of France."

Now I caught on. Jouvet was claiming the diamond for France even though it was still in the hands of the Adairs.

Jouvet went on.

"A German officer stole the Blue Danube when the Kaiser's armies took Paris in 1871. He eventually settled in the United States where he passed it to an immigrant Irishman named Patrick Adair to discharge gambling debts. Neither knew the diamond's true value. Patrick discovered what he had when it was appraised.

"The diamond remained at the Adair estate in northern New Jersey until the family placed it in a Dore vault in New York store for safe keeping. It was then moved to New Jersey, to Dore's vault in Morristown, and that is where it is now."

"Forgive me, Minister," I said. "But I'm not too sure of the point you are trying to make."

Jouvet waved his hand.

"Let me explain, Max. Our understanding is that the English are claiming the diamond because India was part of their Empire. The Germans say it's theirs because they captured it during the Franco-Prussian war. And now the American government is filing a lien against it because the Adair enterprises owe back taxes. And naturally, Rajeesh Kumari is stubborn in his insistence that the Blue Danube belongs to him as the sultan's direct descendent. Or, at the very least, he wants India to own it. But, the Blue Danube belongs to France," the deputy minister concluded firmly.

So, that was the bottom line. Jouvet wanted the diamond.

"We have not vigorously pressed our claim up to now, but we will. Like everyone, we remain vitally interested in the Blue Danube now that it is to be the subject of litigation. And you, Max, have a fiduciary responsibility to make sure that the Blue Danube is returned to its rightful owner if it ever goes astray."

"You mean a responsibility to France?"

"To the French Republic. You are still a Frenchman. You must place your patriotism above personal gain and greed."

I learned something at that luncheon. Irrespective of who really owned the rock, he wanted it for France or for himself, depending on his own level of greed. Jouvet did not intend to let me to step in his way. How he would reckon with our IRS who would have first dibs on the rock to satisfy Adair tax delinquencies was a question I avoided to prevent embarrassing the minister. My take on Jouvet's discourse was that he knew or believed that something had already happened or was about to happen to the Blue Danube.

The Adairs were not fools. Family members must have known that the French government, if not Jouvet, was eying the Blue Danube. And certainly they would have known that a back tax due bill could expose the diamond to seizure. At the very least, Henry and Colin Adair would have arranged to keep it out of sight and out of reach. But somehow, whatever they did or were planning to do, I should have been kept in the loop unless they were conspiring to steal the diamond for themselves.

From that point of view, its reported transfer from Colin to Henry, with all other stateside Adair assets, made sense. At the very least, it would make my claim or my daughter's claim to the Adair estate for difficult to press when the time arrived. What didn't make sense was an Adair plot to bring the Blue Danube to France where it would be so much easier for Jouvet to grab it.

"Does my position conflict with yours as the gem's family custodian?"

Jouvet's question caught me off guard.

"I don't follow."

"Well. Your wife was an Adair, even if she was adopted. That gave her a share in the Blue Danube. My understanding is that before you married her, you refused to sign a prenuptial agreement giving up your claim by marriage to the gem and the rest of the estate in the event she died."

"That was at Colleen's urging," I explained. "I married Colleen for love and not for money. She said she would decide who would get what."

"So you would be willing to sign such a document today?"

"What an odd question, Excellence. Why should I sign away my rights to something I didn't own? When my wife died, she left no will as far as I can see. My answer is no. I have my daughter to consider. She is Colleen's blood descendant. The courts will have to decide the issue when the time comes."

Jouvet murmured.

"Yes. When the time comes."

The conversation and lunch ended there.

The Blue Danube diamond, like its namesake river, generated a continuing stream. But it was an income stream for the Adairs from business ventures built on debt collateralized by the Blue Danube. Financing their enterprises would have been impossible had they not possessed the stone.

Two questions nagged me. Who was Henry's silent partner, Emile Barco, the ghost with the money, the connections and the name on the shipping documents that evidenced receipt of the cargos on airway bill One Zero Seven? And, what was La Salle's real interest in this matter. Whatever was his game, Pierre was playing his cards close to the vest.

Were there other diamonds like the Blue Danube? My daughter asked me that once, and that prompted me to do some research.

I could appreciate the deputy minister's interest in the Blue Danube. But it was not the only giant stone in the world. Most giant diamonds originated in India. The Regent diamond was over four hundred carats. It was discovered in India in 1700. It was cut down to 140 carats and sold to the regent of France and was now at the Louvre. It was a bluish stone and I often wondered what happened to the rest of the diamond. My guess was that smaller gems, from one to ten carats, were cut and sold for amounts exceeding the value of the Regent.

Another fabulous gem was the Koh-i-Noor, or Mountain of Light. It ended up in England where it finally came to rest upon the Queen Mother's crown as the Cross Formee. This particular stone was a brilliant white diamond. The Orloff, a big one at 195 carats, ended up in Russian hands; and

The Sancy, a rare Kimberly yellow diamond weighing 53 carats found a berth at the Louvre next to the Regent. Only the Hope diamond, a light blue stone, came to grace the Smithsonian in Washington D.C. In my heart of hearts, I thought it would be nice if that some day the Blue Danube could become the Hope diamond's neighbor.

The largest diamond on record was a mutant discovered in the Transvaal in 1905 weighing in at more than 3100 carats. It was a yellow diamond of the Kimberly variety and was cut into smaller stones. Again, the sum of their parts exceeded the whole in value.

That left the Blue Danube. The scuttlebutt in the trade backed Jouvet's contention that it came from the Great Mogul. Many eyewitnesses over the centuries swore to its existence and to its size and experts agreed it weighed two hundred seventy nine carats and corroborated historical records claiming it was first sighted in the twelfth century when the Islamic Moguls invaded India. It was last seen, allegedly, by a French soldier and explorer named Jean Baptiste Tavernier in the seventeenth century. However, the stone was never on public display.

The rumor that the Great Mogul was cut into two diamonds, one of which was the Blue Diamond owned by the sultan Kumari, survived the centuries and was accepted as gospel. I had no reason to question it, but nothing was known of the other half's fate.

Quite frankly, I was more intrigued by the Blue Danube's potential than by its intrinsic value. I stood to earn a small fortune in the event it was stolen and I recovered it: ten percent of its insured value. But if I did get my hands on it, why not keep it and either sell it on the black market or have it cut and then sell off smaller sized gem stones? Or perhaps I should press my dead wife's claim to her share of the diamond. That too would generate a nice cash flow that could last years.

My eyes widened. I had been blind sided. Of course! How stupid of me! Siphoning off uncut stones from African shipments was the way Colin Adair was able to pay his stateside bills. His trusted people were the mules who brought them to Otto who cut them into gems, sold them and then deposited the proceeds, most likely in an offshore bank for Colin's account, perhaps in the Bahamas. Carl might have discovered the scheme and decided to blow the whistle. It was conjecture, but it was logical under the circumstances. But how did Johnny Cork fit in the scheme? I saw him as a dim witted courier or mule but not as Haussmann's traveling partner.

La Salle and I left Jouvet at the Ritz where he had another appointment and walked out to the street. He confided before we parted company that he was not fanatical like Jouvet about his claim to the diamond for France.

"My business is to solve cross border crimes like smuggling, theft and murder. The proper ownership of the Blue Danube, if it is not legally the property of the Adair family, is a political question. In this context, nothing belongs to anyone. Everything is negotiable. In fact, I could look the other way if you somehow acquired the stone, Max, as long as you lead me to Carl Haussmann's killer, and perhaps remembered me in your old age. Even Colin's diamond smugglers can be winked at for their cooperation and for the proper consideration if Maison Dore and the Adairs can be exposed. And who knows, Max. The Blue Danube could be our passport to the good life in the islands where we can live happily forever after."

That was a leading statement if I ever heard one.

"I'll see what can be done, Pierre. I do know people in very low places, you know."

I was never close to the Adair twins before or after I married Colleen, but I was friendly with Brian Donovan, Larry O'Leary and Mike Surrey. We were drinking and golf buddies. Henry did not play golf, but Colin, who served with us in the army, always joined our annual reunion and tournament.

We grew up together, went to the same schools, went into the army and eventually married and lived in the same county. Henry skipped the draft by moving to France and I saw him only when I traveled to Paris on business.

I left La Salle to return to his office and started walking to my hotel when suddenly I stopped short. A grabbing pain in the pit of my stomach took my breath away and I had to lean against a lamp post. I had some antacid tablets in my pocket and popped one into my mouth. I was about to move on when there was a tug on my arm.

"Monsieur Max?"

The only person who ever called me by that name was the concierge at the Maison Dore building..

"Monsieur Max, are you ill?"

I blinked several times.

"Gaspard. Gaspard Lancet. What a pleasant surprise! No. Thanks. I'm fine.

Are you returning to Maison Dore?"

We started walking slowly together. Gaspard Lancet was a handyman way beyond retirement age. He was short and squat, wore a beret over a mop of white hair and sported a bushy moustache. In blue overalls and jacket, he was the typical old fashioned French worker.

"I am not with Maison Dore," he confessed. "Monsieur Dore fired me at the request of monsieur Adair. He said I was too old."

"You're retired now?"

The former concierge shook his head.

"No. I am too young to retire. I will have plenty of time when I die. I am starting work at the justice ministry."

"Doing what?"

"Sweeping floors." Gaspard sighed. "There is little demand for old men."

"What about money?"

"I have a pension. It pays the rent in an upstairs room and all my expenses. Otherwise, I am broke until I start working."

We stopped in front of my hotel where I took out my bill fold.

"No." Lancet shook his head in protest. "I cannot accept charity."

"Your pride will kill you," I said.

"What are you talking about? I am in my eighties."

"How long do we know each other, Gaspard?"

"To the War? Since you were a small boy?"

"A long time, my friend. You took care of me. And you continue to look after my interests. How is your family?"

"My wife has passed on, like yours, monsieur Max. My kids and grand children live in the south."

I pulled out a thousand dollars in hundred dollar bills.

"Here," I said. "This is a loan."

"I will pay you back," Gaspard insisted.

"Yes, you will," I agreed, pressing the money into his hand.

"By the way, is age the only reason you were fired?"

"Monsieur Adair was at the office with his partner who was friendly with a former customs official at the airport who now works as a waiter at a bistro he owns in Basse Terre. The partner said his talents were being wasted and suggested that Maison Dore hire him. Monsieur Adair spoke to monsieur Dore who hired the waiter and fired me."

"What does the business partner look like?"

"Tall and thin, a goatee and long dark hair in a pony tail. He wore dark glasses and I think his hair is a wig. Monsieur Adair called him Barco, a truly strange bird."

"Would you like to come into the hotel for a drink?"

"Oh, no. The Westphalia is not for people like me."

"Well then. Why do you call Barco a strange bird?"

Gaspard shrugged.

I repeated La Salle's limp hand gesture and description.

"Comme-ci-comme ca?"

Gaspard did not respond.

"What about Henry," I asked. "How did he look when you saw him last?"

Gaspard stared at me.

"He usually looks terrible. But he recently began looking healthy. It was a remarkable transformation. He appeared fine the day I was fired."

I gave him a business card.

"I'm flying back to the States. Call me collect if necessary. Let's stay in touch and give my best to your family."

II
NEW JERSEY

5

Pyramid Scheme

No brain surgeon was needed to figure things out. Johnny Cork, Brian Donovan, Larry O'Leary and Mike Surrey might take an occasional trip to Ireland but never to the European mainland. That was simply not their bag. Colin's Irish mafia was in the diamond smuggling business and Pierre La Salle wanted to break up the ring and maybe cut himself into a bit of the action.

However, Jouvet had the Blue Danube on his mind. He wanted to get his grubby hands on it and was willing to buy my help with a fat, no-show job. Complicating matters was Carl Haussmann's murder and Johnny Cork's disappearance. It was one thing to engage in cross border theft and smuggling, but murder and material witnesses who vanished played poorly with national and international law enforcement agencies. What was curious was the fact that Jouvet, by virtue of his lofty position as a deputy minister, seemed to have little interest in law enforcement matters.

My immediate problem was simple. I didn't want to sell out my friends even if they were diamond smugglers. La Salle must have read my mind by suggesting a way out. I could make a deal on his behalf.

I was pleasantly surprised to find Mike Surrey, short and stout and with the map of Ireland and a perpetually elfish grin pasted to his face, waiting for me at the airport in Newark upon my return from Paris. Good old Mike. He was never without a joke.

"Hey, Max," he said, grabbing my carry on bag the moment I cleared U.S. customs. "Did you hear about the Lufthansa flight that went down over the Atlantic?"

I was caught off guard and braced myself to hear about an air disaster.

"No. You're kidding. What happened?"

"The plane was going down when the captain made an announcement over the intercom from the cockpit. 'Passengers on the right side of the aisle will find life jackets under their seats. All passengers on the left side, thank you for Flying Lufthansa!' Gottcha!"

And he burst out laughing.

Mike's only fault, besides his constant jokes, was booze. He was a drinker and martinis were his favorite beverage. He would have several eye openers at breakfast, run errands for a few hours, and then head for a restaurant that served alcohol before the noon hour.

Mike Surrey had only one leg and was one of my closest buddies. Whatever his personal problems he was always in a good mood and was never without a smile. We were in an airborne unit during out stint in the service and once, when we were making a drop, he had the misfortune of landing before me on the top of a machine gun nest. We took out the nest but the encounter cost him a leg.

Janine had apparently asked him to pick me up and, not wanting to refuse, he had commandeered Brian Donovan, the headwaiter at the Bernardsville Club hotel owned by Colin, to do the driving.

Tired, coping with an upset stomach and a cramped left arm, I jumped at Brian's offer to stop at the restaurant for a soft drink and an antacid on the way home.

It was then that Mike Surrey informed us he was not drinking that day.

"I went to see a doctor," he explained. "No more booze if I want to live."

"Drink and die, or suffer and live," Brian Donovan quipped.

"I should give up eating," I responded. "I feel like shit."

"You look like shit," he noted. "That's the trouble with all of us," he went on as we waited for my belongings at the baggage carousel. "The Irish drink themselves to death and the Jews eat themselves to death."

"Isn't that the truth," I said, pulling my bags off the turntable. "Thank God for the invention of whiskey, or else you guys would own the world."

Mike laughed lightly.

"Tell you what. You don't eat and I don't drink. We can have tea and crumpets," he said.

"I'll drink to that," said Brian.

I liked Mike. At parties, whenever the question of how we met came up he would say, "We met in some gin mill when I accidentally stepped on his fingers." The truth is that we met long before any of us had vices.

Mike's marriage to Arlene, a next door neighbor's daughter, was sudden. It was called a shotgun wedding in those days. They were in their late teens and she was pregnant. Since they came from very Catholic families, abortion was out of the question. They had to get married.

Arlene was a fine but not very bright woman who produced three sons. In my opinion, Arlene was homely as a teenager, and unlike fine wine, she did not improve with age.

Mike played the field after his marriage, even after he lost his leg. But he always made sure to get home for the late news. I felt sorry for Arlene. She was a devoted wife and mother. She worried over the fact she had produced no daughters, realizing that sooner or later her sons would move away as in the cliché: 'A son is a son until he gets a wife; a daughter is a daughter for life.'

She need not have worried. Her sons never left home. The oldest, a college graduate, about my daughter's age, never married, and Janine swore he was gay. I think women have a sixth sense about things like that. What was really unusual was that the kid never held a steady job and lived at home. Unlike his father, he was ill tempered and nasty. The middle son, a college drop out, was unemployed. He too lived at home. He was short and skinny and as mean as his older brother.

Mike's wife, when she was pregnant with her third, prayed that if he was to be a boy, he would find an occupation close to home, like maybe become a priest. I had to smile inwardly but sadly. Her wish came true. He never left home. He was born retarded. The funny thing is that he ended up with a paying job at a local occupational center for the handicapped. Mike used to joke that of his three sons, the retard was the main support of the family.

Once a week, I'd collect Mike at his home in the morning and drive down to the shore for a brief ride on my boat. I had to make sure that we would be back at the slip in time for us to be at the Blue Marlin in Sea Girt by noon. I would order one sandwich and a coffee, and he would order a small salad and a martini.

By the time we were done an hour later, he was finished with his second or third martini and would fall asleep, snoring soundly, while I drove us home. On the way, we would stop at the occupational center for his retarded son. Now, some retards are nice; others are obnoxious and mean. This one was nasty and loud and would roughly shake his father out of his drunken stupor as we approached their home. When we reached the driveway, Mike would stumble out of the car followed by his drooling son.

I'd sit in the car and watch them wobble up the walk to the front door that mysteriously flew open to let them in. The door stayed open for a few seconds and then slammed closed, and I would sit there for a few more seconds before driving away, wondering what awaited them in the black hell beyond.

I shuddered. I kept thinking of the hospital corridor and the slamming door at the hospital in Paris where Carl Haussmann died. Death was all too damn final.

"How's business?" I asked.

Brian peeked at me through the rear view mirror as he drove.

"Larry says it's not bad, Max," he replied. "But I'm telling you it could be much better. The problem is that no matter how much we make, it all goes. Larry doesn't talk much, but he's worried."

"Expenses?"

"Hardly. This place is a cash cow. But it's the only one, and Colin milks it for his other operations. He has other restaurants, you know, and a hotel in Delray, Florida, and a bunch of other things, like office real estate. They all lose money except the restaurants and hotel and even they show no profit on the books."

"Is someone cooking the books?"

"That's the other thing," Mike Surrey interjected. "Colin and his brother have this company in the Bahamas that now owns this place and everything else in the States. Fifty percent of all revenues from the hotel and from Colin's other businesses are paid as a general administrative overhead expense charged to the Bahamian holding company.

In the best of times, it's hard to break even. And to make matters worse, Colin has this investment bank in Florida that sells participation shares to dealers at a steep discount. The dealers resell the shares at markups to sub-dealers who add a final markup on sales to their customer base. A piece of each action goes to the investment bank which uses the money to make more high risk investments.

"It's a pyramid scheme that colors his books black. Most of those ventures go south. So more shares have to be sold to pay off those shareholders who want out. No matter what, he's bleeding red ink. I'd say that his back is against the wall and everyone, from clients and creditors to the IRS, are lining up with loaded guns. It can only get worse."

"Man. Take away the booze and you become a financial wiz."

Mike temporarily lost his smile.

"This is no joke, Max. I'm worried. If Colin goes down, we all go down."

He and Brian Donovan exchanged glances through the rear view mirror, thinking perhaps they had said too much.

"Is that why you guys have gone into the diamond smuggling business?"

"You have to let that go, Max. We're trapped. Larry tells us what to do, and he gets his marching orders from Colin."

"Carl Haussmann is dead," I said. "The French think he was murdered. And Johnny Cork has melted away in Paris. What's more, Interpol is wise to you guys."

"What are you going to do?" Brian asked.

"Nothing. Not right now. I'm not going to sell out my friends."

We reached Colin's hotel restaurant a half hour later. The grand circular bar was full but it was too early for dinner and the restaurant section was nearly empty.

Brian led us to a corner table where he had a waiter bring out a serving of tea and biscuits on fine china in a sterling silver tray.

Larry O'Leary, the restaurant's manager came over and sat down with us while Brian went off to change into his head waiter's tuxedo.

"How are things, Larry? The family's ok?"

"Surviving. The wife and kids are fine. I make sure they're recession proof. How's with you, Max, and your daughter and her family?"

"I'm getting younger and they're getting older. I guess Colin's not around. How's his wife?"

"Eva? She great, and her kids are doing fine. I think they've retired."

Larry shook his head in dismay..

"They don't work and they're always after her for money. So Colin lets her and the kids have anything they want. And that's not good for them. They should have gotten jobs years ago."

"Why doesn't Colin send them a road map and the help wanted section of the papers?" I asked. "That should give them a hint."

Larry laughed.

"Colin would, but not Eva. She says her kids remind her of you."

I nearly choked on my drink.

"They're Colin's handiwork, not mine," I insisted. "And Eva had to have been a willing accomplice."

"Eva is always a willing accomplice," said Mike Surrey, his blue eyes dancing.

I decided to change the subject.

"Talking about Colin, where is he?"

"He's in the Bahamas with Henry," Henry replied. "How was Paris?"

"Not so good."

There was no other way to put it. So I told him the story.

"Carl Haussmann, the diamond cutter and appraiser, is dead. He may have been murdered. And John Cork, who went with him, has dropped out of sight."

Larry's smile evaporated.

"That's not good news."

"Mike and Brian know. I told them."

Larry O'Leary, tall, suave and silver haired, the consummate restaurateur, was Colin's right hand man and grew up with us in the same neighborhood. He and Colin Adair were close friends and when Colin took over the hotel from his deceased parents he made Larry his general manager.

Mike Surrey interrupted.

"I want to hear about the women in Paris," he said.

Brian Donovan had finished changing and came over.

"What Mike wants to find out if you tried to make it with Nicole Colbert while you were there."

I evaded the issue.

"Too busy."

An old priest and family friend of the Adairs happened by on his way home and overheard our conversation.

"Perhaps it's time you remarried, Max," he suggested.

"I'm curious, Father," I said, sipping my tea and swallowing a pill to settle my stomach. "Have you contemplated marriage before becoming a priest?"

The priest nodded.

"Often and even after I became a priest. But doing God's work was more important. However, I strongly recommend marriage. It's good to have someone to love and to hold as the nights get long. It might be good for you, Max."

I shook my head sadly.

"That's wishful thinking, Father. I lost my wife fifteen years ago. She had breast cancer. Not that I was ever a great bargain of a husband, but I held what was left of her in my arms when she died, just the way I did when we first met. We had a daughter, but I never had a son."

"Did you love her?"

"I suppose I did. So many things had happened between us, as they do with other couples. Probably everything would have been fine had she lived, but that's wishful thinking. I'll never know because she's gone. At the end, I wonder if I held her out of love or out of pity. And then, for whom was the love and for whom was the pity? More for her, or more for me?"

"You've never considered marrying again?"

No. I've had girlfriends, and I still have one; her name is Gladys. Marriage is not a good idea for me. It creates kid problems and estate problems, and so on."

"Then what do you do for love and sex?"

"What do I do for love and sex? How can I put it? Sometimes I have trouble distinguishing one from the other, Father. I remember an incident when I was in the service. I was on leave in San Francisco. Have you ever been there? It's one of my favorite places. It's a little like Paris, in the sense that it's a great walking town. Paris is bigger, though.

"I usually ended up in Frisco on leave. Most guys went to Saigon, or to Thailand, or Japan or all the way back to Honolulu for their R & R and to get laid, but I went to Frisco. I had a steady hooker there.

"She wasn't a street walker; she was more of a call girl type. She worked by appointment and charged anywhere from fifty to a hundred dollars, which was a lot of money back then, especially for me. I would call her answering service all the way from Asia to make that appointment. And I never missed a date except once when I was in a firefight and got hit and couldn't make it. So I sent her a money order so she shouldn't feel stood up.

"She was a gorgeous dame, frizzy black hair like a sheep, milk chocolate skin and a great body. One year, a few days before the start of the Christmas holidays, I was on furlough. I called her up and made a date for Christmas Eve. She said she was available. Now, you have to understand that Christmas can be one of the loneliest days of the year for the prostitutes, unless they can go home, which they usually can't do. Their johns and their pimps are gone and they're left to shift for themselves. When I arrived at her place, I told her while she was showering that I had only enough money for dinner and a one night stand. She never said a word. She threw a wad of bills over the shower curtain thick enough to choke a horse.

"It's been a good year, Max," she said.

"We had a fast one right then and there on Christmas Eve before going out together for midnight mass at a big cathedral on a hill and then returned to her apartment where we hit the sack and stayed there until a few days after New Year's, breaking only for meals, showers, and a New Year's Eve party at some hotel.

"When it was over, I asked her to marry me. She refused. I'll never forget her words.

"A cat and a fish may fall in love, but where are they going to live?"

"I left that morning, and when she closed the door behind me, it was as if a door had slammed shut on the rest of my life.

"I don't know what happened to her? I never saw her again. She should be in her sixties by now, if she's alive at all.

"If you had to ask me the difference between love and sex, I would have to say I have no idea. I can safely say I love my daughter. As for sex, I go to New York or Atlantic City to clear my tubes. A good hooker or call girl does the trick, if you pardon the pun. The up front price may be high, but I save money and emotional involvement in the long run. But as I get longer in the tooth, my trips become fewer. So I don't play the field much anymore. I don't like steady girlfriends either. They think they're wives and make claims on body and soul. There has to be a better way. Let me know when you find it, Father."

Larry smiled.

"So, what are you going to do, Max?"

I sighed.

"Oh, I don't know, Larry. Maybe, I'll steal the Blue Danube for myself."

The words must have struck Larry the wrong way because a pained look came over his face.

"Oh, don't worry, buddy. Before I steal the diamond, I have to get myself some new teeth. I have a dental appointment tomorrow. I also want to ask you guys something."

"Shoot."

"What can you tell me about an airway bill with the numbers One Zero Seven?"

Mike Surrey swallowed hard.

"What did you say?"

I pretended to make light of the matter.

"Interpol thinks that you guys are moving diamonds. Of course, I know it's not true. You've got to be sober to do that and you guys are Irish."

Brian shook his head.

"I don't know, Max. If you're saying that Interpol has the goods on us, what does denial get us?"

"A fair trial and a long prison sentence," I answered. "But there's no need to worry about that if you guys are clean or ready to deal."

"We're between the proverbial rock and a hard place," said Larry. "We owe our jobs to Colin. If he sinks, we go under, our jobs, our homes, everything. We're not actually stealing anything. We're only peeling off inventory before it's sold so that Colin can pay his bills. We get paid nothing for what we do. We get our expenses and our regular pay. Nothing more."

"That's very noble, but you're going to have to deal."

"What's the deal?" Brian asked.

"A quid pro quo. You guys come clean and you stay out of prison. Interpol might even let you keep your diamond gig if it finds Haussmann's killer."

"I thought Haussmann died in France," Mike Surrey said.

"That's right. Heart attack induced by a diabetic fit from being given the wrong medication. Interpol wants the killer."

I was feeling better and asked Brian to call me a cab.

"Think about it, guys. I think it's a good deal."

"I'll drive you home, Max," Mike Surrey offered.

"Thanks, Mike. But you go home where you belong. I'll be fine."

6

Rite of Passage

I never thought Colin's Irish mafia would be helpful in shedding light on the picture of international business and tax fraud that was slowly emerging from the shadows. But I counted that Larry O'Leary at least would report my inquiries to Colin who would be tell Henry. Either one or both of the twins would then have to make a pre-emptive move soon to avoid prosecution. I was also counting on word getting back to Mel Solomon and Sol Weinberg, who were bound to be dragged into this mess.

Needless to say, it had not been my intention to spearhead the unraveling the Adair empire but La Salle was very clever. He had sandbagged me into his corner with no way out. But secretly, I was overjoyed at the chance of seeing the Adairs brought down a peg or two.

However, my mind was currently elsewhere. My upset stomach continued and was aggravated by a nagging toothache. To increase my aggravation, I arrived home to find Janine waiting for me with a constipated look on her face. I thought she was again going to bring up the subject of a will.

I was wrong this time. She simply wanted to say she was worried because I was late and that she was leaving with her husband and kids and driving down to Busch Gardens in Williamsburg for a long weekend. She merely wanted to know if I would be all right.

"You have booze in the liquor closet," she commented before leaving. "But I don't see food in the fridge except for some old cheese and rotting fruit. You need to go shopping, dad," she said.

"I'll do that this weekend," I grunted.

"And get a haircut," she added.

"I'm trying to save the few hairs I have left."

"And change your underwear. I bet you're wearing the same pair of shorts I washed before you left for Europe."

"Why? Am I going out on a date?"

"Gladys will be pissed if you see her this weekend the way you look."

And we left it at that. A quick kiss and she was gone.

Falling asleep for what I thought would be a quick nap brought me to the late morning of the next day. I moped about for a while, grew tired and tried napping, but this time I couldn't fall asleep. The kitchen calendar reminded me that it was Friday, February twenty seven, and I thought it would be a good idea to pay my monthly bills. That took less than an hour, including the walk down to the mailbox.

That done, I huffed and puffed my way back up the driveway to answer a telephone ring that could be heard outside the house. I wished I had never picked up the receiver. It was Gladys reminding me that we were supposed to go to the mall later.

It was odd but she never bothered to ask about my trip. I begged off, and she said she would go with her girl friends and call me later. I began to have doubts about this relationship.

I kept my appointment with the dentist who cleaned my teeth and inserted a removable bridge he had prepared months ago. He said the toothache was from poor dental hygiene and that I should keep flossing.

That cramped feeling in my left arm returned. Back at the house, I skipped dinner, broke with protocol and took my shower then instead of waiting for morning, put on fresh underwear, and for good measure I packed a duffel. Feeling much relieved, I dropped off to sleep.

Midnight found me awake and in a sweat. Something wasn't quite right. And so, I dragged myself to my feet and made the call to 911.

For the longest time, people asked me how I knew to make the call. I had no good explanation.

"A guy knows. It's a rite of passage. And a guy never forgets the date," I always answered. For me, it was Friday, the twenty seventh of February.

I ended in Morristown Memorial but the way there was convoluted to say the least. The police came with oxygen and a pill, and I felt better. An EMS vehicle came next and took me to a local hospital where I knew they didn't do hearts. Furthermore, I had a feeling that my insurance didn't cover that particular health care facility. I was by then feeling better and opted to return home over the loud protests of the emergency room attendants.

That morning, after a few hours of sleep, I checked the physician list in the new manual sent by Sentinel to their health plan subscribers. After dressing, I called Brian Donovan for his advice.

"Hold on a minute."

Brian left the phone for a few seconds.

When he got back, he suggested, "Larry says to see Harry Silver. Larry says he's the best cardiologist in the county. Here's the number."

I called, and was told Dr. Silver was away but that I could meet with Barry Benson, the covering physician, at the hospital's emergency room. The drive to Morristown Memorial's emergency room took ten minutes but the wait took an hour before the doctor showed up. The duty nurse told me to get into a hospital gown. I refused, saying that I was waiting for Dr. Benson. But she continued to insist that I don the gown.

"I'm leaving," I declared finally, and started for the door.

"Oh, no you're not," a voice barked. "You're staying!"

I turned around and found a youngish, dark haired, pleasant faced chap in a brown sport coat and khaki slacks blocking my exit. He eyed me quickly from head to foot.

"I'm Barry Benson, Dr. Silver's associate," he said. "And you look awful."

"I fell good right now," I replied.

"Tell you what," he continued. "You come with me. I want to take some video pictures and put you through a stress test. If you pass, you go home. No charge. Fair enough?"

"And if I fail?"

"You stay and pay."

I took the stress test and failed miserably.

The pictures showed two arteries that were 50% and 85% blocked, Barry Benson stated. By chance, my packed duffel was in my car, but the doctor, afraid that I was going to bolt, wouldn't let me out of his sight. He checked me into a hospital room where I gave him the car keys.

Once he made sure that I was in bed and connected by a mess of tubes to some sort of body stabilizing machine, he went out to the car and returned with my bag.

I've been having minor heart attacks, he explained; nothing serious at the moment but it could turn nasty. There was minimal damage at this point and I was lucky to have received a warning shot across the bow. A short, simple procedure was needed. No open heart surgery, but one in which two stents are inserted into the heart from a tiny opening made under the right side of the groin. An angioplasty procedure, he called it.

"You won't even be knocked out," he concluded. "You'll be sedated but conscious. You must be awake to move your arm as we guide the stents in. We're going to do you on Monday and you'll be out Tuesday."

So that was it. I was finally caught. It reminded me that many years ago when I was young and my uncle lay dying.

I visited him at the hospital and he said something unusual.

"The end is near," he said, "when the demons of your past come dancing at your feet."

"What end?" I had asked.

"The end. When you see that wall and you can't avoid it."

It was weird. I never saw the agony on his face until now and I wondered if at last my own number was up. I now understood exactly what he was talking about. Well, at least I had paid the monthly bills.

I called Gladys from the hospital but all I got was a recording. Annoyed, I left no message.

I called my own number for messages and there I found one from Gladys. It was not what I expected. It was a "Dear John" message saying that in view of the fact that marriage was not on my horizon, she felt it was best that we part company. I cursed with a smile on my face.

There was once a Russian girlfriend in my past. I should have stuck it out with the broad, maybe. At least she was great in the sack. Who knows? And before her, there was a Eurasian woman, and before her there was Nicole Colbert, and before her…. Who the hell remembers.

But one of my early flames was Eva who ended up marrying Colin. I was either the greatest winner or the greatest loser in the world.

So here I was. Gladys was no longer an option; the Russian was gone; my daughter was away and left no number. I wanted to get laid at least one more time, but the nurses were either too ugly or too young. The food stank, and I couldn't go to the bathroom without carrying around a tall pole to which was attached a plastic bag that pumped strange fluids into my arm.

Nor could I drink or smoke. Life was really beginning to suck. My sole contact with the outside world was a bedside phone.

I had to call someone, and finally I settled on Larry O'Leary who I knew would be working. We connected, and I explained my predicament.

"Is Harry Silver doing the honors?"

"No. His associate, Barry Benson."

"He's good also. Welcome to the club."

"What club?"

"I had my heart attack five years ago. Benson and Silver treated me too."

"Oh."

"Is there anything I can do?" he asked.

"No," I replied. "Benson says I'll be home Tuesday."

"You will; that's for sure. They do heart work there," he said. "They'll put you on the third floor of the Jefferson Wing."

"How do you know?"

"That's where I was. And oh, did a priest or rabbi visit you yet?"

No, why? I'm not dying."

"That's what I mean. You're not. The word would be out if you were and one of those yo-yo's would have popped in to say you're going to a better place."

"So?"

"That means you're going to live."

"Thanks, Larry. I'll keep that in mind."

So much for my wallowing in self pity.

That Saturday night was nevertheless one of the longest of my life, longer than the night my wife gave birth to Janine, but not as long as the day she died in my arms.

I couldn't sleep well. I had to stay on my back because of the tube. A nurse came by every four hours to give me a pill, and in my helpless state I started thinking how fragile was the fabric of life. One moment you're here and then you're not. I thought back to my army days.

Most of my buddies, like me, left the service alive and well. We had a few losses, to be sure. Colin went in with two first cousins who never made it, but they never knew what hit them. Mike Surrey lost his leg, but other than that, he survived. Some who didn't make it died of one ailment or another, a heart attack, liver failure, prostate cancer, diabetes, and things like that. One was a skydiver and died when his chute didn't open, and another died in a shark attack on a salvage operation in the Caribbean. The rest of us did well except for John Cork who never made a steady living.

Johnny Cork was part of our operation. He and I were points, the first men out of the bird, so to speak, the guys who snuck ahead to ferret out trouble.

Colin? He was our explosives expert. Mike Surrey was supposed to be my backup but he was knocked out of action early on and Johnny Cork, who was Colin's close buddy, was teamed with me. After we were discharged, Johnny went to work for Colin who could rely on him to do things that no one else could be trusted with.

I can't say I disliked the service. I had some of my best times. I had all the women I wanted and more spending cash in my pockets than I have today. I thought I was immortal and nothing would ever happen to me. I even liked the food. Many people hated army food, but I liked it.

Very early Sunday morning my daughter called. She had apparently called home, and when there was no answer, she called Larry.

"I'll leave right away," she declared.

"That's sweet, cookie," I said. "But there's nothing much you can do for me. You don't get much of a chance to get away as a family. Just stay where you are, and I'll see you Tuesday when you get back. That's when I'm going home."

However, Janine was not the only person Larry spoke with. He must have called everyone he could think of. A flower bouquet arrived from Eva Adair which a nurse arranged on the window and then passed me the phone as it started ringing.

I was overwhelmed. It was Eva.

I had a picture in my mind. I saw her, sitting at the telephone table near a mirrored vanity, her legs crossed. She was a tall, blonde woman with a soft, feline face and a statuesque body with a dancer's legs.

"Where are you?"

"Close enough, Max. Do you want company?"

"Always."

"Then the good fairy will grant your wish. I'll be right over."

Eva must have been on the floor because she appeared at my bedside less than a minute later. She gave me a tearful hug and settled down on a chair next to me.

"You big jerk," she said. "Why didn't you call me when it happened?"

"After all these years? I didn't think of it. Besides, I wasn't feeling that bad. Any way, thanks for the flowers."

Eva nodded. She had flown up from Delray and abandoned her Florida wardrobe for a sweater and slacks outfit over which she had thrown a long mink coat. Her blonde pony tail bobbed up and down over its high collar.

"I had to come up anyway to review the books. When Larry called late last night to say you were sick I decided to take an early flight. Max, you need someone to look after you."

"Janine does that."

"Oh yeah? Where is she tonight?"

"In Williamsburg. I told her to stay there."

"Oh, Max. You're such a fucking martyr. When are you going to grow up? Where's Gladys?"

"She gave me the boot."

"It's a good thing she did. You deserve it."

"How are the kids?" I asked.

She giggled happily and gave me a lingering kiss on the lips.

"Spoiled," she replied. "And they're grown up. And they have bad eyes, just like you, Max. Isn't that funny? They have to wear glasses. I think that's why Colin hates you so."

Larry must have related our Friday conversation at the restaurant to her.

"Aw, come on, Evie," I whimpered. "I'm a sick man."

"I also spoke with your doctor. He said you're going to be better than new. I need you healthy to help me out of the mess I'm in."

"Does it have to do with the business?"

"Yes. But I'll know more when I go over the books. But don't you worry about that now. You just concentrate on getting back on your feet."

"Where's Colin?"

"He flew to Paris from the Bahamas with his brother. He has to help him sort things out. Anyway, lets forget Colin for now."

An old question kept prying on my mind.

"Eva," I said. Level with me. We dated for a long time. I even gave you my school ring. How come you never gave me a tumble?"

"You mean get romantic and all that?"

"I suppose."

"You were nice to go out with, Max, and lots of fun, especially in the sack. But you had no purpose in life. You were shiftless. A woman needs a sense of security and a feeling of stability to build a nest and raise a family."

"And Colin filled the bill?"

She smiled sadly.

"It was a trade off. Good marriage or good times. I went for the gold. Let's face it, Max. You always said I was a gold digger. My real problem is that I never realized that Colin reserved his jollies for other women."

She sensed the surprise in my face and elaborated.

"Colin is a two-timing bastard. I'm looking for a way out of this marriage. You're going to be my way out."

"How is that going to happen?"

"You'll see. For starters, you and I can move on from where we left off."

Here was an opportunity I was not going to pass up.

"I'm out of here on Tuesday," I said. "Will you come collect me?"

"You're sweet, Max. I remember when we used to date. You'd ask what time you should come to 'collect me'. That's what I found cute about you."

"I had more hair those days."

"And I was a real blonde."

"What are you going to do after you dump Colin?"

"I have to stay afloat somehow. What about you when you leave here?"

"Well, when I get out of here, I'm either going to press my claim to a piece of the Blue Danube or steal it and take you away from all this."

I was joking abd bragging at the same time.

"Why Max, I never thought you'd have it in you to do something like that. We'll have to talk about those crazy plans of yours."

Larry showed up just then with a box of chocolates and some cigars.

"For you, Max." He showed me the goodies. "Benson says you can't have them anymore. So the sweets go to Eva and I'll smoke the cigars."

Visiting hours were over and they left, promising to return the next day. I felt much better to say the least, and went to sleep at last, determined that I was going to come through this effortlessly, pull myself together and return to becoming the Adonis I never really was.

Dr. Benson was at my bedside bright and early Monday morning with the results of the blood work done over the weekend.

"You've been bad," he declared. "High blood pressure, high cholesterol, a bit of chronic colitis, a touch of diabetes, and you also have a slight case of epilepsy."

"Epilepsy?"

"Epilepsy! You've probably been experiencing wild mood swings with short, wild fits of shaking mixed with cold sweats without giving them much thought. I see some antacid pills near the phone. How long have you been taking them?"

"I thought it was all part of growing older. I've been taking them for years. They work."

Barry Benson shook his head.

"No. They don't work, and you're not old; you're just dumb, and you've got your head buried in the sand. Look. I can fix your ticker. Pills will take care of everything else. But if you want to live, you need a life style change. Start by losing weight and exercising. Think about it. You're going in this afternoon."

I took a closer look at the physician who obviously seemed to relish what he did for a living.

"What made you decide to be a cardiologist?" I asked out of the blue.

The doctor thought about the question a while before responding.

"I became a doctor because that's what my father did, and he followed in my grandfather's footsteps. But do you know what my real love is?"

"No. What?"

"Scuba diving."

"Scuba diving?"

"Yep. Scuba diving. I'm a licensed scuba diving instructor, and I recently passed my last exam to qualify me for commercial deep sea diving. I have a plan," he continued. "After another year of this, I'm going to pack it in and move to the Caribbean and start a marine salvage operation. Maybe you should also think of changing the way you make a living. You might live longer. You might even be happier."

He gave my shoulder a light tug before leaving.

"You'll be good as new," he concluded. "This is a simple procedure. It's what you do afterwards that counts."

All of a sudden, nothing much mattered anymore. I was being drugged and prepped for the operation, and I paid little attention to a cascade of calls that came in throughout the morning. It was just as well.

One of the calls was from Pierre La Salle. He too had received word of my plight and urged me repeatedly not to worry. I asked about the Blue Danube affair and I could hear him laugh over the phone.

"It is a strange case, my fine fellow," he remarked. "Your government has informed us it plans to place a lien on the diamond for unpaid taxes and has asked for a court order to seal the Maison Dore vault in Morristown. This is only the beginning. The Adairs and your government will be locked in court for months before the matter is settled. So relax, Max, and get back on your feet. We have plenty of time. And do not forget Jouvet's offer. It remains open."

And so it went. I was by now too sedated to care. To this day I can barely recall Eva, Larry O'Leary, Mike Surrey and Brian Donovan dropping by in the long basement corridor with the light tan walls moments before I was wheeled on a stretcher by two attendants through the double doors leading into the operating room. I only remember closing my eyes and straining to hear the doors bang shut as I went through. I missed the banging door but I did hear a humming sound of what seemed to be a compressor or generator or maybe a respirator working in the background.

A philosopher named Descartes once said, "I think. Therefore I am."

So long as I kept thinking, I would stay alive. But what if I went brain dead and stopped thinking? What if I flat lined? What then?

Nothing unusual happened during the operation. Although sedated, I was not asleep. And there was none of that business where people said they flat lined and passed through a great white light before returning to life. The only light I saw came from beams over the operating table and I kept hearing the whirring sound of that distant compressor or respirator.

The operation was simple. I obeyed orders, shifting positions and raising my arm on command.

"Raise your arm, Max. Raise your arm!" I heard the doctor say.

"Higher, Max. Higher!"

The doctor repeated the command several times during the operation.

I felt discomfort but little pain. I distinctly recall the doctor making small talk with his associates as he rummaged for what sounded like silverware in a drawer and I thought someone was playing piano on my right thigh and groin area.

There were two episodes of unbearable pressure on my chest. During the second crisis, I cried out, "Tell my wife I love her!"

The doctor asked me afterwards about my wife and I explained that I must have been delirious because she had passed away years ago.

He smiled.

"We have to be careful, Max. Men often call out a woman's name when they're on the table. We're never sure if it's a wife, mother, or a girlfriend."

A while later, when I was lying still groggy on the stretcher with Eva at my side in the outer corridor, Barry Benson came out of the operating room with something in his hand.

"You're all clear," he declared. "An eighteen wheeler could drive through your arteries."

He placed a pair of defibrillator paddles on my chest.

"Here. Use these if you don't feel good."

I was too sore to laugh, but I did manage a weak grin.

"Who is taking this guy home tomorrow?"

The doctor looked directly at Eva.

"I am," she replied, and Barry Benson gave her an envelope of pills.

"Make sure he takes these," he ordered. "One a day until he sees me in a week." Turning to me, he said, "You'll keep until I see you again."

Another half hour passed and I was back in bed where I was instructed to lie on my back without moving for six hours. A weight was placed on my abdomen to ensure compliance. Eva surprised me by giving me a long soulful kiss and said she would be by tomorrow with Janine who had called her from the road while I was in the operating room. Life, after all, was not so bad.

I had to go to the bathroom. An orderly came by who helped me stagger to the private toilet in the room. I looked into the full length mirror and saw a pale, drawn, misshapen creature with shadowy bloodshot eyes staring back at me. I was black and blue and grotesque. I groaned at the sight, finished my business and swore mightily that this experience would never again be repeated.

7

Doorbell

Late Tuesday morning, I wobbled out of the hospital sandwiched between my daughter and Eva. The recovery process began with a discouraging cup of watery soup and a tasteless salad at a local eatery while a couple at the next booth feasted on steak and potatoes.

Eva personally supervised my recovery and rehabilitation. Mornings were devoted to physical therapy, afternoons to chores around the house and at the office, and evenings to exercises in culinary restraint.

Summarily, I could eat anything I didn't like and drink anything I hated.

The results were astounding. I began losing weight immediately. I would have given up this Spartan life but for the after-hours rewards that Eva's company offered me. There were also the periodic checkups. Barry Benson was out much of the time and in his absence I was attended by Harry Silver.

Dr. Silver seemed older than his associate. I had heard that he had started his professional life as an internist and only lately turned to cardiology after becoming board certified to do heart surgery. To say the least, I was unimpressed when we met. He wore his hair in a ponytail and seemed totally bored with my situation, conveying an impression that he had no interest in any of his patients and that if he had any choice he would rather be running a bed and breakfast at some seaside resort.

He went through the motions of giving me an examination and then gave me several envelopes filled with pills.

"What are these?" I asked.

"The usual," he answered. "Anti-cholesterol, high blood pressure pills and something for your diabetes and a mild sedative for epilepsy. But the best thing for you is diet and exercise."

"Aren't these medications available by prescription at a pharmacy?"

"Sure they are. But these are free. You come here when you run out and I'll save you money."

"Well, give me some prescriptions anyway, in case I run out while I'm out of town."

The doctor grumbled as he wrote out the pharmacy prescriptions. But something about his behavior made me suspicious.

"How many refills?"

Silver's eyes narrowed.

"A year's worth. Why? Are you leaving town?"

I shrugged my shoulders and replied, "You never know."

As much as I liked Barry Benson, I started distrusting Harry Silver.

Other than to get back on my feet, I had no plan, but Eva did become an increasing presence in my life. I don't think either of us thought in terms of a so-called relationship but there it was. She kept a condo, a two bedroom Florida apartment in Delray Beach not far from an old hotel called the Poinciana that Colin bought a few years ago.

The Poinciana was on Atlantic Avenue, the town's trendy shopping and dining thoroughfare than extended from the highway to the beach on the ocean side of the causeway. A three story, sand colored stucco structure, it was probably built in the early nineteen twenties when terra cotta roofs and imitation Turkish or Moorish minaret towers were popular sights at celebrity hotels. The Biltmore in Coral Gables had them as did the Breakers of Palm Beach, although those of the Breakers tended to be more Gothic.

The Poinciana's watch towers had bright red maroon domes, matching the the maroon awnings over the guest room windows and the three maroon and gold livery awnings over the veranda and guest entrance four steps up from Atlantic Avenue's street level.

Eva's condo was next to the Del Rey Resort Tower hotel across the road from the beach. It was a great place for a clandestine relationship and I was soon a frequent flyer between New Jersey and Florida.

The Blue Danube diamond went on the back burner for a while. Sentinel had major clients in the area who were always lodging claims for lost and/or stolen high priced jewelry, and Mel Solomon asked me to temporarily take over for a retiring agent. The company also had a maritime division and Mel gave me the added job of investigating marine claims. That plum came with a membership at the Delray Yacht Club where Colin kept his yacht.

If Eva hated her husband, she remained a loyal business partner and dutifully managed the Poinciana and His South Florida Trust operation in his absence. The investment banking house was Colin's big interest. With offices in Fort Lauderdale and Delray, Eva managed both places with the help of Mel's peripatetic vice president, Bill Ford.

South Florida Trust owned skyscrapers in Fort Lauderdale and Miami (which housed the Sentinel and Centurion insurance companies) and was itself owned by Island Investments, an Adair owned corporation in the Bahamas that enjoyed tax free status. It did not take perfect eyesight to see that if Colin was working a tax scam, Eva was not far behind him.

At the Delray Yacht Club I befriended the president of the accounting firm who audited all the Adair books which had by now been subpoenaed by the IRS through a court order. He essentially confirmed what I had learned from Colin's Irish mafia back in New Jersey, namely, that all his businesses were syphons designed to suck cash from the States to the Bahamas. In addition, Sentinel was a principal South Florida Trust investor and client.

Much to my surprise, so was Victor Nishkanian, the owner of the Carnival diner across the street from the Poinciana and an old friend of mine.

Luck was with me. Once, when I was in Delray, Otto Katz, who I hadn't seen in months, showed up unexpectedly at the Poinciana. I found him at the lobby bar and we greeted one another like long lost friends.

"What brings you to sunny Florida, Otto?"

"Vacation, Max. Actually, I'm on loan from Kumari. Colin Adair invited me here to appraise some estate jewelry. He also owed me for some services I performed."

"Did these services involve cutting illegal diamonds?" I asked.

Otto almost spilled his drink.

"What the hell are you talking about?"

"It's only a rumor, old buddy. It comes from Interpol."

The big man knew the jig was up. He ordered me a drink while he regained his composure.

"What's in it for me if I talk?"

I was taking a chance here.

"Immunity, if this thing gets nasty." I smiled benignly. "How about it?"

He started talking, and his waterfall of words never stopped and confirmed my scenario of the events that had transpired up to now. He took a deep breath when he finished.

"I never made an extra penny on the deal. I was paid my regular salary by Rajeesh Kumari with my travel expenses paid by Sol Weinberg. He wanted to help Colin pay his bills and keep Sentinel solvent."

"Was it a love affair, or what?"

Otto shook his head.

"No charity, Max. Raj and Sol are slowly worming their way into Colin's and Mel's businesses. This is a cheap, painless way to take over, diamond by diamond. Every transaction increases their stake. If this goes on long enough, they'll end up owning everything."

And then it came to me like a message from above.

"You know, Otto. We should give thought to stealing the Blue Danube for ourselves. Once it's in our hands, we can make a deal with the devil, with the IRS, with anyone. If some of you guys stand the chance of going to prison on a diamond smuggling charge, we might as well all go to prison for something worth while."

Otto's eyes narrowed.

"I don't think we'll be caught, Max, if we do it."

"Is that a prediction or a prophesy?"

"It's certainty. Not if the heist is done right. Speak to Mike Surrey. I've had a similar idea and spoke with him. He knows the Morristown Dore building. All we need is find a legitimate reason to see the diamond. Since you're a part owner, you can force the issue and ask to see the stone. We can do the rest."

"We'll need more than Mike Surrey," I said.

Otto gave me a bland smile.

"You'll want all of Colin's mafia, some police allies and your faithful old diamond cutter, me."

I made a point of seeing Mike on one of my trips home. He confirmed his talk with Otto and indicated he was ready to take the plunge if we were. I told him that I would think about it. Mike Surrey was a veritable encyclopedia. He knew everything about everyone and was a history book when it came to the Adair family.

He told me that Colin's great-grandfather, Patrick, the one who acquired the Blue Danube, came to the States from Ireland in the late 1800's. He used the diamond to leverage the purchase of a crumbling inn in Bernardsville. He restored it, renamed it the Bernardsville Club Hotel, adding a restaurant that became a Morris County fine dining fixture.

Patrick married and had two sons, Patrick Jr., and Sinclair. Patrick Jr. ran the Bernardsville place while Sinclair opened a second location, the Blue Marlin, in Seagirt.

Sinclair and his wife had no children of their own. However, he and Frank Hague, Jersey City's political boss, were friends. Once a year, Hague would send his cronies and backers down to Seagirt for a day of sun and fun at the beach topped off by a night at the Blue Marlin. Women were brought in to entertain the more important guests. One of the girls was a waitress named Josephine who became Sinclair's mistress and restaurant manager. His wife found out, so he went across the inlet to Point Pleasant and opened another eatery that he called Joe's and turned it over to her.

There was an apartment over the bar and they lived there. Josephine soon became pregnant and gave birth to the twins, Colin and Henry. Sinclair's wife died at about the same time that Josephine passed away and old man Sinclair died shortly after. Before he passed on, he formally adopted his sons and made them legal. That part I knew.

But Josephine was not his only girlfriend. He had another who lived in Bay Head and got her pregnant as well. The woman gave birth to a girl who he named Colleen and also adopted. I dated Colleen when we were in school but I always preferred Eva, having even given her my old school ring to wear. When Colin made the moves on her, I started dating Colleen seriously. And when Colin and Eva married, I married Colleen on the rebound upon leaving the army. Our wedding was at the Bernardsville Club and was hosted by Patrick Jr., and his wife. It was strange that they would host a wedding while still grieving the loss of their two sons. Perhaps it was because they felt that life had to go on no matter what. But that feeling, in retrospect, made no sense at all since they died in an apparent murder-suicide pact a few days later while we were on our honeymoon in Bermuda.

It was a tragedy that has pressed my mind from the day it happened. Patrick Junior's two sons, who were by definition Colin and Henry's first cousins were several years older. When they joined the army, Colin went in and the rest of us followed except Henry who ran off to France. The cousins were blown up by land mines in an operation commanded by Colin. It was the same ill conceived mission that cost Mike Surrey a leg. That war had no winners and to learn of our wedding hosts' deaths while on our honeymoon brought the conflict to a horrific close.

The official story, the one hawked by the district attorney and published in the papers was that Patrick shot his wife and then himself. The details filled in for me by Mike Surrey was that Tom Lyons, who was a rookie cop at the time, reached the scene after being called by Colin who was on the property with Johnny Cork when the killings took place. Tom was then quoted by the press as believing a third person was at the house, an angle that was pursued and went nowhere.

Colin's official statement was that they were visiting his aunt and uncle and had come up on the bodies inside the house when they broke in after no one answered the door. It just so happened that Patrick Jr. and his wife kept no guns and knew nothing about them, an interesting tidbit that was ignored. Also ignored were the facts that they had no health, emotional or financial problems. The one weapon found in Patrick's hand in fact belonged to Colin, an old 32 caliber revolver. If it was not a murder-suicide incident, it had to be a double-murder. But no prints other than Patrick's were found on the gun and the prosecutor's office refused to bring charges, ostensibly for a lack of solid evidence. And so, Colin and Henry lucked out, as did Colleen. They inherited everything on the Patrick Adair side, including the Bernardsville hotel and Patrick's share of the Blue Danube diamond.

I was in a win-win position. My wife was not into intra-family feuding. Her idea was to keep the peace and wait, making sure that Janine's interests were protected. As for myself, being comfortable with my lot in life, I went with the flow. Besides, being the object of Colin's scorn and ire, especially after Eva's kids were born, brought me satisfaction.

I had the best of all worlds. I was married to an heiress, had a daughter and was able to continue tapping Eva on occasion without the inconvenience of being married to a gold digger. It never dawned on me that Colin would take action on his suspicions even though it was well known that he harbored a deep streak of paranoia and was wary of everything and everyone.

Mike Surrey said it best.

"Colin is threatened by competition even when it doesn't exist."

Mike had it right. I was Colin's invisible competition and he knew it.

Colin had a secret desire. Like Carl and Louis, he wanted to be more than he was. Being an inn keeper was not good enough for him. He had visions of grandeur and had the notion that high society blue bloods with up turned noses would not cozy up to him due to the nature of his business and ethnic background.

How he got those airs was a mystery. He and Henry were the bastard sons of a philanderer and a harlot and like most of us he had few bragging rights about pedigree.

Colin nevertheless felt a need to reinvent himself. He positioned himself as an investment banker and financier who as a sideline owned a chain of high class eateries. There, well heeled clients could be entertained with vintage wines and champagnes, top shelf liquors and the finest cuisine prepared by the best chefs and served by white gloved waiters in tuxedos.

Profits were used to branch out into the financial services industry and high rise office real estate into which clients were smooth talked into investing or in lending money. Brian Donovan filled in the details through his friendship with lawyers and accountants who represented Colin and dined regularly at the Bernardsville restaurant. He was even able to supply me with a paper trail by having many important financial records purloined and copied. Whatever motive he had for being cooperative, I didn't ask.

Larry O'Leary was less open, maybe because he had more to lose than Brian or Mike in turning on Colin. Nevertheless, little by little, a fascinating picture was emerging. Fifty percent of gross revenues from all operations were remitted to Island Investments which owned the stock in Colin's stateside enterprises. This meant that his stateside businesses either barely broke even or ran big losses while Island Investments enjoyed high tax free profits. Whether this was a real crime was a question beyond my competence to answer. One thing was sure. Many people were going to take a financial bath when this wonderful river of cash would dry up.

When Eva was in Delray, I would stay at the Del Rey Tower and she would come over or I would go to her condo, or sometimes we spent the night at the Poinciana for a change of pace. We had many good times and I even began thinking that I might be falling in love again.

Love? I wasn't sure. Infatuation? For sure. Temporary blindness, was the phrase Janine used to describe my affair.

But true love it wasn't, at least not yet. Something was not right. However, not once did Eva bring up the subject of the Blue Danube. I found that to be refreshing yet curious.

That didn't puzzle me as much as her husband. Colin was conspicuous by his absence. If I was in New Jersey, he was in Florida. If I was in Florida, he was in New Jersey. If I was in Jersey in the morning and in Florida in the afternoon, he was in Europe or the Bahamas or making the rounds of his restaurants and other businesses.

Eva was forever making excuses for his being away and after a while I stopped asking. The same with Henry Adair. He was constantly on the road. Sightings had him looking fit; others had him ill and dying. He was always somewhere else. It was plain that I was being avoided like the plague.

It was a few months after my hospital discharge that I began thinking back to Carl Haussmann and Johnny Cork. In particular, I wanted to retrace the steps Johnny had taken prior to his departure for Paris.

Johnny Cork lived in an old houseboat on a swampy stream off the New River west of the Interstate on the outskirts of Fort Lauderdale. His constant companion was an old dog named Doorbell, was so named because it barked whenever someone came to the door. Johnny was forever being hounded by bill collectors. Doorbell would bark when they arrived and Johnny would dive out a rear window and take off in his dinghy.

"Who's taking care of Doorbell while Johnny is gone?" I asked Eva one fine day out of clear blue sky.

Eva reacted as if she had been hit by lightening and tried an off-the-cuff response.

"I think Colin sends one of his guys to clean the place and feed the dog."

She sensed my skepticism by and elaborated.

"Yesterday, my brother, Frank, went with dog food."

"Does he still drive for Jake?"

She nodded.

The explanation seemed satisfactory but I decided to pay his houseboat a visit anyway after speaking with Jake Santana over lunch at the Poinciana.

"It's funny that no missing persons report on Johnny Cork was ever filed," Jake noted. "Neither was one ever filed in France."

"This case is weird," he went on. "La Salle called me a few weeks ago to go have a look see and I asked a friend down in Broward County to go check but he hasn't gotten around to it. Broward County is outside our jurisdiction so I can't send anyone down officially. Broward County doesn't speak to Palm Beach County. But you can go have a look see."

"Eva says Colin's guys look after the place, or maybe Frank."

"Eva's brother? Maybe. I don't bug him about what he does on his own time. I don't even like the guy. I keep him on for Eva's sake. Now Colin's guys are George Lerman and Ed Houston who he shares with Mel Solomon, and I don't think dog watching is their thing. In any case, I'll tell Frank to pick you up after lunch at your hotel."

Frank Barton. As lithe and tall as Eva was, her brother was short and built like an ox. He showed up at the Del Rey Tower an hour later and we were off.

It took us a half hour to make the trip to Fort Lauderdale on the Interstate.

We turned off the highway at Broward Avenue and drove west. The Fort Lauderdale skyline shrank behind us and we were soon threading our way around boat yards, trailer camps, small factories, warehouses and marine salvage operations in the marshy flats along the New River.

The sky was cloudless and the afternoon heat was stifling. It was so hot the ground in front of us shimmered as we approached a rundown marina filled with derelict vessels parked under the shadow of an overpass.

"How was Doorbell the last time you visited?" I asked Frank.

"I haven't seen Doorbell since Johnny flew to Paris last year," he replied. "I was going to drive him to the airport to catch a flight to Newark," he replied, "but Larry O'Leary was in town and said he'd do the honors. John does work for Colin when he's sober. Colin or Eva, or one of the hotel workers, are supposed to take care of the dog when Johnny is away."

We stopped in front of a deserted houseboat that was listing on one side and slowly sinking into the weed-covered mud around it.

Frank seemed unnecessarily nervous so I had him wait in the car while I went over to the decaying vessel to have a look. Ordinarily, Doorbell would have been barking incessantly but only silence greeted me.

I entered the houseboat and there on the floor in the middle of the room was Doorbell, its small decomposing body with its throat cut lying in a rust colored pool of dried blood.

I stepped over the dog and walked gingerly over the crumbling floors and searched the rest of the houseboat. It was filthy and reeked of rot and was filled with accumulated dirt and garbage. Except for poor Doorbell, there was no sign of violence and the mess was pretty much untouched.

Eva's story was a fabrication. Either she knew something and was not talking or she knew nothing and simply made up a story to keep me off her back. Her way of handling situations beyond her understanding was often to simply ignore them.

But the reality was that whoever picked up Johnny Cork either returned to slit Doorbell's throat or had someone else do the job. This could only mean that John Cork had been booked on a one way ticket to Paris.

I walked out into the blinding sunlight and returned to the car.

Frank looked at me sideways from the driver's seat.

"Find anything?" he asked.

I thought of lying to Frank, saying that Doorbell was nowhere to be found, but on second thought, I felt that he would soon find out the truth and that moreover, he might have himself done the deed.

"Doorbell's dead," I replied.

When I got back to the hotel I called Jake and asked him to have Doorbell picked up for an autopsy.

"I want to know how long the dog's been dead," I told him.

Jake Santana was furious.

"Autopsy a dog?"

He nevertheless arranged to have an anonymous call made to the Broward County's public health authority which had the houseboat declared a health hazard. Doorbell's body was removed, and view of the fact that it was knifed to death, the place was dusted for fingerprints and an autopsy dutifully performed.

No incriminating prints were found, but the autopsy revealed that Doorbell died around the time Johnny Cork left to catch his flight to Newark. None of this lead anywhere because it was known that very often Larry and Frank would take turns watching Johnny's place when he was away or being dried out at some detoxification center.

"What now?" Santana asked a few days later.

"Nothing. Inform Interpol, that's all. The only crime we have is a case of animal cruelty."

"You know, Max. Maybe you should drop the whole thing."

"I don't follow."

"Listen. How long do we know one another?"

"Ten? Twenty years?"

"More than twenty, if you count our time in the service. So, listen. We have a dead man in Paris who may have been attacked in New Jersey and died in a foreign country. That's a jurisdictional dispute. We have a man who vanished in thin air, and who knows why. No crime there."

"At least not yet."

"And we have one lousy mutt with a slit throat. Anyone could have done that."

"So?"

"You have a lot going for you, Max. Maybe you should go on about your life and leave this thing alone."

"Have you made any deals with Colin, Jake?"

Santana looked down and then stared directly into my eyes.

"Everyone deals with Colin. If he goes down, we go down. Look, I own a security company that Colin financed. We move cash and securities for him to the Bahamas. That's how I can afford a nice house and good things for the wife and kids. I'm branching out on my own, but I need a few months time. We're all in the same boat, me, Brian, Larry and Mike. We're at that time of life when we have big bills to pay. We know Colin is going down. All we want to do is to stall for time. Then you do what you have to do. What do you think, Max?"

The detective was almost begging at this point. I slapped him on the back and said, "Don't worry, Jake. I'll keep quiet and lay off for a while. I also have an idea."

"What's that?"

"I've been talking to Otto Katz and Mike Surrey about the idea of stealing the Blue Danube for ourselves. We can then make a deal with anyone we want, or in the worse case scenario, we can have it cut up. As I told Otto, the sum of its parts could bring more than the whole. But we need confederates to help us pull it off."

Jake's face brightened.

"I don't know if I'd look good in prison orange, Max. However, it might be our only golden parachute."

"A diamond parachute, Jake. A big diamond parachute."

"I have to think about this," said Jake.

"No rush. Meanwhile, there is one question hanging on my mind."

"What's that?"

"Colin Adair and Johnny Cork were always tight. Any idea why that was?"

Jake Santana shook his head.

"I've often wondered about that. They're total opposites and yet they stuck to one another like glue. Go figure."

We shook hands over our tacit understanding and parted company.

8

Unsolved Mystery

I returned to New Jersey the next day, arriving home in time to receive an overseas call from Pierre La Salle.

"I hear that you have been busy, Max."

Good old Pierre. He never missed a beat. I brought him up do date about everything I had learned, including my trip to Johnny Cork's houseboat, but I omitted my conversation with Jake Santana. It made no difference. La Salle was fully acquainted with Jake's extra-curricular activities.

"Interpol has a net around Maison Dore, Sentinel, the Adair twins and all the players small and large," La Salle informed me. "It is but a matter of time before we pull in the net to examine our fish. The little fish, we may set free in return for testimony. The rest will go to prison for many years."

"How much time before you draw the net?" I asked.

"Certainly in the next few months."

"Is there wiggle room for the big players?"

I could picture La Salle's smile at the other end.

"Jouvet wants the Blue Danube. As far as Interpol is concerned, there is always wiggle room except for murder. There, we have no wiggle room."

Then he continued.

"I have other news, Max."

"What is that?"

"We found out that Carl Haussmann had a history of heart problems that went along with his diabetes."

"That's old news," I reminded him.

"Correct, my friend. But what is new is that he was never treated in France for his condition. He was treated in your country."

"Do you know by whom?"

I could hear La Salle over the phone rummaging through papers and files on his desk.

"Ah yes. One moment. Ah, here it is. His treatments were being supervised by a medical group called Madison Medical Associates. Two physicians are in the group, a Barry Benson and a Harry Silver. Can you do me a favor and find out more about them?"

"Damn!"

"What did you say, Max?"

"Dr. Benson treated me and Dr. Silver gave me my pills."

There was dead silence for a long moment before La Salle finally made a comment.

"Perhaps, Max, you should consider changing doctors."

The conversation ended on that note.

Nothing was to be gained by going crazy over La Salle's revelations, and I had to assume that he was following professional instincts which were not going to be compromised by self interest. At least, I was glad to know Pierre was still actively pursuing Haussmann's murder investigation.

I should have had the brains to back off from what could easily become a misadventure. There were other jobs I could find that involved little or no risk. Or, I could retire. I had enough money. And insofar as protecting my daughter's interest in the Blue Danube, that could easily be left to the courts and an attorney skilled in such matters.

However, assuming the courts validated my claim to a share of the stone, no guarantee existed to reserve a chunk of its value for me or for Janine after creditors' claims were met. After the battles ended and the dust settled and the lawyers paid and all debts liquidated, what would be left? Stealing the Blue Danube was beginning to sound better and better.

Oh, well. That was life. A visit to Tom Lyons, now a detective inspector for the county specializing in white collar crime, was in order. One phone call reached him and he told me to come to his Morristown office.

He gave me a hearty handshake, ushered me into a small office behind a partition and pointed to a thick file of papers tucked unevenly between a dog eared folder on his messy desk before sitting down.

"Getting busy again, Max?"

Tom Lyons was way over six feet and could have passed for John Wayne in his prime. Big and broad shouldered with conservatively trimmed gray hair, he had a large friendly face and twinkling hazel eyes behind a pair of glasses.

The rookie cop's blue uniform that I remembered had long been replaced by a tan sport coat, shirt, tie and dark brown slacks over wing tip shoes.

"You were wearing glasses when we last met," he noted.

"It was two years ago," I said. "A stolen jewelry case, I think. I went for an operation after that to cure my astigmatism. It worked."

"You didn't like glasses?"

"Vanity, inspector. Sheer vanity."

I pointed to the file on his desk.

"What's with the paper?"

"Oh, that? We've been following the Carl Haussmann case in cooperation with your Interpol friends. I figured you'd surface soon or later. How are you feeling these days?"

"Better, thanks."

Tom Lyons leaned way back in his swivel office chair and peered at me through the bi-focal part of his glasses.

"So, what can I do for you?"

I'd like to probe your memory about the deaths of Patrick Adair and his wife about twenty years ago. It happened shortly after Colleen and I were married. As a matter of fact, we were on out honeymoon in Bermuda."

"I know that or else you could have been a suspect."

"How do you figure that?

Colin Adair and Johnny Cork were at the house. There was a third person with them."

"Do you know that for a fact?"

"You bet. I interviewed Cork at the house and several times later on, but he was drunk most of the time and wasn't very helpful. I also interviewed Colin but he denied anyone else was there. But he was lying and covering for someone. He lied to me and he lied to the DA's office. Why the DA dropped the case is beyond me."

Tom took a deep breath and shook his head sadly.

"Unfortunately, the DA is long gone and everyone else involved with the investigation is either dead or retired. But I'm telling you, there was a third person at the house."

"Any real proof?"

"A school ring. It was on the floor next to an open window in the back of the house. You'd be our man except that you were in Bermuda when they died. Did you lose or give the ring to anyone, Max?"

I shook my head.

Is the case still open?"

Tom lost his smile.

"It's an open case as far as I'm concerned. There's no statute of limitations on murder. Why are you interested?"

"How does a man with no small arms experience shoot and kill his wife and then himself."

Tom nodded.

"It happens rarely, but it happens. We would have liked to have performed an autopsy but the bodies were cremated right away."

"No graves?"

"No.

"You still have the gun?"

"A 32 caliber job. It's in our inventory. The police keeps evidence forever around here."

"It's a hunch, but can you check to see if the weapon was designed for a right handed or left handed person?"

The detective leaned forward.

"Man. I never investigated that angle. But it wouldn't matter. Those revolvers were generic. It would be almost impossible to tell if the shooter was a left or right handed. What are you getting at?"

"Here's the thing. Old man Patrick was a southpaw like me. I don't know much about guns, but lefties fire weapons differently than normal folks and create opposite pressure on the trigger when they squeeze it. This may be grabbing at straws in the wind, but it's worth a shot, if you pardon the pun."

He stopped talking suddenly and looked at me through lowered eyes.

"Are you sure you're not setting yourself up to grab the Blue Diamond if Colin is put away?"

I got up and prepared to leave.

"Thomas," I said. "It's a thought. Otherwise, I'll have to stand in line with everyone else if something happens to him. But you've been hearing too many rumors."

Tom Lyons leaned back again and laughed.

"And there are many, Max. So do keep me posted about the larceny in your heart."

He tapped the top of the file lovingly.

"One of the pieces I can't fit is Eva's part in this case. Can you shed any light on her? I hear the two of you have become an item, especially since her old man is away so often."

"Is that illegal?"

"Not for you. You're a jolly widower. In her case, it's called adultery. But that's besides the point. I need information about her involvement in Colin's operations."

"Hard to say. If I was her, I'd be up to my eyeballs."

Tom Lyons escorted me to the office door.

"Let's keep in touch, Max. And let me know when you finally decide to grab the Blue Danube. I'd like to be the one to order you a tailor made prison ensemble unless we can make a deal."

A few weeks later I took a call from Otto Katz in Florida. He was flying to Newark airport and staying overnight at the Marriott to catch the next Paris flight. He sounded anxious and wanted to meet. It seemed like a good idea and we agreed to have coffee at the hotel grill that evening.

I found him in a booth slouched over a cup of coffee on the table. Another cup of coffee was waiting for me.

I slid into the opposite seat with a perfunctory greeting, expecting to make small talk, and was surprised when he came straight to the point.

"Interpol wants to interview me in Paris," he blurted out.

I tried to maintain my cool.

"Who contacted you?"

"La Salle's assistant."

"Simon Perez?"

"Yes. He was vacationing in Florida and delivered a message from Pierre La Salle. I called La Salle and he confirmed he wanted to see me and talk about my role with Kumari and Maison Dore. Am I in trouble, Max?"

I burst out laughing.

"Otto. You're over-reacting. You and I, we're small fish. La Salle doesn't want us. He wants to trap Haussmann's killer whoever that is, and he wants to stop the illegal international diamond trafficking that Kumari, Dore and the Adairs are engaged in."

"What about tax fraud and money laundering?"

"Also, but I think the feds are more interested in that angle."

"The justice ministry people also want to speak to me."

I rubbed my chin.

"That would be Jouvet. Tax evasion is a crime in France too."

Otto threw up his big hands.

"But I wasn't alone. I was doing my job."

I tried my best to calm him down.

"No doubt about it. But you're clear, as long as you get La Salle on your side. Throw him a bone. Suggest that you'd like to include him in a plan to steal the Blue Danube. He's up to his eyeballs in debt. He'll jump for joy at the chance to retire rich."

The big man relaxed.

"You think so?"

"I know so. Now, answer me this. Was anyone at the viewing of the Blue Danube who was not supposed to have been there?"

"Larry O'Leary stood in for Colin Adair. But now that you ask, there was someone waiting outside the vault…."

And he went on to describe Johnny Cork.

"….What I found strange was that when the inspection was completed, Carl Haussmann left with Larry O'Leary and that guy standing outside. What was that all about, Max?"

"I have no idea. But if I were you, I wouldn't volunteer that information."

Otto's angst could not be completely soothed but he was definitely in a better frame of mind, especially when I said I was still warm to the idea of stealing the Blue Danube.

"Certainly you're joking," he said happily.

I shook my head.

"I'm becoming more serious every day."

He seemed extremely happy as he returned to his room.

I was home an hour later to find Janine waiting up for me at the house in a mild state of agitation.

"Where were you?"

"At the airport," I said. "Having a coffee with Otto Katz."

"The big Santa Claus guy in the green corduroy suit?"

"That's him. What's up, cookie?"

"I don't know what you're up to, but Tom Lyons called me at my house. He said I had to find you. Call him back, dad. He gave me his home number."

I took the note and called the number. Tom picked up right away.

"Where the hell were you?" Tom demanded to know.

"At the airport with Otto. He's going to Paris to meet with La Salle."

"Great. Now, let me bring you up to date. I found the gun we were talking about. We still have it."

"Yeah, so?"

"We had it tested and examined. It has apparently been used often, probably for target practice, and the trigger squeezes ever so slightly to the right."

"Well, let me ask you this. If Patrick was a leftie, why was he using a right handed gun? That doesn't make sense, does it?"

"No it doesn't," said Tom. .

"So, now what do we have?" I asked him.

"A theory. If Patrick didn't do it, we have Colin Adair, Johnny Cork and a third person, presently unknown."

"And we have a gun and a ring."

III

DEADLY INTERLUDE

9

The death of Louis Dore

A school ring and a gun. The ring was mine and the gun once belonged to a member of the Adair family. I had given the ring to Eva and who knows who used the gun? Was she Tom Lyons' unknown third person? I didn't have the guts to try and find out. How do you ask a woman you are currently screwing if she committed a murder more than twenty years ago?

Life crawled at a snail's pace. Days became weeks and weeks rolled into months and soon the green hills of northern New Jersey were covered with snow under the soft melancholy light of winter. By Christmas, I was back to an earlier self, pounds lighter and feeling trim. Colin and Henry were still playing cat and mouse and I was getting bored and beginning to find some of the nitty little details in my relationship with Eva annoying. I was falling out of love.

Thus, when Pierre La Salle called early in the new year to inform me that Louis Dore had committed suicide, I relished the news as an opportunity to get back in action. Pierre thought that Louis killed himself over the loss of his partner. I wasn't so sure, unless they were lovers. He never missed a step after Carl died. Louis inherited Carl's half of the business and replaced him with Otto Katz on a contract basis to cut and appraise diamonds. This new arrangement was good for Kumari who increased its stake in Dore as the price for giving Otto to Louis on a permanent loan basis.

But now we had new circumstances. With Louis gone, would Maison Dore go to Henry Adair? It bothered me that a prosperous business like Maison Dore should fall into the hands of a draft dodger who with his brother might have also been the architects of Carl Haussmann's murder. I wanted to fly to Paris to see things for myself.

I called Mel Solomon to tell him my plans. He was out of town and was connected to Bill Ford, his CEO.

Needless to say, he was not thrilled at what he called my "meddling," but he grudgingly went along.

"Don't get lost and don't break the bank with your expense account like you usually do," he said. "And remember. You work for us not for anyone else."

Then out for nowhere he added, "Since you've been a little out of sorts, go see your doctor before you leave."

A chronic hypochondriac and habitually prone to suggestion, I made an appointment to see Barry Benson for a checkup. Again, it was Harry Silver who was at the office. He gave me a clean bill of health.

At the end of our session, he asked, "Have you been taking your pills?"

"Yes," I lied.

"Then take these with you and take one whenever you board a flight. In the event you are out of whack, they will stabilize your system."

He gave me a small envelope of pills which I promptly threw in my pocket. I was beginning to accumulate a pill collection.

A Concorde jet landed me at Charles De Gaulle International Airport on a cold afternoon with fog beginning to set in. But it was not quite a fog. It was more of a thick haze that enveloped the city's gothic architecture in a ghostly shroud and left the tops of buildings and churches barely visible in the dying half light of winter.

Night falls early in Paris during the winter months and it was dark by the late afternoon when I finally caught up with Pierre La Salle in his office after trying unsuccessfully to reach Henry at Maison Dore.

"You look younger, Max," Pierre remarked.

"Thanks," I replied. "I'm losing weight, but I can't say that I'm enjoying life more."

"My sources say you are seeing Eva Adair. Business or pleasure?"

"Lust, Pierre. Lust covers business and pleasure and some pain."

"Ah. One cannot have everything, my friend. You must decide where you stand and what you want otherwise you will have pain with no business and no pleasure. Now, tell me what you have been doing."

I proceeded to carefully brief La Salle about all the events surrounding the discovery of Doorbell's death, including my discussions with Jake Santana and Tom Lyons. Pierre listened politely until I was finished.

"And of course there was your encounter with Otto," he added with a knowing wink.

"Yes. Did he call on you?"

"He did, and he told me everything. What is more, he has learned quite a bit since he started doing work for Dore and has become very cooperative. He has become, what do you say in English, a double agent?"

"You mean a stool pigeon?"

La Salle laughed.

"Whatever, Max. But, you will be happy to hear that it was on the basis of his information that Interpol prevailed upon the police to have a warrant issued for the arrest of Louis Dore. What a pity he died before the warrant could be executed."

"Will Otto avoid prosecution?"

"Oh, yes. I promised him that."

He waited to make sure I understood the extent of his generosity before going on.

"I have also been speaking with Jake Santana and Tom Lyons, as you must be aware, and they essentially corroborate your analysis. We are dealing with a nest of vipers and a conspiracy circling around the Blue Danube diamond. I believe Eva is one of them. And if she is, you must stay with her and play dumb. It is best not to terminate your relationship with the woman. This is a waiting game, Max, and breaking up with her at this point will make her and the other vipers suspicious."

The Interpol director went on to tell me about Louis's death, that he had shot himself in the right temple and that the gun was still in his hand when he was found. According to La Salle, the police and Jouvet dismissed the incident as a suicide.

"My problem," he said, "is that since Henry and Jouvet run in the same social circuits, I must go along and cannot publicly question the cause of death."

"You have doubts?" I asked.

"Yes."

"So do I, Pierre. When I was in hospital with Carl Haussmann, Louis pulled a handkerchief out of his left pants pocket and wiped off his brow with his left hand. That makes him left handed. Why would he have killed himself with his right hand?"

La Salle agreed.

"I thought of that too. My interpretation is that this was a contract killing, and the killer simply assumed Louis was right handed."

"What else do we have on the table, Pierre?"

"A Paris court has appointed Henry as executor over the Haussmann and Dore personal estates and made him Maison Dore's legal administrator. The other complicating factor is that Blue Danube's status, including yours, must stay in limbo until the estates are settled and the Adair family's tax situation in America is resolved. We have also confirmed that Colin transferred title to the gem and all his businesses to his brother for an undisclosed amount. This throws another big monkey wrench into the works. Has Eva ever mentioned anything about Colin's transfer of property?"

"No. She keeps talking about divorcing Colin."

"That is strange, is it not?

"So, what do we have, Pierre?"

"A grand plan, Max. Its relies on many crimes, smuggling, theft, murder, money laundering and securities and tax fraud. And it all has to do with the Blue Danube diamond and keeping the Adairs and Sentinel afloat."

La Salle leaned back in his chair and sighed.

"What is new at your end, Max? Do you have anything else to report?"

I related to the Interpol director what I had learned from Brian Donovan, Mike Surrey and Otto in the past several months.

"There is a pattern," I summed up. "Uncut diamonds are shipped to Maison Dore in Belgium from Africa and paid for in cash. Those not kept by Maison Dore are smuggled to the United States by Colin Adair's people where they are cut into finished diamonds by Steve Anders and sold through Kumari who sells them for cash in international markets. Kumari keeps a commission and deposits the balance in an Island Investments account in Nassau. Some of those proceeds go to pay current Adair bills.

"Now for the interesting part, Pierre. All the Adair businesses in the States pay a full fifty percent of gross revenues as a management overhead fee to Island Investments. We call this profit shifting from a high tax country to a low tax area. The high tax country would be the United States. The low tax area would be the Bahamas, a tax haven. But the best is yet to come. South Florida Trust uses capital raised from investors and deposits made by clients to collateralize loans for down payments on the purchase of commercial real estate, restaurants and hotels with heavy mortgages made by Centurion and independent creditors insured by Sentinel and secured by the Blue Danube.

"Nothing makes money because of the fifty percent charge on income by Island Investments. With volatile financial markets and office space going begging, the only winner is Island Investments who will end up a few billion dollars richer with the worse possible case scenario being that ownership of the diamond may have to be surrendered. After the dust settles, the Adairs and this guy Emile Barco can live happily forever after."

"Can we make a case?" La Salle wondered.

"Only if Colin's Irish mafia is granted full immunity in any court of law and a full pardon for all sins, past and present."

"That is a tough bargain, Max. However, it can be done."

"Great. Now, have you made progress in finding John Cork?" I asked.

La Salle shook his head.

"Yes and no. A man answering his description was seen in Basse Terre but we have nothing more."

"Then he must be in that neighborhood."

"Not quite. I asked the Paris police to launch a search when I learned that your John Cork has been traveling again. It seems he managed to fly to your country and then return. He went through our customs about two weeks ago and left again a few days, this time on a flight to Canada. In any case, Jouvet found out about my search request and stopped it. He said a more discreet search would be made through his office."

"Why is Jouvet interested in Cork's fate?"

"Do not be so suspicious, mon ami. In view of the Blue Danube's delicate status, the minister's position is logical."

"Strange. Do you suppose Johnny Cork is the one who murdered Carl and Louis?"

"My dear friend. We have no reason to suppose he did not. But my queries are being blocked and I am not anxious to be forced into retirement. I need the income. My ex-wife has expensive tastes."

"Is Henry still making himself scarce?"

"Yes. But more interesting than him is Emile Barco. According to Interpol research, he comes from Alsace. We are still trying to learn how he came to acquire that estate in Basse Terre."

"Damn!" La Salle had bested me again.

He grinned.

"You see, Max, I too have friends in low places."

"You score on this one, Pierre. Tell me. Do you have friends at customs?"

"You mean when Carl arrived in Paris? The official who examined Carl's bags quit the next day. His bags were sent to Maison Dore. He himself went to work for Maison Dore but quit after a few days. We have been searching for him but he seems to have disappeared without a trace. About Carl's bags, the only thing we found were what was left of the pills that killed him."

I dug into my pocket and threw the envelope of pills Harry Silver gave me before my trip.

"Do me a favor, Pierre, and have these checked out."

"Ah, you are on to something."

"Not yet, Pierre. Just have the pills analyzed. Now, where are we?"

"We are nowhere. Mel Solomon says the diamond will be inspected once the courts give their blessing. Right now, we watch and wait. Agreed?"

I shrugged.

"I suppose, although Mel never spoke to me about inspecting it."

"He probably will. Now, I have something for you. You may have heard that there has been a movement by the Chirac government to compensate the surviving orphans of French Jews who were sent to the death camps by the pro-Nazi Vichy government in the Second World War. I thought you would like to know," he added.

"I'm not so sure," I replied.

"Are you writing off the past?"

"Not exactly. But the past makes me uncomfortable."

"I would be willing to initiate the necessary applications if you wish."

"You know, I'm not sure I care to revisit my childhood."

La Salle persisted.

"This is not about history. It is about money."

"How much money?"

"The amount has not yet been established. But the government is talking about the equivalent of a lump sum of thirty five thousand dollars per person or monthly payments of three hundred seventy five dollars."

"Is that a fair price for the loss of my mother?"

A long moment of silence followed.

Finally Pierre said, "Life has no value, Max. It is priceless. The money is atonement. France did not anguish over its wartime behavior until Chirac became president and took personal responsibility for what happened to France's Jews."

"How about dedicating the Arch of Triumph to the Holocaust's memory?"

The Interpol director erupted into cynical laughter.

"You over reach, my dear friend. France builds monuments to its victories, not to its defeats. Take the money, Max. Then if you wish, slap us on the face with it."

"You're right, Pierre, as always. I'll go for the money, and I don't wish to slap anyone. What happened is finished. We've all moved on. So start the paperwork. The money will at least pay for a few good dinners."

"Yes, but not too many good dinners. Paris is expensive, you know. Of course, we would be overjoyed to have you as a permanent resident."

"To be frank, Pierre, I love the place but it brings bad memories. However, I will visit to pick up my checks."

Another laugh.

"Do not rush. That may take years. We French do not write checks easily. I hope to see you many times before then. In the meantime, I will send you application forms. That will also give you time to consider Jouvet's offer."

"Offer? Oh, yes. What do you make of it, Pierre?"

"String him along, Max. Jouvet wants to buy your trust and services. We must find out why."

"Then tell him I'll have an answer by Bastille day. Fair enough?"

La Salle rose to his feet and extended his hand.

"Thank you, Max. Now I have some personal information."

"Oh?"

"Yes. Do you recall your childhood years in France?"

"I try not to."

La Salle smiled understandingly.

"I have been assembling a dossier on you, Max. A file I think you call it at home. It has to be done to pursue your claim against our government. Were you aware that your mother worked as a clerk for the French security police in Basse Terre during the German occupation until she died.?"

"I never heard that, Pierre."

"And did you know that her husband, your blood father, was a Basque from Gascony who played Jai-Lai?"

"That I knew."

"He apparently left the country just before the war."

That's right," I said in a strained voice. "He cut and ran and left us."

La Salle shook his head and rose to his feet.

"No, Max. He did leave, but he tried to return a year later. He made it to North Africa where he joined the Free French movement and fought with the Americans in the campaign against Rommel. He was killed in early 1943. It is all well documented. He was also rich in his own right because he was a champion player before the war.

My face was warming and I felt it necessary to interrupt La Salle.

"Why are you telling me this, Pierre?"

"Because he bought 200 acres of forest land in Basse Terre where your mother lived for a while. I found the deed. I wonder if that is not the same land now occupied by Emile Barco, Max. And if it is, we must ask is how and why its title was transferred from your family to Barco."

"I'm going to leave it to you to find those answers, Pierre. In the meantime, tell me what happened to my mother."

She divorced your father and remarried shortly after the Germans entered Paris in 1940. Shall I go on?"

"Yes, please."

"I believe it was to keep her Jewish identity secret that she then married a German intelligence officer while her father and uncle fought in the French Resistance in the Basse Terre hunt country. She died in early 1944."

"Basse Terre seems to hold many interesting secrets," I said. "How did she die?"

"She was tracking German troop movements for French resistance fighters in the Sologne forest around Basse Terre when she was caught and shot."

A long moment of silence followed. La Salle's voice became more subdued when he continued.

"The pieces of the puzzle are slowly coming together, Max. Give me time, Max, and I will be able to piece your family history together. It is sad, true. But it is not altogether bad. Both your mother and your father gave up their lives for what they believed, each in their own individual way."

"What was the name of the German officer who married my mother?"

"That, I am still trying to find out."

La Salle gave me a gentle tap on the shoulders.

"To paraphrase you, Max. We must live and move on. But I will keep you posted."

There was certainly enough said to justify a good long cry. I tried my best to keep my composure and my smile, thanked him and shook hands.

"By the way, have you met Gaspard Lancet yet?" I asked.

"One of the first things he did when he started working here was to come see me and tell me the story of his life. He is probably waiting for you as we speak. But careful with him. People bent on revenge make poor associates. Well then. I do hope to see you again soon, perhaps for Bastille Day."

"Perhaps, Pierre, perhaps."

Then suddenly he asked, "Are you seriously going to make a run for the Blue Danube? Jake, Otto and Tom have been talking."

"Oh, I'm not a jewel thief, Pierre. I just want what's mine and Janine's. But I do want to bring down the house of Adair and help you solve some murders along the way. Who knows, Pierre. Who really knows."

"You must be patient and allow the investigation to run its course. I would not do anything dramatic until the rats come up for air. But if you decide to do engage in such an entrepreneurial adventure, I might very well be interested in joining you and the others in a partnership."

La Salle, although basically honest, wanted to keep his options open. He was also painfully aware that his chain was being pulled from high up and so he was telling me obliquely to run my own investigation but not to forget him in the event I planned to pull a fast one. At the very least, we were on the same wave length and it did seem as if he was trying to safeguard my interests.

"In the meantime," La Salle concluded, walking me to the door. "If you need entertainment, call Nicole. She continues to ask about you. Who knows, we could even double date, as you say?"

I shook his hand again, slapped his back and left.

On the way out, I made a point of running into Gaspard Lancet. The old man was going off shift and was heading for a local bistro on the opposite corner of Place Vendome. I joined him, bought him a cognac and brought him up to date.

"What do you make of all this, Gaspard?"

"It stinks."

"What makes you say that?"

"Oh, I am sure La Salle is clean and doing all he can. But he has a job to protect. Jouvet is another story. He has an elegant life style, too expensive for a mere deputy minister. There may be inherited money; I am not sure. I hear that Emile Barco also comes from money."

"La Salle says Barco is from Alsace."

"True.

"Only child?"

Gaspard held up three fingers.

"Three brothers. One went to America; one died here; only Emile is left."

Gaspard looked me over.

"You look different," he noted. "You have lost weight. Are you well?"

"I had a heart attack shortly after leaving Paris last year," I replied. "I'm fine now. Do me a favor, Gaspard.

"What is that?"

"I want to find out what is going on at Barco's estate in Basse Terre. Have you friends or family in the region who can make a few discreet inquiries?"

"I have a cousin who is still alive. He would love being a spy. He has little else to do."

"That would be great, Gaspard. There is also something about Jouvet that I cannot fathom. Just keep an eye on him for me and let me know if you detect anything unusual."

10

Standoff

Pierre La Salle had neatly exploded my perception of the past. My history as I knew it was destroyed and with it my sense of the present and my vision of the future. Aside from the issue of what had really happened to my parents during the war, I had the distinct feeling that the circumstances surrounding my mother's death in Basse Terre were somehow impacting the present and were destined to shape the future. How or why, I had no idea.

But getting back to the present. Mel Solomon sounded surprised when I called from Paris to inform him that I was returning. But I was even more surprised when Bill Ford showed up with a limo when I landed. It was the first time anyone had ever come for me at an airport and Bill was all bundled up and suffering from a cold. Something was up. Clearly, picking me up was not his idea.

It was cold and raw and even the heat inside the limo could not kill the dampness. A light drizzle was falling and a fog hid the Manhattan skyline as we drew nearer to the massive gray wall of buildings that sprang up like a fortress along the East River.

We had nothing to talk about beyond the usual dull comments about the weather and we sat mostly buried with our thoughts in boring silence.

Happily, the ride ended and the limo deposited us in front of a private club off Fifth Avenue where we were soon ensconced in a small conference room with Mel Solomon and George Lerman, of all people.

The place was supposed to be soundproof but noise from a compressor and jack hammers on the street below penetrated the thick panes of the solitary barred window. What a horrible location for a meeting, a drab room with faded yellow walls on a gray day, with steam from an open sewer line outside billowing up to form grimy beads of condensation on the dirty windows. Despite heat from an old steam radiator rattling in the corner, a damp chill filled the room.

Mel Solomon was his usual blustery self, announcing several times that he had elevated himself to board chairman and made Bill Ford his CEO, a fact already known to the world. Nevertheless, I nodded approvingly and wished them both luck.

I had worked with Mel for many years and felt sorry for him. More pear shaped and flabbier than usual, his heavy, sad face reflected his insurance company's financial woes.

Bill Ford, in contrast, was short and slight. He had a bad habit of biting his fingernails whenever he was nervous. Mel liked and trusted him because he was good with numbers. To me, Bill was a brown nosed climber and a sneak. He was a salaried employee who had to curry his boss's favor to keep his job. I distrusted him and made it my business never turn my back on him.

George Lerman was a question mark. Of medium height, heavily built and balding, he could have passed for a faded boxer or wrestler trying to make a living as a salesman. A former fighter pilot, I had no idea what he really did for a living. What distinguished him from normal salesmen was the gun he kept in a shoulder holster. He insisted he was a free lance investigator but Mike Surrey once confided to me that he, like his partner, Ed Houston, was a hired gun, a hit man, actually.

The two heavies were in fact were a Mutt and Jeff duo. Ed Houston was the taller of the two. Thin with a lined taciturn face and an expressionless dead man's stare, his coldness repelled normal social relations. Both were the type of guys who would be expected to go to sleep with their clothes on. Ed was not at this meeting.

There was a saying among us that went some thing like this: "if George is here, Ed Houston is near."

Mel Solomon started.

"The word on the street is that you've been asking a lot of questions."

Ordinarily, I would have been scared of Mel, but this time I wasn't.

"So?"

Mel was nonplused by my response and Bill Ford had to jump in to help him out.

"You're meddling in things not your business, Max. You're out of line."

"Who says?"

"Henry Adair says you were trying to see him in Paris and Larry O'Leary tells us you've been pestering his guys with a lot of questions."

"I'm just being a good citizen, Bill. I'm sure you'd do the same."

"You're interfering with the Adair family," Mel stated lamely.

"I'm part of the family," I said.

"Only by marriage," Bill qualified. "And your wife is dead."

"So?"

Mel's jaw dropped.

"So?"

"Well, Mel. I finally realized after all these years that everything Colleen would have gotten, one third of everything, is mine in trust for my daughter, Janine. I have a vested interest in making sure that the Adair estate is not illegally milked. That includes the Blue Danube, even if Colin turned title over to Henry which I don't think he can, at least not legally, that is."

"You're crazy!" Bill Ford exclaimed in a loud voice.

"Maybe. But just think. Colin, Colleen and Henry each own one third of the diamond. Colin has the right to turn over his share to Henry but Colleen's share is my daughter's. Whatever affects the Blue Danube diamond and the Adair estate compromises my daughter's stake. If everyone is clean, there is nothing to worry about. You must admit, though. The deaths of Haussmann and Dore happened under odd circumstances and leave many unanswered questions."

Mel turned crimson with rage.

"I could fire you for this."

He went on to remind me that my responsibility was to Sentinel and to no one else and that I had no business flying to Paris on my own to investigate what I believed were irregularities concerning the deaths of Haussmann and Dore.

"Haussmann died of heart failure and Dore committed suicide, and that's that," Mel said.. "I was going to ask George here to run an investigation."

"Don't bust my balls, Mel," I responded tartly. "I went to Paris on my own dime to protect my family interest. It's not your call and I won't turn in an expense account for the trip. Moreover, why would you have George look into the matter if you didn't think there was a problem?"

"George is an expert on these things, you aren't. You're my diamond man and I want to keep it that way."

"Are you telling what I can or can't do, Mel? If so, I quit."

Bill Ford interceded in a softer tone.

"What Mel is saying is that we want to count on your continued support in this thing. We need George and we need you."

Mel relented.

"That's right. A mess is unfolding as we speak and Sentinel is vulnerable. Business is bad enough as it is. We are being hosed by all the weather related casualty claims we've had to make good on these past two years. If that isn't bad enough, Sentinel holds policies on the Blue Danube diamond and just about on everything else the Adairs own or claim to own. If Adair goes belly up and if the Blue Danube falls out of our reach, Sentinel is through, and so is your daughter's interest, I might add."

I played a hunch.

"I hear that Henry Adair and this Emile Barco have stock in Sentinel. They must have put in some money."

"Where did you hear that?" George Lerman asked.

"I keep my ears open," I replied.

Mel waved his hand.

"Let's put it this way. They gave me money. I gave them a few preferred shares in return. I made the same arrangement with Sol Weinberg. But let that subject pass for now," he said.

"What happened in Paris?" Bill Ford asked nervously.

"Simply put? Let's say that I know for a fact that Carl was murdered, and I know for a fact that Louis was murdered. And I know for a fact that Johnny Cork is a suspect in both murders. I'm also wise to that diamond smuggling operation the Adairs are running. Should I continue?"

Mel raised his eyebrows.

"How did you learn about that?"

"I'm a diamond guy, remember?"

"What about Louis Dore?"

"Louis is left handed. But the wound was on the right side of his head."

"You're sure?"

"Positive."

Mel turned to George.

"How does that square with you?"

A strained expression crossed Lerman's face. He had somehow convinced Mel that Louis's death was a suicide as the French had decreed it was.

"I was there," George insisted. "I saw the body with the police. What the hell does this guy know about murder?"

"Nothing," I interrupted. "But I know right from left. By the way, George. What were you doing in Paris?"

"Colin sent me to meet with his brother and with Emile Barco."

"About diamonds?"

"It's none of your business."

I shrugged.

"Suit yourself," I said. "But did you know that this Barco guy has a 200 acre estate in Basse Terre?"

"What's Basse Terre?" George asked.

"Shut up," growled Mel. "What about it, Max?"

"Who issued the title insurance on the property, Mel?"

"Why, Sentinel did. It was part of the deal when he helped us out."

"Oh yeah? And did you guys do the title search?"

Mel was ashen faced.

I sat back in my chair and turned my attention to Bill Ford.

"So. What's going on at your end, Bill?"

The insurance executive sighed.

"We're in deep shit, Max. Colin Adair is broke. We need the Blue Danube diamond to stay alive, and that's more important than anything else. The IRS is on our side on this one. They want to slap a lien on it to satisfy Colin's tax bill. The IRS may let us keep the rock if we agree to pay his back taxes."

"Have you broached the subject with Colin?"

"No," Bill Ford answered. "We learned from his attorneys and accountants that he missed several meetings with the IRS. The government is ready to pounce. We want to make a deal before that happens."

I agreed.

"That sounds real good, Bill. Why don't you speak with Eva?"

George threw me a question from left field.

"Do you carry a piece?"

"No. Why?" I asked.

"You're going to need one when Colin finds out you've been screwing his wife."

I was unfazed, pissed, but unfazed.

"Well, George. I have no idea how you like your sex, but with me, as a bachelor, all women are in season, including Colin's wife. Now, I don't like guns and I do hope Colin doesn't come after me. So, we're going to have to keep this little secret among us, aren't we!"

"I heard a rumor, Max," said Mel.

"What's that?"

"I heard you might want to make a run for the Blue Danube if you can't enforce your legal rights."

"So?"

"So. I'm asking you nicely to back off if that's your plan. I want first shot at it. You back my claims and I'll back yours and your daughter's as heirs to the family estate. Is it a deal? At least, for old times' sake?"

"Not a problem, Mel. It's a deal. For old times' sake."

"What do you plan to do now?" Mel asked.

I looked at my watch and got up.

"Nothing. Now, who's taking me back to Jersey?"

Bill Ford demurred but George Lerman offered to do the honors. He drove and I sat next to him.

Neither of us said anything until we reached the Jersey side of the tunnel.

It was George who broke the silence.

"You want some advice, Max?"

I shrugged.

"Go ahead."

"I take it you don't like me. I personally have nothing against you, but I do what I'm paid to do, and sometimes someone gets hurt. I really don't want to see you get hurt, but you will if you stick around."

"I wish I could back off, George," I said. "But things have happened and I have to stick around. That's just the way it is."

"That's life," George continued. "A friend is an abstraction of the mind. A buddy is real, but buddies are temporary conveniences."

"Like marriage?"

"Maybe. Like marriage. Buddies come and go. In this world, there are the the living and the dead. Our mission on earth is to stay alive as long as it's possible. That's all. Everything else is bull shit. In the end, death gets us all. It's the great equalizer. That's why I attend every funeral, for friends and enemies alike."

George turned the limo into the interstate. He was on a role and I had to let him go on.

"Have you ever seen that picture of jungle animals drinking together down by the river?"

"Many times."

"Well, that's us. Like we were sitting around the table at Mel's club, or when we get together for a wedding, a funeral or a family gathering or some reunion. Those are short periods of truce. We drink, eat and then return to the jungle to find our next meal."

"Since when did you become a philosopher?" I asked.

George's voice turned nasty.

"Don't mess with me. This is good advice. Treat everyone as an enemy and you'll have allies on demand. Treat everyone as a friend, and one of them will kill you. You need to be nice to me, Max. Who knows. You might even need me to fly you somewhere one of these days."

He turned and winked at me.

"Thanks, George. I'll keep that in mind. Now since you're so smart, how did you think this meeting went?"

A faint smile crossed George's lips.

"Oh, I don't know. It looked like a standoff. At the very least, you scared them."

I was home before I knew it.

"Take care of yourself, Max," George said. "I hope I don't have to see you again from the wrong side."

I was relieved. If there was a contract on me, George was not holding it, at least not yet. We still had a truce.

11

Shootout

The significance of the exchange at the New York meeting lay in what was not discussed. A full year had gone by since the Blue Danube was examined by Carl Haussmann. Not once did Mel or Bill Ford bring up the contractual obligation to inspect the diamond in the Dore vault in Morristown. I could only think that tie ups in the courts were blocking and delaying the stone's annual inspection.

The first thing I did early the next morning after a good night's sleep was to call Tom Lyons to see what progress he had made in checking out where Patrick Adair and his wife were cremated.

"It's a dead end," Tom moaned over the phone. "The funeral home where the arrangements would have been made closed down ten years ago and we can't find any records."

"Where does that leave us?" I asked.

"Nowhere. Exactly nowhere."

My next move was to apply for a gun permit and the right to carry a concealed weapon. Once I received the paperwork informing me that I was good to go, I went over to see Mike Surrey. He kept a snub nosed 38 caliber revolver in the house which I asked him to lend me.

"Are you going to war, Max?"

He gave me the weapon, a shoulder holster and several boxes of cartridges.

"Maybe," I answered. "I ran into George Lerman the other day."

Mike sneered.

"Bad news. He and Ed Houston do cleanup work for the highest bidder and they're great shots. You don't want to be in their cross hairs."

I explained my situation over lunch to Mike and for the first time in many years he managed to stay sober.

"I'm afraid I may have put you and Brian at risk."

"Forget us," said Mike. "We were glad to come clean. The only reason we fell in with Colin was because he threatened to fire Brian and blackball him in the hotel restaurant industry if he didn't work with him on this diamond caper. Brian would have trouble finding work as a dishwasher at an all night diner were Colin to let him go. Let's face it, Brian has a wife and three kids in high school and college. He needs Colin."

"Then what if Colin finds out decides to get rid of him?"

"Brian and I talked about that. Do you remember Colin's first cousins?"

"Yes. They were killed in action. They stepped on a land mine."

"Right. We were there. I had the area map and looked it over before giving it to Colin. The mine field was marked. He ordered the boys to take that piece of terrain but never told them of the mines. He killed them, Max. Brian and I are positive. Just as we're positive he murdered their parents."

What a surprise. I wasn't the only one who thought Colin could be a killer. "How come you're keeping quiet? What's he have on you?"

"What can I say, Max. He pays me so I can keep my retarded son out of an insane asylum. And he pays me so I can keep boozing. I'm a jacket and tie drunk, or haven't you noticed. There's no way I can hold a real job."

"Better drunk than dead?"

"Not quite, Max. Brian and I have a fat insurance policy. We're worth more to our families dead than alive. We discussed the whole thing. That's why we're cooperating. Fuck Colin, we say! If he kills us, our families will be rich."

I took a deep breath.

"What about Larry O'Leary?"

Mike Surrey rolled his eyes.

"He has bigger problems. He has an expensive wife and two unemployed spoiled brats. Colin keeps him afloat. He has to stay with him.

"Do you think Colin wants to kill me?"

Mike smiled.

"He should. You stand between the twins and sole control of the diamond. That's why George is going to be your shadow. Colin and Mel want to keep their eyes on you."

"Why do you say that?"

"It's simple. The Blue Danube is fair game. Mel wants to make sure you don't stray. If you do, you die." Suddenly, his face lit up.

"Have you ever considered the possibility that the jewel was a fake."

"A fake?"

"A fake. I'm not saying it is, but let's assume it is. Who would know it's a phony if it's never appraised?"

"But it was inspected and appraised, many times."

"So it was. But suppose the Blue Danube was appraised many times by a so-called expert and declared genuine but after all was said and done, it was still a piece of glass. Whoever ends up with it then sells it, maybe to France. That fuckin country has nothing but the Eiffel Tower and a monster ego. The frogs will put the rock under glass at the Louvre as a national treasure and no one will be the wiser. In the meantime, someone puts you away before you discover the fraud. End of story."

"That sounds like a stretch, Mike. Don't you think? Is there a reason to believe the Blue Danube is fake?"

Mike Surrey laughed.

"Not at all, buddy. I think it's real for only one little reason."

"What's that?"

"I hear you're still thinking of stealing the diamond. Why would you steal a worthless rock?"

"Idle chatter. Nothing serious."

"Whatever you say, but don't buy green bananas for a while. And in case you're going for the gold, let me and Brian know. We'll join you."

I didn't know whether or not to take Mike Surrey seriously at this point.

Anyway, I was glad when my gun permit arrived, and I spent a few weeks at a range familiarizing myself with the ugly nuances of shooting at people.

The handgun became my steady companion.

Mike Surrey returned to his old drunken self and one late morning wanted to go for a drive. That was his code term for wanting to get to a bar early. We were about to leave when my cell phone rang. It was Eva. She was calling to say she was in New Jersey and wanted to have lunch.

"I'm with Mike Surrey," I said apologetically.

"Not a problem," her cheery voice replied. "Bring him along."

"Where to?"

"Let's try Troy's. It's in Basking Ridge. I've haven't been there yet."

"Sounds good," I replied and looked at Mike. "Troy's, Basking Ridge. You know the place?"

He pointed to his chest.

"Moi? There is no bar that has escaped my eye. It's near the Great Swamp. Follow me, partner, and take your gun, just in case."

I mumbled something but obediently strapped on a shoulder holster inside my blazer and tucked Mike's revolver into it.

It was mid winter and the day was cold and colorless. The drive took us through the Basking Ridge estate country where large homes were scattered over generous spreads of land. The brown landscape slowly gave way to pine woods hugging a dark, narrow road that eventually lead through a desolate landscape littered with the brown twisted stumps and branches of dead trees. It ran through a swamp at the end of which stood a run down house and two cars parked in a gravel lot next to it. A hand painted sign on a post announced that this was Troy's.

Eva was waiting inside at the bar when we arrived. We were the first guests of the day and Eva, well organized as usual, had selected a table for us. A waiter came over and sat me with my back to a slightly open window while she sat down opposite me and next to Mike Surrey. Above and behind them on the wall hung a painting illuminated by a pale ray of light from the window.

A noise from the parking lot caught my attention. I thought it came from a car idling outside but forgot about it when a short, slope shouldered waiter in an apron came by to take our orders. He had an accepting manner and stood by patiently as we painstakingly studied the menu.

Finally, for all our dawdling, Eva ordered a glass of wine while Mike asked for his usual martini. I asked for water. The waiter disappeared and returned a few moments later with our drinks and then took an order for three tuna fish salads, again after much discussion and mind changes.

"So," I asked. "What's the occasion?"

"I inherited this place when my parents died, Max. And now Henry wants to start a new business here once he straightens out his citizenship status. Colin and Larry O'Leary say that it has good potential. What do you think, Max? I need your advice."

It was odd that Larry, who was in the business, would suggest buying an eatery in the middle of nowhere. It also seemed pointless to ask my opinion. I knew nothing about restaurants. However, the news about Henry's possible return peeked my curiosity.

Henry was a draft dodger. He bolted for France the moment his number came up and Colin enlisted. Why France? That's hard to say. He and Colin were French majors in school and became fluent in the language, but Henry had some sort of intellectual love affair with the culture and tried to speak French as often as he could.

When we dined together, he'd hold his knife and fork like the French, knife in the right hand and fork in the left. He made a point of never switching it to the right hand like we do. He could have run off to Canada. Lots of guys ran off to Canada, but he ran off to France, and that's where he stayed.

Personally, I found him irritating and never missed him. He had a habit of trying to bait my linguistic skills by insisting on speaking to me in French. I hated draft dodgers and was glad he left.

Henry's sojourn in Paris earned him success. His failing health was a steep downside. He came down with cancer and at one point was at death's door until he started treatments at a cancer clinic in the Biminis where Colin went often to see him. Colin had apparently found a doctor there who claimed to have a treatment for several forms of cancer. It involving drinking something made from an apricot pit extract mixed with other potions. It was similar to a therapy given to some famous movie star a long time ago. The cancer killed him anyway.

It was strange. The twins and I rarely communicated openly. We were at war but the conflict was invisible.

Not so invisible was Eva's rage when she heard I was marrying Colleen. She never attended our wedding, using the excuse that she was pregnant and not feeling well. We were supposed to have gotten together as two couples upon our return from our honeymoon but our cruise ship was delayed by a storm and in the meantime Patrick Jr. and his wife died.

Colin got Eva, and Henry eventually got Nicole, although I was by then long married to Colleen. Aside from those contrived family socials at holiday time, I occasionally ran into Colin at our army unit's annual reunions which took the form of golf outings in Florida. However, I had missed the last few engagements due to schedule conflicts.

I think the last time I saw Colin must have been four or five years ago when he and Eva began spending most of their time in Florida. And were it not for the heart attack that rekindled my affair with Eva, I would most likely have retired.

And now there was this lunch with Mike and Eva in this godforsaken gin mill that made a pretense of serving edible food.

She was taking her first mouthful and Mike was just about to finish his first martini when a shadow moved across the painting on the wall behind them.

Eva screamed. Mike froze. I drew Mike's revolver and spun around.

Two shots rang out, one from my weapon and one from the window. The glass in Mike's hand shattered and the painting behind him fell. The sound I heard next was that of automobile tires screeching.

For whom was the bullet intended?

For Me, Mike Surrey or Eva?

Mike feverishly worked his cell phone and the police arrived within minutes, lights flashing and sirens wailing, and good old Tom Lyons walked into the room with his usual slight swagger.

"What happened, Max?" Tom Keys asked after the restaurant was secured by the usual yellow crime scene tape.

"Did you short change someone on an insurance claim?"

"Beats me," I answered. "All we were doing was having lunch."

The detective looked at Mike Surrey who was now at the bar working on fresh martini.

"What are you doing here, Mike? This isn't your territory."

Mike was too shaken to reply and Eva rushed over to his rescue.

"I invited them here," she said. "We're thinking of fixing this place up."

"You want to keep this place?"

"Yes." By this time Eva was clinging to me like a Siamese twin.

"What the hell is here besides swamp?"

The edge of Tom's question was dulled by the monotone of his drawl.

"My husband thought it might be a good idea. I asked Max to come with me because he has a good eye for things like this. Mike Surrey came along for the ride."

"You could have asked Larry O'Leary," Tom noted. "He knows the food and beverage business."

"He was busy working today."

"Fair enough. Now, who shot whom?"

I recounted the episode from my perspective and finally, taking Tom aside, I said, "I frankly don't know what the hell is going on."

Tom looked sideways at Eva and Mike.

"Neither do I," he said. "Why is this restaurant open anyway? It's been closed since your folks passed away. It's supposed to be closed."

Then he asked, "I suppose you have a permit for the gun, Max?"

I nodded, described the weapon and told him it was on loan from Mike.

"Well, you guys got lucky," he exclaimed. "The shooter missed but Max's shot scored. Blood spots on the ground run from the window to the parking lot and tire tread marks suggest a getaway vehicle. My hunch is that there were two people, the shooter and the driver. We'll find them. Good shooting, Max."

Tom wanted to question the waiter and the kitchen staff but by the time he and other police officers checked the back, they were gone. It was as if they never existed. Tom concluded they had they had followed a pre-arranged escape route through the swamp.

It turned out that the bullet that came through the window lodged itself in the wall behind the painting. Days later I learned that it had been fired by a nine millimeter pistol. The car in question was a rental and was returned to Newark Airport. Tom said DNA tests on blood found outside Troy's might reveal the shooter's identity.

It also turned out that the two cars parked at the restaurant were inoperable junks and had been there a while. That raised the embarrassing question of how Eva got to the place. She claimed she took a cab but could not remember the cab company.

A motive helps when trying to narrow a list of murder suspects who would have gone to the trouble of staging an elaborate assassination plot. No clear cut motive stood out, at least not yet. However, whoever called the shot must have thought that my death was sufficiently important enough to require the help, however unwitting, of others. But the hit man hired for the purpose had to be a rank amateur who couldn't shoot straight. The shooter was no George Lerman or Ed Houston.

I was driving home from the gym one day when a call came in on my cell phone, which could ostensibly make and receive calls from anywhere in the world.

"Ah. I see that my phone can speak to your phone. Technology is fun," I heard him say.

"What can I do for you, Pierre?"

"Those pills you asked me to have examined, Max?"

"Yes?"

"They are identical to the ones that killed Carl Haussmann."

"Thanks. I always suspected that. Anything else?"

"Not much. Everything is at a standstill and tied up in the courts."

Another week passed. Tom Keys made further investigations and was concerned to the extent that he offered to provide me and my daughter and her family police protection. He was certain, as I was, that whoever tried to make the hit would try again. He was considering offering the same security to Mike Surrey and Eva. To say the least, we all accepted, for whatever that protection was worth. However, with Eva he was merely going through the motions. He was convinced she was part of the a plot to kill me and, much to my chagrin, I had to agree.

"It's an easy problem is, Max," Tom observed sarcastically. "Eva set you up, using herself as bait. Once we link her with the shooter, the driver and the unknown restaurant staff, we'll have a case."

"Seems like a slam-dunk," I sneered in response.

I checked my calendar. The date set for our old army unit's annual golf outing was approaching. This year, it was to be held at the Delray Beach Golf Club followed by a banquet at the Poinciana. There was no way I was going to miss the function.

Colin, as our former commanding officer, was to be our guest of honor. At last, all the rats would be in one place. I was also sure Mel Solomon, Sol Weinberg, creditors, Interpol and the IRS would be there with questions to ask and subpoenas to serve. An interesting day was in the offing.

12

Disappearance

Eva was unfazed by Tom Lyons' suspicions and decided to fly south and prepare for the tournament and subsequent party. Whatever else she might be,
she was a gutsy woman. I drove her to the airport.

Over a fast food dinner at the terminal I ventured to ask.

"Who actually had the idea to have you take a look at that gin mill in the
swamps?"

Eva bowed her head and confessed.

"No. That place was my own idea. Colin doesn't give me the right time of
day anymore. He's broke and I feel I'm going to lose everything. I thought I
might be able to work a deal to run the place with Larry O'Leary or maybe
with Brian Donovan. I have to pay the taxes on the land; I might as well do
something with it."

If Eva was lying, she was very convincing.

"Have you spoken to Colin recently?"

"No. I rarely see him. He spends his time fishing between Florida and the
Bahamas on *Obsession*, that yacht South Florida Trust owns."

She was either desperate or a great actress.

"I thought this restaurant on the edge of the Great Swamp would give me a
fresh start up here and that I could count on your support."

"But what about the Poinciana? Are you going to lose that?"

She smiled coyly.

"I have a secret, Max. I bought out Colin a year ago."

"How did you do that?"

"Simple. Colin needed cash. I had Victor Nishkanian bankroll me."

"Vick? Doesn't he still own the Carnival Café?"

"Yes. But he's been after the hotel for years. He backed me in return for half of it."

I was impressed. Eva could not be accused of lacking brains and guts. Here was a woman who knew how to land on her feet, even if she lied on occasion.

"This way, with Troy's, I would be keeping my feet in both Florida and New Jersey if I lose the Bernardsville Club."

"What's going to happen to Colin?" I asked.

Eva's lips made an ugly curl.

"Who cares! I'm going to divorce the bastard whatever happens. He'll be going to be served with legal papers at the banquet."

She must have seen the concern written on my face. Aware of my aversion to confrontation, her face softened and she placed my hands in hers.

"The next man who becomes my husband will be rich, Max. I guarantee it. Who knows, it might even be you, if you ever decide to remarry. But right now, I need your protection. You're smart and fast and you act decisively. Too bad you weren't that way when we met."

She gave me a lingering kiss and whispered.

"Who knows. The Blue Danube may be in our future."

I was tempted at that point to bring up the subject of my school ring but I kept my mouth shut.

Eva made her flight to Florida, leaving me to realize at long last that no matter how much I was drawn to her, she was a heap of trouble looking for a place to land. It was my bad luck that she was so damn attractive.

I was home, packing my bags for Florida when Tom Lyons called.

"I hear you're going to Delray, Max."

"That's right," I confirmed. "How did you find out?"

"Jake Santana called to say Colin missed several tax court deadlines and that a federal arrest warrant for him has been issued. I want to go down there myself to see the fireworks and take in some golf. Janine gave me your flight schedule. I can be on it. Do you need a lift to the airport?"

"You bet."

I told him to pick up Mike Surrey on his way to my home.

Tom's call was premature and he didn't have to bother picking up Mike. No sooner did I hang up the phone when it rang again. Eva was at the other end. Her clear voice was slow and serious and I sensed that something terrible had happened.

She chose her words with unusual care.

"The golf outing will have to be postponed," she said.

"What happened?"

"*Obsession* blew up on the way to the Bimini islands. Colin was on it. I think he was killed."

There was nothing more to say.

So much for the Delray showdown and all the maneuvering. And so much for Eva's divorce plans. She was now a widow. This was a classic example of an extenuating circumstance derailing the best and the worst of all human intentions.

Later, Eva called to ask if I would come down to Delray for a gathering of friends in a tribute to Colin's memory in the near future. She went on to say there could be no funeral until his body was recovered and a cause of death established, but that a simple memorial luncheon would be an appropriate gesture.

I asked if she wanted me to fly down right away to keep her company.

"You're sweet, Max. But you stay where you are. There are a few things I need to take care of here first." As an after thought she asked. "Are you going to examine the Blue Danube any time soon?"

"I'll tell you before I do anything."

Her voice was all business now.

"As a widow, the diamond is ours."

"That's not my decision," I reminded her. "Henry is still alive."

Eva was undeterred.

"If your appraisal and authentication goes well, Max, you could end up a very wealthy man. We could live happily forever after, like in the story books."

I smiled, perhaps a little sadly.

"Yes," I echoed. "Forever after."

I hung up the phone and immediately called Tom Keys,

"The trip is off," I informed him.

"Heard all about it. Santana just called. How did you find out?"

"Eva phoned. She also mentioned the Blue Danube."

The detective laughed.

"She's the original goldbrick," he stated. "Well, this thing is going to get very messy before anyone gets anything.. Anyway, I'll be in Florida when you are. I have questions that need good answers. As a matter of fact, I can ask you two questions now."

"Shoot."

"Who besides Eva wants you dead?"

"That's a tough one, Tom. The Blue Danube has three owners, Henry, Colin and me on behalf of my daughter, Janine. It could have been Henry or Colin. Eva gets her share through Colin, so it isn't logical that she would try to have me taken down before Colin died unless she was also planning to kill him next. And then she'd also have to go after Henry. I don't think she's that kind of a serial killer."

"No. Eva's in on the attempted hit. I'm positive. Her story is just too damn weak. Troy's was shuttered until two days before you guys got there. It had no operating license and all we found in the kitchen was a portable coffee maker and a microwave. You weren't supposed to walk out of there. By the way, did Mike Surrey give you his theory about the diamond being a fake?"

"He did. And he said I might be at risk if I appraised the Blue Danube and found it wasn't real. That theory would hold water if the diamond was bogus which I don't think it is. Carl Haussmann knew his gems. Eva?"

"Was Colin a jealous type?"

"You mean my thing with Eva? The whole world seems to know."

Tom Keys drawled on emotionlessly.

"I ask questions, Max. That's what I get paid for. Your affair is no secret, and Eva herself doesn't go to great pains to hide it."

"Well, she did say several times she might leave Colin, but I never took her seriously."

"You should have, buddy. Jake Santana says she filed papers in Florida a few weeks ago. Listen. I have a theory. If Colin is crazy jealous and knew the two of you were having an affair, he would have done something about it a long time ago and Eva would not have been involved in setting you up. So the angle about jealousy is out. My hunch is that the divorce bit is an act and that he and Eva were working together to get you out of the way. If the divorce action is for real, then Eva is working her own deal with someone else to take you and maybe even Colin and Henry down."

"So, what do you suggest?"

"We wait and see. If Colin is dead and another attempt is made on your life, it means that Eva has a contract out on you."

"That's very encouraging, Tom."

I could not dispute his logic.

"Anyway," he continued. "Santana is working on this angle with La Salle and on the health thing with Felix Styles, the police chief in Bimini who is checking out the cancer clinic Henry goes to."

Good cops are like dogs. They never let go once they get their hands on a bone. Tom Keys, Jake Santana and Felix Styles were good cops and Pierre La Salle was a master cop.

So, what did we have? A missing person, two dead people, one dead dog and an attempted murder. And now the man who might have had answers to many provoking questions was blown away on his yacht.

I reviewed the situation with Mike Surrey over lunch the next day who was in seventh heaven over the news of Colin Adair's mishap. I figured that Brian and Larry O'Leary would also be overjoyed. At the very least, Mike was so happy that he didn't drink and stayed amazingly sober while I talked. When I was through, he shook his head.

"There's a price on your head," he said, passing his hand across his throat for emphasis. "It might be over that damn diamond or over something else or both, and in both cases, Eva is in the loop."

"How does she fit in the picture?"

"She is the picture. Eva may need you but she doesn't want you and maybe now she doesn't even need you. The problem is that you're blind sided each time a broad spreads her legs for you. You probably even remember the first time you got laid."

I smiled as fond memories returned.

"It happened when I was a teenager," I said. "I had an uncle in New York who took me to a whorehouse for my birthday and got me laid with a two-dollar hooker. It was sloppy. And yet it was strange and wonderful. After it was over, I asked for more, but my uncle got pissed and we left. I guess he couldn't afford the extra two bucks. But, even if I didn't like the experience, I probably would have gone along just to appear normal."

Mike Surrey sighed.

"I guess marriage is about that, acting normal," he noted. "It doesn't matter if one's head and feet are screwed on backwards. A person has to suck wind and pretend to be normal, whatever that is. Marriage and family grant the appearance of normalcy."

"I've done that. Is that what you did?"

Mike Surrey drew back. I had inadvertently struck the wrong note.

"I married because I had to, old buddy. The woman was pregnant and very Catholic. Abortion and children out of wedlock were not options. But getting married was the worse thing I did in my life. It has created my hell on earth. I thought of suicide but it's against my religion. I've thought of ramming my car into a tree but I don't have the guts."

"So, what are you going to do?"

Mike smiled mischievously.

"I'm going to drink myself to death. But what you need is a major life style change. We both need it. Who knows. It might save you life sand save my soul. We need to go through with the idea of stealing the Blue Danube.""

"You win, old buddy. What's the action plan?"

"Have a lawyer go to court and push your claim to the diamond, insisting that it be inspected and appraised. It's way overdue anyway. Once you get into the Dore vault in Morristown to examine the Blue Diamond, you steal it."

"That simple, huh?"

Mike Surrey guffawed.

"You need a plan. But it's simple. The Morristown store is in a stand alone building that's over a century old. The last time it was wired was thirty or forty years ago. The circuit breaker box is in the cellar with access from the parking lot in back."

"How do you know that?"

Mike's eyes twinkled.

"That building belonged to my folks. Remember? They had it rewired so they could sell it. I did the electrical work. I also installed Dore's security system. It has never been changed We'll shut off the electricity, disable the system and create a blackout."

"We'll have partners, you know."

Mike Surrey laughed.

"I can live with that, especially if some of them are cops. We can use some official protection."

IV

FLORIDA

13

Delray

The on again-off again golf outing in Delray was on again. Eva did not want our golf outing, which had become an anticipated annual happening, to be canceled. After a socially acceptable period of mourning, she mailed out invitations calling the faithful to an eighteen hole round of morning golf at the Delray Beach Golf Club to be followed by a testimonial luncheon at the Poinciana.

"Heading to Florida again?" My daughter inquired when she found me at home packing a duffel and assembling my golf gear.

"Yes. It's too damn cold here. It's got to be warmer in Florida."

"Any news about Colin?"

I shook my head.

"The story hasn't changed. Colin's boat blew up with him in it. He's part of the seascape now." I flicked my fingers. "Just like that!"

"I guess Eva is not so grief stricken if she's going ahead with the golf outing."

"Life goes on, cookie. Besides, this isn't a funeral. It's a testimonial, like a sort of roast."

Janine shuddered.

"This sounds grisly to me."

A long moment of silence followed before she asked, "What actually happened to Colin?"

"From what I've been able to put together, he was headed for Bimini alone on *Obsession* to meet up with Henry when the yacht blew up outside the cut leading into the harbor between North and South Bimini islands."

"Any wreckage?"

"You're too delicate, Janine. You mean body parts. I called Felix Stiles, the Bimini police chief. He said the explosion was so intense that the yacht was splattered over a one mile zone. Colin would have been first incinerated and then granulated. There wouldn't have been morsels left large enough to use as chum."

Janine seemed unconvinced.

"Are you sure this isn't a hoax, dad?" Her perspective was sanguine as she continued. "Give this thing a few weeks and the shit is really going to hit the fan."

"In what way?" I asked.

"The bottom line is always money and who gets what. I bet the guy didn't have an updated will."

"I don't have one either."

Janine looked at me as if I was crazy and she was probably right.

"Your situation is not complicated," Janine reminded me. "You have no siblings and you have only one daughter. Me. By the way, when do I get the Blue Danube?"

"Soon."

Janine's eyes widened.

"Are you going to kill Henry?"

"No, cookie. I'm going to fight him in the courts."

"I don't understand."

"I'm having our lawyer lodge an action to allow me, a diamond expert and part owner, to inspect and appraise the Blue Danube. This is being done as we speak. I've also instructed him to start proceedings to advance our claim to a full one third share of the stone. Colin had no right transferring its title to his brother without my consent."

"So you're going to stand and fight, dad?"

I nodded definitively.

"Damn right."

"What about Eva?"

"What about her?"

"If you marry Eva, we get two thirds of the diamond, unless she kills you first."

"That's not funny, Janine."

"How is Henry?" Janine asked.

"Don't know. He has to survive his cancer if he has it at all. I get different stories. But he's been having a good life and has grown rich in his own right. And having no one to support makes him richer."

"Are you sorry you had a daughter instead of a son, dad?" Janine asked.

"Of course not. I'm happy you're here and that you made me a grandfather. I wouldn't have it any other way."

After my conversation with Janine, I called Morristown Memorial Hospital to find out if Barry Benson was making his rounds. He was, and a half hour later I caught up with him in the coffee shop.

He was his usual chipper self.

"You look great, Max. What brings you here?"

"I'm trying to track down an associate of mine," I said. "From France."

"Oh, I know who you mean. A jeweler. I think Haussmann is his name."

"Yes. Carl Haussmann."

"Yes. I've seen him at our office. He's Harry Silver's patient. Colin Adair referred him to Harry. Our medical office handles all of Colin's employees and associates under his health plan. I've seen Carl's file. He has a bad ticker and diabetes. How is he?"

"He was fine the last time I saw him, doctor. I was trying to get his address and telephone number."

I followed Barry Benson into the corridor.

"Call Harry. He's at the office. He'll give you the information."

"Thanks, doctor. How are things otherwise?"

"Pretty good, Max. I finally bought a place in the French West Indies for my marine salvage business. You'll have to come down and see it. By the way, are you taking your pills?"

"I sure am, doctor. I sure am."

"Good. Make sure you get them from a drug store. Harry's samples are too old. I want to make sure you make it to the islands."

He gave me a good natured shoulder punch.

I reported my conversation with Barry Benson to Tom Lyons who quickly began investigating the Adair, Haussmann, Silver connection. I also told him that the Delray function was on again and that I was heading for Florida.

"I heard," was his curt reply. "I'll be there."

No sooner had I hung up on Tom when the phone rang. It was Otto Katz at the other end. He had arrived at Newark Airport from Paris and was waiting for a flight to West Palm Beach.

"Mike Surrey and I will meet you at the airport," I said.

The three of us caught the same flight. It was only half full and we were able to sit together by an emergency exit that had ample stretching space. It was an early morning flight that put us into West Palm before Eleven.

Mike felt good that morning. It was important to take early morning flights with him. Lunch was the climax of his day, and we had to reach a place that served booze by noon. But this trip was different. He stayed stone sober, and that gave us two hours to plan our move on the Blue Danube.

Frank Barton met us at the airport in Fort Lauderdale when I landed.

Ever so formal, he said, "Welcome to Florida, Mr. Gordon, Mr. Surrey and Mr. Katz."

And he grabbed our duffels under his brawny arms.

"Mr. Surrey and Mr. Katz will be staying at the Poinciana and Mr. Gordon, you will be at the Del Rey Tower on the beach. Inspector Santana is waiting for you there. Have you all brought your clubs?"

"They should be with my bags on the carousel downstairs," I said. "Isn't the luncheon at the Poinciana? Why am I staying at the Del Rey?"

"We thought you would be more comfortable there."

We dropped Otto and Mike at the Poinciana and a few minutes afterwards I was at the Del Rey where Jake Santana and Pierre La Salle were standing at the livery entrance with Tom Lyons.

"Who told you I was coming to town?" I asked them.

Jake Santana pointed to Tom.

"Guess who. Besides, we have to talk."

"Tom here says you've become good with guns," Jake said after I had checked in and we had settled down at a table near the pool.

"I'm decent," I replied dryly. "What's the lineup on the course?"

Jake explained that the two lead foursomes would be Colin, Jake, Vic and I in the first and Ed Houston, George Lerman, Larry O'Leary and Mike Surrey in the second. Sixteen more foursomes were playing in the tournament.

"What's the schedule?" I asked after my bags were sent up to the suite and we had repaired to the bar.

"Eva is having everyone over tomorrow afternoon," Jake replied. "That gives us a morning of golf. We thought of canceling but she said it was out of the question. She said Colin would have wanted us to carry on."

"Who's standing for Colin?" Tom asked.

"That wouldn't be cool," said Jake. "Felix is here but he won't be in our group. He'll play in O'Leary's foursome in Mike Surrey's place. We want to have a missing man formation in our foursomes, so Mike will be our team caddy and drive the cart with the clubs. Pierre here and Tom will play with Solomon and Weinberg. We have 72 players this year, so it's going to be a shotgun start, one foursome to a starting tee. That should speed up the game. We'll have to move fast to avoid being trampled."

Jake ordered a round of drinks and we began to relax.

"Eva told me a little about what happened, but not much," I said. "What do you know, Jake?"

"It's sad but much of it doesn't make sense."

Tom's eyebrows rose.

"How's that?"

"*Obsession* was powered by a two heavy duty recently inspected diesels. Diesel powered boats rarely blow up; that's why the industry has gone from gas to diesel on large yachts. We've all been on the yacht, and so have you. It's filled with redundant, failsafe systems. One could drop a grenade into the fuel tanks before anything happened, and then that would probably be a fuel fire and not an explosion. There should have been time to send a May Day signal."

"Any trace of the boat?" Tom asked.

"Nada, amigo! It was pulverized. Felix tells me they found an oil slick and the usual debris, but nothing on which to base a positive I.D."

Tom's head shook in disbelief.

"You mean to say that a yacht evaporates with no I.D., and we're claiming that it's Colin's boat and that he was on it? Funny, isn't it? How do we know that's what actually happened?"

Jake scratched the bald dome of his head.

"We don't. We know less today than when Haussmann died."

La Salle shook his head.

"Whatever you think, I think. I have no new ideas."

I tried a different tack.

"How did Eva learn about Colin?"

"She says Henry and Felix called her from Bimini. Felix confirmed the call and the conversation. Henry made the call from his office. Incidentally, Felix told me that Henry looked fine. It seems those treatments worked for him."

"That means Henry is in the Bahamas. Is he here for the luncheon?"

"Not a chance. He's afraid of being arrested as a draft dodger."

"Damn, Jake. That was years ago. No one wants him today."

"Henry told Felix he tried to get a visa through the American Embassy in Nassau. It was denied because his draft situation was never clarified. So he flew back to Paris this morning."

I grumbled under my breath.

"How convenient."

"What was that?"

"Nothing," I answered. "Nothing."

Then I added, "I hate draft dodgers!"

Jake smiled.

"Are you sure you don't hate Henry because he stole your girl in Paris and married her?"

Tom Lyons changed the subject.

"That's not the issue, Jake. We have two possible murders in Paris...."

"Oh, Haussmann and Dore were murdered. We have no doubt," Pierre La Salle interjected.

Tom went on.

"And we have a guy, John Cork, traveling like a ghost between the States and Europe, an attempted murder in New Jersey and a key witness who has been blown up. They are linked together through a diamond smuggling ring and one very large diamond. Since we can't talk to Colin, we need Henry Adair to talk to us."

"And to complicate matters," I added. "I'm going to steal the Blue Danube. And I'm going to need your help."

There was a long moment of silence.

"You're going to do what? Tom asked.

"You heard me. I'm going to steal the Blue Danube," I repeated.

"We could arrest you just for saying that," said Jake.

"You could, but you might be missing out on a good thing."

And I proceeded to lay out my plan in broad brush strokes. It was basically the one Hans, Mike and I developed on our flight. When I finished, Pierre La Salle asked the obvious question.

"How much are we talking about, Max?"

"A lot of money, Pierre. A lot of money. This particular stone is a perfect blue diamond of about 149 carats. On the street it's called fancy blue and it carries a wholesale per carat value today upwards of $300,000. If you do the math, that comes to more than $44 million. That's about what we would net at the very minimum if the Blue Danube is cut into smaller stones and turned into jewelry like rings, necklaces and earrings."

"Who would do the cutting?" Jake asked.

"Otto Katz," I replied. "He has to be a partner."

Tom leaned back.

"How many partners are we talking about in this gig?"

"Six. That's over $ 7 million per partner. There are four of us here. Our fifth partner is Mike Surrey. He's an electrician and knows the Maison Dore layout in Morristown because his family owned the building before selling it to Haussmann and Dore. Otto is our sixth partner. We need him because he's the best diamond cutter in the business."

Pierre La Salle took a sip of his drink and asked the next obvious question.

"And what must we do to earn our shares, Max?"

"Nothing in particular, and nothing out of character. Mainly, I need you to grease the skids and look the other way once the theft is discovered."

"How are you even going to get close to the diamond," Jake Santana asked.

"My attorney is suing to allow me to inspect and appraise the diamond with Otto. That should happen real soon. Your job is to make sure that Otto, Mike and I make it out of the country with the diamond."

"That's an awful risk you're asking us to take," said Tom.

"True," I replied. "We could go to prison. But if we succeed, we'll be very rich. What about it, gang?"

"It sounds good, Max," said Tom. "What about Eva?"

"She's not a partner."

"And Henry?"

"There's Henry and Emile Barco, the invisible man. They're bound to make their own play for the diamond. We have to beat them to it."

"That's an invitation for you to be killed," said Jake.

"I'm already on someone's short list," I replied. "So what difference does it make?"

"Max has a strong argument," La Salle pointed out. "If Henry and Barco steal the Blue Danube, Max will pursue them for the 10% bounty. Either he will kill them or they will kill him. That is a high risk proposition and we, my friends, end up with nothing but aggravation. If he steals the diamond, they will chase him down and again, either he or they will die. But we will be on his side and the risks will be lower. We may also end up being much richer than we are today. Consider me in, Max."

"Same here," Jake Santana declared.

"Affirmative," said Tom Lyons.

We shook hands and toasted to our new partnership.

14

Reunion

A gunslinger enjoys popularity. Word of my encounter with a shooter up north in New Jersey had spread and I suspect that Eva, Tom Lyons and Mike each in their own way contributed to adding embellishments that soon turned a failed hit into a heroic gunfight. By the time I reached the golf club I was basking in the limelight of being the man of the moment.

Frank Barton came by early the next morning with Jake, Felix Stiles and Mike Surrey and took us to the Delray Beach Golf Club a few miles inland.

Mike had once been Colin's restaurant manager back north until drinking forced his resignation. That was how Larry O'Leary ended up with the job.

Mike was now, to use his words, "fully semi-retired, doing charity work and devoted to hobnobbing with politicians and other important folks."

Drinking was the reason he stopped playing golf. He used to be a scratch player despite his fake leg but he had not played in years since his day ended at noon and that meant getting on a course by seven in the morning. It was partly for his sake that our games were always timed to end before lunch.

But now he was a man transformed and stayed sober for the entire game.

Mike took one look at me when we reached the clubhouse.

"You look a little peaked," was his observation. "Are you ok?"

"So far so good," I assured him. But in fact my stomach was acting up.

"Did I ever tell you what the guy who jumped off the top of the Empire State Building said?" Mike asked.

"No, what?"

"When he passed the bartender looking out the window of the 44th floor grill?"

"No, what?"

"So far so good."

Everyone laughed and even I couldn't resist cracking a smile.

We reached the course in threatening weather and time was pressing.

"Shotgun start," announced Larry O'Leary, turning his head skyward.

I liked golf. Not that I was good at it. I struggled to play in the 90's. Yet I found walking a seven thousand yard course refreshing and therapeutic. And now I walked, club in hand and my golf bag in Mike Surrey's cart.

The game reminded me ever so much of the old infantry assault lines when squads would split up into four man teams who would then spread out along a line of fire in brush or tall grass to slowly converge on a target.

The choreography was chillingly similar. In golf as in battle, we advanced at a snail's pace and then in spurts. Once we finished teeing off and walked down the sides of the fairway to locate our balls, we would patiently await our turns before slamming them again to the green. The game progressed cautiously. We advanced in a vague formation through and around assorted obstacles until the golf balls found the green.

For me, reaching the green was the goal and the putting game was largely anticlimactic although granted it was crucial to winning. Any golf game can of course only have one winner, but I felt that since we all reached the green at about the same time without sustaining real casualties, everyone won.

I noticed we were no longer young. It was a silent understanding among us that except for pictures of children and grandchildren, old photos betraying the years and the combat of flesh against time where time always won were not to be shown. War stories too remained buried in our memories.

Victor Nishkanian was there. He always fascinated me. A thick head of carefully coifed wavy hair, prominent sideburns and a well-groomed beard framed a pair of eagle eyes over a heavy curved nose. He looked more like an ancient Assyrian warrior than a Florida businessman.

He ambled over to me after the game and observed diplomatically, "I see life has been good to you, Max."

I was oblivious to what he meant.

"Thanks." I said. "I do try to make a living here and there."

Vic laughed.

"Let me put it this way. I have watched you play. You have dropped a point off your game for every pound you lost."

I smiled at his remark.

"But I'm not here to comment on your healthy eating habits. How friendly were you with Colin and Eva?"

Victor was of medium height, so I had to bend my head to listen better.

"How do you mean?"

"I mean that Eva and I have mutual interests. She and I own the Poinciana and I gave her cash to pay Colin, but he died before she could pay him and before we could settle his other loans from me against which he pledged the Blue Danube diamond."

"Isn't it in the Dore vault in Morristown?"

"That's my question. It should be there, but I have my doubts."

Vic looked around anxiously to make sure no one was listening.

"How do we guarantee that the diamond is there to satisfy creditor claims?"

"That's a tough one, Victor. What are you suggesting?"

"I'm suggesting that I may need your help. After all, you do have a claim to the Blue Danube in your own right."

"I haven't thought about it, but I'll help you anyway I can."

"Getting back to you and Eva. Will you be marrying her? You two make a nice couple, and I think I would prefer you as a partner over anyone else."

His voice faded when Jake Santana came over with the other foursomes to congratulate Vic for having won the tournament.

"How's the winner?"

Vic was the game winner and everyone took turns shaking his hand and slapping him on the back while Larry O'Leary announced in his usual formal cordiality.

"Lunch is at Two, gentlemen. We have to change and get going."

He turned to me and asked, "How's it going, Max? Too bad we have to meet this way."

"There'll be happier times," I promised.

Larry gave me a nudge and a wink.

"Oh yeah? When?"

Ed Houston, who was cleaning his clubs with George Lerman, looked up.

"You have to give us the secret for losing that beef, Max."

Pride began swelling in my chest.

"You look pretty good yourself, Edward. You're as thin as a rail."

"That's the funny thing," he said. The doctor says I have diabetes. I can't figure it out."

It was odd, I thought. That's what I was told as well. Indeed, I recalled the cardiologist mentioning at one of my checkups that heart problems can be induced by diabetes.

"Who did you go see?"

Ed Houston shrugged.

"Some guy up north named Harry Silver."

"Do yourself a favor," I told Ed. "Let me know before you start taking any pills Harry gives you."

Ed Houston shrugged.

"Why?"

"I might save you a trip to your own funeral. At least, let me see the pills."

George Lerman was standing next to Ed Houston. Once again he reminded me.

"You stay healthy, Max, you hear?"

Felix Stiles, the police chief from Bimini, was nearby. He too had served with us before returning to the Bahamas where he was born and eventually went into police work. Short and thick and with a halo of closely cropped hair around his head, a slightly off-center Groucho Marx type moustache over lips puckered into a grin gave him an impish air.

He greeted me with a firm hand shake.

"It's a long time since you were in Bimini, Max," he said. "You should come over one of these days so we can get in some fishing."

"I'd like that, Felix," I noted. "Hopefully, I'll have better luck getting to Bimini than Colin."

"Not funny, Max."

"I know. But this is a not a fun time. You know, Colin could have flown to Bimini instead of taking his yacht and being blown up on the way."

"On the way?" Felix squinted. "He wasn't on the way to Bimini. He was leaving Bimini!"

"Oh?"

"Yes. He checked through our customs the day before, spent the day out in the yacht fishing with his brother, returned to the harbor where he dropped off Henry and then departed for Florida. Henry was in my office when we heard the blast. It happened about fifteen minutes after the yacht cleared the cut between North and South Bimini."

"Damn!"

"Say what?"

"What about the clinic where Henry was receiving his treatments?"

"I'm curious about that, Max. I'm checking it out. Believe me, Santana, Lyons and La Salle share the same concerns. Something isn't right and we intend to find out what that is."

His words were comforting. They made me aware that I was not alone in questioning the events of the past year.

Jake cornered me on the way out of the country club.

"Tom Lyons, Pierre La Salle and I had a meeting yesterday after you left."

I feigned disinterest.

"We're in," he said. "You tell us what you need."

It was the best news I heard in a long time.

An hour later, we reassembled at the Poinciana where Eva had arranged a buffet in the ballroom that seemed more fitting for a celebration of life than for a wake. The rain that threatened never came and the sun was out.

Pierre La Salle was standing on the hotel porch looking at the sky and smacked his lips.

"Beautiful weather, Max. We don't have weather like this in France, not even on the Riviera. Did Jake speak to you?"

I nodded.

"I have to go in," he said with a smile. "Otto is here. I want to see him."

Pierre slapped my back, a stiff smile pasted to his lips.

"By the way, Max. Those pills. Were they from Harry Silver?"

"How did you know?"

The Interpol director smiled secretively.

"Never underestimate the investigative police powers of the state, my dear old friend."

La Salle slapped my back again and followed a bellhop inside.

I nodded and moved on. Now I knew exactly how Carl Haussmann died. I wondered how long it would be before Tom Lyons would be paying Harry Silver a visit.

It was late February and the height of the tourist season. From the veranda I could look out on the streets teeming with shoppers making the rounds of the upscale boutiques and shaded sidewalk cafes.

The street crowd spilled over into the hotel lobby and its adjacent bar and restaurant. This section of Delray could have sprung out of a Paris street scene painting to which some clever artist added a tropical touch with palm trees, banyans and brightly colored floral shrubs. Given any day or evening in the high season, Delray was overflowing with aimless throngs of people milling and walking and being watched by even more people cramming the cafes. This day, the crowds were thicker than usual.

The lobby, always a busy place, was filled with wicker and rattan chairs and tables standing on terra cotta floors next to potted palms whose ferns reached up to the fans and chandeliers hanging down from the high ceilings. There were two indoor restaurants, several bars and a ballroom off the lobby that opened out back into a garden atrium and parking lot. Eva chose to hold the luncheon in the ballroom and atrium.

A short, stocky man in a brown blazer appeared out of nowhere, huffing and puffing under the weight of an over filled duffel in one hand and a rum drink in the other.

"Hi. I'm Stanley Short from the IRS."

He went on to explain he was on vacation and thought he would drop over to pay his respects. He confided he had already belted down a few drinks and had his eyes on a tall brunette making her way to one of the inside bars.

"You're Max Gordon, aren't you?"

"Yes?"

"I'll catch up with you later, Max. We have to talk."

He disappeared into the hotel, chasing after the brunette. I never saw him again at the party.

Even Rajeesh Kumari showed up under the pretext of having to visit his retail stores in Miami.

"It is nice to see you," he said, a grin covering his gleaming brown face.

"Your friend, Otto, says many good things about you."

"He does?"

"Yes. He says you are a man to be trusted."

"Indeed!"

"Yes. I would like to use your services to help me procure the fabled Blue Danube diamond. It belongs to my family. I am willing to pay for your good services and to buy out your interest."

"And what services are that?"

Rajeesh peered at me through his thick glasses. The grin never left his face.

"I want to you to make sure the diamond ends up in my hands. I will take care of the other details."

"What details?"

"Simple, Max. I have always wanted to see the Blue Danube returned to its ancestral home in India."

"You mean to your ancestral home, don't you?"

"Exactly. I am willing to pay dearly for the gemstone. Henry has offered to swap me the diamond for my business."

"Are you sure you want to do that?"

"Yes. It works for me and it works for Henry who will be able to merge Maison Dore with Kumari. At the same time, my friend, Sol Weinberg, will take over Sentinel in return for a promise to discharge all of its debts. I need to make sure nothing happens to the Blue Danube. I will match Sentinel's ten percent commission based on its insured value to make sure it stays in safe hands, assuming of course that you renounce whatever claims you think you have, however dubious they may be, to the diamond."

"But what about the IRS?"

"Stanley Short? He is a good friend of mine. I can work with him. Are you dependable? Otto vouches for you."

"If I'm reading you right, you're talking about doing some serious stuff, Rajeesh. I'll have to think about this. Anyway, I'll let you know."

So. I wasn't the only one with wicked ideas.

Rajeesh Kumari kept smiling as he walked away to mingle with the other guests at the reception.

The affair was a classy, high profile gesture to Colin's memory and to his family's success over a century. It was also a tribute to Eva who looked more radiant than ever as she presided over the luncheon in a simple black dress and small veil to partially screen her face and turned up blonde hair. I marveled at her stamina and the way she graciously exchanged a few words with each of the well wishers who lined up to pay their respects even if there was no body.

When my turn came, she took me aside and whispered into my ear.

"I'm glad you're here, Max. What are you doing tonight?"

The question left me tongue tied. I blurted out some reply about being free and added, "I'm flying home tomorrow."

"You're at the Del Rey Tower, aren't you?"

"Yes."

"I'll be there for dinner," she said.

I was about to say something more when she turned away to speak with Mel Solomon who was towering behind me. Next to him stood Mel's old friend and competitor, Sol Weinberg, chomping on his usual cigar. Here they were, the big fat schlemiel and the little fat schmegegi.

"Long time no see," Sol said, shaking my hand.

"Must be a few years," I noted.

Sol grinned.

"Don't you regret not working for me, Max? Think of all the aggravation Mel has been giving you."

"Don't tempt him," Mel Solomon chimed in. "He'll ask for a raise."

He grabbed my hand.

"How's everything, old buddy?"

He kept pumping it and wouldn't let go until he finished what he had to say.

"That was cool work back up in New Jersey. I like your guts. Stay alive, will you, and take your cues from me, you hear? Play your cards right and you'll end up rich and famous."

Poor old Mel. He didn't have too many more pots to piss in. At least he knew how to put up a front.

He stared at my jacket for an instant.

"Where's your piece? Surrey loaned you his gun."

"I don't like guns."

"Carry one anyway. You never know."

"Take Mel's advice, Max," Sol added.

"I want you alive and healthy when you come work for me."

I laughed.

"I'll try to stay alive." Then I asked Mel. "Where's Bill Ford?"

The Sentinel chief dropped his hand.

"Out with a dislocated shoulder."

Eva appeared anxious to keep the line moving and I quickly moved out of the way.

Sol and Rajeesh cornered me later and asked me about my arrangement with Sentinel.

"I have no exclusive deal, Sol," I replied. "Nothing in writing. I'm a free agent. It's just that I've always done work for Mel. What's on your mind?"

My company insures Rajeesh Kumari. His business competes head on against Maison Dore. He wants two things. He wants the Blue Danube which he believes belongs in his ancestral home in India. He also wants to acquire Maison Dore to expand his markets. And I want Sentinel. We need you on our side."

"Yes. And I said I'll think about it. But I can't promise anything."

The noise level rose and the well wishers grew boisterous in measure with the flow of liquor. The afternoon wore on. I was never that much of a party animal and I was bored if not tired. Without saying another word to anyone, I located my golf bag in a storeroom, slipped out of the hotel and was about to hail a cab when I found Victor Nishkanian at my side.

"How about coffee at the Carnival? It's across the street. I'll drive you back to the Del Rey later."

Protest was pointless. There was something bothering Vic and I thought it would be a good idea to listen. Besides, coffee in the relative quiet of a diner in the late afternoon would be a welcome relief.

A few minutes later we were at a window table where a waitress came over promptly to take our order.

The diner was another landmark. It had a long horseshoe counter and an assortment of odd sized tables and booths spread over two rooms. Waiters and waitresses took no cash; everything had to be settled at the cashier's counter near the door. Vic's wife manned the cash register by day and Vic presided at night, sharing his shift with two adult sons and a daughter.

It was a twenty four hour eatery with a standard diner menu where food and coffee were served in heavy platters and thick cups with ample portions of toast and rolls. The tables and booths were plain and the walls were filled with cheap prints of famous paintings. Here and there hung the art works of local artists looking for customers. Chrome, Formica, black vinyl, and pink neon trim mixed with cheap brass chandeliers, hanging planters and ceiling fans created an eclectic bohemian atmosphere.

We ordered coffee and the waitress returned a minute later with two mugs and a plastic pitcher filled with hot coffee. I came right to the point.

"What's up?" I asked.

"I'm going to lose a lot of money over this, Max." Vic replied.

"Why is that?"

"I think Eva is going have trouble handling her husband's debts."

"What about the diamond? Doesn't it collateralize the debts?"

"It's supposed to. But I have my doubts. I keep hearing that Henry may have bought Colin out, including the Blue Danube. That's bad for me. My deals with Colin were mostly done on a handshake. I do own some paper on his hotel and restaurants up north but that's not enough to pay me back. And I hear a deal is the works to have Kumari get the diamond in exchange for Maison Dore and for Centurion to get Sentinel. That leaves me and all the other creditors out in the cold."

"So, what do you want me to do?"

Vic leaned forward to press his point.

"Listen. Mike says you and Eva were once an item and you're seeing her again. All I'm asking is that you speak to her and find out what's going on. I'll pay you…"

I shook my head.

"That was many, many years ago, and the clock isn't turning back on this one. But I do appreciate your offer, and I'll speak to her. There's no need to pay me. I'm in line for part of the diamond and I plan to keep my eyes on it. And if it's stolen, I'll make plenty getting it back. That's the business I'm in. Either way, I won't forget you."

"You're an honest guy, Max. I'll settle for that."

Then he asked, "How's Mike?" he asked. "Has he stopped drinking?"

"Could be, Vic. Could be."

I shifted to another subject.

"I saw Sol Weinberg at the hotel. How close is he to Mel Solomon?"

Vic leaned back.

"He's a shark and smells blood. If Mel's empire folds, he wants to pick up the pieces."

"What about George Lerman and Ed Houston?"

"They wouldn't touch you. It's too obvious. I'd watch the small potatoes. They'd be tempted to bite your ass for a price."

"You make me feel good, Vic."

He rose to his feet.

"Come. I'll drive you to your hotel."

15

Dinner

Everyone had an angle and I was glad to have kept my mouth shut. There would have been no gain in making everyone more upset than they were by telling them that I was staking out my own claim to the Blue Danube.

It was all too much. Back at the Del Rey, I went directly to my suite where the message button on the phone was lit. I lifted the receiver and accessed the voice messaging system.

There were two messages. The first was from Brian Donovan who said he needed to see me and was flying down. The second was from my attorney who advised me that he had finally obtained the necessary court injunctions that would get me access to the Blue Danube.

I was too tired call back. I hung up the phone and fell asleep.

It was not quite sundown when the telephone's persistent ring woke me up. It was Eva.

"Do you want dinner or are you having your period?"

I smiled.

"My dear woman," I said. "I'm always having my period. Where are you?"

"Downstairs in the lobby."

"I'll be right down. Meet me at the bar. We can dine at the hotel."

It took less than five minutes to shave, freshen up, throw on some clean clothes and run downstairs and across the pool area to meet her. It would have taken less time but a stabbing pain hit my right side, like a rib cramp. It made me stop by a beach chair and gasp for air. The pain left as suddenly as it came and, giving it no further thought, I made my way to the lobby where I found Eva sitting at the hotel lounge bar.

She was in the same outfit I had last seen her in earlier in the day except that she had removed the veil covering her hair, which was still turned up. I had to admit. She was as beautiful to me as the day we first met.

"That was many years ago," she reminded me later over dinner at the Del Rey's indoor restaurant.

"And we were much younger."

"And not very smart," I added.

"I remember what you used to say, Max. I think it was in Spanish…"

I raised my glass of scotch in a toast.

"I said, 'Salud, amor y dinero, y tiempo para gastarlo.' Health, love and money, and time enough to have it all."

"That was very sweet, Maxie. I thought I'd never hear those words again."

"And I thought I would never hear the name 'Maxie' from your lips again. You make me feel young again."

"How long has it been since we first dated?"

"Long enough."

"Do you keep company with other women when I'm not around?"

"Ask my daughter. She's my watchdog."

Eva was edging around some subject she obviously wanted to bring up and I was trying my best to be on guard against her next broadside.

"I'd like to be the one for you, Max."

"Like when we were young?"

"What happened to us?" she asked. "Why didn't we stay young?"

I shrugged my shoulders.

"You placed your bets on Colin. You thought he was a winner, like you told me. And he was."

"You had no direction those days. I didn't know what you wanted. Colin had a family business. He offered me love and security. We went over all that. But Colin is gone now, and you're here."

I stared down at my hands before meeting the stare of her hazel eyes.

"All I ever wanted was a wife and family. I always figured I'd make a living. But you did well. And now you may end up being a rich widow."

"Well, yes. But no real family life. I was going to get a divorce but now I don't have anyone to divorce. The funny thing is that you can end up a rich widower if you play your cards right."

"I'm sure there are worthier candidates than I."

"I'd consider Larry O'Leary and Jake Santana. Larry knows the hotel and restaurant business and Jake is all around savvy."

It was obvious that Eva had given much thought to life after Colin.

"They're married with kids," I protested.

"In name only," Eva responded with indifference. "They would divorce in a flash if I gave the word."

She snapped her fingers.

I had my doubts about Jake jumping ship. He had too much of a sense of balance and order in his life. Besides, he was already in the bag as one of my partners in our plot to steal the diamond.

Larry O'Leary was another issue. To the outside world, the O'Leary family was perfect and successful. The cracks in their picture of marital bliss were invisible to the human eye. Larry invited me to a birthday party for his daughter Simone about six years ago. It was glitzy to say the least and media photographers were on hand to take pictures family togetherness at its best.

Larry's kids suffered from a near fatal disease. I read a column about the illness once. It was genetically inherited and called, "Influenza!"

Simone and her brother Jason had just returned with their mother from the semiannual children's fashion show in Florence, Italy, and were showing off in their latest wardrobe purchased from Franconi Necci whose stores were in Milan and Paris. The clothes were tailor-made designer originals that must have cost several thousands of dollars per outfit. Larry, passing behind me at the party, clapped my shoulders and laughed.

"How would the world know I'm successful if my kids buy off-the-rack clothes?"

I had to agree. Simone and her mother had on pink, thigh-high dresses a-la Lili Pulitzer, and Jason was in a silk suit and lizard loafers similar to those his father was wearing. The younger generation was unabashedly mimicking the older one. These teenagers were being groomed for success, although I overheard a Neiman-Marcus buyer at the party snort to a companion.

"The only people who buy these clothes are parents who treat their kids as fashion accessories."

Larry's wife caught me near the exit when I was about to leave.

"Don't they look wonderful, Max? I think good clothes build self-esteem. Do call the next time you're in town, dearest. We can do lunch."

What Eva didn't realize was Larry's debt load that forced him to tie his fate to Colin's luck. With him gone, it made sense in a perverse way for Larry to go for Eva. He could hitch his fortune to hers and probably make enough money to still take care of his family. It was difficult for me to keep in mind that Eva was an accessory to an attempted murder.

"But if you and I were married," I heard Eva say, "we would own a full two thirds of the Blue Danube."

There it was, neatly laid out for me. It was either me or Larry. It was my call. She preferred me but Larry would do. She was a determined woman and a great salesperson. She kept talking of the great life we would have, and Colin's body was not yet cold. It did not even exist.

I was perhaps being overly analytical. Shellac and varnish can cover knots on wood quite well. The immediate and the superficial were what counted and scratching away at these veneers of life was not smart. I once read that the Greek philosopher Socrates claimed that the unexamined life was not worth living. He was probably wrong. Perhaps life was not worth examining too closely and only the unexamined life was worth living.

"Do you like being a grandfather?" Eva asked suddenly.

"I used to hate the sound of the word," I exclaimed. "It sounds like old age. But from you it sounds great. The answer is yes. I like it."

"I have two kids," Eva complained. "They make me feel old. I wish I could start over."

"Don't we all? But you're still beautiful."

"You know, Maxie, there was a time when I would have followed you to the ends of the earth, and I still would if the chance came up again. Didn't you once have a girlfriend in Paris, before you met Gladys?" I know you're finished with Gladys, but what about her predecessor?"

"That was a fluke, an accident. I was still married, although my wife was sick. Anyway, it didn't last long. She married Henry. I guess that makes me a two-time loser."

Eva was inching again towards the subject of marriage and I tried hard to avoid the subject. Marriage was an attractive prospect but I wanted to be able to make that move at my own initiative when my mind was clear.

I looked at my watch.

"Listen, I'm glad we got back together, even under these sad circumstances, but this is a bad moment for us to talk about the past."

"Could we then look forward to a future? I could use someone to help me in the hotel-restaurant business now that Colin is gone."

"Maybe, Eva. Maybe. I'd like that. But, I'm telling you beforehand, I don't want any part of your family business."

She shifted gears.

"Don't be greedy. I'm thinking of a general manager for starters."

"Oh?"

That was a new one on me.

"What about O'Leary?"

"He's the one who recommended you. He wants to retire."

"Have you spoken to Victor? He says Colin owes him money."

Eva blushed, and it took several moments before she recovered her composure.

"Nish is a snake," she snarled. "He owns half of the Poinciana and Colin owes him a few dollars, so he's trying to muscle into my affairs."

It was interesting how fast Eva's personality could change.

"How does this mess leave you financially?" I asked.

"Very rich. All the businesses on this side of the Atlantic are mine once I settle with Henry. If Colin's death is ruled an accident, I end up with a fat insurance settlement that Sentinel has to pay. Colin's deal with Nish is to turn the Blue Danube Diamond over to him if the debts aren't paid. That's not going to happen. Neither am I going to let Henry take what's mine. I'll see him in court first. I owe my husband that much! I also understand that people are suspicious about the diamond. Well, it can be seen anytime as soon as a official death certificate on Colin is issued and the courts give the sign."

This woman was sharp.

"It's been way over a year," I said. "A visit is way overdue."

Eva shook her head.

"That won't work right now. Henry's U.S. attorney obtained a court order sealing the vault until Colin's estate is settled. Who knows, I might have to ask you to steal the Blue Danube, Max."

She laughed. She was obviously unaware my attorney had beaten Henry's attorney to the draw.

"I'm joking of course," she said.

"Of course. However, why should I steal something when part of it already belongs to me?"

I laughed back, but my comment was poorly received. Eva's smile faded and she became all business.

"There are three of us. Henry, me and you. We can play together, Max, or only one of us will ever get the diamond. I promise you that!"

Eva was about to press her point but must have sensed my reluctance to discuss the matter further. She leaned forward and gave me a peck on the forehead.

"You're tired, and it's been a long day. Let's call it a night. I too want to get some sleep. And in the future, you can stay with me. It's much nicer than the Del Rey."

Looking back on that evening, I couldn't decide whether I was romancing a woman whose goal was to survive and took love as a bonus or whether I was rolling in the grass with a viper with passionate fangs filled with poison.

A noise outside my suite's balcony got me up shortly after dawn. I pulled myself out of bed and shuffled off to the balcony. Down below several police officers were retrieving a body from the pool.

I threw on some clothes and rushed down to see what was going on. Jake Santana and Frank Barton were already there in a huddle over the body when I reached the pool.

"What's going on?"

"It's Brian Donovan," Jake replied. "He was flying down to see you."

Poor Brian. Whatever he had wanted to tell me must have been important enough to have him killed. I hoped for his family's sake that he had paid his last life insurance premium.

"He left me a message last night. How did you know?"

"We checked your messages. You never erased them."

"How did he die?"

"He was strangled and thrown into the pool between two and three this morning."

"How did he get here?"

"That's what we have to find out," said Jake. "Larry was supposed to pick Brian up but he never got to the airport. He was with Eva at her condo."

"Not so," I protested. "He's wrong. I was with Eva."

Jake smirked.

"Only for dinner. We verified that."

"Then who picked up Brian?"

"You didn't. That's for sure. You were snoring so loudly, I thought you were creating a disturbance."

"So. While the cops are watching me, Brian gets himself killed. Tell me. Why are you guys following me anyway?"

Jake's smile disappeared.

"You might not believe this, Max. But a few of us would really like you to stay alive."

"I'm sorry, Jake. I was out of line. Brian didn't deserve dying the way he did."

"No one deserves to die," said Frank. "But we'll get the killers."

"Killers?"

Two, Max," Jake explained. "Brian was garroted. There was a driver. Brian was in the front passenger seat; the killer sat in the back seat, placed a wire lace around his neck and strangled him. He must have known his killers. The body was brought here and thrown in the pool, maybe to send you a message. This is not good for tourism, Max."

16

The Deal

Brian Donovan's body had to stay on ice in Delray while the investigation into his murder ground on. I decided to stay until it was over and almost forgot about going home. But Spring came early in New Jersey and finally my daughter called to say it was as warm up north as it was in Florida. She added that she had picked up my mail and that a brown envelope had come from Paris. I asked her to open it.

La Salle was as good as his word. The envelope contained documents to be completed in triplicate in application for the monies that France was offering to pay orphans of the holocaust in France. I told her that I would fill out the forms when I returned.

I met Mike Surrey in front of the Poinciana and we went into the hotel for lunch. Larry O'Leary was there and he joined us.

The mood was subdued in the absence of Brian Donovan despite the bright sun outside.

One thing the Adairs had was a sense of history expressed by preserving a consistent image in all their hotels and restaurants with period architecture and furnishings while adding contemporary essentials like climate control and computers. Several broad steps lead from the street to a covered, wrap around porch in front of double-hung doors that lead to the lobby and the registration counter that crouched under the stairwell leading to the rooms on the second floor. To the lobby's left was a spacious dining room and circular bar done in mahogany and walnut tones with a mix of Federal and Victorian motifs. To the right was a sitting room with chairs and card tables set around a fireplace. The arrangements were not unlike those at the Bernardsville Club hotel.

I was in the midst of explaining what I was being offered by the Chirac government and complaining about its mendacity to my attentive audience, concluding with the usual cliché, "Too little too late," when Larry suggested sympathetically that I should consider donating the money to charity.

That didn't go over well with me.

"Charity begins at home," I countered unintentionally with another cliché. I then added.

"I'm broke. My daughter is always asking for handouts and I'm saving up for a new girlfriend. My women have expensive tastes."

"The problem is that your short arms can't reach into your deep pockets."

Tom Lyons had come by and overheard my tirade. He came over to our table and continued the hounding.

"Max has to be frugal. That's the only way he can afford nice things."

Here was humor I never saw in him before. I gave Tom the international sign of ill repute. He feigned insult and sat down.

"Why don't you marry again?" Mike asked. "You're my oldest buddy. You need a steady woman to take care of you and keep you going."

"The only thing any woman is going to do is take care of is my money," I retorted.

"You were seeing someone else along with Gladys weren't you?" Larry inquired. "At least for a while?"

"Some Eurasian or Russian chick, wasn't it?" Mike recalled.

"Tell us about it," said Tom

I nodded.

"That thing goes back many years. But it went nowhere. I was seeing the two of them. When it started, Gladys was recently divorced and had small kids. She didn't want to remarry because she was afraid she'd lose her alimony and child support. The Eurasian broad was also divorced but she had no kids. She wanted to marry, but she was too pushy and a little unbalanced.

"When we first met, she was Eastern Orthodox with a touch of Buddhism. She celebrated Christmas and New Year's Eve a week after we did and she always insisted on following the major Asian holidays. That worked for me. I could divide my time easily and not miss a stroke, if you pardon the pun.

"Everything changed when she discovered the credit card and also wanted to start spending the regular Christmas holidays, including New Year's Eve, with me. Naturally, I couldn't be in two places at the same time. It created timing problems.

"On top of that was a slight matter of deception. I didn't want the women to get pissed; so I never told either of them that I was seeing another. To keep my stories straight, I had to make sure that when I went somewhere with one, I went to the same place with the other. That means I saw every movie twice, every play twice, and went to every vacation spot twice, once with one broad and again with the other.

"I also had to keep each set of friends and relatives apart, and that meant I had to run in two social tracks and keep two separate calendars. You don't know what stress is until you try it! And of course there was the marriage thing. All dates would end with a fight over marriage. And if I stonewalled, she'd sulk and sulk and sulk. I had to call it quits."

"I remember her," Larry recalled. "You two had dinner a few times at the Bernardsville place."

"That's right," I went on. "We broke up soon after. But then Gladys started talking marriage. Her kids were getting too old for her to keep getting child support and her ex husband dropped dead one day while he was jogging and she lost her alimony.

"But you want to know something else? I took a close look at her. I like women to give me a thrill, a tingling feeling. All she was giving me was a chill. And then there were all those shopping forays. I didn't want to end up with bills and a high maintenance woman. Anyway, she's gone.

"You know, those two broads gave me a lot of stress. I'm convinced now that the real reason I ended up with a heart attack was stress. I'm not going to do that again."

"Maybe you'll meet someone in Paris when you go collect your stipend," Larry suggested.

"Has anyone heard from Henry?"

Larry shook his head.

"Eva does. They communicate by fax, phone and e-mail. I thought she hated him. They were never in touch like that when Colin was around. She wanted Henry to come over and help her out with her business, but there's no way he can get here until his old draft status is cleared. She says he's working on it, but that won't be anytime soon."

"Even for a funeral?"

"That's the thing, Max. Colin isn't officially dead. Eva can't even place an obit in the papers."

"Did you hear about the old woman who lost her husband?" Tom asked.

"No, what about her?"

"This woman's husband dies and she has to make up an obituary. So she calls the paper and tells it to write, 'Herb is dead.' The copy editor tells her she can have up to six words for the minimum charge. She thinks it over for a while and then instructs him to write, 'Herb is dead. Cadillac for sale.'"

We all laughed. Larry then turned to me and said, "Oh, by the way, Eva said you're thinking of a career change."

"Me? Not me. She told me you were thinking of retiring and wanted to know if I wanted your job."

"She offered me a spot here," Larry confided. "I told her I'd consider it if I ever turn into an orange. What did you tell her?"

"I said I wasn't making any career change. So don't worry, Larry. I'll stick to what I'm doing for a while. I'm familiar with the routine. I like it."

Eva was a cunning woman. She would have me at the Bernardsville place and Larry at the Poinciana, two managers she could trust. It was here that I resolved to begin distancing myself from Eva. I suspected that a dangerous pathology was infecting her brain. Her behavior was simply not normal.

I returned to my hotel room to pack and started pondering my next move. A hit man was on the loose; Brian Donovan was dead, and I was a target. There were plots to unravel, murders to solve and a diamond to steal and I had no idea how to proceed. Making off with the Blue Danube was the easy part. Mike and I had worked out the details and we were ready to spirit the stone away from its cozy Morristown vault. Making the plan work was another thing.

There was a knock at my suite's front door while I was thus wallowing in a pool of self pity, despair and doubt. I peeked through peep hole. It was Tom Lyons. Someone was with him who Tom introduced to me as Stanley Short from the Internal Revenue Service. It was the same Stanley Short from the Poinciana.

"Come in, guys." I invited them into the living room kitchenette area where they sat down on the bar stools around the peninsular serving counter.

"Soda, coffee or water, guys. That's all I have. It's too early for booze."

They settled for water.

"We met the other day, I think." I told Stan Short.

"That's right," Stan agreed.

"We have a problem and need your help."

In contrast to Tom, Stan Short was short and stocky and wore an ill fitting dark blue suit over a cheap white-on-white shirt. An easy smile softened the bureaucratic, bean-counter image of his wardrobe.

"I take it that this isn't a social call."

"It is, Max. It is, and it's also business," said Tom. "Stan and I thought we should have a chat. We've been reviewing this Blue Danube business with La Salle and Santana and we've come up with an idea."

"What's that?" I asked.

Tom smiled blandly.

"Mel is concerned about the insurance policy on the diamond that Sentinel holds. So is Weinberg who wants to buy him out. I don't blame them. But that's not my thing. My thing is the rising body count."

"So am I, Tom, Did La Salle tell you about Harry Silver and his poison pills?"

"Yes. I'd arrest him if I had more evidence. The other problem is that his chain was being pulled by Colin and now I'm sure it's being pulled by either Henry or Eva. I can't arrest Harry without tipping my hand on the others."

Stan Short coughed.

"That's where I come in," he said. "Aside from the murders and violence, we have a small matter of tax evasion and tax delinquency."

"That's what I hear," I said. "What about it?"

Stan smiled.

"Our mutual friend Colin Adair was about to be arrested when his yacht blew up."

"That's life, or the lack of," I noted. "What now?"

"Colin was in trouble long before his yacht blew up, and he knew it. The SEC was after him; we were after him; some of his smarter clients were after him, and his creditors were on his tail. Now that he's gone, the money is gone and the only assets left is real estate and the Blue Danube diamond which is bottled up by all that litigation. The IRS can't get close to it until we get a court order. And Henry Adair isn't helping either. He's blocking every move we make even though he has his own wealth. He claims the Blue Danube was titled over to him by Colin and that he has the papers to prove it. To cap it off, your lawyer was able to obtain a restraining order superceding all other court actions, including those of the IRS, until you inspect the diamond."

"You have to get in line," I said. "A lot of people want to get their hands on the diamond. And so do I. One third of it is mine. I'm using the legal system to protect my interest. That's the American way, Stan."

"I realize that," he replied. "But the IRS can play hard ball with everyone including you, Max. Therefore, I want to let you know that the IRS has filed a lien on the Blue Danube to satisfy its own claims. It's going to be your claim against ours."

"How does Eva fare in this mess? What does she gain or lose?"

"Nothing," Stan replied. "She worked a deal with this guy, Nishkanian. He got the Poinciana and in return she took cash and a healthy equity interest in the hotel. The deal also has a golden parachute. If he dies, she gets the hotel back. That makes sure his family stays out of the picture."

"What about the investment business?"

"She's the president all right, but only as an employee. Colin had all the stock and took personal responsibility for all debts. But those debts were never collateralized with property. He was the ultimate swindler. Everyone took him at his word."

I scratched my head.

"So. What do you propose?"

Tom and Stan glanced at each other.

"We know what you're about, Max," said Stan Short.

"What am I about?"

"The word is that you may be thinking of stealing the Blue Danube."

"You're kidding. Part of that stone is mine anyway."

I'm not saying you're going to go for it, Max. That's the word on the street. So, we want to let you know the IRS has first dibs. You're a hired gun and bounty hunter. Oh, we know you don't chase people down; you go after lost things, expensive things."

"Like diamonds," Tom interrupted impatiently.

"Look, Max. I might as well level with you. We told Stan what we were planning, that you had put a team together, meaning us, and that we were going to help you steal the diamond. I think Stan has a much better idea. He wants to propose a trade."

"That might work," I said. "if you look at this thing my way. I'm a ten percenter. If the Blue Danube disappears and I'm hired to recover it, I get ten percent of its total insured value, irrespective of my and any claims to it. And if I'm not hired to recoup it, I'll find it anyway and I'll cut it up and sell the pieces. I'm not good at math, Stan, so you'll have to help me out. What's ten percent of a 149 carat stone?"

"The Blue Danube is priceless," Stan said.

"Exactly," I said. "I'm not greedy either. Ten percent of a priceless gem sounds better to me than life on the run as a diamond thief. So, I'll tell you what since you came here to deal. I'll trade my interest in the gem for a mere

$100 million worth of perfect uncut diamonds and renounce my claim forever."

Stan Short's mouth dropped to his chin.

"And that can be after taxes. How's that for being generous."

"That's being un-American," Stan complained.

"Why? Isn't optimizing one's economic opportunities a corner stone of our capitalist system? I'll sweeten the deal a little, Stan. If the diamond is stolen from your custody, I'll recover it for nothing. Do you feel better now?"

Tom sighed.

"What do you think, Stan? I think we can live with Max's offer."

Stan Short hesitated.

"We can do $100 million in perfect blue white diamonds," he finally said.

"No settings."

"Ok. No settings."

"Wholesale"

"Wholesale."

"And tax free?"

Stan pursed his lips.

"Come on, Stan," I insisted. "The IRS probably has a few billion dollars in diamond inventory confiscated over the years that it can't unload. This gig is going to cost you nothing."

Stan smiled for the first time.

"Deal," he said. "We're talking conflict diamonds from Africa that have already been confiscated and are being held for our account by Belgian customs as part of the Adair estate on which we have a lien. Belgian is ready to release them to us."

"So what's the hitch?" I asked.

"No hitch. The IRS can't be caught with conflict diamonds. It's bad news. But the Blue Danube is clean. We can seize it without fanfare. We'll authorize Belgium to release the diamonds to you the moment you release the Blue Danube to us. At the very worst, it will end up at the Smithsonian. This trade is good for you and good for us. It's a win-win for all of us."

I noticed Tom throwing me a wink and a nod. He must have had worked out the framework of an agreement with Stan, Jake and Pierre before coming to see me.

"Deal," I repeated. "Now you, Tom. What can I do for you?"

Tom Lyons looked at me through narrowed eyes.

We still have murders to solve and we think Eva is the key. She may be able to shed some information about what's going on if you press her."

"Are the restaurants and hotels in trouble?"

Stan shook his head.

"We're going to look the other way for the time being. We don't want to start a recession by closing everything down. But some of the people there are dirty; we need to ferret them out. Eva can be helpful. You also know Henry Adair. He knows stuff we don't know, Stan pointed out.

"I haven't seen Henry in years."

"You've never seen him during your trips to Paris?"

I shook my head.

"I did. But all contact stopped when he married my former girlfriend, Nicole. And even before then, I never considered him a friend."

Tom smiled.

"Look. You're in a position to help us. We spoke to La Salle and he fully understands that. Mel Solomon also keeps score. He realizes he's in a corner and can't get out. He'll be ready to deal."

Stan Short smiled like a cat that swallowed the canary.

"Mel was Colin's silent partner. So was this Armenian, Nishkanian. Colin may be dead but these guys will be doing hard time if we close in on them with a fraud charge. And there's someone else. Henry has some sort of an angel working with him, a silent partner like Nishkanian, who has his hands in every business touched by the Adairs. But we have no I.D. on him. And then there's Eva…"

"Eva?"

"You bet. We can nail her as an accessory if nothing else."

"There's also this thing about Colin's death," Tom went on. "I spoke to Jake Santana and Felix Stiles who think Colin's yacht could very well have been sabotaged. If they're right, we have another murder on our hands. Eva is beneficiary to Colin's life insurance policy and stands to get ten million dollars if his death is ruled accidental. But there's no payment if it's suicide or murder. So it's important that you stay close to her. She may have been behind all the killings beginning with Carl Haussmann. But you watch yourself with her, you hear. Scorpions make poor house pets," Tom Lyons cautioned.

"Anything else?"

Stan Short nodded.

"Yes. In case you need an expert diamond witness, Rajeesh Kumari has offered us his personal diamond specialist to help you appraise the Blue

Danube. We'll go with you and the Kumari representative to see the thing in the flesh as soon as your court order comes through."

"Who's the Kumari man?"

"A diamond cutter named Otto Katz. What do you think?"

I stretched my arms.

"It sounds good to me."

There was nothing more I could say. Having Otto inspect the diamond was like having a bear sample honey. The question was: was it still necessary to steal it with this new deal on the table? It was amazing how much and how little Stan Short knew.

I reviewed the subject later with Tom Lyons.

"La Salle is the guy who approached Stan. He thought this was a better way to make a small fortune without going to prison."

"I assume Jake has been clued in?"

"Yes. We're keeping the six way split we agreed on. The difference is that we don't have to steal that damn gem. The moment Otto gives it a clean bill of health, Stan grabs it for the IRS and customs in Belgium releases their consignment to you. La Salle figures those diamonds will bring better than $200 million once they're turned into jewelry. We'll miss the high adventure of stealing the Blue Danube but we won't have to cringe each time the door knocks and we won't have to hide in a god forsaken place like a bunch of fugitives."

"That's too bad, Tom. The Caribbean could be a nice change of pace."

"It could be, Max. With my job at a dead end and my kids grown, moving to the Caribbean sounds good. But now I'll travel first class instead of running like a thief looking over my shoulder."

V

NEW JERSEY

17

Doubt

I was barely home in New Jersey a few days later when the Blue Danube diamond suddenly burst into the headlines. An enterprising young television reporter had latched on to the Colin Adair incident as an unsolved mystery and began an investigation. He periodically reported his progress on the late night news. The stories started with a trickle of recaps about the explosion at sea and expanded to stories about the Blue Danube diamond. It soon turned into a torrent of unending media gossip fanned by pundits and talking heads who painstakingly examined every big and small event and rumor under their editorial microscopes.

The legendary diamond was the largest in history, they claimed. They were wrong. It was not the largest; there were larger ones. They said that the Hope diamond was larger. Wrong again; the Blue Danube was larger. The Blue Danube was stolen; as far as I knew, it was safe and sound. It was creating a foreign policy crisis. That was a stretch.

The stories went nowhere. They were boringly repetitive and were greeted by stony silence by all directly or indirectly connected to the gemstone. This was a private party and the common aim was to keep it that way. Failing to gain traction since the media was unable to cajole anyone into admitting or saying anything, the story slowly died and the reporter was sent grazing in greener pastures. However, Tom Lyons and Jake Santana did some snooping and found that the media had been fed the rumors by Frank Barton, Eva's brother. I wondered what his game was.

All of a sudden and at least to me, Frank was no longer Eva's lame brained brother, but a co-conspirator in the Blue Danube affair. A grand scenario of designated hit men working as couples was forming in my mind. All I needed were faces to fill the blanks. I had suspects now, including Frank Barton, but I wanted to air my ideas with someone I trusted. Pierre La Salle was my best bet but he was with Stan Short in Belgium taking inventory of the diamonds that were going to be exchanged for the Blue Danube. And when he was not in Belgium he was in Paris wrestling with Maison Dore's tangled fortunes.

I would have thought that Maison Dore, with the deaths of Carl and Louis, would have been gone belly up, left rudderless and financially foundering as it was. However, it never closed its doors and even expanded operations with Henry Adair's management under the scrutiny of the French courts. I came to suspect that Emile Barco, and perhaps even Rajeesh Kumari, worked to keep the business healthy. Rajeesh, I could understand, but Emile's motives for being in the picture escaped me.

The high-end jewelry boutique business in general had many large cash and carry transactions. They supplemented credit card and/or check sales, and Maison Dore was known as the place to sell priceless gems for cash. It was commonly understood in the trade that transactions leaving a paper trail were recorded but that most cash deals were kept off the books. The business was not labor intensive and could easily be run by two or three principals. It did not take many people to carry cash to a vault or to an off-shore bank, buying off prying tax collectors in the process with generous gifts. Colin's stateside enterprises and Sentinel also kept muddling along. Was Emile helping them all to survive in order to augment his own fortune and cash flow?

La Salle had once put it this way.

"His Basse Terre estate produces little income, Max. But he must still pay property taxes and maintenance expenses, and they can be formidable. A bit of diamond smuggling can make a big contribution to overhead."

There is nothing like litigation to fan the fires of survival. More law suits were bound to fly and some were bound to land on me. Preventative steps were needed. Waiting a week, I resigned my position at Sentinel. I liked Mel but felt I had to maintain a respectable distance. In the back of my mind, and although I prayed my feeling was wrong, I felt he was somehow implicated in the plot to kill Carl Haussmann. Insofar as my own court action went, I was armed with an open ended court action that was good for one year and one which pre-empted all others. I could pick my time to inspect the Blue Danube and have it authenticated. Stanley Short was happy. This was one action that the IRS was not going to contest.

Mel Solomon didn't want to lose me entirely and understanding that I had an arrangement with Stan Short who made me a fee paid consultant with the IRS's fraud division, he appointed me to Sentinel's board of directors. Three quid pro quos came into play. First, with a seat on Sentinel's board, I was able to help the company peel off assets that were not part of its core business in order to keep it financially healthy. In return, Mel gave up all his claims to the Blue Danube and agreed to cooperate with the feds' tax case against Colin Adair's estate. In return, he received immunity against any possible civil or criminal prosecution. He was a wise man.

What was odd was Bill Ford. He was not to be seen anywhere. I found out later that he took an extended leave for health reasons. That made me more suspicious than ever.

The second quid pro quo was for Eva. The feds agreed to limit their action against South Florida Trust and Island Investments and leave the hotels and restaurants alone. In effect, they threw South Florida Trust into receivership and assumed its management and brought criminal money laundering charges against Island Investments in the Bahamas. That action effectively froze its international transactions until the case finished making its way through the Bahamian, U.S. and possibly even through international tribunals. As an added bonus, they offered Eva immunity from prosecution. But in exchange, and after much angst and trepidation, she had to surrender her rights to the Blue Danube and assign them to the IRS.

Stanley Short had scored a victory and Eva had breathing space. That left Henry Adair. His attorneys were obstructionist and continued throwing road blocks. They were unsuccessful and Eva and Mel Solomon were no longer in a position to block the government's fight to get its hands on the diamond.

The third quid pro quo involved Vic Nishkanian. With Eva's blessing, I met with him in Florida and laid out the situation, informing him that the feds were prepared to fight him for the diamond and level other charges.

"Eva is agreeing to pay you back with interest for all the money you lent Colin and invested in his banking house, but you have to give up your claim to the diamond."

Vic paused.

"I can't do that," he said.

"If you persist in your claim, you'll have the IRS on your back. They want first digs on the rock."

Vic pondered the situation for a few moments and then asked, "What's my guarantee?"

"Luck is the best guarantee, plus my word, if that helps. This is a deal I'm cutting for the feds. This is part of it. I aim to make it work. What do you say, old buddy? You'll get all your money back, but it's going to take time. Are you in?"

One last pause.

"All right. I'm in."

These negotiations completed, I signed up for a daily exercise schedule at a local rehabilitation center. One thing there I found fascinating. Most of the people working out on the treadmills and bikes were men. They were of all ages and all physical types. Some were young, some were middle aged, and some were old. There were fat men, skinny men, tall men and short men, but there were few women. Heart disease was an equal opportunity killer.

There were meetings to attend. Sentinel's board of directors gathered at a New York hotel and reelected Mel Solomon as Chairman and kept Bill Ford as CEO. The board also voted to sell a fast food franchise to a foreign buyer for cash. Meetings in Bernardsville occurred more frequently and zeroed in on cash management with a view to constructing a viable payment program for Victor Nishkanian.

And then there was Interpol. La Salle finally called to say he was satisfied with the ways things were going but indicated that Jouvet continued to insist that the Blue Danube belonged to France.

"No matter," he said. "Interpol supports your government's position along with yours."

"I'm curious about something, Pierre."

"Yes?"

"Has the investigation of Louis Dore's death been completed?"

"It was ruled a suicide, Max. I am not questioning the ruling at present. I say, however, that it was murder. I will reopen the inquiry at the right time."

"Any word on Johnny Cork?"

"Not yet. However, I spoke to your friend Gaspard who claims he saw him in Basse Terre."

"That's where Barco has a place, isn't it?"

"True. However, Basse Terre is a big place. He could be anywhere. But do not fret. He will be found."

"Perhaps, Pierre," I said, "But listen, I have something I want your opinion on." And I went on to give him my idea of hit teams operating in pairs.

"Fascinating," La Salle exclaimed. "How does your theory work?"

"Let's go back to Carl Haussmann. I believe two people were involved: one was Johnny Cork, the other may have been the driver and the one who killed his dog."

"Why kill the dog?"

"Because it makes it appear that Johnny was earmarked for termination. I think that Cork knew his dog had to be killed to throw everyone off his trail and that he has become a roving hit man for whoever has him on contract."

"Who else is he working with?" Pierre asked.

"Don't know off hand," I replied. "But I'd wager that whoever killed Louis Dore was also one of a pair and probably Americans who were unaware that Louis was left handed."

"What about Brian Donovan?"

"Same story. In his case, we know there were two hit men, one who drove and one who killed the poor guy. Same scenario in the attempted hit on me. There was a shooter and a driver. I think we're talking about either two or four hit men working in pairs. Two pairs make more sense than a single pair. "I was thinking along the same lines," Pierre noted. "And I agree with your assessment of John Cork. But to fill in your theory, Max, we need three more hit men and their handler or handlers. Call me when you are closer to the end of your interesting painting."

I felt more confident for a change and my life was back on track. But while things were looking up for me, Mike Surrey's health was going downhill. It started after I told him that our planned heist was off. Even though I made it clear to him that I intended to include him in my deal with the feds, he began to slide. I kept to the strict and narrow but Mike returned to the bottle.

For sure, Brian Donovan's murder unnerved him, and the longer it stood unsolved, the more depressed he grew. But there had to be other reasons. At a local bar, in one of his more lucid moments, our conversation drifted to the subject of Colin Adair.

"I liked Colin, sort of," Mike remarked. "He was a little like you. He didn't give a damn about anything."

"That's the way I remember him in the service. He was our sabotage and demolition expert." I said. "Do you remember the combat engineer slogan, Mike?"

"That I do," Mike answered proudly. "Essayons."

I nodded. "Let us try."

"I was out before you," Mike reminded me. "What happened when you were mustered out?"

"Oh. That wasn't a happy scene, old buddy. We thought we'd be treated to a hero's welcome so I wore my uniform and my medals. Well, when I got off the bus in Newark, I was greeted like I was a mass murderer. But you want to know something else? I would do it all over. No doubt about it. The hell with them! They should rot in Hell!"

Mike disliked controversy and started talking about Colin again.

"He had talent," he said. "He could make explosives out of dirt and would walk straight down the middle of a fire fight and toss grenades around like hockey pucks. Weren't you his point man?"

"That's right."

But there was something that Mike Surrey said that shook me up.

"Colin had a thing for women," Mike said.

"Don't we all?"

"That's not what I mean. He had a broad," Mike confided. "She didn't drive. He couldn't take her to one of his restaurants because that would be dumb. So he had me drive her to a buddy's restaurant across from a motel. I'd leave her there and tell the headwaiter what was going on. Colin would arrive later. They'd eat and then go to the motel. Each year at Christmas, Colin would go see the headwaiter and give him a thousand dollars and a note on which he wrote, 'Thank you for your understanding.'

"The affair went on until the broad fell in love with the headwaiter. The last thing I heard is that they got married."

"And lived happily forever after?"

A drunken leer filled Mike's face.

"Something like that." He swayed and I had to steady him.

"Did Eva suspect anything?"

"Hard to tell. I don't think she cared what Colin did as long she got laid often. She didn't need Colin for that. She did fine on her own. I was working at his place at the time and she would come by looking for action. And she wasn't particular with whom. I tapped Eva several times. So did Larry and little Brian Donovan. We all took turns with her. One thing was for sure. She loved sex. We nicknamed her Sally Cream Cheese."

"That's a funny name."

"That's because she was so spreadable."

Mike's revelation devastated me and I didn't know how to take it. But it was his next statement that through me for a loop.

"But you want to know what I really think?"

"What?"

"I don't believe Colin actually liked women. He had a reputation here at the restaurant for hitting on the young male waiters and busboys."

"You're joking."

"No. I think he liked clean, young boys and an occasional woman on the side. I ran into Colin's old girlfriend a few years ago. She said that all the time she was with Colin he never touched her. I guess they just stayed in the motel and watched television. I don't know."

His voice faded.

It was not exactly what I wanted to hear and I did my best, with difficulty, to dismiss the conversation from my mind.

Mike and I continued going out for lunch but I never again discussed any personal matters with him. It was a recurring scene. Pick him up in the late morning. Go for a drive and arrive at a bar by noon. I said little while Mike babbled about the times he had, the business deals he put together and all the women he had.

Fact merged with fiction. I'd have my usual soup and salad while Mike would have his martinis. I watched and listened. His eyes grew misty, then distant and then more vacant as the days wore on.

Mike Surrey was liked by everyone who stopped to bend an elbow at the bars we frequented. Even Tom Lyons developed a fondness for him. But we could only stand by helplessly and watch his deterioration with distress and sadness in our hearts.

Would it ever end? Mike Surrey resisted our attempts to have him seek out medical counseling. I called his wife but all she could do was cry. We plotted to kidnap him and take him to a hospital or to a detox center, anyplace, but a lawyer we consulted admonished us. He said all we could do was to cut him off and take him home. We did that one day and delivered him to his wife in a delirium, screaming, crying, and begging not to be sent to hell.

That same evening, his wife called to say that Mike had a nose bleed that wouldn't stop. She became hysterical. I called Emergency and raced to his house, arriving in time to greet the police and an EMS truck. Mike was taken to the hospital where doctors began working on him immediately. It was too late. His bodily systems failed and he was placed on a respirator.

Mike Surrey lay there in bed under a light yellow sheet drawn up to his neck, breathing serenely, eyes closed in sleep and the hint of a smile on his face.

It was impossible to forget my last exchange with Arlene after Mike had been settled in.

"After Mike is stabilized, we're going to get him cured once and for all and once he's well, we're all going to go out and have a big party, with grapefruit juice. Won't that be great, Max?"

"It sure will, Arlene. That would be great."

Mike's wife left to get a coffee and I went back to the hospital room to see how Mike was doing.

"He looks all right now," I observed to an attending nurse. "He's resting quietly and seems to be breathing normally. Maybe he'll snap out of it."

The nurse shook her head.

"No. The respirator is doing the breathing for him."

That night the generator powering the respirator failed and Mike Surrey's tormented body released his soul at dawn, Easter Sunday.

18

Memories

Mike Surrey was murdered. Tom Lyons was convinced of that. According to his investigation, the generator system never failed; it was disconnected. Tom had the entire intensive care unit combed for finger prints. Fresh prints were found. They were Harry Silver's and an arrest warrant was issued.

Tom could have saved his breath. On a hunch, I went to the medical office building where Barry Benson and Harry Silver had their practice. The work day was over and the office staff had left for the day.

Strangely, the office door was unlocked although there was no one inside. I let myself in and wandered from room to room until I found Harry Silver sprawled on the floor of his private office. He had been killed with a single shot between the eyes. In the next office was Barry Benson, sitting quietly on a chair behind a desk. His head was thrown back and his arms lay dangling at his side. His eyes were barely open.

Barry was breathing heavily. Still he managed a weak smile when I barged in. On pure reflex, I called 911 and asked for two EMS vehicles.

"You're alive," he noted in between his labored breathing. "I guess you never took those pills Harry gave you."

"No. I never took them. How did you know about them?"

"Harry took up pharmacy before he decided to be a doctor. He has a small lab out back where he mixed powders for a hobby. A cleaning girl dropped some compounds. Harry was making his hospital rounds and I was covering the office. She was scared and came running to me, expecting to be fired. I told her not to worry and to go home. I picked up the stuff and on a lark I ran some tests. That's how I found out Harry was making pills that induced heart failure."

"When was that, Barry?"

"Just after you took off for Paris. Our office records show you came in for an examination. Harry gave you a batch of pills but no fresh prescription to fill. That's when I put it all together."

I pointed to his arm.

"Did you just do something stupid, Barry?"

The physician nodded sadly.

"It's over for me, Max. You're going to need another cardiologist."

"But why, doctor?"

"I kept quiet about Harry, thinking I was jumping to conclusions, but he was selling those pills on the side to Frank Barton. He sold him a batch a few days ago."

"I don't get it. What's between Harry and Barton?"

"I listen to the same gossip and news you do, Max. I know all about the Blue Danube diamond, you and your on-going fight with the Adairs. Harry Silver was high one night and confided that he gave Frank a mess of pills at Colin Adair's request for a ten percent stake in a new venture called South Florida Trust. I knew Colin. He was my patient, and I learned that those pills have killed at least one person so far."

"What about Mike Surrey? Whose patient was he?"

Barry Benson started sobbing.

"Mine. Poor guy. I couldn't do anything to get him off the bottle. I pulled the plug on him when I heard he was in the hospital. I'm glad I did. He was finished."

"But the cops found Harry Silver's prints, not yours."

A sly grin broke across Barry Benson's face.

"I disconnected the machine earlier and asked Harry to go check on him. That's how his prints ended up the ICU. I put a frame around him."

"Who shot Harry Silver?" I asked.

"Ed Houston. A few hours ago. He said Harry was trying to poison him."

Barry laughed weakly.

I reached for the phone again.

"You don't have to die over this, Barry. Whatever you did to yourself can be reversed. I'm going to make sure you get to work your marine salvage business in the Caribbean."

"Thanks, Max. But, don't bother, Max. I'm dying. You know those pills? They're not bad."

He started coughing as Tom Lyons and an EMS team barged in.

Tom took the doctor's pulse.

"We'll save him."

Within seconds Barry Benson was given several spoonfuls of a brown goo from a bottle. He threw up a storm and was whisked away to the hospital to have his system pumped out.

Tom pointed sternly at me.

"You heard nothing, understand?"

"How did you find me?" I asked.

"I followed and was listening outside. You're good at sniffing out snakes. And don't worry about the good doctor. The moment he's back on his feet, I'm going to ship him off to his favorite island paradise. We don't need him facing embarrassing questions that can ricochet over us."

"Too bad Colin's dead," I remarked. "He was behind all this. I wonder what his real game was."

"Forget Colin. We want to find out what Eva is up to before you end up on her platter."

"Me? After all I've done for her?"

Tom Lyons laughed.

"Did I ever tell you my snake joke?"

I shook my head.

"Well, this dude goes into the woods and hears a voice. 'Will you please take this rock off my head; it's crushing me,' the snake says.

"So the dude removes the rock and the snake bites him.

'Why did you do that?' The guy asks. And the snake answers, 'Because I'm a snake.'

"You see, Max," concluded the detective. "We are all what we are, just like you are what you are."

I felt responsible for the deaths of Brian Donovan and Mike Surrey. Yet, there was nothing I could do. As Tom Lyons said after Barry was taken to the hospital, everything was conjecture and hearsay. There was little rope with which to hang anyone on anything. The Donovan investigation in Florida too was at a dead end for the time being. At least, Barry Benson was alive and would survive to keep his practice.

"We'll have to keep fishing," Tom said. "Benson will be better for us free than in prison."

"What about Ed Houston? Are you going to pick him up?"

Tom shook his head.

"What for? He killed a crooked doctor who wanted to kill him. What we need to know is who wanted Houston out of the way and why. Incidentally, Max. La Salle called to explain your hit man theory. I'm buying into it since it's the only one we have at present but I'm leaving Ed Houston and George Lerman out of our list of suspects."

"How come?"

"Too obvious. But what I can't figure out is how Ed Houston knew Harry Silver was a poison pill dispenser."

"I told him," I answered.

Beauty is a curse that casts a spell, someone told me a long time ago. But what was beauty? Beauty was beguiling. It had an energy that sapped the soul and consumed the heart and twisted the mind and made us do strange things. Beauty could be in a thing or in a person. The Blue Danube diamond was beautiful and desirable and it was a thing. Eva was beautiful and she was a person. Somehow, I had become obsessed with both the Blue Danube and Eva.

Much as I was obsessed with Eva, I was equally obsessed with life and I managed to keep at a healthy distance from her, being all too aware of the temptations that tugged at my body. Besides, Mike Surrey's tales about her did much to dampen my enthusiasm for her.

Eva reminded me a little of Nicole Colbert. Nicole was earthier though. She was well stacked, had long frizzy blond hair and blue gin and tonic eyes that camouflaged a cash register mind when she considered things seriously. She was a beauty consultant for a cosmetics company when we met in Paris and made a decent living managing their counters at Galeries Lafayette, a large department store on Boulevard Haussmann behind the Paris Opera.

In those days, I stayed at the Grand Hotel on the Boulevard Des Capucines and dined at the Café De La Paix which was part of the hotel. The restaurant is still there, but the hotel is now the Intercontinental Grand.

It was occupied by the German army's high command for northern France during the war and housed a Gestapo unit. It may be a coincidence but the Grand Hotel Krasnapolski in Amsterdam was also Gestapo headquarters. The surveillance agency was never a bargain to the human race, but at least it had good taste in picking hotels for its operations and officers' billets.

I wasn't familiar with the hotel in Amsterdam but the Grand in Paris was not such a good location for the Germans. They were a smart people, but I don't think they ever suspected until after the Normandy invasion in 1944 that deep under the Grand was a network of ancient tunnels and sewers that were part of the old city and crisscrossed Paris. Several of these old passages made their under the Seine River to the catacombs miles away on the far side of the Left Bank.

This underground highway helped French resistance fighters to move about the city like ghosts and make lightening strikes against the occupying forces without detection. These hit and run attacks went a long way to bleeding the Germans dry.

I was part of a gang of street urchins who worked as spotters for Gaspard Lancet who was a local resistance leader. I don't think our acts ever softened German resolve to hang on to Paris, but its morale must have suffered when officers were kidnapped in full daylight and then dragged below to be killed.

My first encounter with Nicole was coincidental. Not merely beautiful, she was smart and lively. She was dating Henry Adair when we met. They were together at a party hosted by the Paris chapter of the American Legion.

The American Legion was founded in Paris in the first World War, and Legion Post One opened for business near the Avenue Des Champs Elysees in 1918. I joined the chapter when I left the service mainly because they had good parties, cheap food and booze at PX prices, all very important to me in those days.

Nicole and I had a special chemistry. We made eye contact and it was love at first sight. Henry and I got drunk and we got into a fight. He won; I lost, but Nicole took me home that night and patched me up. I woke up in the morning with a headache and Nicole at my side. I needed aspirin and Nicole said we could buy some at Le Drug Store on the Champs Elysees near the Arch of Triumph.

Back in the sixties and seventies, Le Drug Store was a popular hangout and open all night. It was Nicole's favorite haunt. There, she introduced me to the city's night crawlers who gathered at Le Drug Store at sundown for a French version of steak and beer, and then gravitated to other watering holes before returning very much later for what passed for servings of bacon, eggs and American style coffee.

Nicole and I hung out with a mixed bag of American expatriates, local businessmen, minor hoods, government workers, politicians, office workers, models, prostitutes and pimps. We would go to Le Drug Store after she left work for the day and then walk to the American Legion hall to check out the action there.

The Legion Hall was a sanctuary for expatriate Americans caught in a time warp who were trying to relive their war days. For them it was a place to fire up fading memories over cheap beer and liquor, watching scratchy black and white documentaries and war movies. We joined them with other shadowy party animals to have a good time.

Off duty marine guards from the American Embassy came for the women who came in droves to be picked up. And of course there were the usual prostitutes and street walkers who found their way into the crowded smoke filled bar and party rooms.

There was Madelaine, a plump, raven-haired girl from Marseilles. She was a regular at the Legion. I could never figure out what her real action was. She favored short skirts and revealing blouses and never wore underwear so that a heavy thatch of black bush between her meaty thighs was one of the hits of the night. Her specialization was an exotic dance that ended with running off to the bathroom with someone to perform a variety of sex acts with the door ajar so that everyone could peek.

Another hanger on was a red headed Russian woman named Katyana, a self-proclaimed intellectual and scholar of classical literature. The widow of a former Russian nobleman, she was financially independent and had a big apartment on the Left Bank where she would bring a stable of lovers. She also entertained guests there on Sunday afternoons. The gatherings began as poetry readings and philosophical discussions about the meaning of life and moved on to sex and drugs. I went to several of her poetry readings until some drunk set the place on fire. She was never seen again.

Then there were two bisexual twins from Germany who were built like a couple of Wagnerian women. They favored group sex with male and female combinations randomly drawn from the streets. Their orgies lasted until one of them came down with gonorrhea and died. Gonorrhea and syphilis were grisly diseases and they, not AIDS, were the sexual scourges of the day.

The most beautiful woman I met, however, never went to the American Legion. She preferred to meet her marks at Le Drug Store. She was a tall, statuesque brunette. She approached me one evening when Nicole was not looking. I was going to make a play for her when the bartender informed me that she was a transvestite.

I was much younger and easily survived the abuse of working all day and partying all night. But as the saying went, it was real and it was good, but it was never real good. I indulged in the excesses of the night mainly for Nicole who I thought was having fun. It took us both a long time to realize we were getting bored.

I visited Paris often after things at home began to deteriorate following my discharge from the service. Doing business in Europe was an escape from my domestic situation. That was probably how and why Nicole entered my life.

She was my steady whenever I was in Paris. She had an apartment off the Boulevard Raspail in Montparnasse on the far end of the Left Bank and invited me to stay there. It was tempting, but for some reason I stuck to my digs at the Grand, and later at the Westphalia, although I did contribute to her upkeep.

Our relationship was hard to define. I toyed with the notion that perhaps she was my mistress. Mistresses were commonplace in European capitals, especially in Paris. The city was accommodating and easy to get around. It was not unusual for a man to have a wife and family in one part of town and to keep a mistress in another. He could pat the wife on the ass, compliment her for the fois gras, and then run across the boulevard, so to speak, for a matinee with the mistress in her apartment for which he paid the rent. And when the arrangement was no longer satisfactory, he might install the woman in a boutique on a fashionable boulevard where she could make a good living for the duration. Many former mistresses eventually married. I didn't know what happened to the rest. Nicole ended up with a bouquet of flowers and the boutique after she and Henry divorced.

Nicole was something special and I even got her a diamond ring. That part was easy because I was already in the business. We made the usual rounds whenever I visited Paris, from Montmartre and Sacre Coeur to Saint Germain and Saint Michel on the Left Bank. We also did the obligatory museums and historical sites, but slowly broke the habit of visiting our old haunts. Perhaps we were outgrowing them. We starting having dinner at the Café De La Paix, go for drinks at Harry's New York Bar on Rue Daunou around the corner from the Westphalia, and then return to the hotel for the night.

Our relationship necessarily cooled when she decided to return to Henry Adair who had in the meantime proposed marriage.

They married and I took their union in stride. Heartbreak came when word reached me that she was pregnant. I was married. I had a family and didn't have the guts to break it up. I think Nicole secretly knew I was a coward and would never leave my wife who was by then seriously ill. She never pursued the issue of our developing a permanent relationship. Anyway, I never saw her again after she went back to Henry. Getting married, building a home and raising a family are important to women, and those were the things I could not offer her at the time.

I could have called Nicole after she divorced Henry. It was out of laziness and stupid pride that I never called. Pride. Just plain stupid pride!

My liaison with Eva was nevertheless ending and I think she knew it also.

There was also business to address which I kept away from her view and that certainly sour our relationship. What made her truly unhappy was that I was no longer a good source of information fore her.

I was still curious about Emile Barco, Henry's silent partner and on this matter I kept Eva in the dark. I asked Stan Short to see what the IRS could come up with. Stan thought he might use FBI back channel connections with Interpol operatives in Europe and the Caribbean.

Marcel Jouvet was also a bit of a puzzle, especially his relationship with Rhone-Fayette. Something about the government official did not ring true and I couldn't put a finger on it. Again, Stan promised to see what he could do. I related my conversation with Stan to Jake Santana and he agreed that getting the FBI into the picture might be a good idea.

One evening, when I was supposed to meet with Eva, she called to say that the catering manager at the Poinciana took ill and that she had to cover for him at a function. She asked me to wait for her at the Del Rey and that she would return later.

I waited in my room where I fell asleep. She never showed and I didn't wake up until the following morning.

I called Eva at her condo when I awoke. A recording came on after a few moments to advise that the number was disconnected. My next call was to the Poinciana where I was put through to Larry O'Leary who corrected me when I mentioned the affair Eva had to cover for the catering manager.

What catering manager? What function? The catering manager was away on vacation and there was no function. Larry said he had flown in yesterday to take over the management of the hotel. The telephone at the condo was disconnected because the condo had been sold. Where was Eva?

"She flew to Paris this morning," Larry said.

I was dumbstruck and could only speculate that Henry's health took a turn for the worse and that Eva went off to see him.

19

Arrangements

Blows to the ego can leave lasting wounds. Colleen often told me I was a fool. I should have taken her more seriously. Why the hell did she have to die on me? A good woman who keeps her man in line is hard to find and I had to admit that without her it was like being on a rudderless boat.

I took the first available flight north to New Jersey and was home before dark where I found Janine waiting with tears in her eyes. Her husband, it seemed, was being transferred on short notice to Singapore for a two-year assignment and they were being flown out within days. Would I be all right with her out of the country all this while?

I bravely wished her all the best and said I would get along. It was not my way to be paranoid but it was a strange coincidence that she would be sent to a foreign country for an extended period of time with no prior warning. There was little I could do to prevent the move. My immediate support network was evaporating. Brian Donovan and Mike Surrey were gone; Janine was going. I was being isolated.

Quick action was needed. I knew Otto was with Pierre La Salle in Belgium examining the conflict diamonds designated for us, so I called and explained my predicament.

"That is not good, my friend," said La Salle. I could overhear him relating my situation to Otto who mumbled something about a place called Jakarta.

"I think we have a solution," said Pierre. "Treat your children to a vacation in Jakarta. It is a very nice city in Indonesia. They can sight see and visit with some of Otto's relatives."

That's why I liked Pierre. He did on occasion have simple answers to some very complex questions.

Subsequent conversations over a more secure line laid out the strategy.

"This move to Singapore has Marcel Jouvet's stamp, Max. I fail to grasp his reasoning, but he has a powerful position on Rhone-Fayette's board and can make things happen. It is obvious to me that he wants to split up your family. Here is what I propose."

And he went on to explain what we were to do. My daughter and her family would keep the Singapore tickets and buy a separate set of airline tickets to Jakarta where Interpol had an office and Otto had a relative in the shipping business. My son-in-law would have an interim job at Interpol while my daughter and the kids stayed with Otto's relative for an undetermined period of time. They would in this way stay out of the line of fire.

Janine invited me to her home that evening where I broached the idea over dinner. My son-in-law was reluctant at first, being unwilling to jeopardize his career. He went along at last when Janine pointed out in no uncertain terms that to go to Singapore might end up ruining all our lives.

A few days later, I returned to Florida to investigate an insurance claim in Fort Lauderdale where I stopped for lunch at Jackson's bar to meet with Jake Santana and Felix Stiles.

Jackson's billed itself as a steakhouse. Eva and I frequented it when we were in town. It was an ultra chic lunch and dinner hangout for the city's 'haves' and the wannabe crowd. The restaurant was done in mahogany and walnut with high ceilings, chandeliers and cheap reproduction art of the great masters. A meet and greet lounge area allowed cigar smoking directly to the right of the entrance. The bar area was lined with sofas and love seats around coffee tables leading to a bar whose seats seemed always occupied by young women in dark cocktail dresses surrounded by lounge lizards. The food was so-so, the service was mediocre, and the noise level was high, but it was very popular despite the contrived atmosphere.

"Are you guys drinking your lunch or what?" I asked.

Jake turned on his bar stool and gave me a toothy grin.

"How are you doing, Max?"

"Not bad," I replied. "How are things, Felix? What brings you here?"

Jake downed his drink.

"You want to tell him, Felix?"

The Bahamian police officer cleared his throat.

"Something about Henry and Colin when they were in Bimini has been bothering me," he said. "Colin actually cleared customs in Bimini at dawn. I wasn't there but our duty officer definitely says he came through, stayed until the afternoon and left. Fifteen minutes later, the yacht blew up. Henry was with me when it happened."

"We know that," I indicated. "That's what you said in Delray. What else is new?"

"That's the thing, Max. Henry flew in the night before and then flew out again the next day on the late afternoon flight. He never went for treatment."

"That's a short reunion."

"I would have figured that he might have been upset about his brother's being on the yacht and would have stayed for the rescue mission. Instead, he took a Chalks seaplane flight to Paradise Island an hour later to catch an evening flight to Paris from Nassau. That's not normally how a brother acts. I also did some checking with your embassy in Nassau. There's no record that Henry ever went to the embassy for a visa to fly to the States."

Jake threw me a toothy grin.

"How do you like that, Max?"

Felix shrugged his shoulders.

"I don't know. We're not terribly advanced in the Biminis, Jake, but we do have computers and are wired in like you guys. I was doing a records check on Henry Adair's draft status. I happened to run across an inquiry made by your Tom Lyons. He was doing a background check on Henry. So I called him. He tells me that Henry's draft status was cleared up years ago with an assist from a French government official."

"Who's the official?" I asked.

"Your detective friend didn't know. He thought it might have been an Interpol official. He followed up by calling Pierre La Salle who says that the intercession came from someone high up in the French justice department who testified that Henry was engaged in intelligence work on behalf of the CIA in cooperation with the French government. What do you think of that, Jake? I'm surprised you never picked up on this information."

Jake fell silent and at first did not respond. Then he blurted out.

"I did pick up on that relationship between Henry and the CIA, damn it!"

The toothy smile on his face disappeared.

"What happened?" I asked.

"I passed the information to Mel Solomon who told me there was nothing to it and that I should forget the whole thing. His response bothered me. So I ran the rumor by one of my CIA contacts who confided that they had Henry in their sights for his smuggling operations through Maison Dore but since there was no foreign policy issue involved, they dropped the case. The word floating around that Henry was an operative for the CIA was a smoke screen. And La Salle hinted as much. He point blank said that Henry was protected by the French government. I figured out that I was poking into a hot potato and I backed off."

"Anyway," Felix concluded. "Henry was good to go anywhere he wanted anytime he wanted."

I grimaced.

"Henry couldn't have been grief stricken by the whole affair if he never bothered to show up for his brother's testimonial luncheon."

"What we have," Jake concluded, "is a bunch of circumstances packed over a pile of coincidences. I'm lost."

"I'm curious, Felix," I asked. "How far out at sea did Colin's boat go up?"

"Just past the shallows. That's about a mile out, where the sea is a mile or more deep."

"I know what's on your mind, Max," said Jake. "Don't even think DNA. We'd have to carve up every fish and bird in the Bahamas to make a positive identification." He went on. "And now about your thing with Eva, Max. I think you're going to have to watch your back."

"In what way, Jake?"

"If she's an accessory to anything, you can become implicated, and there'll be nothing we or anyone can do to help you."

I sighed. The flood gates were opening and I was helpless. My mind was cluttered with doubts that could not be allayed and questions to which I had no answers.

I chose to ignore my plight.

"You must have heard, Jake; Eva flew to Paris. Or didn't Larry O'Leary tell you."

My statement was received open mouthed by Jake.

"I haven't heard," he muttered almost unintelligibly. "That's a brand new development. She must be connecting with Henry."

I turned to Felix.

"Have you checked that clinic in Bimini where Henry got his treatments?"

"That's the amazing thing, Max," he said. "I threatened the owner with a subpoena to examine the clinic's records and he started talking non-stop. It seems he is running a phony operation. Henry was treated at the clinic, but the owner conceded there was nothing that could be done for him. You see, Henry had AIDS. He was a dead man before ever going to the Bahamas. He just wouldn't accept it."

"Well, for a dead man he certainly gets around."

A call came in for Jake at that moment. Jake answered the call and his face turned pale.

"We have a killing at the Carnival diner in Delray. You coming, Felix, Max?"

We rushed out into the street, piled into the car and drove with screaming sirens to Delray and parked alongside several squad cars across the street from the Carnival in front of which were drawn police barricades and yards of yellow crime scene tape. A police officer came out of the diner, wringing his hands.

"You have to see this," he said.

We followed him into the empty restaurant and to the storeroom in the rear. There, on the floor, dead, shot execution style, lay Victor Nishkanian's wife and adult children. Victor lay a few yards away, a pistol in his right and hand and a bullet through his right temple.

"This is a murder-suicide on the face of it," Jake exclaimed.

"Could be," I replied. "But why?"

"Whatever it is, it's a massacre," said Felix. "It's horrible. Nish was my friend. I was at his wedding many years ago. I've been to the christening of his kids, to all their family gatherings. How can this happen?"

"We were all there," sobbed Jake. "This sucks. It really does."

The press started to get nasty as they usually do in cases like this. But Jake was lucky. The papers bought into the police murder-suicide story. The news quieted down and the Carnival reopened for business.

But here, there was a strange twist of fate. Since the Nishkanian family was gone, a court appointed trustee and receiver was needed to manage its estate including the restaurant. And naturally, the court wanted a competent party and selected Eva with her experience. And naturally, Eva was in Paris and could not be reached for comment. So it was Larry O'Leary who took on the task of running the diner.

For some unknown reason, perhaps under prodding from Eva, Henry gave up the fight to block the Blue Danube's inspection. The stage was set and arrangements moved forward to appraise the stone.

There was one more critical development. Eva, through her attorneys, had convinced a local court before her departure to issue a death certificate. Colin was now officially dead and Eva was officially a widow. She was at last in a position to collect on Colin's life insurance policy. She was also officially one of the Blue Danube's owners, as she had predicted she would become.

The time had come for me to make my move. I called my attorney to have him set up a time and date for the Blue Danube's inspection and to assemble all the concerned parties. Pierre La Salle was to be in Belgium for Interpol to take custody of the conflict diamonds and Otto Katz would do his thing in New Jersey and authenticate the diamond at Maison Dore in Morristown for Stan Short to whom it would be surrendered. Partly for old times sake and partly out of courtesy I notified Mel Solomon of the appointed date for the Blue Danube's inspection.

20

Last Call

Just before I was to leave for New Jersey Mel Solomon called me and Jake Santana and asked us to come down to Sentinel's Miami offices. He wanted to talk about Victor and his family and of the ramifications of Eva's recently and officially declared widowhood.

Jake picked me up and we were off at high speed for Miami. Strangely, his usual driver, Frank Barton, was not behind the wheel. Instead, sitting there with a faint sneering smile on his face was Ed Houston.

"Where's Frank?" I asked.

"I decided to use Ed instead," replied Jake. He has something to tell us."

We got stuck in traffic along the way and Ed took the portable flasher with the magnetic base and fixed it to the roof. The congestion cleared and we sped on in grim silence. We had no reason to be nervous about the meeting but something was tugging at our innards, hinting that this rendezvous was urgent.

Jake brought up Johnny Cork and Ed Houston on the way.

"I was speaking with La Salle, and we think we know who was working with Cork when he flew with Carl Haussmann."

"Who was that?"

It would have to be someone Carl knew with whom he was comfortable. An element of trust had to be present. He didn't know Cork that well despite the fact Johnny was a good friend of Colin, and therefore he wouldn't have traveled with Cork unless someone else was there to leave him in his hands."

"That's kind of like giving away the bride at her wedding?" I ventured to ask.

"Exactly," replied Jake. "By process of elimination, he would only trust the people he knew. That would include you, Colin, Henry, Colin's wife and her brother, Frank. I checked out everyone's whereabouts from a few days before Carl flew to Paris to a few days after. It turns out that it was Frank who flew from here to New Jersey with Johnny Cork; it was he who picked up Carl's medication from Harry Silver and it was he who drove Carl and Johnny Cork to the airport in Newark. And it was he who killed Cork's dog. My guess is that he got his marching orders from Colin or Eva."

"What about Ed Houston, here?"

Jake made a face.

"You tell him, Ed."

"Frank asked me and George to take you and Brian Donovan down," Ed said. "That was after you told me about Harry Silver. I refused. Figuring that I was now an open target for knowing too much, I decided to send a message and went after Harry Silver after finding out that he was dealing death with his pills."

"Who killed Brian, Ed? Do you know?"

"I'm betting on Frank, but I'm not sure."

"What makes you bring this up now, Jake?" I asked.

"I'm trying to reconstruct the events leading to Carl's death last year."

"What about it?"

"You were supposed to inspect the Blue Danube. Instead, Mel sent you packing for a few days and by coincidence you were drafted by La Salle to look into that load of stolen diamonds in Belgium. Mel was at the stone's inspection, representing Sentinel and the Adair family and Haussmann was there on behalf of Maison Dore.

"It turns out that two days before Frank Barton picks up Johnny Cork at his houseboat, he goes to see Harry Silver for a checkup. That's when Harry sells him the pills for Carl. Everything is set. Frank and Johnny fly north with Mel Solomon on his private jet with Larry O'Leary. Tom Lyons found all those names on the flight manifest filed away at Morristown Airport. The jet lands and Larry takes off for Colin's restaurant and reports for work but the others pick Carl up at Colin's home and take him to Maison Dore in Morristown to meet up with Otto Katz and inspect the diamond. The rest is history.

"To make a long story short, that assignment La Salle gave you is the one that blew open a conspiracy to hold together the Adair and Sentinel empires. That's why anyone connected to the conspiracy is being murdered one by one.

Dead witnesses can't testify. I'm hoping that's what Mel wants to see us about. He knows something we don't and break this case open for us."

Jake sounded almost weary.

"I hope all goes well when you and Otto inspect the Blue Danube. Is Tom going to be there?"

"That's the plan."

"What about La Salle? Is he in Belgium?"

"Yes. He's ready."

"There are only five us now."

"Yes. Let's try to keep it that way," I said hopefully.

Jake sighed.

"I can see the roses," he said, "but I can't smell them yet."

Traffic was light and we were able to make good time. Over to our left and past the towns filling the region's flat panorama, loomed the high rises of Aventura, Turnberry, North Miami Beach and Bal Harbor. To our right were the warehouses and strip malls that eventually gave way to the squalid slums of Liberty City. Miami's corporate towers, barely a shadow on the southern horizon, now reached for the cloudless sky.

I knew the city well. The old Orange Bowl was buried in the bowels of the new glass towers that had become Miami's permanent landmark and symbol of its prosperity. Most of the taller and more spectacular buildings faced the the turquoise waters of Biscayne Bay. Many of those shiny new buildings were owned by banks and insurance companies. Some were boutique banks and investment houses that catered to a select, private clientele and offered an assortment of esoteric offshore services like South Florida Trust.

One of the newest towers, on Brickel Avenue south of the Miami River, belonged to Centurion. A taller, neighboring structure belonged to Sentinel. Mel Solomon's offices were on the building's top floor overlooking the bay and Miami harbor. The Sentinel building was surrounded by police and an EMS van with flashing lights was standing by when we arrived. Jake Santana nervously flashed his badge to a couple of indifferent officers who ushered us into the lobby where Don Goodwind, a short, fat detective with a wheezy voice from Miami-Dade homicide, was huddled with two EMS attendants.

He stuck out a thick paw in a handshake.

"We must stop meeting this way, guys," he quipped. "How are you, Jake? Max, you too. Long time no see."

Jake lapsed into Spanish.

"Que paso?"

Don nodded his head to the high ceiling.

"Upstairs."

We followed him to an elevator and went to the penthouse floor. The door opened up into a spacious office whose floor-to-ceiling windows filling the outside wall overlooked Biscayne Bay. A large desk was centered in front of the windows and slumped over it was Mel Solomon, his head resting on a fancy decorative blotter, eyes and mouth open, dried blood on one side of his face and a revolver gripped tightly in his right hand. A hand written note lay next to his head.

Don Goodwind lifted the note with a pair of forceps and showed it to us.

I looked at it and without realizing what it said I read the note out loud.

"You win, Max. May you rot in Hell!"

My face turned beet red.

Jake Santana smirked.

"I guess Mel thought your plans for the Blue Danube were something to die for, Max." he joked sarcastically. "He killed himself over them."

This was undeniably a suicide and Mel Solomon wanted the world to know that I was the cause of his misery. At least there was no need to find a killer this time around.

His death did leave one question, however. If Mel Solomon, Tweedledum the schlemiel, was dead, what was Sol Weinberg, Tweedledee the schmegegi, going to do? More important than second guessing Sol's intentions was the issue of the mounting body count. When would it stop?

Carl Haussmann and Louis Dore were murdered; so was Brian Donovan, most likely for feeding me information. The same thing could have happened to Mike Surrey except that Barry Benson beat everyone to the draw. It was a mercy killing that exposed a murderous physician on the take. Harry Silver was gone, but he was no great loss. Mel Solomon took his own life, and that was too bad. I kind of liked him. Nishkanian and his family were brutally t murdered, and that was pointless. And of course, old Colin had to be added to the list.

The direct hits bore the imprimatur of one or two kill teams. But if Colin was the grand architect of those killings, he was gone. The kill teams were still in circulation. Were they now without portfolio or were they receiving their marching orders from the likes of Eva or Henry? Not that I didn't believe them possessed of homicidal leanings to offset their utter lack of moral judgment; they just didn't seem capable of developing a grand plan involving diamond smuggling, financial fraud, money laundering and murder leading to retaining control of the Blue Danube.

Mel Solomon's suicide convinced me that it wasn't over a fear of being accused of murder. Killing was never his bag. He took his life because he was afraid that whatever I was to find in Maison Dore's vault would close him, and life as he knew it, down.

There were three possibilities that might have compelled Mel to end it all.

The first was that the diamond was a fake and he knew it. The second was that it was real and had been lifted when Carl inspected it, and Mel was in on the theft. The third possibility was that the diamond was a fake and that Mel knew that also and therefore went along with its removal from Morristown. This could only mean that Otto Katz too was in the loop on that angle.

The failed shooting at Troy's now began to fit a theory. The motive for the hit must have been to keep me away from the Blue Danube more than it was in retribution for having laid bare the stolen conflict diamonds scheme. Could that mean that I was one of the few who never suspected the diamond was a fake?

Another facet of this case presented itself. If I was in danger, so was my daughter and her family. It was reasonable to expect that whoever was after me would be gunning for Janine. The saving grace that the family would be safe, at least for a while. As for me, I had to watch my back and move fast if I was to stay alive and well.

A call from Stan Short reminded me that Otto was in the States and that the date for the consummation of our deal was two days away. I should quickly get my tail up to New Jersey, he insisted. The feds were not wasting any time. It was show time.

Back at the Del Rey I asked the concierge desk to make airline reservations and then called Larry O'Leary at the Poinciana to tell him I was leaving for New Jersey. Larry wasn't there, but I spoke to Eva's brother, Frank, who said he would give Larry the message. Not trusting him to deliver any message of mine to anyone, I called Jake Santana, gave him my itinerary, and then asked him.

"Where's Larry?"

"He went north yesterday. Why?"

"Frank said nothing about Larry being away."

A moment of silence followed.

"You keep to your travel plans," said Jake finally. "I'll call you if you have to make a change."

"Is there a problem?"

I heard Jake laugh over the phone.

"Not if I can help it."

I was airborne the next morning, landing in Newark at noon under a gray and threatening sky. Like Jake, I was liking Frank less and less and sooner or later I felt he would have to be dealt with one way or another. I was had come to realize that if Eva was brewing, he was stirring. Needless to say, I began to regret having told him anything.

My regret was justified. Waiting for me at the baggage carousel was Larry O'Leary. He was uncharacteristically dressed in an old leather field jacket and slacks over hiking shoes.

I shook his hand enthusiastically.

"I'm sure glad to see you, Larry. But I thought you were at the Poinciana."

"There were problems in Bernardsville. I flew back last night."

"Are you my transportation?"

"You bet, Max. I got the word this morning that you needed a ride to Dore in Morristown to inspect the diamond."

"That's right. Oh, by the way. I don't have any bags besides the duffel I'm holding. Walk me to the payphone. I want to make a call."

Larry looked at me suspiciously.

"Who to?"

"Pierre La Salle. He needs to know I'm in New Jersey today."

"Is this about the diamond? I'm supposed to take you to Morristown."

I nodded. Without waiting for Larry to react, I gave him my duffel to hold and placed a collect call to Pierre's private number.

He picked up right away, recognized my voice and lapsed into French.

"Max? Is everything all right?"

"Yes. I said I would call. I'm in Newark."

"Alone?"

"Almost. Are you ready at your end?"

"Definitely."

I hung up, hoping he would understand my message, and followed Larry to the terminal exit door.

"Do you have a piece?" Larry asked suddenly.

"No. I don't carry one on planes."

I took advantage of a pause in the conversation to grip my chest. My ploy was to stall for time.

"Are you all right, Max?"

He leaned forward to help steady me on my feet. I had to stall for time. "Do you mind if we stop for a soda or coffee?"

"Sure, Max. There's a coffee counter over there. Here. I'll help you."

"I'll be fine. Just hold my duffel."

We walked to the beverage concession and ordered a couple of coffees. I rummaged through my duffel and located my pill box.

"I know how you feel, Max," said Larry. "I get that feeling also when I'm under stress."

We continued to talk as the minutes passed. I waited more than a half hour and then said I was feeling better and ready to leave. I said nothing more and followed Larry quietly out of the terminal to the outside lot where he had left a rental car. I made no mention of the rented car and settled into the vehicle's front seat next to him. Rain started falling and we were off.

Larry O'Leary was a New Jersey boy who still had trouble driving around the airport. After a few more wrong turns he found the exit and we were on the Interstate. Another road would have taken us directly to Morristown but he missed the exit and stayed on the Interstate which ran south of the county seat.

"I'm sorry," Larry apologized. "For a moment I thought I was driving to Bernardsville."

"Not a problem, Larry. We can cut through the Great Swamp."

I either tried to keep a straight face and just kept smiling, hoping that Jake had an ace up his sleeve, like sending someone after us. The saving grace was that Larry had a poor sense of direction. He was studying the highway exit markings carefully and gripped the wheel to make sure he would leave the highway the moment the desired exit appeared. The car swerved slightly to change lanes and I happened to notice the butt of a pistol peeking at me from inside his jacket.

Larry drove west for a while and then turned off on a local road that would have eventually taken us to the center of Morristown via the Great Swamp. This was decidedly the long way to town, which was probably what Larry had in mind to begin with. The rain picked up and a fog set in.

Larry's lips were parched and he seemed nervous. I decided to relax and play out this little adventure. I pretended to doze off.

It was pouring when we entered the Great Swamp and visibility was poor. Here, Larry was on home turf. But then again, so was I.

"We're going to stop here for a few minutes and wait until the rain eases up," he said.

He drove the car off the road and down a gravel path through the swamp until we reached a boat ramp used to lower canoes into the water. It was a popular spot on weekends but desolate on weekdays. It was he who, many years ago when we were young and in school, took me to the Great Swamp with a couple of college girls. The party we were to have was aborted when one of the girls discovered a dead body lying in the nearby brush. I never returned to that spot again.

Larry stopped the car at the top of the ramp just as the rain stopped. He slapped the gear shift in neutral and left the engine running, lowering his window to let some fresh air in.

I could have gone for his gun, but I didn't. I leaned casually against the door and smiled.

"So, Larry," I said. "You're the man with a gun, and you know where we are: in a deserted section of the Great Swamp, where we used to bring the girls to get laid many years ago. What's you next move?"

Larry O'Leary shook his head sadly, pulled the pistol out of his jacket and placed it on the dashboard. He laid his right hand on his lap and clenched it in a fist.

"My orders were to make sure you never got to Morristown, but I can't do it, Max. I just can't."

He began to cry and I had to give him a handkerchief to dry his tears.

"Colin is dead, Larry. Who's giving the orders?"

"Colin was a swindler, Max. But he never killed anybody."

"Never gave orders to have anyone taken down?"

"Not Colin. He had to go with the flow, like us. We were blackmailed by our bills. Eva and her brother called the shots."

"Damn it, Larry. What the hell did Eva have over Colin? It couldn't have been money."

Tears continued running down Larry's cheeks.

"Don't you know, Max? It's always money, sex and power. That's all there is and that's all we struggle for. Look at me! If I kill you, I stay solvent and alive and my family ends up being well taken care of. If I don't kill you, I get killed and my family loses everything. But I can't shoot you, Max."

I pointed to the pistol on the dashboard.

"Well, I'm not going to take the gun, Larry. And I have to get to Morristown. You need to tell me what you're going to do."

Larry sniffled a couple of times and straightened out his jacket.

"I've already made my decision," he said. "It's last call at the bar."

Against the foggy backdrop of the swamp where birds on brown branches looked on quietly, Larry grabbed the pistol from the top of the dashboard, thrust its business end into his mouth and squeezed the trigger.

The shot frightened away the birds perched on the trees and George Lerman appeared outside the driver side window.

A car with the engine running was parked a few yards away.

"If we don't make this look like an accident," said George. "Larry's wife will never collect on his insurance."

"How are we going to do that?

George grunted. He removed the pistol from Larry's hand and snuggled it carefully behind the sun visor above the windshield.

"Who sent you?" I asked.

"Jake Santana. He also got word from La Salle and I followed you from the airport. Are we finished here?"

"I have no idea. I'm new at this."

"Then, get out of the car. We're going to ditch it."

George Lerman was a study in cool. He obviously was very experienced in handling these situations.

"I left the safety off on the pistol. It will take the cops a while to find the car and the body, if they ever do. And when they do, who's to say it wasn't an accidental shooting. The idiot went down to the swamp, parked here for a while to shoot some birds, put the gun down, maybe took a nap and let the car roll down the embankment. The gun dropped off the visor and went off. End of story."

"Fantastic," I said.

He shifted the car into neutral with his hand and we pushed it down the ramp, watching it roll into the swamp where it slowly disappeared from sight. A few bubbles made their way to the surface and then there was nothing.

Poor Larry. He was out of his league and had lost his way.

We walked back to George's car.

"Who are you working for, George?"

"Anyone who pays me, Max. With Mel and Colin out of the way, I have to go with the highest bidder."

"Where's your sidekick, Ed Houston?"

"Around. He's in the same boat I am."

George was not about to reveal anything and I had to hand it to him. He was a true professional. I tried another tack.

"You guys know everything. I went to pay to John Cork's houseboat some time back. Someone killed his dog."

George shrugged his shoulders.

"I told you before. I don't do dogs."

"What about John Cork? I hear he's still in Paris."

"I hear that too."

"Is he dead?"

"No. He's sick. Colin said before he died that John had a disease, TB or something like that."

"Tuberculosis? That's contagious. But I hear it can be treated and even cured. I heard that Henry has AIDS. What about Carl Haussmann and Louis Dore?"

George's mood turned sour.

"You ask too many questions, Max."

I changed the subject.

"What's your deal with Jake Santana?"

He laughed.

"No deal. He pays and I and Ed Houston play. But this was pro bono. Jake and a few dudes pooled their funds to protect their interests by keeping you alive. Where to now?"

I took a deep breath.

"Morristown," I said.

21

Gone

The encounter with Larry made me more apprehensive than ever about the meeting in Morristown to inspect and re-authenticate the Blue Danube. The weather cleared for our drive to Morristown and by the time we made it to Maison Dore on South Street the sun was shining. George Lerman found a parking spot along the town's tree lined square and maneuvered the car into the space, leaving the motor idling. Two blocks away, two squad cars filled with cops were positioned seconds away from Maison Dore whose display windows covered the entire block. Tom Keys and Stan Short were also there. They stood near the front entrance, making small talk. Now and then, they would look up and down the street nervously and check their watches as they waited for me to appear. I couldn't see if Otto Katz was there yet. I assumed he was because Stan seemed completely relaxed. Then I saw the reason why. Several men in blue suits and red ties were congregating close by. IRS or FBI agents, I guessed. Stan Short had covered his bases well.

"This is it," said George Lerman. "I'm out of here."

"Where do I find you?" I asked.

"I'll be around," he said. "And don't forget. If you ever need a plane and pilot, I'm your man."

I got out of the car, not fully understanding what he meant or implied.

"Thanks."

He grunted and drove off.

The vault where the Blue Danube Diamond rested was no place to bring up what happened in the Great Swamp. I was not the worse for wear and nei-

ther Tom Keys nor Stan Short referred to my tardiness. Tom, the ever obser-
vant cop, pointed to my feet.

"Did you walk from the airport, Max? You have mud on your shoes."

He had me on something. He knew it, but he could not guess what it was.
I wanted to tell him, Then, it dawned on me that Jake Santana might have
called him. But no. If Tom had received a call from La Salle or Santana, he
would have had the police rescue me and George would not have been there.
Tom was clueless, at least right now.

Tom and Stan followed me into the store where Otto was talking with Joe
Kelly, the store manager. With his Santa Claus face and his grizzly bear frame
stuffed into his usual green corduroy suit over a wrinkled open collar shirt,
Hans stood out from the rest of us inside the fancy jewelry retailer. He shook
Joe's hand firmly.

"It is a long time since last year, my friend. I trust everything is in good
order?" He asked loudly in his German-Dutch accent.

"We have up-dated our security system," replied Joe. "And you, Max. It's
good to see you again."

"Same here," I said. "Are we ready?"

Otto laughed nervously and was perspiring, and I could sense that he was
definitely surprised to see me.

"Ready for love and war." Otto said

"And diamonds?"

"One diamond in particular," he replied. "Shall we do the dance?"

Otto pointed to the back of the store as Joe Kelly stepped up to greet me.

"You'll like what we did here since your last visit, Max," said Joe.

"That was two years ago, Joe. What did you guys do?"

"We installed a new security system. It opens the vault when it recognizes
certain registered fingerprints pressed against the exterior vault scanner. The
door shuts automatically once someone is inside and reopens when the same
prints are placed on the interior scanner. There's a five second grace period
between the vault's opening and closing. Once inside, we're locked in until
someone with the right prints lets us out."

"Neat. When did you get it?"

"In time for Carl Haussmann's inspection a year ago January. We bought
the system from a Sentinel subsidiary. Mike Surrey set it up for us. You were
in Belgium at the time."

"Whose fingerprints is the scanner programmed to recognize?"

"Carl Haussmann, Mel Solomon and mine. Yours were to be registered but your heart attack got in the way."

"So, who gets into the vault now that Carl and Mel are dead and I'm not registered?"

The Dore manager pointed to himself.

"I'm the only one who gets in and out until this mess is sorted out. If you check the vault door's computer records, this will be the first time the vault will be opened in over a year."

"He's opening the vault for the IRS," Stan Short said. "We plan to attach the diamond today," he continued. "The moment you and Otto authenticate it, we're seizing it for unpaid taxes. You won't ever have to bother with the Blue Danube again."

"Sounds good to me."

I looked at Otto.

"How about it, old buddy? Shall we get started?"

"It's now or never."

"Yes," I agreed. "Once a year the diamond comes to life, like the mythical phoenix. It rises to tell us all that all is well with the world."

"Great poetry, Max."

We gravitated to the vault area behind the showrooms on the street floor. The small talk in the heavily guarded and brightly lit back room shrank to a few monosyllabic words and evaporated into a dead silence when the Dore manager placed his hand on the scanner. The heavy door opened silently and we quickly entered the steel vault. Seconds later it slammed shut. It was the same slamming sound I heard when Carl Haussmann was wheeled into the operating room at the hospital in Paris.

On a table in the center of the room was a large mahogany box illuminated by ceiling strobe lights. The jubilant store manager, eager to demonstrate how well his new security system worked, lead us to the table. We stood still for a few moments, trying to figure out what to do next.

"You're the man of the moment, Stan," I said. "It's your call."

Stan Short turned to Otto.

"You're our neutral, outside expert. You start the process."

Otto placed a large trembling hand on the box, unlatched the lid, raised it and took a peek. He blinked.

He took another look and his eyes widened.

He opened the box wide for all of us to see and placed it back on the table and waved his arms.

"Empty!"

"Empty?"

Stan Short pushed his thick neck forward and stared into the box.

"Empty!"

Tom Keys took a look.

"It's gone! The diamond isn't here. Gone!"

The Blue Danube was gone.

Of course! The whole picture sprang to life in color while Stan Short was frantically trying to reach La Salle on his cell phone to abort the Belgium end of the deal. The Blue Danube had been purloined last year. That's what Carl Haussmann had wanted to see me about and that's why he was killed. He had somehow been conned into participating in its theft without realizing that he would be murdered and relieved of the diamond upon arriving in Paris.

The grand design finally surfaced. A master plot to spirit the diamond away to France must have been hatched years ago by the Adair twins as part of a huge swindle to wipe out their friends and associates and to safeguard their interests. Now I knew why Carl Haussmann wanted to see me. He must have had a pang of conscience and was prepared to spill the beans. That explained his call to me. He had the stone and was scared out of his mind and afraid for his life. How right he was! And this was why Larry was paid to stop me.

Pandemonium broke loose at Dore's Morristown store. Alarms went off and police cordoned off the South Street entrance while Stan Short, red with rage, made frantic calls to La Salle in Belgium to have him abort the release of the conflict diamonds.

Suddenly, all lights went out. I found a wall and pressed my back against it. I stood motionlessly and listened to the shuffling, scampering and hollering around me. Somewhere in the darkness, I heard Tom Lyons curse and Stan Short scream as they collided, trying to find an emergency light. Local police and federal agents scurried about with guns drawn and blinding flashlights trying to focus on moving objects, light switches and circuit breakers.

The entire fracas was over in minutes, but it felt like hours. Miraculously, the lights went back on. The store was in shambles but everything was intact, and Tom Lyons immediately began searching for Joe Kelly and Otto Katz.

Tom Lyons saw me, still pressed against the wall.

"You stay right where you are," he barked before running down the back stairs.

I waited patiently.

Joe Kelly was easy to find. He was lying at the bottom of the cellar stairs, his neck broken. Otto Katz was another matter. He had left through the rear door leading to the parking lot behind the building and was nowhere to be found.

Reconstructing the theft was easy. First was my trip to Belgium while Mel and Carl snuck the Blue Danube away from Dore's Morristown store. Otto Katz, Joe Kelly and Mike Surrey were their immediate accomplices and of course the rest of Colin Adair's Irish mafia had to have been seduced with the promise of lifelong wealth, unaware that they had signed their death warrants when they joined the scheme.

When it was finally over, after the police and feds left, the store closed by court order, and Tom Lyons unable to find any good reason to detain me, I was allowed to go home. Yet, it was clear that I was in deep trouble. Larry was dead. His family would soon notice he was missing and call the police. Tom Lyons would waste little time connecting my muddy shoes with Larry's disappearance and that would propel him to my doorstep with embarrassing questions.

I called Pierre La Salle to explain my plight.

He sounded amused over the phone.

"We are surrounded by vipers, Max. But not everything is lost. If the Blue Danube is not in America it must be in France. We will find it and we will be rich, one way or another. There are more of us than of them."

"It boils down to a killing contest, doesn't it? Winner take all." I said.

"Yes, my friend. It is coming to that."

"What if we were out of the way, Pierre?"

"Then they would start killing one another. That is normal."

"What do you suggest?"

"I suggest you come to Paris. I need you here and I need you alive."

Tom Lyons called me later. He had wasted no time. An APB was issued for Otto Katz's arrest on suspicion of murder and grand theft, and a warrant for Johnny Cork's arrest for the murder of Carl Haussmann was transmitted to Interpol for execution through the police in France. He followed up officially by enlisting the services of the FBI and Interpol in the hope of recovering the diamond.

"As a matter of fact, Max, I'm seriously thinking of asking the DA's office jump into this with a grand jury investigation.

He snorted.

"That might happen anyway." And then he added, "All deals are off. I hope you understand that."

Stan Short also called. He was understandably furious and cryptically told me that everything was off.

The IRS, done out of its treasure, was out for red meat. But Stan had his work cut out for him with Mel Solomon's death and was too busy to fixate on the Blue Danube. His new job was to referee Sentinel's dismemberment and the sale of its parts to satisfy IRS and other creditor liens. To this end he was talking with Sol Weinberg at Centurion to broker a deal.

Sentinel's breakup and the theft the Blue Danube effectively terminated my career and position as the diamond's caretaker for the Adair family. All I was left with was my one third claim to the gemstone, and that I was not going to surrender.

I expected Jake Santana, Pierre La Salle and Tom Lyons to duck for cover to avoid the glare of publicity that was bound to follow the international theft of a world famous diamond. I was right.

Jake had his hands full with the Donovan and Nishkanian murders and calls for his resignation were beginning to mount.

Tom Lyons too had problems. There was the unsolved business at Troy's. On top of that he had to deal with Larry's wife who demanded to know what happened to her husband. It didn't help when his body was found, despite the fact that it was ruled a terrible accident. His death nevertheless prompted an investigation, leaving Tom to be pilloried by a bad press.

Pierre La Salle was taking heat as well. Haussmann's and Dore's deaths were re-classified as murders and, to complicate matters, someone called the American Embassy to complain that John Cork, an American citizen and a murder suspect, had disappeared in Paris and that nothing was being done to find him. And making things worse, the top brass at Interpol was giving La Salle flack for not solving the case of the stolen conflict diamonds. His career was on the line.

The best defense is an aggressive offense. La Salle was right. There was no no choice but to go to Paris and find the Blue Danube, assuming it was there. Once in my hands, my options would be clearer.

I called Pierre again to review my situation and options.

"We must find the Blue Danube," he said. "But I must stay low and leave you to do the leg work for me. I am sure the diamond is here, Max. Colin is dead. That leaves Henry and your friend Jouvet who has something going with him and with Emile Barco."

"What makes you say that?"

"That offer from Jouvet. A reason was behind that offer. After all, do you truly believe that France needs an aging investigator for a no-show job? You have been asked to bug off in so many ways, Max."

"To wit?"

"We start with Eva's overtures at the hospital when you were sick. Looking back, it was obvious. She put your head between her legs to shut you up. Do you think she only wanted an orgasm?"

My face was hot and I was glad Pierre could not see me blush.

"There is something even more troubling," Pierre said solemnly.

"What's that?"

"You son-in-law's sudden transfer. Your whole family is on the other side of the world. They wouldn't know for months if you were to disappear. This transfer was a ploy designed to isolate you. That had to have been Jouvet's work."

"Is Otto Katz working with Jouvet?" I asked.

"That possible connection is being investigated," Pierre replied evasively.

"Damn it, man! Janine could be in danger with Otto's relatives in Asia."

"No," said Pierre definitively. "Fortunately, we were able to deflect that."

"How is that?"

"I never trusted Otto. So, I took the liberty of having your daughter and her family sent to my Caribbean property behind Otto's back. He does not know where they are and continues to believe they are in Asia. They are safer than ever and everything is under control."

"I hope so, Pierre. I hope so. But tell me. What made you distrust Otto?"

"I will tell you in Paris, Max. You know, summer is here and Bastille Day is coming. It is a good time for us to finish our business. You could also look up your old girlfriend when you get there."

"Nicole Colbert? I haven't seen nor spoken with her in years."

"See her, Max. She has a clothing store on Rue Saint Honore around the corner from Place Vendome and has an apartment upstairs. Do you remember that she was pregnant when you dropped out of the picture?"

"Vaguely."

"Well, she gave birth to a son."

"Healthy?"

"Yes. He is an actor and makes a living playing minor roles at the Comedie Francaise in Paris. His name is Michel Colbert Darcy. She gave him her first husband's last name, the man she married when she was sixteen years old."

"I never knew she was married once before. How long did that last?"

"Less than a year. They were too young."

"So. Who's the father?"

"Don't know. It might be Henry. Or, it could have been her first husband."

"How do you know all this? Have you've been dating Nicole?"

"Don't be so touchy, Max. I am seeing her cousin, Christine. But anyway, Nicole is well and asks about you. Go see her, Max."

"Do you think she would speak to me after all these years?"

"It is worth a try. You could reignite your romance."

"I don't need more romance in my life, Pierre."

"Nicole could be helpful, Max. She doesn't much care for her ex-husband."

"How come? Didn't they have this son you're talking about?"

"It's not his, Max."

"What did you say?"

"You heard me. The kid is not his."

"Whose is it, then? This guy Darcy?"

Pierre became more insistent.

"See her, Max. Her store is called Chez Colbert on 209 Rue Saint Honore. It is the same address as your suite number at the Westphalia."

VI
PARIS

22

Rendezvous

Packing a few things, I made airline reservations and booked my usual suite for a two week stay at the Westphalia. The day of my flight, I called Maison Dore in Paris, leaving word that I would like to meet with Henry Adair on Sunday or Monday. His secretary said she would relay the message. I also called Pierre La Salle and left a message indicating that I would be in Paris the next morning.

I landed at Charles de Gaulle International Airport in time for breakfast on Friday, and seeing Pierre La Salle waiting for me on the other side of customs was a pleasantly unexpected surprise. It was sweater and jacket weather but the sun was out and the air warmed as we drove closer to Paris.

"Anything on Otto Katz?" I asked.

"Nothing, Max. And in case you are wondering about Gaspard Lancet, he too seems to have evaporated in thin air."

"What about Johnny Cork?"

Pierre laughed.

"John Cork, the global scapegoat. He is somewhere around us, Max. More people have been traveling using his name on faked passports than we have spies. But I think that now that we can assume the Blue Danube is in France, and now that you are here, all the rats will surface and we will be able to pick them off one by one."

"Am I the bait, Pierre?"

"Yes, my friend. You are the bait. But I do hope to keep you alive."

This was all giving me a terrible headache, but something else was on my mind and I thought this would be a good opportunity to unload it on the Interpol director.

"I have a recollection that has bothered me for many years, Pierre. I think it happened when I was a kid here and I thought that maybe you could place the scene."

"Can you describe it, Max?"

"It is a railroad station waiting room. It has steel girders that spring from the walls like flying buttresses to support a high vaulted ceiling around a huge glass dome at its epicenter through which light floods the room."

"I think I know train station," said Pierre. "Have you more specifics?"

"Yes. The waiting room has only one way in and one way out, through an entrance guarded by a heavy gate or portcullis that drops from above. It has to be made of metal because the thing always drops with a loud clang.

"I had a dream about the place last night. The station is filled with people frantically dragging their belongings in makeshift bales, trying to clear the gate to the tracks before it closed. Those who make it disappear into a steam filled platform where ear splitting whistles and the chug-a-chug pounding of loco-motives drown out all other sounds."

"Is that in your dream?"

"Yes. All of a sudden, all motion stops as if frozen in time. I panic and ran to reach the gate before it drops, but I'm too late. It falls with a loud clap of thunder and I start crying like a baby. As a matter of fact, my eyes were wet when I awoke. But that's not the issue, Pierre. This has been a recurring dream over the years. I know the place is real and that I've been there; I just don't know where it is."

Pierre smiled knowingly.

"You're describing a railroad station in Paris, Max. Trains there run north, and a high speed one goes to Brussels. I take it on occasion. Vertical gates drop down to block access to the tracks when a train is leaving. It is a safety measure. Those gates were there when you were a kid. Your nightmare may be recalling a bad childhood experience. As long as you wake up from your dreams, you're fine."

"Thank you, doctor," I said. "What can you tell me about the rest of the stuff?"

"The train station is the Gard du Nord and it is still in operation. The trains run north to Le Havre and other port cities on the English Channel.

You may have been there when you were an infant, Max. As a matter of fact, I know you must have been there."

"How do you figure that?"

"I have researched your past in some detail, my friend. That is the station from which your father left for Le Havre. Your mother was probably there with you to see him off. Under ordinary circumstances, the occasion would be sad. In your case, it was traumatic, and now you are for recalling that bad childhood experience."

"What else do you know, Pierre?"

"Quite a lot, my dear old friend. The name Barco is a Franco-German name, as you know. We spoke of his background before. He is one of three brothers. My research shows that one brother moved to your country."

"You had mentioned that," I said.

"True. Did I mention that this brother changed his name? That is the reason he could not be traced. He changed his name to Barton, married and had two children."

"Don't tell me. Eva and Frank Barton!"

"Exactly, Max. Colin Adair's widow and his brother-in-law. But the second Barco brother is more interesting."

"Why is that?"

"This second Barco was an officer in the German army and is the one who married your mother. He became her second husband and inherited the land in Basse Terre when she died. That brings us to our friend, Emile Barco, the third brother. He changed nationalities in 1945 and becomes a pure Frenchman and claimed the Basse Terre property as the sole surviving heir. By then your father is dead; your mother is dead; your step father is dead, and there is no record of your being alive since you too have changed your name. And so Emile Barco obtained title to all that land by default.

"Do you now understand what this is all about, Max? It is Emile Barco who wants you dead, having found out through his niece and nephew that you are alive. Not only are you on his case on account of his connection to Henry Adair and the Blue Danube diamond, he knows you will be after him for his Basse Terre estate which is legitimately yours."

Pierre La Salle looked out his car window.

"Ah, the Westphalia. We have arrived."

La Salle dropped me off in front of the hotel and we agreed to meet later in the afternoon after I had freshened up. But by the time I was checked in, it was noon. What a bombshell. The day was going too fast for my mind to catch up.

The tourist season was at its peak. The hotel was jam packed and the lobby resembled a refugee camp with guests trying to leave bumping into new arrivals trying to register.

I raised my head above the crowd to see if I recognized anyone and thought I was seeing things. It was Bill Ford. He was trying to edge his way out the hotel door and had obviously seen me.

"Bill," I called out. "Bill Ford."

It was too late for him to leave unnoticed. He turned around and I gave him a stupid wave of my hand. He tried to look surprised, acknowledged me with a weak smile and slowly elbowed his way to the registration counter through the maze of tourists.

"Max. Great to see you. Haven't seen you in ages."

I stuck my hand out and grabbed his in a handshake that made him wince. It was strange because I had barely squeezed his hand.

He recovered rapidly and asked in breathless rapid fire sequence, "What are you doing in Paris? Are you staying at this hotel?"

"Yes. What about you?"

"No I had to see someone here. I'm at the Meurice."

"Pleasure?"

Bill Ford shook his head.

"I wish. It's business."

A voice behind me called as Bill was talking.

"Max Gordon?"

I turned and found myself facing Simon Perez, La Salle's assistant.

"Simon. It's good to see you. What brings you to the Westphalia?"

"I was here for a quick lunch. I just returned from Disney World and am working today to make up for lost time."

We shook hands and I introduced him to Bill Ford who seemed slightly embarrassed.

"Pleased to meet you, sir," said Bill.

Simon squinted slightly.

"Were you not on my flight the other day? Two of your friends met you at the airport when we landed."

Bill shook his head.

"No. It must have been someone else. We've never met. I took a cab here."

Simon shrugged his shoulders and smiled innocently.

"I must have been mistaken. I apologize."

"You aren't working this coming holiday week, are you, Simon," I asked.

"Yes. Pierre is on vacation and I have to keep open his office."

"That's great, Simon. We should get together."

Simon Perez smiled.

"We will, Max, perhaps sooner than you think."

We shook hands again and Pierre's assistant took off, constantly looking over his shoulder at Bill Ford. A bellhop came up with my suitcase and took it to my suite.

Bill seemed suspicious.

"Do you know this guy?"

I felt it was best to level with him.

"He's an administrative assistant in Pierre La Salle's office."

It was obvious that Bill Ford, although he was remotely acquainted with Pierre La Salle, knew little about nothing Interpol's staff. I was just as happy to keep it that way. It was also equally obvious that Bill lying about not being met at the airport.

He looked at his watch.

"Listen. I'm running late and have to run. Call me. I'm here for a few days. We can have a drink."

"I'll do that," I said, giving him a handshake that again made him wince slightly.

Few Europeans and Americans were in evidence at the hotel this holiday week. Neither were any French tourists to be seen. Most of the guests and visitors in the lobby were African, Asian or Latin American. Several families from Arab countries were at the hotel on a shopping spree. Husbands in suits and wives in traditional chadors, their eyes following their small children as they darted in and out of luggage, waited patiently to register. I must have stood out like a sore thumb.

"It is for Bastille Day," the bell hop who had taken up my duffel to the suite noted when he returned for his tip.

"Tourism is at its peak these next few weeks. This is also a busy shopping season."

He pointed to the suitcases around which the children played.

"Do you see all that baggage? Most of it is empty. The Arabs come here to shop and buy the things they cannot find at home. At this time of year they are the mainstay of the luxury trade. They come here with empty suitcases and leave with them full. I usually hate the Arabs, but they spend a lot of money here."

The bellhop stared at the tip I offered him and declined it.

"Oh. Monsieur, you must need the money more than I. You keep it."

And he stalked off.

I sighed, and was about to make a mental comment about the ingratitude of the human race when Simon Perez appeared out of nowhere.

"Do not be too harsh on Jacques," he said. "He is an Interpol agent who is here to watch your back. My boss planted him here."

"I suppose I should be honored at all this protection."

"I also wanted to warn you about your friend, Bill Ford."

"He's not really my friend, you know."

"I understand. But you should understand that he was on my flight and he was met at the airport."

"By whom?"

"By Gaspard Lancet and Otto Katz. I recognized them. Moreover, Interpol has been tracking their movements."

"They make a strange couple, don't you think, Simon?"

"Yes. But Pierre believes they can lead us the Blue Danube."

"Gaspard?"

Simon nodded affirmatively.

"Yes. I must go now. We will be stay in contact."

I went up to my suite where an envelope was on the telephone table next to the bed when I entered. I opened it and found a written message. It was from Henry Adair's office. He was returning from a business trip and agreed to meet with me upon his return. He would leave a message giving the time and place.

Bill Ford, Otto Katz and Gaspard Lancet. What an amazing trio. And good old Henry Adair, finally agreeing to see me after all these years. And Johnny Cork, still alive. Life only two certainties were uncertainty and death.

I walked to the suite's front window which was directly across the street from Maison Dore. The firm occupied the entire four story building. The retail store on the ground floor was lit up and I could see that business was brisk. Somehow, with or without me, and with or without the Blue Danube, the world would go muddling on.

On a lark, I called Marcel Jouvet's office. He was in and personally took my call.

"Monsieur Gordon. This is a welcome surprise! When did you get in?"

"This morning, Minister. I wanted to see La Salle."

"The director is away. May I be of assistance?"

"I wanted to talk about the latest developments concerning the Blue Danube diamond."

"Where are you staying?"

"The Westphalia. Are you free for lunch?"

"Not free, my friend, but available. Are you paying?"

"How about the Celadon here at the hotel?"

"I shall be over in a few minutes."

The Celadon was a quiet, formal restaurant to the right of the lobby and bar that was now filling with guests loaded down with packages from the morning's shopping. The restaurant, when it was not hosting the out-of-town crowd, catered to the same high-powered clientele that routinely made the rounds of the exclusive dining rooms at the Ritz, the Lotti, the Meurice and Intercontinental. The food was gourmet, expensive and spare. I rarely dined there unless it was on the expense account.

Fifteen minutes later, Marcel Jouvet and I were seated at a corner table and chatting over a bottle of red wine and an appetizer tray.

"You look wonderful, Max. You have become as thin as I. We could be brothers, or, father and son."

That last comment rattled me but the deputy minister was unaware of my consternation and went straight to the point.

"What can I do for you, Max?"

"There is a strange situation surrounding the Blue Danube, Minister. It has disappeared from the Dore vault in Morristown. I have reason to believe that it is in Paris."

Jouvet listened attentively, all the while devouring the appetizers set in front of him. The waiter came with the main course and poured more wine into our glasses.

Jouvet noticed I was barely touching my food.

"You're not eating, Max. You must be upset."

I said nothing.

"I understand your concern, Max," Jouvet said. "If the Blue Danube has indeed been stolen, it will become an international incident. Every police agency in the world has already been placed on alert. And I assume that your own career is in trouble. The problem is that I do not consider the diamond as stolen. It has been returned to its rightful place."

"What do you mean, minister?"

"The Blue Danube was returned to France by one of your associates over a year ago and kept at Maison Dore here by Henry Adair who returned it to me a few days ago."

The deputy minister smiled.

"However, the reality for you is that your life is in danger if you remain here. You have many enemies. But the Blue Danube diamond is the property of France. You must leave Paris and renounce your claim to the diamond, my friend."

It made no sense trying to argue with him. I should not have been shocked, but I was numb with shock. All I could do was to be adamant.

"I can't do that, Minister."

"What a pity. In that case, are you familiar with the name Ed Houston?"

"Yes. He is an independent investigator."

"Then you will be glad to know that we have detained him upon his arrival here a few days ago. He is the one who returned the Blue Danube to France."

This was bizarre but I played along.

"Can the diamond be seen?"

Jouvet smiled mysteriously.

"Perhaps. We can return to that subject later."

The fix was in. Jouvet had placed a frame around Ed Houston who Jake or Pierre La Salle must have shipped to France to give me backup. The minister was tipped off, had Houston arrested and charged him with stealing the gem last year, masterfully removing suspicion from poor old Carl Haussmann and Otto Katz, and leaving Johnny Cork alone to face a possible murder charge, if he was still alive. Insofar as Ed Houston was concerned, every murder and mishap connected to the Blue Danube could end up being pinned on him.

I decided to dance around the subject.

"May I see him?"

Jouvet leaned forward.

"I have no objection. Would you care to see him now? I can also show you where the Blue Diamond rests."

I almost choked on my food.

"Yes," I finally said after a long pause.

Jouvet smiled.

"We will see him now. He may tell you things he has chosen not to tell us."

A self satisfied smile crossed his thin lips. He wiped his mouth and chin with a table napkin and rose from the table.

A waiter came over with the bill which I charged to my suite.

"Will there be anything else, sir?"

"No," I replied lamely. "Everything is delicious, as usual."

23

La Petite Conciergerie

I numbly followed the deputy minister into the street. The Rue de la Paix, bright and warm under the mid July sun, swarmed with cabs, scooters, cars and limousines whose horns screamed at the jay walking crowd that mingled with shoppers and vacationers who were now pouring in for the coming Bastille Day celebrations.

Cartier, next to the hotel, was unusually busy and so filled with customers it looked as if it was having a going-out-of-business sale. It was all a blur. My chest tightened, a sensation I had not felt in months. I took a few deep breaths and the pain went away.

A brisk walk took us from the Westphalia to the justice ministry and in a few minutes we were at La Petite Conciergerie. Jouvet pressed a buzzer on the gray stone wall and the door was swung open by a guard on watch inside. He saluted, admitting us into a narrow dimly lit corridor with closed doors on either side. One of the doors was open and we could see in passing that it led to a small airless cell with a tiny barred window facing the inner yard.

"This was once a prison," Jouvet explained. "It was supposed to become a museum but the project was stopped for budget reasons. Today, we use it mainly for storage."

We walked to the end of the corridor and exited into the fortress yard. It was enclosed by walls topped with barbed wire and watch towers. At the far end against the Rue Cambon wall stood a small windowless two-cell guard house, each cell with its own iron door.

It was not the guard house that caught my attention. In the center of the courtyard, silhouetted against the sunny sky, stood a tall guillotine. Several men were fussing about and testing it. A heavy, slanted, razor sharp blade reflected the sun's rays and glared down to grimly remind us of its bloody history. On the ground, in front of it, was an empty wicker basket.

"Is that thing still used?" I asked.

Jouvet rolled his eyes and replied.

"No. France has no death penalty."

The guillotine was being tested. At that moment its blade was released and it came thundering down with a resounding crash. The empty wicker basket jumped and fell over on its side.

"So, what's with the guillotine if there is no death penalty?"

We stopped briefly for Jouvet to explain.

"It is simple, Max. It is a fetish that France indulges me with. There is no death penalty for ordinary capital crimes. However, we do have executions in camera for exceptional crimes against France. Crimes like treason, sabotage and assassination. Crimes threatening the national security. For those crimes we hold a secret trial so as not to arouse the public or excite the media and then we use this guillotine. It is quick and private with no witnesses."

"No last rites for the condemned?"

"Truly unnecessary. However, no one has been guillotined in years. So, we amuse ourselves with mock executions on Bastille Day. Mannequins and an occasional cadaver are used to simulate reality. This year, a cadaver has been chosen and I will release the cord. What more can a lonely old man ask for? It will be my holiday entertainment."

Jouvet winked.

"But there is time, Max. There is still time for that special crime to occur."

His voice trailed off and we walked to the guard house's front cell.

"The American is in here."

A guard at the door released the outside bolt.

"Incidentally, Max. My offer from a few months ago is still good. Come work for us or go home. It could be your smartest move."

My mood hardened.

"Shall we go in?"

Jouvet shrugged his shoulders.

"As you wish," he said.

We entered the cell and a low wattage lamp automatically went on. In the amber light between the gray shadows was a cot chained to the ground next to which was a plain wooden table over a long forgotten dirt covered grate. The room smelled of dried urine and accumulated grime and had probably never been cleaned in its centuries of use. The stench didn't seem to bother Jouvet but it almost made me gag.

A guard who had entered with us whispered something into Jouvet's ear.

The deputy minister shook his head.

"What a pity."

He turned to me and explained.

"What a shame, Max. The guard informs me that the poor man is dead. It was perhaps a heart attack."

A body was lying on the cot. Sure enough, it was that of Ed Houston. Poor Ed. The world would never know the story he had to tell.

"What about the Blue Danube?" I asked.

"It rests on a table in the adjoining cell," replied Jouvet. "You will see it in time but not today. I want you and an independent expert to authenticate the diamond. That will happen very soon, Max. You will do that for France."

Jouvet left the guard house and returned a few minutes later with several stretcher bearing guards and a physician who took the body's pulse.

The doctor shook his head.

"Dead," he confirmed.

Ed Houston's body was whisked away and Marcel Jouvet returned to his unflappable self.

"At last I have a cadaver for my guillotine," said Jouvet, relishing his grisly sense of humor. "Unless you want to grace it."

Jouvet fished in his pocket, produced two tickets and gave them to me.

"I have something for you and a companion. Two tickets for the season's last performance of Carmen tonight before the Garnier opera house closes for the summer. You will enjoy it."

The tickets made me suspicious but I took them anyway.

"Whose were the tickets for originally?" I asked.

"Henry and Eva. They were engaged last week. It was to have been my present to them but they are out of town."

"That's too bad."

"And oh, I am hosting a few friends at a pre-theater reception at the opera. Feel free to join us."

"Sounds interesting. What's the occasion?" I asked.

"Join us and you shall see."

I took the tickets, murmured my thanks and limply followed him out the door. His announcement about Henry and Eva hit me like a sharp slap on the face and I could feel my cheeks smarting. A few minutes later, alone in the bright sunlight of Place Vendome I let the tears well up in my eyes and began to cry.

A story Gaspard Lancet told me when I was a kid on the Paris streets kept spinning in my head. It had to do with an incident that took place during the French Revolution. A method of mass execution was needed to dispose of the thousands of people who were sentenced to death. The usual drawing, quartering and disemboweling process took much too time and was very gruesome and messy. Moreover, since it had been favored by the monarchy it was therefore to be reviled. It was not in keeping with the spirit of the revolution and the purity of the new republic. Hanging was an acceptable alternative but death often took up to a half hour to occur. It was not practical for putting thousands of dissidents to death rapidly.

A certain local doctor Guillotin came to the rescue in the name of speed and efficiency by urging the use of a recently invented industrial cutting machine as a fast and reliable instrument of execution. The device became known as a guillotine. One was erected in what today is Place De La Concorde, a traffic round-about between the Champs Elysees and the Tuileries Gardens.

With the Bastille prison destroyed during the revolution's opening salvoes, condemned prisoners were penned both in La Conciergerie and in La Petite Conciergerie. From there, they were transported in horse drawn cages to the guillotine. No one could escape from the main prison because it was on an island. But one night, a prisoner discovered a sealed opening in the floor of one of the holding pens in the annex. It lead to sewers and tunnels that had once formed part of an older, medieval street system. He pried open the cover and several hundred prisoners escaped, ruining the Paris mob's entertainment for the next day.

I stopped. This lapse into old history was an intellectual exercise leading nowhere. My problem was that I had too much useless knowledge and not enough good judgment to deal with the rigors of survival. I was literally alone in Paris with my back against the wall and I was fretting about an old city and its secrets under my feet. I was an expert on its historical trivia and could recite its many obscure human dramas. I knew all about Paris, its past and its present as I did about many places and many things but I could not find my own direction. I was lost, forever reading people and events the wrong way. Things happened under my nose and I never knew what they were or what they meant until long after they were over.

I was outmaneuvered by all, outsmarted by Jouvet and outfoxed by Henry and Eva and good old Frank. This was like a chess game going bad. I was still king but many of my strong pieces were gone and I was being constantly checked. One more ill conceived move could be my check mate.

The sound of jack hammers cutting through concrete reached my ears along with the whirr of a compressor that drove the drills. Across the square a street maintenance crew was finishing up for the day.

Finally, I decided to go buy a suit, or perhaps a tuxedo, one that could be worn to a final performance at the opera and began walking to the Rue Saint Honore where Nicole's store was located.

I was intercepted along the way by a black Mercedes sedan. Inside the car was Simon Perez, the bellhop, Jacques, from the hotel and Pierre La Salle.

"Get in, Max," La Salle requested. "I hope you do not mind our meeting this way, but I must keep a low profile. And now, tell us how lunch with the deputy minister went."

La Salle and his spies were at work again. They were terrific at finding out things but seemed utterly incompetent in solving crimes. I was beginning to have misgivings about him and his shadowy entourage.

I jumped into the car and related my adventures from the time Pierre and I parted company before noon.

"Ed Houston may be dead," the Interpol director said. "But Paul Lerman is safe. He arrived on a flight after his friend and we were able to hold him for his own protection. He will be very important to us in a few days."

"How does Bill Ford fit with Gaspard Lancet and Otto Katz?" I asked.

"We are not sure, but we will find out. But you will be interested to know that Frank Barton, Eva's brother, is in Paris. The problem for us is that we may have several loose cannon to deal with, each with a personal agenda."

"So, Pierre. Where do we stand?"

"Well, my friend, all the jackals, including ourselves, are closing in for the kill. If you are in Paris, it is because the diamond is here, which Jouvet had admitted. The final act is at hand, Max."

"It is?"

"Oh, yes. It is. And Jouvet is setting it up. We must wait and see."

"Exactly how does Jouvet fit into this picture?"

"We will know soon, Max. Are you going to pay Nicole a visit?"

"I was thinking about it."

"Good. Say hello to Christine if she is there. They should be packing as we speak."

I was puzzled.

"Why is that?"

"I do not want them caught in the middle when push comes to shove."

"I guess you're doing the right thing, Where are you sending them?"

"They are going to spend a few weeks in the French West Indies where I have a small property. They will be safe. It is a precaution, like the one we took with your daughter and her family."

"I am assuming my daughter is safe," I said. "I have only your word for it."

"I am positive, Max. So tell me. What is your schedule this evening?"

"The deputy minister gave me tickets to the opera. I hate opera."

"You trouble, Max, is that deep down you are very superficial. Go to the opera. It will be good for your soul. Perhaps you can convince Nicole to go with you. And oh, Max?"

"Yes?"

"Watch your back. Too many of your American friends are here."

"Maybe they just want to be in Paris for Bastille Day, Pierre."

24

The Suit

There was an emptiness in my stomach when Pierre La Salle left me a few blocks from Nicole's place. I couldn't put a finger on my malaise but it had much to do with my being robbed of all initiative. I was reacting to events and reading from a prepared script with no control over the destiny of others let alone my own.

Nicole Colbert was easy to find. Chez Colbert was one of several specialty boutiques surrounding an off-street courtyard that could be reached through a driveway under a porte-cochere. The courtyard was small, each store limited to two parking spaces, and was a nineteenth century version of a strip mall that catered to the so-called carriage trade prior to the days of the automobile.

I was nervous. It was years since I last saw her and I didn't know what to expect and what to say. I almost hoped Nicole would be out or too busy to see me. I hoped that if she was there, she had grown ugly. I was wrong on all counts.

Through the store front display window adjoining the door I could see two strategically placed racks of men's suits, slacks and jackets flanking a tie and jewelry vitrine and a counter filled with carefully folded shirts.

The store was empty. A car was parked outside, a bright and shiny lemon colored Mercedes roadster convertible.

A bell chimed when I entered.

The door closed softly behind me, leaving me to stand like a fool, trying to figure out what to do next. I went to the racks and pretended to look busy by browsing through the rows of suits.

My hand accidentally touched the sleeve of a brown suit jacket.

"Try the dark blue one, Max. You look terrible in brown!"

I spun around as if shot.

"Nicole!"

Nicole Colbert stood in the back of the store, near a hallway that lead to a small office under a flight of stairs leading upstairs. She stood there, hand on hip, critically watching my every move. She was in a black, knee length dress that hugged her still attractive figure and accentuated her curly blond hair. The signs of youth were still there, albeit enhanced by the latest advances in cosmetology. The face, once smooth and round, was more clearly defined and slightly lined. The eyes, once soft and dreamy, were harder, more penetrating and more calculating. But her voice still had that slightly shrill edge, and she had the same gin and tonic blue eyes.

And she was truly beautiful. Why Henry Adair let her go was beyond me.

"Well. Aren't you going to kiss me hello?"

I moved timidly to the doorway and we exchanged light cheek kisses.

"Are you running for political office, Max? Is that the best you can do?"

We kissed again, and this time it was slightly more passionate before I pulled away.

"Damn it, Nicole, it's been years."

"So? You're still a man, aren't you?"

"I…I didn't know how you were going to receive me after all this time."

Nicole stepped over to the front door and hung up a 'closed' sign.

"Did you expect me to slap you, Max? Or perhaps kick you out? Besides, your associate, Pierre La Salle called to say you would be by."

"Pierre is a good mind reader."

"And so am I, Max. You are in trouble."

"Yes. I'm having problems, How did you hear?"

"My poor old Max. Always scared and evasive. It is my womanly instinct. Besides, word gets around. Pierre has been calling constantly. So has Otto Katz, your old friend. They seem worried about you."

"Why? What did Otto want?"

"I am not sure about him but Pierre has an ulterior motive. He has eyes for my cousin, Christine."

"Did I ever meet her?"

"No. She moved here from Marseilles after you left. She lives here with me. She has gone out to do some last minute shopping. I think Pierre and Christine are in love because they are talking about marriage."

"How did Pierre and Christine meet?"

"Oh. Christine was working for Kumari. It was Otto who introduced her to Rajeesh Kumari who started dating her. She dropped him for Pierre when she stopped working."

She looked me over carefully.

"Your clothes are too large."

"I lost weight," I replied.

"It's about time," she said. "Dieting?"

"Sort of. I had a heart attack."

Nicole was silent for a moment. Her voice softened.

"I was never told."

"It wasn't important. It was a slight tremor, a warning shot."

"Is there anything else I should know that your friend never told me. How is your family?"

"My daughter is married and has two children. My wife died shortly after you and I parted company. I assumed you would have heard."

"I am so sorry, Max. I was never told. You should have called."

"I thought about it but you had just become engaged to Henry and I didn't want to queer the deal between the two of you."

"Why not," Nicole shot back. "You did once before."

"The truth is," I said, "is that I was uncomfortable about bouncing back to you so soon upon my wife's death. I felt I made a decision for us to part and made up my mind to live with it."

Nicole pointed to the back office.

"Do you wish tea or coffee?"

I nodded and followed her to a small kitchen next to the office. She filled a tea kettle with water and placed it on the electric stove.

"It will be ready in a moment."

We sat down around a small table upon which she laid down two cups and saucers, a spoon and a container of instant coffee.

Nicole's voice was insistent.

"Tell me what is going on, Max. Is it about Henry?"

"Sort of. He and I have a score to settle over a diamond."

The calmness of my own words gave me a chill. Even Nicole could not say anything for several moments.

"Pierre believes you and my ex-husband are on a collision course and that Henry may use us as hostages to keep you at bay or as decoys to draw you into the open. Is he correct?"

That was a possibility I never anticipated.

"He's right. It might have been a mistake for me to come here."

Nicole went on.

"No. I am glad you are here. But Pierre wants to play safe. He is sending us to the Caribbean. He wants us to stay there for a while. What do you think?"

"You should go, and the sooner the better."

"That is what we think. We are leaving tomorrow. Is your dispute about the Blue Danube diamond?"

The kettle began whistling. The water had boiled. I parceled out a spoonful of instant coffee in each cup and Nicole poured the water.

"It's supposed to be but I'm not sure."

Nicole took a sip of coffee.

"When you get right down to it, the diamond is the good reason, Nicole," I said. "But basically, the real reason is because I hate the guy. I always hated him. That stone was stolen a year and a half ago and I aim to get back. It will be my trophy."

"So Pierre is right. You are after it. It is a priceless gem, Max. Henry has a right to his share."

"Maybe. But Henry doesn't have it anymore. He turned the diamond over to a guy named Jouvet."

"Marcel Jouvet? The deputy minister?"

"You know him?"

"You and Henry are crazy. But you are on a vendetta. Pierre explained the entire Blue Danube business to me, including some strange plan several of you had to either steal or exchange it for a bunch of African stones. You are all crazy. But for my part, I do not want to see you killed. I lost you once; I do not want to lose you twice. Marcel Jouvet is not only dangerous; he is crazy. He keeps a guillotine as a toy and beheads animals for amusement."

"I know, Nicole, and I'm sorry. I have to see this thing through. I'm dead if cut and run now."

"Max. I have never seen you this way. What has happened to my shiftless wanderer, my party boy?"

I smiled.

"I'm too old to keep gallivanting around the world. I'm tired and my body doesn't have the moves anymore. I want to settle down and live out my years in quiet retirement if I can leave Paris alive. But right now, I have things to do and I don't want to see you hurt. You'll be much safer in the islands. I'll find you there when I'm finished. Pierre says he sent my daughter and her family there."

"Yes. That is what he said. Christine and I will be sharing the same house."

"In that case, you will be easy to find," I said.

Nicole's face lit up in a smile.

"Do you promise?"

"Yes. But let's talk about the store. Who'll care for it while you're gone?"

Nicole shook her head.

"Summer vacations start after Bastille Day. The retail business dies until the end of August. Closing this shop will save me money. Besides, I own the buildings here and receive all the rents. It was part of my divorce settlement. That is not what worries me."

"What then?"

"Rajeesh Kumari and Otto Katz. They frightens us."

"I thought you said Christine worked for Kumari."

"That is part of the problem. Christine will no longer have anything to do with Rajeesh. She does not trust the man. And she trusts Otto even less."

"Why is that?"

"Otto dated Christine for a while until they had a falling out and she started going out with Rajeesh. Christine became pregnant. She was not seeing other men and was convinced that Rajeesh was the father. He refused to marry her and introduced her to Henry. He said Henry would marry her to continue the Adair name. When she threatened to have an abortion, he had her arrested for having stolen diamonds from his business and said he would drop the charges if she married Henry.

"Interpol entered the case when a police investigation discovered that the the diamonds came from a lot originally stolen from a Belgian shipment from Africa. That is how Pierre met Christine. Interpol became involved and Pierre had all the charges against her dropped."

"What happened to Rajeesh?"

"Absolutely nothing, Max. Kumari was too well connected. The case was buried. Christine went for her abortion and has been with Pierre ever since. But in the last year, Otto has been pestering us to report on what Pierre and you are doing under the pretext that it is for your protection. He calls here at least once a week and in the last month he has been calling almost daily. I hope that when we return from the islands, he will leave us alone."

A strained expression filled her face and she stopped to drink her coffee.

"I take it that Christine didn't like Henry," I said, trying to continue the drift of the conversation.

"It was much more than that, Max. The rumor was that Henry had come down with AIDS."

Nicole shuddered, finished the coffee and poured herself another cup. She was on the verge of tears.

"Then, his health seemed to improve. To add insult to injury, he called me a few months ago to have dinner. I refused. He never liked women when he was my husband. I saw no need for another platonic relationship."

I was taken aback.

"Henry didn't like women? But you were dating before we met."

Nicole started crying.

"We never slept together, Max. We never had sex. You were not much of a bargain, but at least we made love. I went for you because you were a man with feelings for women."

"Then why the hell did you marry the guy?"

"I thought he was just waiting to be married. I had one failed marriage as a teenager and I wanted to try again. I wanted you but you had baggage, family and a sick wife and were not ready for commitment. Henry had no baggage."

"So, what broke up the marriage, Nicole?"

"Henry told me he needed a wife to be respectable in society. He agreed to marry me because I was already pregnant with my son. He said he wanted to have a son to make his family complete and to have someone carry forward the Adair name in France. It was the same arrangement Rajeesh offered Christine years earlier on Henry's behalf."

"Damn, Nicole!" I don't understand."

"You are thick, Max."

She started to cry.

"Henry is a homosexual."

Nicole was sobbing and excused herself for the bathroom, leaving me to sit glumly and stare at my hands. She returned a few minutes later and cleared the dishes from the table.

She smiled coyly.

"You are going to ask me about my son sooner or later, Max. I might as well tell you. My son is your son."

I could not suppress a broad grin.

"Is he handsome like me?" I joked.

Nicole laughed.

"You are such an arrogant jerk, Max."

But she couldn't stop beaming.

"Michel is my baby. My big beautiful baby. He turned twenty one a few months ago. And he is so handsome, Max. Like you were once."

I smiled.

"I'll take that as a compliment, Nicole."

"I am sorry, Max. But you know what I mean."

"Not a problem. What's he doing now?"

"He is an aspiring actor. Right now, he is on tour with a theater group. He should be back soon."

The tone of her voice turned serious.

"My son's last name should properly bear your name, Max. It should be Gordon," she concluded with finality.

"Michel Joseph Gordon, or Michael Joseph Gordon in English, in addition to his current name."

"That would work," I said.

"Is that a marriage proposal, I am hearing?"

"How about a date first when I meet up with you in the islands?"

"No more dates. I have had too many dates. Do you love me, Max?"

"I don't think I ever stopped loving you."

"Then I will not stand in your way. I will wait for you if you love me that much."

"All right. This is a marriage proposal. Will you marry me?"

"Yes. I will marry you if that is what you really want. We can be married in the islands," she said dreamily.

Nicole paused and checked the kitchen wall clock.

"I know you are too shy to ask," she said sarcastically, "but since I will not see you again for some time after tonight, I am free for dinner."

I took the hint.

"Will you have dinner with me? I also happen to have opera tickets. It's the season's final performance of Carmen."

"That is what I like about you, Max. You react well to cues thrown in front of your face. You should get a job reading the news on television."

"That's one retirement job I haven't yet considered. Where shall I collect you?"

"Are you still at the Westphalia?"

"Yes."

"I will come over. Final performances at the opera are black tie affairs. Do you have a tuxedo?"

"No."

"I will bring one. Pierre and Christine are going out tonight and we can meet them after the opera. I was going to tag along with them since we are leaving for the islands tomorrow but now I would rather go with you. It may be our last night together for a long time."

I was about to leave when she asked, "Are you not forgetting something?"

Grabbing her in my arms, I kissed her, more passionately this time.

"Come upstairs," she said softly. "I have something for you."

I followed her upstairs and felt good again.

25

The Opera

It may have been that I had a superficial mind set. It was all too simple and too quick. A dead romance rekindled with the spark of few extemporaneous remarks ended with an accepted marriage proposal. I did not even bother to think about the impact that my reunion with Nicole might have on my family and on the rest of my life.

An hour later I was whistling my way back to my hotel. Reality set in when when Gaspard Lancet intercepted me along the way near the Ritz.

"I saw you and your friend with Marcel Jouvet at the ministry," he said.

"You are the eyes and ears of the world," I noted. "Is there anything or any-one you do not know?"

Gaspard grinned broadly.

"I am from the little people, monsieur Max. We function many levels below your class. We are the ones who execute your commands, go through your garbage, wipe your ass and clean up after you. We are the chambermaids, the bell hops, doormen and waiters. I am friends with every concierge in Paris. "For example, from the ticket agent at the Garnier Opera, I learned that the deputy minister, Marcel Jouvet, purchased a box for tonight's performance. Yours is directly across from his."

"Do you also have a guest list?"

"Yes. Henry Adair and his new fiancee, Eva, have been invited but they are away. The proprietors of Kumari and Centurion are in town and have also been invited. Is there anything else you wish to know?"

"Jouvet gave me those two tickets for the box you are talking about."

"Are you going?"

"Yes."

For someone claiming to know everyone and everything, it was odd that he never mentioned that Pierre La Salle would be at the opera with Christine. Maybe he didn't know everything. It was just as well.

"I saw you at the ministry with Jouvet," he continued. "You must realize by now that you are in great danger."

His constant harping was beginning to annoy me.

"That's old news, friend. Is there new information?"

"Yes. I have located the Blue Danube. I have seen it."

"Where?"

"It was in one of the rooms in the guardhouse of La Petite Conciergerie."

"Is it still there?"

"No. It was moved today. I found out that it was taken to Basse Terre in an armored car. I spoke with the driver when he returned."

Gaspard was too obvious, but I played along.

"I'll pay you to help me get my hands on the Blue Danube. Can you lead me to it?"

"Will that make me a millionaire?" Gaspard asked.

"Yes. If I live."

The old man scratched his head.

"I will help you," he said.

I returned to my suite to rest up for the evening where my thoughts turned to Nicole. I had mixed feelings about our reunion. The truth was that I never gave Nicole much thought after we broke up and I began wondering if my sudden marriage proposal was not a knee jerk reaction to my ill fated affair with Eva or a way to get even with Henry or both.

In this rare moment of truth I realized I was a failure in life. Not exactly a failure in life if creature comforts are a measure of success but I was a failure at life. That was different than being a failure at making a living. The basis of my failure was my inability to find one woman, a life's partner, with whom I could be happy for the duration. That was the problem. I had no woman to give me direction. Perhaps Nicole would be the answer for me.

I shaved, cleaned up and then catnapped for a couple of hours until Nicole arrived in a black knee length dress and high heels and her curly blonde hair falling gently around her neck. Draped over an arm was a tuxedo. There was no longer a doubt in my mind. She was the woman for me.

Nicole took several steps back as if admiring her handiwork after I was dressed.

"You look good," she remarked. "A pity you never wore a tuxedo when we were dating."

"If I knew that's how you got your jollies," I quipped, "I'd have worn one to bed every night."

She drew up close to me and flicked a finger under my chin.

"Is that so?"

And so we left arm in arm and made our way through the busy streets until we reached the opera house a few blocks away.

Night comes late to Paris in the summer months and it was light outside as we moved through the crowds congregating in front of the Garnier Opera's imposing facades.

Ordered built by Napoleon III on the style of la Grande Epoch and intended to showcase the Second Empire's splendors, it was garish and massively built as a "temple of the bourgeoisie," according to its critics. Location and design however had a more practical goal. Its many exits were intended to provide escape routes for the emperor in the event of an assassination attempt.

The opera house itself was built in the center of the city's main shopping district and was surrounded by broad streets and boulevards leading away from the main square to ease the emperor's hasty departure. The idea was that by curtain call department stores and boutiques would have closed and the streets and avenues would be clear of traffic. The theory was never tested. Napoleon III was deposed and the opera house was not completed until some years later.

Nicole and I walked up the many steps and into one of the half dozen high arched entry ways lining the front of the building. Inside, where two rows of ticket counters kept the lines moving rapidly, an attendant in full livery edged over to my side.

"You are Max Gordon?"

I nodded affirmatively.

He placed a printed invitation in my hand and announced.

"The deputy minister of justice is hosting a reception and is requesting the pleasure of your company. Will you kindly follow me."

We by-passed the ticket counters and were taken up the ornate ceremonial staircase to the Grand Hall, or Grand Foyer, as it was called, outside the main auditorium. Two reception halls with vaulted ceilings flanked the main Grand Foyer. One was the Salon de la Lune and the other was the Salon du Soleil.

Chandeliers, marble, gold, statuary, burgundy, red and green velvet drapes and furnishing were everywhere.

"Whorehouse chic," Nicole explained as we were deposited in front of the Salon de la Lune, the "Loon Room," as I nicknamed it.

Frankly, I was nervous about taking Nicole to a reception hosted by Jouvet who I figured by now always had a hidden agenda.

Luck was on my side. Wandering outside the salon was Pierre La Salle with a pleasingly plump dark haired woman clinging to his arm. I guessed that the woman was Christine.

Nicole waved and we made out way over to them. I never expected to see Pierre at the opera, and of course seeing him with Christine was even more unexpected.

Christine smiled coyly at me.

"You must be Max Gordon, my cousin's fiancé."

Nicole certainly wasted no time in telling her cousin of our engagement.

Pierre grinned.

"I thought this might be a pleasant way to meet and then to leave gracefully later tonight," he said.

He dropped his voice to a whisper and looked around carefully.

"I also want to make sure the women are seen here tonight by our mutual friends in the event their home is being watched."

"How come?" I asked.

"The girls are not returning home, Max. They are packed and ready to go. From here they go in my car to a private charter that will fly them directly to the islands. You and I can finish our business here without having to worry about their safety."

Pierre had figured out all the angles.

Still, I preferred not to have them at Jouvet's reception.

I explained the situation to Pierre and he agreed.

"I should not be there either, Max. We shall wait in our box. But, remember that we plan to leave at intermission."

Nicole was reluctant at first.

"Will you be long?"

"A few minutes."

She agreed and, watching them go off in the opposite direction, I heaved a giant sigh in relief. They would somehow be ushered into the box; the curtain would rise; and once inside they would stay put until intermission. I could get in but they couldn't get out. That was how the Garnier Opera worked.

They were gone less than a minute when Marcel Jouvet, in a tux and a glass of champagne in hand, appeared at the entrance. He was all smiles and waved me in.

"Max, you're here! Come in. I want you to meet some people."

I followed him into the busy reception hall where waiters in black tails and white kid gloves darted among the guests handing out champagne, wine and finger food. Many of the guests were political hanger-ons but I recognized more than a few of them. In some ways, it was like a homecoming day at school.

Sol Weinberg was in a corner, chomping on a cigar, chatting with Bill Ford who kept throwing me sidelong glances. Close by, engaged in an animated conversation with a tall brunette, was Rajeesh Kumari. And not too far away, talking with some blue suited men from the American embassy, was Stan Short.

Stan Short. I never expected to see him in Paris. He broke away from his entourage and came over.

"Jouvet said you'd be here this evening. I had to be in Paris for business and thought I'd take in some culture," he said.

I smiled understandingly.

"Actually, the deputy minister called this meeting." he blurted out.

"I like meetings," I said, and I followed him into a smaller meeting room nearby where Jouvet, Sol Weinberg, Bill Ford and Rajeesh Kumari were already seated around a small table with two empty chairs, one for Stan and one for me. On the table was a spread of pastries and several bottles of wine.

"No real drinks tonight?" I asked, sitting down next to Bill Ford.

Rajeesh Kumari's best grin covered his face.

"It's good to see you again, Max. No real drinks. This is serious."

I looked around.

"Where is Henry Adair and his fiancée? I thought they might be here."

"They are still away," Jouvet explained.

"How about Henry"s partner, Emile Barco?"

Jouvet took me aside and whispered into my ear.

"Henry sent word that it would be his pleasure to meet you for Sunday lunch at his usual bistro in Basse Terre. Can you make it?"

"Yes. Where in Basse Terre?"

"Basse Terre is a small town. It has only one bistro. You will not miss it."

I nodded. It was a trap and both Henry and Jouvet knew I was mule headed enough to step into it.

"Well? Shall we start the party?"

Jouvet pulled away, coughed and began.

"We. have reached an agreement on the Blue Danube diamond. It has taken a long time, Max, but at last we have a satisfactory understanding."

His gaze fell on Stan Short.

"Would you like to bring Max up to date?"

Stan smiled benignly.

"I'll try." He caught his breath and started. "As you know, Max, Sentinel and the Adair enterprises in the United States, aside from being bankrupt, owe the IRS millions of dollars in back taxes, not to mention interest and penalties."

And he went on to laboriously recite the lengthy history I already knew, leaving me to wonder where this was all going.

"And so we decided to make a deal," Stan concluded at long last.

"What's that?" I asked.

Stan Short had a self satisfied expression on his face.

"It's the best way."

Sol Weinberg jumped into the conversation.

"Yes. My company will pay off Sentinel's and Colin Adair's taxes and debts. In return, we acquire Sentinel."

Rajeesh Kumari added.

"And my firm will be transferred to Maison Dore in exchange for the Blue Danube diamond which will be returned to my family and to the home of its ancestors in India."

"Where does that leave Henry Adair, Eva and the Adair enterprises on both sides of the Atlantic?" I asked.

"It leaves them flush and free of claims," Bill Ford replied. "They get a fresh start."

"An early wedding present, if you will," Jouvet offered.

Deciding impulsively to play out a hunch, I leaned over and bumped into Bill Ford's shoulder. He winced slightly, just as he did at the Westphalia, and shied away.

"Yes," I repeated. "What about Emile Barco? What's in this for him?"

Jouvet explained.

"Henry and his partner Emile Barco acquire Maison Dore and Kumari, and all the Adair businesses in your country. And of course, Henry surrenders the diamond to Rajeesh Kumari, as we said."

"Of course. I suppose this means that Henry has the diamond."

"Yes, he does," Jouvet confirmed. "He will step forward in time."

"But if he has the stone, it means it was stolen to begin with."

"That no longer matters," said Stan Short. "All the suspected thieves are dead. What we're looking at now is a mere shift of physical inventory from one country to another."

"What about France's claim to the Blue Danube?"

"France renounces its claim," declared Jouvet. "It is time for us to move on, Max."

"And. what about Otto Katz? Is he out of a job?"

Sol Weinberg shook his head.

"Not at all. He has a standing offer to work for me once he straightens out his legal problem in New Jersey. And so do you, if you're interested."

"That's very generous, Sol. I'll have to think about it."

I looked at my watch.

"I think the opera is about to start, gentlemen."

Bill Ford looked squarely at me.

"Don't you have any questions, Max?"

I shook my head and rose to my feet.

"No. You've given me more answers than I can use."

"We don't want you to feel you were working for nothing," said Sol. "Part of the deal is for Henry and I to pay you one million dollars for all the great work you did. It's the least we can do."

"And naturally, we expect you to renounce all claims, past, present and future to the Blue Danube," said Jouvet. "I am referring to that pre-nuptial agreement you never signed before marrying your wife. That has left your claim to part of the Blue Danube up in the air. Your agreement to our offer makes any claim null and void, Max. I would imagine that a million dollars is proper compensation?"

I shrugged my shoulders.

"In other words," I said. "You are offering me a million dollars now for me to renounce my claim to one third of the value of a priceless gem. Now, if I don't sign, your deal cannot go forward. It could actually be bottled up in the courts for years."

"That would be very unwise for you not to agree to sign, Max. A million dollars is a lot of money."

"Not enough for me to get out of your way."

"We could possibly increase the amount."

Rising to my feet, I added,

"Possibly. Think about it and get back to me."

Jouvet got up also.

"We will, by midnight, on the eve of Bastille Day."

"Is anyone here going to the opera?"

"No," Jouvet answered. "I thought this would be a nice place to meet. We have a party at the American embassy that Stanley Short is hosting. You can join us after the opera if you wish."

I started to leave, stopping by Rajeesh Kumari who was smiling widely at me through his oversized glasses. He was apparently jubilant over the deal that had been struck.

"Raj," I said. "As they say in India, bonne chance, old buddy!"

26

Ambush

So that was that. Either the diamond was history or I was history. I found the box where Pierre La Salle and the women were sitting and awaiting the start of the opera, and sat down next to them.

Nicole looked annoyed.

"It took all this time for us to be seated," she complained. "And after we were seated, we were not allowed to leave the box."

"That's too bad," I replied. "You didn't miss much."

She read my face too well.

"Is everything all right, Max?"

"Yes. Let's enjoy the performance."

The story line in Carmen was simple and I had seen the opera many times. An attractive local hooker is jailed and a young prison guard is assigned to guard her. He becomes infatuated. She talks him into helping her escape, pledging her love. Once free she spurns him for a more flamboyant and popular bull fighter.

Something told me not to wait for the piece to end. On the balcony across the auditorium from us was the box reserved by Marcel Jouvet. It was empty except for Bill Ford who occupied one seat.

Nudging Pierre and then Nicole, I said in a low voice.

"Don't look. But see that guy in the box on the other side?"

Nicole stared through her opera glasses and passed them to Christine who took a peek while we engaged in 'let's pretend' talk.

Finally, she returned the glasses to Pierre.

"That's Bill Ford," I said.

Pierre took a look.

"I know him," he said.

"He was at Jouvet's little party," I said. "He has a bum shoulder. I'm sure positive he was the guy who took a pop shot at me at Troy's back in Jersey. I think he has a contract on me. That's why he's in Paris."

"I think I am getting the picture, Max. What do you want us to do?" Pierre asked.

"Nothing. Ford is watching me and he's watching you guys. You keep to your schedule. I'm out of here at the start of intermission and going back to the hotel. You stick around a while. Then you guys take off before the end of intermission."

"You will need help," said Pierre.

"And you need to get the girls out of the country."

We sat back and watched the performance which dragged on and on while Bill Ford kept sitting in his box, watching and waiting until the curtain fell to the sound of enthusiastic applause.

I wanted to be obvious. We went through the charade of parting company, making sure that Bill Ford's eyes were fixed on us.

Nicole blew me a kiss.

"Max?"

"Yes?"

"I love you."

Walking brazenly out of the box, I beat the intermission crowd to the street and began walking slowly to the Westphalia.

Twilight had turned into night. The streets off the main avenues away from the plaza around the opera house were deserted, poorly lit and covered by a shiny slick from a light rain. Store fronts were shuttered and black garbage bags were piled on curbs waiting for the dawn pickup.

As expected, Bill Ford was a block away on the Rue de la Paix and on my tail. I made a right turn and ducked into the Rue Daunou, a side street near the Westphalia. I had no gun. I was counting on local knowledge and hoped to lose him in an off street. It was the wrong move.

Had I turned left on Daunou, which intersected the Rue de la Paix, I could have ducked into Harry's New York Bar or into any other of the open late night bistros.

But it was too late to change course. Ford was at the top of the street and I knew it made little sense to try and outrun a bullet. I stopped and turned to face him as he reached me and drew a pistol from inside his jacket.

"You wouldn't shoot a man with no teeth, would you Bill?"

And with those words I pulled the removable bridge from my mouth and threw it in his face and landed a fist in his mouth.

He fell backwards, landed on his back and dropped the pistol. Somehow he recovered and jumped to his feet and tried to recover the weapon which I had in the meantime kicked out of reach.

I was about to run when a black Mercedes sedan with no lights pulled up behind him. I heard a dull pop and Bill Ford collapsed in the gutter. This time he lay still.

Two shapes bounded out of the Mercedes and one of them knelt down next to Bill Ford. It was Simon Perez, La Salle's administrative assistant. The one holding a silencer equipped pistol was George Lerman.

George looked down at Bill's motionless body.

"Dead?"

Simon took Bill's pulse.

"Dying."

Simon looked up at me.

"Just as La Salle thought, Max. You will lead us to our killers."

He took Bill's pulse again and felt his neck.

"He is very doubtful."

I got down on my knees and placed my face close to Bill's.

"Who put you up to this?" I asked.

Bill Ford gasped for breath.

"Eva and her brother, Frank. They pay and I play. I have no choice."

"You were the shooter at Troy's, weren't you? Was that their call?"

He nodded weakly.

"What about Nishkanian and his family?"

Bill Ford shook his head.

"Frank arranged for that."

"What about little Brian Donovan?"

He started coughing.

"Frank and Otto Katz killed him. Otto also did Joe Kelly."

"How did you get sucked in, Bill?"

Grabbing my lapel, he groaned.

"Money, Max. It makes us do strange things."

"What do you have against me?"

"Nothing. Nothing at all. You were assigned to me. Don't ask me why. I don't know. You must have pissed off a lot of people, Max."

A faint smile crossed Bill Ford's lips.

"But Colin also had it in for you for a different reason, Max. He was real pissed when he found out that you were the one who got Eva pregnant."

I grabbed Bill by his shirt.

"What did you say?"

"You heard me, man. Eva's kids are yours. Live with it."

I let him go. I understood perfectly now. The Blue Danube was never the real issue with Colin. Poor bastard. From his point of view I had stolen his self respect and manhood by forcing him to be a surrogate for my progeny whose paternity I had denied and ignored all these years. And of course, his wife Eva didn't care one way or another. She had her motherhood, she had Colin's money and shared his claim to the diamond and she had all the affairs she wanted. What else could a woman desire? Love?

And Henry. He married Nicole and that gave him an instant family and the bourgeois respectability that was so important in conservative French society. It was good for her too. She was a mother with money, position and security that lasted even after she and Henry went their separate ways.

And she bore me a son. That was not too shabby. I made a mental count of my inventory. I had a daughter through Colleen, a son and daughter with Eva and a son with Nicole. I had four grown kids and two grandchildren and I wasn't yet retired. Me. A total fuckup who couldn't make a living and went through life with an open fly. How funny. How sad.

That left Marcel Jouvet. What the hell did he want with me? Was it about the Blue Danube or was it about something else? I could not guess what that something else could be, but the killings that started with the murder of Carl Haussmann were certainly over the Blue Danube and the other stolen gems and not over me.

I was convinced by now that Colin and Henry, and maybe Jouvet and this Emile Barco, were behind them all in their grand get rich-stay rich scheme. Greed had forged improbable unions of convenience and that same greed was just as quickly dismembering them, leaving a lengthening trail of bodies in its wake.

Emile Barco had an entirely different agenda. He needed me dead to protect his interests in Basse Terre, and here, Eva and Frank were his angels of death. That agenda paralleled but had nothing at all to do with the Blue Danube.

"Tell me, Bill. Who killed Doorbell?"

Bill Ford closed his eyes and whispered, "I did."

Simon Perez felt his neck again.

"Dead," he sighed. "It is too bad. Deathbed confessions are garbage."

George Lerman went back to the Mercedes and returned with a body bag draped over his shoulder.

"Don't stand there, guys," he said. "Give me a hand with this thing."

Simon and I helped him stuff Bill's body into the open bag.

They zippered it, tossed it into the car trunk and slammed it shut.

"What are you doing here?" I asked George.

"Don't worry, Max. You won't get my bill. This is on Jake Santana."

"How did you find me?" I asked them.

"We have been circling the neighborhood for hours," Perez replied.

"That's right," George added. "And now we have to pick up La Salle and some women near the opera house."

He shook his head sadly.

"It's going to be a long night. Here, take Bill Ford's piece. You'll need it."

Simon Perez placed another object in my hand.

"What this?"

"It's a sensor, Max. It's on and La Salle wants you to keep it in your pocket so we know where you are. What is your schedule?"

"I'm going to my suite to get some much needed sleep. Tomorrow, I'm relaxing and Sunday I'm going to Basse Terre. According to Jouvet, I'm supposed to meet up with Henry at a local bistro. It's probably a trap but in that trap I'll find Henry and that not too far away I'll find Johnny Cork and the Blue Danube diamond."

Simon concurred.

"It is a trap."

"Right, and I plan to walk into it. And hopefully you guys won't be too far behind."

27

Overtures

I was dog tired and made it up to my suite almost in a trance where I fell on the bed like a dead weight.

It was late Saturday afternoon when I was aroused by the phone ringing. It was La Salle who called to say that everything was fine and that he would be over later for dinner. It was his way of announcing that the women were on their way to the West Indies. I felt much better now. A good hot shower, a shave and some fresh clothes and I was good to go.

I put on my blazer and took the elevator down to the lobby to ponder my next move. Standing with my hands in my pockets next to the elevator, I found myself faced with a difficult decision. Should I go for a walk, have dinner now or wait for Pierre? The decision was made for me.

I was about to go out when, standing in my way in spiked heels and a gray afternoon suit ensemble, blond hair curled over her head, was Eva Adair.

In a way, I wasn't shocked. She was bound to surface sooner or later. But her presence now left me cold.

"It's good to see you, Eve. What brings you to Paris besides Henry?"

"You, Max."

"Me?"

"Can we talk, perhaps at the bar?"

"I would, Eva. But I'm tired. I'm not in a mood for a drink."

"Can we talk in your suite, then?" She asked coyly.

Refusing her was pointless. I was too tired to resist her overtures.

"Let's go," I said.

The elevator was small and an Arab family, back from shopping with bags and boxes, filled the cavity. We wriggled into the narrow space inside the elevator where Eva's body rubbed against mine, leaving me to wrestle with mental images of what would happen next.

Was this to be a set up? A sexual encounter? A tearful confession? A joyous reconciliation after convincing me that she had done nothing wrong and that I had misinterpreted her motives and misjudged her as a human being?

The elevator moved slowly, agonizingly, groaning under the weight of the Arabs who could have used generous doses of deodorant, and deposited us mercifully after what seemed an eternity in front of my suite.

The suite was actually a small apartment. The hallway door opened into a vestibule lit by a chandelier and furnished with a table and two arm chairs. It also featured a small closet where guests could hang their up outer garments without cluttering the suite.

A door to the left lead to a service corridor that circled an inner courtyard where room and linen service could be discreetly provided without using the guest hallways. Another door on the right lead to the living-bedroom suite that overlooked the Rue de la Paix through a pair of French doors that opened to a balcony. Behind the living room was a two-room bathroom-vanity combination with a window whose glass was opaqued to block the view of the unsightly inner courtyard.

The suite was done in French empire style, the walls decorated with period art. The bed, a huge king sized affair, was flanked by an ornate wall mirror. Above an elegant sideboard facing the bed was another gilt framed mirror that reflected an unopened bottle of scotch, two glasses and a bucket of ice, left earlier by the hotel.

Eva went over to the sideboard, threw some ice cubes from the bucket into the glasses, opened the scotch and poured it over the ice. She gave me one glass and took another and loosened her hair, allowing it to fall smoothly around her shoulders.

"To us," she toasted.

"To you," I said, taking the glass and taking the smallest sip.

So here we were together, one more time, Eva Barton, the former grieving widow of Colin Adair and now hooked up with is brother, Henry. Good old Eva Barton, the former Eva Barco and the niece of Emile Barco, formerly of Alsace, a strange Franco-German whose brother married my mother, if Pierre was right. What a strange world and what a weird turn of events. Eva, Frank and I were actually kin, kissing cousins, I think it was called.

I had to assume that she knew what I knew and that she too owned a piece of not only the Blue Danube but a piece of the Basse Terre property as well.

I had to laugh. George Lerman was right; we were all predatory animals in the jungle of life.

She was about to remove her suit jacket and skirt but I shook my finger.

"I don't think so, Evie. I'm not interested."

She drew back with a pained expression on her face.

"Why, are you having your period?"

"That's a bad joke, Eva."

"Then what is it? You never turned down a little pussy before."

I slapped her across the face and she fell on the bed, crying.

"I could have you killed for this."

I laughed hoarsely.

"Then why don't you?"

She regained her composure.

"I like you and I think we can still make a great team."

She climbed off the bed and straightened out her clothes.

"Is that why you left Fort Lauderdale without saying anything?"

"There was no other way. I wanted to see John Cork. He's sick."

Eva was a convincing liar.

"So, that's it," I said. "You flew to Paris to see Johnny Cork."

"And to marry Henry."

"Why?"

"The Blue Danube. I have to protect my interest now that Colin is gone."

"I would imagine your share would have been protected as his widow."

"Right. Except that Henry has the diamond. I figured that out a long time ago, Max. As his wife, I get everything when he dies. It's double insurance."

"How did you figure it out, Eva?"

"I found out from Colin's guys. They couldn't keep their mouths shut."

"So why come here for a screwing?"

"We have something special, Max."

"Oh yeah? What?"

"My kids are your children, Max. You sure liked to fuck me back in the old days, Max, didn't you? Well, that's what you get. You get kids."

"What the hell else do you want me to do with women, Eva? Throw rocks at them? And your kids. So what if they're mine as well. Should I adopt them now? They're adults and rich in their own right."

"I thought you loved me."

"Love? You come barging into my life with a phony bill of goods and you hang me out to dry for Henry and now you say that I'm the father of your children and that I should take you seriously? Be real, Eva!"

"I love you, Max. But I have to protect myself before protecting you."

"That's crap. You're not here to protect me. I don't need protection."

"I'm here because I care about us and our children."

I shook my head.

"You're not stupid and I'm not crazy. You didn't come up here to get laid because you're horny or in love or concerned for two grown children. You're too smart for that. What are you here for?"

Eva drew back.

"You're right, Max. I thought this would be a nice way of asking you to get off our backs. You'll be killed if you don't back off and I don't want to see that happen. Henry sent me with some papers for you to sign."

"What papers?"

"They're like the prenuptial agreement you never signed with Colleen. It's about signing away your right to the Blue Danube and to all other assets and properties owned by Colin and Henry Adair and Emile Barco."

Here was the clincher at last. I was to lose my claim to the diamond and to the Basse Terre land in exchange for the right to live, maybe.

"Who is Emile Barco, Eve?"

She ignored my question and laid a stack of official looking papers on the bed..

"Sign the documents," Eva insisted.

"If I didn't sign then and I didn't sign yesterday, why should I sign today?"

"For Nicole's sake."

"So that's the ticket. You bastards are going to kill her."

"You must renounce your claim."

"Too many people died because of that damn stone, Eva. All that killing must stop."

"Then you'll sign?"

"Never! As for Nicole, good luck finding her!"

Eva was not to be deterred and tried another ploy.

"Be practical, Max. We can have a good thing together. Henry is staying in France and I'm going to go back to Florida to run the stateside businesses. Henry doesn't care what goes on there. You and I can do our own thing. You can be my manager. What the hell is Nicole to you?"

I smiled.

"Well, maybe not everything."

"You're a good man, Max. You know how to take care of things, and you know how to take care of women. I like that."

"Maybe we do have a future after all."

I was lying. Walking over to the French doors facing the balcony, I swung them open, looked out upon the bustling late afternoon crowd below and wondered if Eva had learned that Bill Ford was dead and that I had his gun. I was sure she suspected that if a confrontation had occurred, it did not go according to plan. After all, I was alive and here. How stupid of me. Of course. Eva was here to get me killed!

I was about to turn away when I thought I detected a movement behind one of Louis Dore's apartment windows facing my suite.

"How did you know I was going to be at the hotel?" I asked.

"Henry told me."

I left the window and walked over to the sideboard.

"Let me ask you this, Eva. Who bankrolled Mel Solomon when he started Sentinel?"

Eva sounded annoyed.

"How should I know? It was some Frenchman. I have no idea. The only thing I heard is that Mel received cash and that in return he gave up forty percent of his equity in Sentinel. The Frenchman was in on all of Colin's and Nishkanian's investments. What does that have to do with anything?"

"If cash was moved from France to the States, then payments were also in cash and moved from the States to France. Who was the bagman? You?"

Eva screamed.

"You blind jerk! We were all bagmen. Johnny Cork and all of us."

"Well, if Cork is in trouble, who's gunning for him?"

"No one. John is sick."

"If he's sick, he must be somewhere."

"I heard he's in a nursing home south of here in Basse Terre."

"That's hunt country. How the hell did he get there?"

"I don't know. The home is on an estate that belongs to one of Henry's French friends."

Eva calmed down and that loving smile returned.

"I'd rather talk about our partnership."

"I have to find the damn stone first. It was last at the justice ministry."

She shook her head.

"No. It's on Emile Barco's estate in Basse Terre. That's the Frenchman I was talking about."

The trap had been set and Eva was part of the bait. I was to be killed here or in Basse Terre.

"Are you sure?"

"Yes. Henry took me there. I saw it with my own eyes."

"Will you go with me?"

Eva was purring like a kitten by now.

"Let's kiss on it?"

"We could. But I'm curious about Emile Barco, Eva. Why didn't you ever tell me he was your uncle?"

I thought she would blow her stack but she managed to keep her cool.

"I didn't know if you would love me as much if you knew I was German," she replied calmly.

She came up close and placed her arms around my neck and pushed her lips into mine. We were by the front window where we stood embracing minutes before she rested her head on my shoulder.

The angle at which we stood allowed me to see her reflection in the mirror next to the bed. The softness was gone, replaced by a look of sheer disgust and contempt only poorly masked by a steely smile and gritted teeth as she maneuvered me with my back to the window. Damn broad! She had been out to get me from the beginning. And it was never over the Blue Danube; it was over the Basse Terre estate.

"So, tell me Eve," I asked. "Whatever did you do with my school ring? Did you drop it in Patrick's house when you murdered him and his wife?"

"You fucking idiot," she screamed. Veins began swelling in her neck and a venomous expression covered her face.

That was not what distracted me. It was a roving red dot on the wall. I held Eva tightly and swung her around to the almost inaudible sounds of two toy balloons bursting in the distance. Letting go, I dove to the floor.

Eva swayed slightly and an almost loving smile crossed her lips when she fell over me. She lay still and stared at me, her arms around my shoulders, as if waiting for a round of sex. Then slowly her arms relaxed. A whimper left her open lips and she closed her eyes. It was over.

I got up and peeked out. Frank Barton, in a light blue blazer was dodging the late afternoon crowds and the chaotic traffic in a fast dash across the street and on his way, most likely to check his marksmanship and to finish the job if necessary.

What a charmed life I had. Two bullets for me and Eva caught them both. How generous. If I somehow survived this, I swore to devote the rest of my life to charity work.

Anyway, Eva was dead and although I could not shed a tear, I had to make some cool moves if I was to see the next day. No wonder she told me all she did. She had known all along I was not to leave the hotel alive. What I didn't understand was why she would tell me John Cork's whereabouts if I was supposed to be killed. Could there have been an alternate plan to get me to Basse Terre if the first one failed?

I blamed Henry for many things, but somehow I never gave him credit for having a satanic mind combined with such Machiavellian skills. It could be that I underestimated him or that perhaps his own chain was being pulled and rattled by either Emile Barco or Marcel Jouvet.

Pierre La Salle would be arriving for our dinner engagement in one or two hours but Frank would be here within minutes. I figured he would take the stairs and be winded and off his guard, expecting Eva and not me to open the door. I was right. There were four knocks, two long and two short. I decided to act first and ask questions later.

Swinging open the door, I pulled Eva's brother in and slammed his head against the vestibule wall. The door closed and I kept slamming his head into the wall until he fell in a heap. It made no sense stopping. Frank was younger and more powerful. If he got up, he could easily kill me. He had to go. A kick to the head knocked him out. I jumped on his back, grabbed his head and wrenched it around like a chicken until his neck cracked.

VII

END GAME

28

Escape

I had problems. Here I was with two bodies in my suite and nowhere to go until tomorrow. Instinct suggested that creating distance between myself and the bodies was a great idea. The trick however was to leave undetected.

La Salle would of course wait in the lobby, but the chambermaid who did the evening's turndown service was due soon. She would find the mess and she scream and carry on and then call hotel security who would summon the police, leaving Pierre with a mess to explain. I had to leave with the bodies.

That Frank shot and killed Eva was not an issue. He had the incriminating gun and the bullets from that gun were in her body. No great murder mystery to solve. But what about Frank? Did he break his own neck by ramming his head against the wall? The police was bound to want to ask me about that and other things.

I changed into more comfortable street clothes, picked up my duffel, turned off all the lights and went to the bathroom window. I opened it and looked out over the tiny balcony into the darkened atrium. A fire escape ladder lead to the balconies below and eventually to the courtyard on the ground floor. It was late afternoon and the bathrooms on the other floors whose windows faced the courtyard were unlit. Hotel guests occupying suites like mine were either still out or napping and not yet getting ready for dinner.

Below in the half light I could see that the courtyard ground was littered with garbage bags awaiting pick up. This was the start of the long holiday weekend and trash from housecleaning and the restaurant could be expected to accumulate for days since there would be no garbage collection until after the Bastille Day festivities. The Celadon was just now setting up for dinner and therefore its trash would not be emptied through the courtyard fire door until late evening. And housekeeping would not be dumping guest room trash until the following morning. This was my only opportunity.

I had already determined that leaving the bodies in the suite to be found by housekeeping's turn down service was not an option. That meant having the police on my tail within hours, at least by the next morning. Removing them might give me a few days' time to finish my business and perhaps catch up with Nicole and my daughter in the Caribbean, assuming that Pierre was to somehow come through for me.

The window sill was low to the floor, making it easy to edge Frank's body on to the narrow balcony and topple it over the railing. It landed on top of the trash with a soft thud. Eva's corpse was lighter and it fell on top of Frank's with a squishy sound. This was truly good riddance to bad rubbish. I threw her handbag down after her.

The suite showed no signs of violence. The rounds that struck Eva left no blood. Frank died of a broken neck that could be blamed on his fall. The gun used to kill Eva was in Bobby's possession and the Paris police would have figure that one out when they found the bodies, and that was not going to be anytime soon.

The two half empty scotch glasses were still on the dresser. I emptied them, wiped them clean and put them back in place on the dresser. But I took the bottle of scotch. The bed did not concern me. It was barely touched, and with the hotel's turndown service, the bed linens would be changed anyway.

The next step was for me to get down to the courtyard and sneak out of the hotel. Doors opening into the street would be locked to prevent burglars from breaking in, making a gracefully quiet exit impossible. Here, I counted on my childhood recollections and hoped they would not fail me.

Old sewers ran under the hotel and I vaguely remembered where they were. I knew that somewhere under the trash was a covered manhole that accessed the underground conduits. What worked once for me once could work again. The goal was to find the manhole, pry loose its cover and lower the bodies into the sewers where they might not be found for many days.

I made doubly sure that Bill Ford's gun was in my duffel, threw the scotch in and checked to see that my flash light worked. I was about to leave when Henry came to mind. He had to be around. I stopped in my tracks and went back to the front window to have a look. The offices were empty, but out in the street and standing against the building's courtyard wall was someone in a gray suit wearing a hat drawn down to hide the face.

I laughed. It was Henry, and if he was here, it meant that his silent partner, Emile Barco, was not far away. Having failed in Paris, they were bound to re-surface in Basse Terre. That had to be where this adventure was going to end.

It was time to go. I left through the bathroom window, closing it carefully behind me, and made my way down the fire escape ladders to the courtyard. An unlocked utility closet nearby yielded a crowbar. I grabbed it and moved quickly to the spot where the two bodies lay sprawled over a heap of black trash bags. I could detect no odor of death. However, a scent, however slight, must have attracted rats because suddenly they appeared, crawling about and sniffing at the bodies in the semi-darkness.

Rats meant they had to have emerged from a hole in the wall or ground. I rummaged through the trash, trying to feel the ground with my feet, until I saw one of the rats duck between two bags. I went to the spot and feverishly scratched the dirt covered ground until I found a sewer lid, old and rusted but moveable.

There was a noise on one of the upper floors and a window opened. I lay still with the bodies and the trash, trying not to breathe. Whoever it was that opened the window closed it and I was again surrounded by a suffocating silence and smell. I waited a few moments and then pried open the lid with the crowbar.

The hole was pitch black but from somewhere down below I could hear the trickling of water. A sewer was down there.

I pulled Frank's corpse to the hole and pushed it in, straining to hear how and where it landed. There was a thump and a splash less than a second later. That was comforting. I calculated the landing to be less than ten feet down.

Next, I dragged Eva's lifeless body to the hole and snaked her face down into the hole, giving her a slap on the ass for good measure as gravity pulled her down on top of her brother. He might have liked that!

My hands felt around the inside of the opening until they came across what seemed to be the rusted rungs of a ladder. I rearranged several garbage bags so that they would collapse over the manhole cover when I pulled it over me and started my descent. Throwing the duffel, Eva's handbag and crowbar into the sewer ahead of me, I lowered myself into the hole and, bracing myself on the ladder, I climbed down carefully rung by rung. I reached bottom where I promptly stumbled over the bodies and fell in the shallow stream next to them.

I cursed. I had stolen Frank's lighter back up in the hotel room and hoped it wasn't wet.

It wasn't and it worked. I grabbed my duffel and made sure my flashlight worked. It too was fine, and so was the bottle of scotch and Bill Ford's gun; it was loaded from last night. I also found matches.

The sewer was part of an old drainage system. The water running along its gutter was fresh and flowed gently downstream from the Opera Garnier to Place Vendome and the Seine about a mile further away.

The tunnel was six feet high, enough for me to stand almost upright so long as I sloshed about in the water flowing in its center bilge. Close by on my right was the entry to a dry narrow upward sloping passage that funneled air to the main sewer. I recalled that it eventually led to a fork, one prong that lead to the Gare St. Lazard, one of Paris's main train station, and the other leading to the Gare du Nord from which ran the train that was to eventually transport my father to his destiny. The small corridor was an ideal site for a fire whose smoke would be sucked and drawn up by the draft through the train stations' venting systems.

No logic existed for what I did next. It was just something I had to do, like erasing a bad memory. I dragged the bodies into the passage, poured scotch over them, and lit a match. The mixture of alcohol, fire and air produced a blaze that engulfed the bodies in a fiery ball and illuminated the main tunnel with an incendiary glow.

I threw the empty bottle back into the duffel and headed downstream, using the flickering light from the fire to guide me.

A steady draft kept the fire alive and drew the smoke away from me. By the time I reached a point which I thought was under Vendome only embers must have remained. The weak light behind me went out and plunged the tunnel once again into total darkness.

The flashlight helped and I found a junction from which tunnels and small passageways spun off in every direction like the arms of an octopus. It didn't take me long to find my bearings. Every step I took brought me back to the war years when these sewers were my haunting grounds. I reached the tunnel under Rue Saint Honore within minutes and by then I had regained my total recall of the old city's subterranean system. A right turn to a flight of stone steps down to a deeper sewer brought me under the complex where Nicole's house stood. There, I found a small cellar like room with a trapdoor in the ceiling. I hoped it belonged to her house and would open into her basement. I tried the door and was right on both counts.

I lifted myself up into the basement and made my way upstairs. Night had set in and the place was empty and strangely quiet. I kept the light off, took off my soiled clothes, bathed and went to sleep.

Waking up at dawn, I took another shower, found a casual sports outfit and a pair of shoes I could live with from her retail inventory, something to eat in the kitchen and looked outside her window.

Her car, the yellow Mercedes roadster, was still parked outside. I found the car keys in a drawer and put them in my pocket, not yet clear in my mind what my next move was going to be.

And then suddenly on a whim I decided to return to the tunnels to see if I could thread my way to the Left Bank. If successful, I could take a livery or a cab to Basse Terre from there or return to Nicole's house and take her car for a nice drive to the hunt country.

It occurred to me that the house might be watched, but that it was Nicole and her cousin who were being shadowed and not me. Henry must have concluded by now that Eva and Frank had ended up second best at the hotel. He would now be waiting for me in Basse Terre. I smiled inwardly. I was not checkmated yet and could still make a few moves.

And so I returned to the tunnels and to revisit my childhood and my old neighborhood, so to speak, duffel in hand and new clothes on my back. The sewer network and its adjacent streets buried in the bowels of the city was the way to move about undetected. The air was cool and damp and very strangely invigorating. The life of a rat might not have been so bad after all.

I backtracked to Vendome where I turned left into a tunnel that bore south to the Seine. This time I knew how to stay dry and stay clear of the gutters that carried running water.

Water began gushing and the walls glistened with moisture, signaling that the river bank was nearby. The tunnel narrowed and went into a downgrade that brought me a good twenty feet under the river bed. The ordeal was like climbing down a black hole on one side and emerging up and out of it on the other side, but it was over in less than an hour.

A spiraled flight of stone steps took me to a crypt-like cavern into which broad beams of light came through the bars of an unlocked iron gate. Two homeless men, circled by empty wine bottles and belongings crammed into bags, dozed on makeshift mattresses of rags and old newspapers. Outside was the Left Bank's river walk where I could see the 'bateaux mouches,' the long, slender 'fly boats' that ferried tourists up and down the Seine, heading out on their half-day trips.

The homeless were ever present along the Seine. I read once that Paris had more than twenty thousand people, men, women and entire families, mostly gypsies, who lived along the river. They preferred the river bank over more secure underground shelters where they would have to compete against the city's permanent residents, the rats and the roaches. It made me shudder but there were probably more rats and roaches crawling under Paris than in any other city in the world.

The brown rat was the main resident. There were millions in the depths of the city and they ate anything in sight. Workers who went underground to maintain the trains and water treatment plants buried deep in the city's belly had to get protective shots. Cave-dwelling freshwater crayfish and scorpions also thrived in the sewers. They had a nasty sting. Then there were hairy spiders who lived in crevices in the walls and the swarms of cockroaches, water bugs, huge biting beetles and other denizens of the darkness that made one pause when contemplating an underground life.

I stepped around the sleeping bums and lost myself among the morning strollers and joggers on the river walk who must have thought I was just another homeless person. Taking a flight of steps to the street over the river walk, I found a bench and sat down to relax in the sun.

It was time to go. After about an hour I hailed a cab to Nicole's house. Her car was still in the same place.

I opened it with the key I found in her quarters, threw in my duffel, opened the convertible top and made myself at home in the driver's seat. It was the ideal car for a Sunday drive to the hunt country under the bright summer sun. In my exuberance, I almost ran over an old man whose back was turned as I was pulling out into the street. Recognizing the face, I stepped on the brakes, rolled down my window and yelled, "Gaspard! What are you doing here?"

This was too much of a coincidence. Gaspard Lancet was the last person I unexpected to see.

29

Basse Terre

"What gives, Gaspard?"

Gaspard turned and grinned impishly.

"Would you kill an old man who has outlived his usefulness?"

He had become as wary of me as I was suspicious of him. I looked at him through the car window and returned his smile.

"Not before you tell me how you knew where I was," I said.

"Knew where you are?"

He threw me a toothy grin.

"I know nothing. I live a block from here." He paused to eye the car before asking, "Isn't this Nicole's Mercedes?"

"Yes," I replied lightly. "The girls are still sleeping and I'm going for a drive in the country. Care to come along?"

Gaspard jumped into the car's passenger side.

"Where to, monsieur Max?"

"South. Henry is supposedly waiting for me at a bistro in Basse Terre near the Sologne forest. You can show me the way."

Thought of the Sologne brought back memories. It must also have stirred recollections inside Gaspard's mind because we were once there together many years ago.

Eavesdropping when I was very young was my nasty habit. That was what I was doing one night in Paris when Gaspard and few resistance fighters were discussing going to the Sologne woods to meet a detail of resistance fighters who were assembling to ambush a German patrol. The prospect of being part of this adventure was exciting and I begged Gaspard to take me along.

In desperation he agreed and I followed him. In his unit was my uncle, the one with whom I lived for a while in the States, and my grandfather. It was a bad move. The ambush failed; my grandfather was killed and the Germans captured Gaspard. Only my uncle escaped.

I was hiding in the brush when a soldier found me. He looked ten feet tall. He might have been shorter but to someone young and small he was a giant. He had a big long rifle and when he came over he prodded me away with his gun butt. I'll never forget his words.

"Allez! Je ne tue pas les petits lapins!" Scram! I don't kill baby rabbits!

I ran off to safer ground where I watched the Germans haul Gaspard away and then high tailed out of there without once looking back.

I was told later that Gaspard spent the rest of the war in work camps for his pain. I often wondered about that German soldier, whether he ever thought of the life he never took.

We headed south on a beautiful scenic drive that wound gracefully around the golden farms, vineyards and old castles on the edge of the Loire Valley. Unfortunately, what began as a sunny day turned cloudy, and when we reached the marshy lowlands bordering the Sologne forest, the sky was very gray and rain threatened. We stopped to raise the car's convertible top.

For centuries, the Sologne was a flat, dismal impoverished backwater until a government water and land management program drained the swamps and restored the ancient pine forests in the late nineteenth century. To transform the region's character from poor to rich, the government stocked the forests with live game for France's wealthy hunting fraternity in the hope that the French passion for the taste of venison and boar would bring the well heeled hunters from Paris to line the pockets of the merchants of Basse Terre.

The strategy worked. A wildlife sanctuary most of the year, the rich came in the Fall and turned the land around Basse Terre into a shooting gallery. In a follow up gentrification program, the French government literally gave land away to people who agreed to build up-scale homes in adjoining areas. If the rumors that La Salle talked about were true, namely, that substantial natural gas reserves lay underground, the poorest pauper with a land stake could end up very rich.

I could understand owning land but big game hunting was never my thing. I was no vegetarian and ate anything that didn't bite back and drank anything I didn't drown in. But I believed in a level playing field. Hunting animals put them at an unfair advantage. The bottom line was that I never much cared for recreational killing.

Gaspard's directions were right on the mark and we reached Basse Terre in the early afternoon. I waited until we were in town before pocketing Bill Ford's weapon.

"Where do I find Henry?" I asked innocently.

"Jouvet says there is but one bistro. Over there."

Gaspard pointed to a low hung building on the corner.

I winked at him.

"You and the deputy minister must be on friendly terms."

Gaspard did not reply.

"How about Otto Katz? You and he are old friends also?

"I do not understand."

"I think I do. But, I've always been curious about one thing, Gaspard. That ambush we got caught in many, many years ago."

Gaspard's voice became guarded.

"Yes?"

"How come everyone, including my grandfather, was killed? My uncle got away and so did I. How come you were the only one who was captured and allowed to live?"

"It was chance," he replied. "Chance is incomprehensible."

"No. It was not chance," I continued. "You know Otto from the war. Otto was the German officer on patrol and you were a pro-German mole inside the French resistance forces. You were a collaborator and that's how that ambush occurred, isn't it? You set up my uncle and grandfather to be killed. And Otto, he's a few years younger than you. I think he's about the same age as Jouvet, isn't that right? Answer me this, Gaspard. What made you a traitor to France?"

"But Otto saved your life," Gaspard said.

"That means he had the pang of conscience you never had," I noted.

Again, Gaspard had no answer.

I pulled the car up against the curb and turned off the engine.

"This is the end of the line for us, old friend," I said.

"What do you mean, monsieur Max?"

Gaspard turned his face away from me and began to perspire.

"Don't bother saying anything, old friend. I just want you to get out of the car and walk away. I don't want to ever see you again."

Gaspard was struggling for words but nothing came out. Finally, he shook his head, adjusted the beret on his head and left.

It was as Jouvet said. Basse Terre had only one bistro and it was open. A waiter in a white jacket and apron was standing by a utensil cabinet near the front door. Its drawer was open and he was humming a tune and arranging silverware in their proper compartments.

I left the car and approached the waiter. He looked up and for a moment he reminded me of someone else, the waiter at Troy's in Basking Ridge, on the edge of the Great Swamp in New Jersey.

I looked closer. It was in fact the same waiter, but he pretended not to have recognized me.

"I am looking for the estate of Emile Barco," I said.

"Emile Barco?" He replied. "His villa is off the main road south of here."

"Who lives there?"

"A very sick American. In a cottage on the property."

"Let me ask you this," I asked. "How often does Emil Barco visit?"

"Mostly on weekends. But he rarely comes here. However, an associate of his, a monsieur Adair, is dining in our private room in back and waiting for a monsieur Gordon."

"I am Max Gordon."

"Then monsieur Adair is expecting you."

And he pointed to the door.

"He is there."

I slipped the waiter a tip and followed him inside. The bistro's main dining room was long and narrow. A bar ran its entire length on one side and booths with red and white checkered table cloths were lined up against the opposite wall. The place was empty save for the waiter.

The waiter motioned to an open door at the far end.

"Monsieur Adair is inside."

"You can wait outside," I told the waiter. "I should be out soon."

The waiter smiled and went away.

I walked in. Seated facing me at a table was Henry Adair, looking tanned and rested. In his Sunday best, well tanned and rested, he was busily enjoying lunch with a bottle of wine.

He raised his head slightly until his eyes met mine but he went on eating, a a little bit faster and more deliberately, cutting a piece of meat on his plate with a knife in his right hand, putting it down and switching it for a fork to pick up the cut slices, again using his right hand.

Finally, after leaving me standing there with my hands in my pockets for what seemed an eternity he spoke.

"Hello, Max. It's been a long time."

"Hello, Colin," I said in a matter-of-fact way, my hands still in my pockets. He looked up, a question mark on his face.

"How do you know I'm Colin," he said.

"The French eat differently. They don't switch the fork from left to right as we do. That's how I know you're not Henry. Your brother tried to be French, but you're an American."

Colin put down his knife and fork in disgust.

"I could never get this stuff straight. Care to join me for lunch?"

"No thanks. I'll stand. Tell me something. How come you covered for Eva all these years after she killed your aunt and uncle?"

Colin leaned back and stared into space.

"Blackmail," he replied. "I couldn't make it with her and she threatened to expose me."

His head and shoulders drooped and his eyes focused on the dinner plate on the table. He started playing with his cutlery.

"I know how I had kids. You were the father and Eva never let me forget it. She rubbed it in every chance she got."

I walked over to the window and watched a two birds chase each other on a tree limb.

"Well," I said. "Eva is dead."

"I figured. You killed her?"

I shook my head.

"No. Frank did by mistake, but I killed him."

Colin smiled, and all of a sudden I could no longer fault him for anything. I was not angry any more.

"That's good," he noted. "I never liked the guy."

"I thought he worked for you."

"I'm not smart enough. I'm a low class con artist, thief and scoundrel, Max, just like you. Henry was the brains, he and this creep, Barco. They called the shots through Eva and her brother. I had all the stateside contacts and went along for the ride. It was great until Henry got AIDS. He was dying, and to keep our businesses afloat, we decided that I would take on his identity and move the Blue Danube to France. It seemed like a good idea at the time."

"It was Henry who got blown up on your yacht?"

Colin smiled.

"Let's call it assisted suicide, Max. That's the way he wanted it. I loved my brother. He was wasting away. It had to be that way. I had him flown to the

Biminis in a private jet. By then he was even too weak to walk. I carried and put him on the boat which was pre-rigged with explosives and set the auto pilot to steer the vessel out to sea where it was blown up by remote control."

Colin took a deep breath before continuing.

"All I ever wanted to do was to protect my business and the guys who worked for me. I didn't understand exactly how dirty this business was until Henry was dying. By then I was caught in this conflict diamond business and a bunch of cover ups that brought on a hysteria of killings spurred on by everyone trying to get their hands on the Blue Danube. By the time you entered the picture, it was too late to bail out. We were in too deep. Even Henry wasn't calling the shots anymore. It was Barco and some buddy of his at the justice ministry, a guy named Jouvet."

"How about this Harry Silver? How did the doctor end up being a killer?"

"He went to medical school in Europe and met my brother and Emile Barco who loaned him money to start a medical practice. The problem is that we all owed something to this Barco guy and soon he owned everyone. Things got worse when creditors and backers who were guaranteed payment with a share of the Blue Danube started looking for payment."

"Was that like 'owning a piece of the Rock,' Colin?"

He smirked.

"Something like that. But Henry wasn't going to let that happen and I went along with him. There was no choice. Once Carl Haussmann, Otto Katz and Mel Solomon lifted the diamond, we had to start getting rid of witnesses."

"Was Eva involved?"

"Yes, but she had her own agenda. She wanted the diamond for herself and would have been in seventh heaven if we all died. Henry and I never realized it until it was too late but she by-passed us and got close to Emile Barco. We didn't know they were related. That's how she became his eyes and ears. Surprised? I guess you never knew either, huh, old buddy?"

"No," I corrected him. "I knew. But I thought Eva went to Paris to marry Henry."

"Wrong, Max. My wife screwed us over. She never came to Paris to marry Henry. She knew he was dead. She came to give me a hard time."

"Damn!"

"You know, Max. You were always a damn pain in the ass. So was Colleen and we did try to get her disinherited years ago, but killing you was never on my mind even though you destroyed my manhood. The thing I don't get is why Barco had it in for you. Emile wants you dead in the worst way and it has nothing to do with the Blue Danube."

"I'm getting the picture, Colin, and I think I know. But since you and I are playing 'show and tell,' where's Johnny Cork?"

"Try Barco's place. We used his name on fake passports so my guys could travel internationally without always using their own names. He's clean. All he did was to give Haussmann bad pills that he didn't know about. He's sick and dying but I'm not ready to pull his plug just yet. You should leave him alone."

"Why, Colin?"

"He's the only friend I have. We're lovers."

I should have been shocked but the fact is that I was not surprised and not disappointed. I wondered if, in his shoes, I would have been that loyal.

Colin put his hands on his belt and I knew this casual encounter was over.

"What's your next move?" he asked. "You know I have to kill you, now."

I walked away from the window and stood in front of him.

"I'm going to let you make the move, old buddy."

Colin needed no urging. His eyes followed mine as his right hand slowly reached for the inside of his jacket. A gun appeared in his hand but I was faster. I drew Bill Ford's weapon and fired one shot.

Colin simply looked at me, smiled, and squeezed the trigger of his weapon twice. I heard two clicks.

"Bang, Bang," he said slowly, a smile still on his face.

His body swayed, sagged and fell to the floor.

Colin was dead and I had shot him. It turned out that the two weapons were of the same caliber and could accept the same bullets. Thus, the way out of my dilemma was easy. I wiped my prints off Bill's gun, placed it in his hand and took Colin's which I loaded and pocketed. A suicide, I hoped the police would declare, although granted that folks rarely shot themselves in the chest or heart. But, switching guns was worth a try. At least it would give me running time.

I was about to leave when the waiter stuck his head in the room.

"I heard a noise. Is it over?"

"Yes, it's over. Monsieur Adair has killed himself."

"An excellent story. Shall I call the police?"

"Yes. Incidentally, did we not meet at Troy's in New Jersey?"

"Oui, monsieur. I was the waiter."

"You work for Barco?"

"Oui, monsieur. I have always worked for him. He pays well and I work well. I was the customs officer at the airport who helped an old man working at Maison Dore smuggle in an important diamond."

"Where is it now?"

The waiter stared hungrily at the money.

"At the Barco estate."

"Not so fast. Did the old man at the airport have a name?"

"Yes. Gaspard Lancet."

"Do you have any instructions for me?"

"Oui, monsieur. You are to meet my boss at his estate."

30

The Barco Estate

A thick fog filled the Sologne forest when I reached the Barco estate. I have no idea how I found the place but it was almost as if I had been there before. A winding gravel path lead around a marsh and ended in a clearing near a small stone house hidden from view by pine tress. It must have at one time been a gate house but now it appeared in disrepair. I parked the car off the road and carefully approached the house.

The front door was unlocked and the place was unlit. The windows were closed and the air was heavy and stifling from the stagnant smell of dirt and sweat. I found a switch, flipped it and found myself in a kitchen from where sounds from a television could be heard from another room. I tiptoed over creaky floors in the direction of the noise until I caught a flickering light from an partially open door. A voice inside was begging for water.

Throwing the door open I walked in, flicking a light switch on the wall. A black and white television set shared a dresser top with a half empty bottle of cheap cognac and an empty oxygen tank lay on the floor. A dust covered ventilator and compressor lay in a corner, their hoses lying on the floor like so many dismembered tentacles. A grimy bathroom was off to one side and another door lead to the rear and two grease stained plastic chairs flanked a rusted hospital bed. There on the urine stained mattress, in unwashed pajamas, lay what was left of John Cork.

He was a living skeleton covered with gray skin inflamed by lesions and sores. Eyeballs sunken in an emaciated head followed my movements around the room. Broken tubes ran from his nose and mouth to his chest and ended there. The stench from rotting flesh and putrefying feces combined with the stale air made me gag.

My eyes filled with tears and when I recovered, a nagging pain filled my heart and I had to gasp for breath and place one hand on the grimy wall for support. I recovered my balance and removed the tubes from John's nose.

"I've got to get you to a hospital," I blurted out.

John Cork shook his head slowly and stuck a bony hand up in the air and grabbed my arm. He reminded me of Carl Haussmann's final moments and I shuddered with fear.

"I'm not leaving here, Max," he whispered. He dropped his grip on my arm and pointed to his chest. "You have a gun, Max, do it. Do it now!"

"I don't have a gun," I lied.

"Then strangle me. Do something."

"You traveled with Carl Haussmann, didn't you?" I asked.

The dying man nodded.

"I thought it was a good idea. Some doctor paid me to go with some pills to make sure he took them for his diabetes. I thought I was doing a good thing."

"Damn, Johnnie. Those pills killed him."

"I know that now," John Cork said. "I didn't know it then. There's a load of them pills floating around."

He propped himself up on the cot and asked for water.

I found a glass in the bathroom, filled it with brownish water from the sink and returned with it to John who gulped down its contents without taking a breath.

"Tell me, Johnny," I asked. "How did you end up here?"

"Colin brought me here with some frog. He said Henry was coming to see me but he never came. Where's Henry? Where's Colin? He's the one who got me into this."

"Colin and Henry are gone, John, and the frog is on the way, most likely to kill us. We have to talk."

"Fuck you," said John Cork defiantly. "Where's Eva? She'll help me."

"Eva is dead also."

I pulled a chair up next to the cot and sat down. A half empty pack of cigarettes was on the other chair. I fished one out and lit it.

"Why don't we just relax, John? Smoke?"

He smiled.

"Man. I'm dying for one."

I wanted to laugh. Instead I inserted the cigarette between his dry lips and he started puffing away.

"This will help you relax. How about a drink?"

He pointed with a long, bone thin finger.

"On the table, there."

I brought the cognac over and gave it to Cork who promptly twisted off the cap with his long bony fingers and took a deep swig. He smiled broadly now but also started coughing up blood.

"Take it easy," I said. "Take it easy. You can keep the booze."

He began to relax.

"Tell me, Johnny," I asked. "What was between you and Colin?"

John Cork emitted a weak howl of a laugh.

"That's a good one, Max."

"I don't understand."

"I've worked for the Adairs since getting out of the army. I'm Colin's runner and lover. How do you think I stay alive. How do you think I get my booze?"

"You have AIDS, don't you, old chum?" I ventured.

"Yeah, I have AIDS," John repeated. "But I'm not sure who I got it from, Colin or Henry or someone else."

"How about Haussmann? Was he gay?"

John nodded.

"So was his partner, that Dore guy. And that fucking frog who owns this place. He's the real queen."

He chuckled weakly in between his sobs.

"The queen of spades!"

"I'm trying to piece together an old story, John. That thing many years ago when Patrick killed his wife and then himself. You and Colin were there when it happened. Was there anyone else?"

His eyes widened for the first time.

"I have to level with you, Max. It was a double murder."

"Colin murdered them?"

Johnny Cork shook his head.

"No way, man. Eva did the killing and she's been blackmailing Colin ever since."

Johnny Cork, with one short statement, had finished the saga of the Adair family by confirming Colin's account of the episode.

"I'm glad you're here, Max. I don't want to die alone."

Johnny was sinking fast.

"Where's the Blue Danube?" I asked.

Johnny Cork closed his eyes and a strange almost triumphant smile came over his worn face. He whispered and pointed through his body.

"It's under your feet, Max."

A shot rang out and Johnny Cork fell back. He was dead before his head hit the pillow and in through the doorway walked Marcel Jouvet, shotgun under one arm. Behind him was Otto Katz.

Jouvet pointed the shotgun at my chest.

"Ah, Max. We meet again. Allow me to introduce myself properly. I am Marcel Jouvet, deputy minister of the ministry of Justice. I am also Emile Barco, good citizen and inspector of the Basse Terre water works."

The unexplainable was now so obvious. Marcel Jouvet and Emile Barco were one and the same.

Jouvet seemed different now. Slightly disheveled, hair out of place, open collared, his eyes were glazed and his voice was high pitched and strained. He looked slightly mad. He glanced down at Johnny's wasted body and shook his head in mock chagrin.

"What a pity poor monsieur Cork will be unable to share our good fortune. And what a pity you never accepted my offer which of course I now revoke."

"Why did you keep him alive in the first place?"

"Moi? It was not my decision. He was a special friend of the Adairs. They did not want to kill him. But now that the last of the Adairs has died, there was no need for your John Cork to continue living. But I congratulate you, my dear Max. You are a tough bird to bring down. Now lay your gun slowly on the bed."

A revolver was no match for a shotgun. I carefully placed the revolver next to Johnny Cork's body.

"You must have come here with a friend," said Otto. "You would be a fool to come alone. Who was it?"

"I don't know, Otto. I thought I had friends but now I see I have none."

"I was a friend, Max. I saved your life once, but I could not do it again."

"You're not a Dutchman, are you, Otto? You're a German. You were the soldier in that ambush during the war. Why the act all these years?"

Otto stared at the floor.

"I had nothing against you, Max," he said. "I could not kill a small boy."

Jouvet snickered.

"Otto always had a soft spot. Letting you to live was almost my undoing. You have plagued me ever since."

I understood perfectly now. It was as La Salle said. Emile Barco's brother was the German officer who married my mother and Otto Katz was a foot soldier in his unit.

"It's not the Blue Danube diamond at all that you're all worked up about, is it, Jouvet, or Emile or whatever you call yourself in your sleep? It's the land we're standing on, isn't it? My mother died and the land went to your brother and from him it went to you. I own this real estate and you want to hang on to it. That's the real issue, isn't it?"

"Right, Max. The diamond does not interest me as much as this land. It is legally mine; I have paid the taxes and expenses all these years and almost went broke. Do you really think that I would allow scum like you to steal this property away from me? No. I have a good name and reputation and will not stand to have them destroyed by the likes of you."

"Why the double life, Emile? Why the charade?"

"I invented the name, Marcel Jouvet, to advance my political career since it would have been difficult to do so as the brother of a German officer. It was my lucky break that I had a cousin in your country who could keep an eye on you and report back to me. What a pity she died. I hear you killed her. But no matter, I have other cousins."

I had to stall for time.

"Were Otto and Gaspard cousins too?" I asked.

"Close associates, Max. Otto came to me after the war looking for work. I gave him a job when he informed me that your mother had a child who was alive in America. As you grew to adulthood, he befriended you in order to keep tabs on your activities. As did your good friend, Pierre La Salle."

Blood drained from my head.

"Pierre?"

Pierre La Salle appeared from the shadows, trim and proper as usual, and made a fast mock curtsey.

"At your service, Max."

Jouvet smiled triumphantly as he explained.

"You see, Max. This trap was laid out years ago but it could not have done without Pierre."

The only thing I could of was how my daughter and her family was doing. Were they being held captive somewhere? Were they dead? Pierre La Salle. This was the ultimate betrayal and I was the ultimate fool.

"It is too bad you had to show up in my life, Max," said Jouvet. "It is an unfortunate conspiracy of unrelated circumstances. And now I assume you would like to see the Blue Danube."

"It's my dying wish," I replied sarcastically.

"Well, it is here, under our feet. Monsieur Katz. Lead the way."

Otto went first with me following. Jouvet brought up the rear. He led us through a trap door in back of the house down to a brightly lit tunnel that descended steeply into the hard rock under Basse Terre's water table.

"Tell me, Otto," I asked said as I walked behind him. "When did you turn against me?"

Otto sneered.

"I was never for you. You ruined my gig in Belgium. I ran the smuggling ring for Kumari and Dore. Did you think your promise of immunity from prosecution would ever make up for my loss of income? You were stupid to think I would cooperate for so little. The world does not work that way. And that idea of stealing the Blue Danube. That could never happen because the stone had already been removed. I went along for the show. But I miss poor Joe Kelly who had to be killed to keep his silence. My true allegiance is to Barco who has promised me a share of the diamond."

After about ten minutes, the tunnel leveled off and ended at the entrance of a huge amphitheater facing a deep open pit that extended the entire width of the cavernous chamber. Stadium lamps in the domed ceiling bathed the vast hall with a soft pastel glow and from the open pit radiated a shadowy amber light that flickered in synch with the churning sound of machines somewhere in its depths.

Waiting for us at the entrance was Gaspard Lancet.

"We are here," Jouvet informed us. "And here is my other trump card."

"What's here?" I asked.

"Part of Basse Terre's water management and sewer treatment system."

Jouvet went on.

"Centuries ago, the Inquisition had a fortress above us. This was a torture chamber for the condemned. Here, were disemboweled and then drawn and quartered or slow fried in boiling oil. Finally when they died, their body parts were tossed into this open pit which was called an oubliette. Those who died were lucky. Those who were still breathing were tossed into the tunnels to be devoured by dogs in search of food."

"We are descended from a fine race of human beings, aren't we?" I noted.

Jouvet shrugged.

"Does it matter? Here is where the Blue Danube rests."

"What's in the pit?" I asked in an effort to stall for time.

"A giant macerator," Jouvet replied. "The oubliette was a mass grave until two hundred years ago when all the remains were shipped to the catacombs to make way for a hydraulic grist mill to macerate garbage from the government buildings in Paris. My job here as Emile Barco is to periodically inspect the works. It is basically a no-show job. The mill is still in operation. Listen. You can hear the pumps and grinding wheels."

And sure enough, the muffled hissing sound from what seemed to be the synchronized action of bellows and pumps in juxtaposition with the meshing of grinding gears and teeth could be heard from where we stood. It was an ancient pump and grinder in action.

"The Blue Danube diamond is hidden in a recessed ledge on the wall of the pit under our feet. Would you like to see it?"

"I can hardly wait."

Jouvet turned to Pierre La Salle.

"And Pierre. You have secured the conflict diamonds?"

"We will, minister. Stan Short agreed to their release. I have the official and original airway bill. We are to deliver the Blue Danube to him on Bastille Day."

"And where is that wonderful airway bill?"

"It is well hidden, sir."

Jouvet grunted and pointed the shotgun at Gaspard.

"Go get the diamond."

Sweating heavily, the old man knelt down at the edge of the pit and reached down. After fumbling for a few moments, he found a box and retrieved it.

"Now, give it to Otto," commanded Jouvet.

Gaspard surrendered the box and stood dumbly with his hands at his side and his back to the pit.

"Thank you, Gaspard," said Jouvet. "What a shame you have outlived your usefulness."

The deputy minister discharged a round from one of the two barrels of the shotgun into his chest.

Gaspard stared at the gaping hole in his mid section where his stomach once was. He teetered on the edge of the pit and fell into foamy brine below where he was caught screaming by the giant macerator's jaws and impaled on its grinding teeth. Otto and I watched speechlessly as his body was diced and sliced, giving Jouvet the breather he needed to reload.

"Open the box, Otto," he ordered.

Otto hesitated.

"Open it!" Jouvet demanded again, this time in a much louder, high pitched voice.

Otto wasted no more time. He fumbled with the lid for a while and finally worked it loose. His eyes were popeyed with bewilderment when he looked inside the box. The bluish gemstone inside was indeed beautiful to behold. But something was wrong. Even in the artificial light, its brilliance should have radiated. The stone had sheen but no sparkle. It was lifeless.

"It is nothing but glass!" Otto announced. "It is a fake!"

A glint appeared in Jouvet's eyes and he beckoned with his free hand.

"Give it here, Otto!"

Otto threw him the box and Jouvet fired another shotgun round that blew off his head, knocking it and his body into the pit.

I burst out laughing.

"Isn't that something, Emile? It's worthless."

I clammed up when I found the shotgun aimed at my chest.

"Shut your mouth, Max," Jouvet sneered. "I know it is a fake."

"You do? I don't understand."

"History, Max. History. I am a much better history scholar than you are a student. There never was a real Blue Danube diamond. There was never any proof as to the diamond's origin. There was merely a legend based on a story told by a sultan who was a Kumari ancestor."

"You're kidding."

"No. That giant diamond, the Great Mogul, that was supposedly the Blue Danube's ancestor, is as real as that pot of gold at the end of the rainbow. It was never actually seen. And you know that, Max."

"But experts have testified to its existence," I countered.

"Wishful thinking. Those were uncorroborated sightings, like UFO's. The Great Mogul is said to have weighed two hundred seventy nine carats. If the rock existed, it would have been too big to hide."

"What about French soldier who saw it?"

"He was lying. He claimed he saw it, but no one else did. How come?"

"Are you saying that the sultan who got his sons back from the French in exchange for the Blue Danube passed a phony?"

"Exactly, Max. There's no proof the Great Mogul was cut into two perfect stones with one of them being the Blue Danube. The sultan had the diamond made of glass to fool the French. The Blue Danube diamond never existed. It was a clever hoax invented a long time ago by an ingenious sultan to save the lives of his sons. The myth has been perpetuated ever since."

I was still in doubt.

"There was no Great Mogul and there is no Blue Danube. If there was a Blue Danube, then somewhere in the world would be its double. Answer me this, Max. Where is it?"

"If what you say is true, why did you go along with the hoax?"

"Ah, my friend. You underestimate me. A fake is as good as real. It has created a fortune and a legacy for the Adairs. It will do so for me. The world need not know the truth. But this land around us is real and I own it. And if your government wants the Blue Danube, we will deliver it. That is why you must die. With you gone, the secret of the Blue Danube will die with you, the land will stay with me, and the conflict diamonds will belong to Pierre and I."

"Did the Adairs know that the diamond was a phony?"

"No. They were true believers."

"Otto saw the diamond in Morristown while I was in Belgium," I reminded him.

"No. He never did. He only swore on the affidavits that he did. He was too lazy to thoroughly examine the diamond. But you, my dear cynic, would have eventually caught on. The diamond's true nature had to be concealed. A real examination would have been fatal. That is why it was removed to France, to preserve the myth of reality."

"Marcel Jouvet by day and Emile Barco by night. That's neat. Was Colin a satisfactory replacement for Henry after he died? I heard that he too was tuti fruti"

Jouvet's face turned crimson with rage.

"I should shoot you like a dog," he screamed.

"Why Marcel? Because you're a fraud protecting a fake?"

"The world is too stupid to appreciate the truth."

"The truth?" I laughed. "The Blue Danube and the legitimate ownership of this land are not the truths you're hiding, Emile. They can survive the truth. The truth is that you're a flaming homosexual covering for a phony gemstone! The exposure would ruin your career and blow your cover. The truth is that you're a crazy old fag who'll never figure out what to do with that thing between your legs before it falls off. You'll die alone with a fake diamond on land you don't own. And as for you, Pierre, you're the ultimate Judas. "You would kill off my entire family with Nicole, her son, and Christine for money."

The deputy minister stepped forward and yelled.

"Hands over your head!"

I raised my hands but he kept yelling.

"Higher, Max! Higher!"

Pierre La Salle stepped forward and jabbed a sharp object into my arm and I passed out.

31

Journey's End

I always thought the expression "may your life be joyous" made no sense. Dying happily was more important than living well. In my case, I came to the conclusion that I was unhappy. I lived well, but I was unhappy about never having experienced the full range of human emotions. Life was flat. It had no feeling or depth. It was a comic book of captioned cartoons on pulp paper that flaked and turned brown and crumbled to dust. My footprints, if they existed, were invisible. What was worse, I had failed Janine and lost my entire family over really nothing that important that anyone had to die for it.

Everything was catching up and pressing on my mind. Maybe it was those demons that I never recognized in life who were now dancing at my feet. Did I hate Jouvet because he was gay? Is that why I hated the Adair twins? Did I hate the friends who had deceived me over a lifetime? Most were dead and could no longer be hated. And yet their duplicity bothered me still.

However, in retrospect they were perhaps merely doing what they felt they had to do to survive in their own version of the world we shared. We could all get along but in the end we had to meet and fight and die. George Lerman, the philosophical hit man said it all. We were all jungle animals in a truce but never at peace.

Right now, nothing mattered but my own survival. I hated to ask, but was I finally checkmated?

I had to get out of the fix I was in and time was running out. The priest left at the end of the afternoon, leaving me to weigh my fate. The sun was still high in the sky and its rays sharpened the shadows cast by the window bars and cut the dull, grayish yellow light in the cell into angular sections that made the room appear off balance. Death for me in Jouvet's mind was a certainty.

Night fell and a low wattage bulb went on in the ceiling above the door. A short time later, two hooded guards, one short and one tall, came in with a dinner of lamb chops and vintage champagne. With my profuse thanks I said I was content and refused the meal. The tall jailor was friendly enough and said they were filling in for the regular guards who were on strike.

"Strike?"

The taller one nodded and answered in a muffled voice.

"All city employees are staging a one day work stoppage to force the government to pay them double for working holidays."

The short jailer asked if there was anything else I needed.

I laughed.

"A pass key," I replied.

They laughed with me and we unanimously agreed that it was a good joke.

They left the meal and the champagne anyway and went off.

I did eat the food and drink the champagne and even tried to sleep but the constant banging of a door and a scratching and scraping outside kept me awake. At last, the door slammed shut with a resounding clang. Suddenly I recalled the source of the sound I heard many years ago. It was exactly as Pierre La Salle had reconstructed the scene.

I was at a railroad station where I was standing with my mother waiting for a train to take my father north to Le Havre where he had booked a berth for himself on a vessel to New York. The Germans were in Paris and those who had visas were leaving every which way they could. My father had a visa and could leave. The plan was to send for us later but that never happened.

The railroad station was a cavernous iron and steel beamed structure built in the era of the Eiffel Tower. It had a high domed ceiling with glass panels to admit light into the bustling waiting room. There, apprehensive travelers anxiously watched an iron grated portcullis that rose when a train departure was announced on a mechanical board or nervously fixed their gazes on the great clock in the center of the room and embraced in tearful farewells when boarding calls were announced.

The vertical gate was usually closed, to deny access to the tracks when the crowds grew too large and unruly. Stone gargoyles perched on the sides of the glass domed ceiling glared down at the pulsating mass of humanity that huddled and waited the long trains pulled by shiny black steam locomotives destined for Channel ports to the north and west.

The call for my father's train was made; he gave us one last hug, picked up his bags and ran for the gate. Moments later it shut with a resounding clang and I never saw him again. Thinking it over I decided that my parents were not so bad after all. They just ran out of luck, like the millions of others who had their lives cut short. We might have been better off staying together as a family.

Who knows. Sometimes in life we do not always make the best decisions. But it didn't matter. It was over. Afterthoughts are too late and I dropped off to sleep.

I entered a dream world where a military band was assembled in front of a tall guillotine and started playing the Marseillaise, France's national anthem. I always liked the tune and its lyrics. It was a call to arms that stirred up the adrenalin. The anthem's fierce fighting words were considerably tamed from the time they were written during the French Revolution's reign of terror.

"Alons infants de la patrie, Le jour de gloire est arrivee." Come, children of the nation, The day of glory is here!

And it went on this way until the climatic refrain was reached..."Marchons mes citoyens! Formee vos battalions! Marchons, Marchons!" March on, citizens! Form your battalions! March on, March on!...

The refrain ended with a noise at the door. It opened wide and in walked Simon Perez and several hooded men.

"Get up, Max. We're leaving."

Was this the cavalry to the rescue?

I never stopped to ask questions. Springing to my feet I followed them out the cell and down the corridor to an old rusted door. It opened and I found myself on Rue Cabon behind the prison where a black limousine was parked and waiting.

We climbed into the limo where Simon Perez was behind the wheel.

"Where are we going, Soimon?"

He did not reply. We drove around the block to Place Vendome. It was the early morning of Bastille Day and crowds of people should have begun gathering for the parade and city wide festivities but the great square was strangely gray and quiet.

Perhaps it was too early, but there was something odd about the building facades. They were crumbling and breaking up with some of them simply disappearing into an amber haze. Was madness overtaking me? Was it a bad dream? But I was awake and could feel the limo's tires bounce over on the old cobblestones of the French Revolution.

I settled back in my seat and saw my daughter, Janine, sitting in a jump seat next to Nicole Colbert, facing me.

"Hello, dad. Is this the way you spend your vacations?"

The driver in the front seat turned around and threw me a wide grin.

"You owe me a fishing trip, Max."

Simon Perez was no longer there. It was Felix Stiles. Someone was in the front passenger seat but his back was turned and I could not see the face.

I tried to make conversation. How could an elaborate rescue scheme like this have been so well and so quickly choreographed?

"We had to move with lightening speed," Simon Perez was saying, waving his hands for emphasis. Now, he was seated next to me.

"Interpol is always prepared, Max, even with traitors in our midst."

And as Simon kept talking and talking, somewhere in the distance I fancied I heard a respirator.

"And of course there was the sensor. That was a big help. And you would be dead without George."

"George?"

He went on and on and on.

"The rest was easy. As you say in America, everything else was history. But now time was of the essence. Only a few days remained until Bastille Day. I wanted very much to mount a rescue mission. But how was that to be done? I knew Nicole's son. He had just returned for the long holiday and I told him our problem. He said we could infiltrate the ministry which would be on a short shift and mimic an execution with his theater troupe…"

Simon kept talking. I kept listening, but his voice was growing deeper and slower and harder to follow. At times, street noises drowned him out. A work crew with jack hammers powered by several compressors and generators created a deafening roar as we drove by.

And he droned on.

"The real challenge was getting foreigners with knowledge of French, of France and of the ways of the French, to coalesce as an integrated theatrical team. And of course they had to learn the language. But something amazes me, Max."

"What's that?"

"When you were delirious and thought it was over, you sent your love to your wife. I thought she was dead, Max. You said she was dead."

Shapes blurred and began dissolving, melting away into a thick brown smog seeping into the limousine. The vehicle stopped and I heard over the background noise the pistons of its powerful engine thumping up and down in synch with my heartbeat. The door next to me opened and I could see the vague outline of the city's gothic buildings silhouetted against a dreary pale yellow sky. A bright white light made my eyes tear and squint. A voice in the distance commanded.

"Raise your arm over your head, Max!"

I raised my arm.

"Higher, Max!"

The passenger seated in front next to Felix Stiles turned around. "Listen to the doctor, Max."

It was Brian Donovan.

"Raise your arm!"

Everyone vanished and Mike Surrey poked his head into the window.

"Hi, Max! Don't worry about Evie. She really loves you. So raise your arm higher, Max. Your life depends on it."

"Higher, Max. Higher!

A crushing pressure gripped my chest, the limo door slammed shut and the light went out.

A hand was on my chest and a light was blinding me. I rubbed my bleary eyes and slowly recovered my senses. I should have stayed with the dream.

The cell door opened and Jouvet, in a blue suit and starched white cuff linked shirt, walked in hugging the box with the Blue Danube under his arm.

"You must forgive us, Max," he said. "Our dedicated public servants have gone on strike. But do not worry. I have asked La Salle to assemble a cohort of standby personnel. There has been a trial last night; you were found guilty and I have signed your death warrant. This execution will go forward."

He definitely looked crazed, his mouth was on the verge of drooling and I wondered how much longer he would be able to hide his insanity behind the position of deputy justice minister before cracking like a nut. Of course, I would be dead before the world found out. Good for the world; not so good for me.

The two hooded guards who brought me dinner followed him in with more guards in black ski masks and hooded gowns over black booted parachute outfits. One carried a shroud, a small black string bag and a plastic body bag. A second held a medical bag. Both wore holstered machine pistols strapped to gun belts around their waists. A third guard was very tall and broad. I guessed he was to be my executioner. The others stood outside the cell door. From the courtyard I heard the scuffle of feet and the muttering of voices. The guillotine was being readied.

The two guards suddenly turned on him. The taller one pulled a gun and pressed it against Jouvet's head. The shorter one grabbed the deputy minister from the rear while a third with a medical bag took out a hypodermic needle and plunged it into Jouvet's neck. The deputy minister collapsed and they eased him on to the bed, the very tall and broad guard catching the box that Jouvet dropped.

It was bewildering and incomprehensible. But whatever it was, the cavalry had really come for real this time, or so I hoped at the very least.

The masquerade was over and the hoods and ski masks came off. It was Simon Perez who tackled Jouvet and La Salle who injected him, and it was Tom Lyons, who I never thought was in Paris, who caught the box that held the Blue Danube diamond and passed it to no other' than Jake Santana who looked at his shorter partner and asked, "Should I hold this for you, Stan?"

"You do that, Jake," said Stan Short. "You're the only one I can trust in this place."

"I don't want the responsibility," said Jake. "I'm giving it to La Salle."

Pierre nodded, took the box and cradled it under his arm. Stan simply grunted.

Damn! I was totally confused.

La Salle was all business. He knelt down, took Jouvet's pulse and looked up at us.

"Dead! The poor man had a heart attack."

He jumped up and started barking orders.

"Place him on the bed and take off his clothes," he commanded, checking the time on his watch.

"You too, Max. Take off your clothes and change with Jouvet."

The priest waved.

"Hurry, Max. We have a show to put on."

I rubbed my eyes.

"Damn!"

The other two guards stood at the door while I frantically changed clothes with the deputy minister.

"Who are you?" I asked, panting while I struggled into Jouvet's pants.

"We have no time for proper introductions, Max," the priest replied. "You will know everything if we survive this adventure. We are all friends."

"We are?"

"You have good friends in low places," said Pierre. "Although I know you do not deserve this attention."

"But how...?"

"Not now, Max," he cautioned. "If we do not rush, there will be no later explanations. Let me just say that you are not the only one who knows the city's under belly. Hurry! We must go."

"Pierre," I started to say. "I must apologize for my outburst yesterday. I never thought..."

La Salle placed a finger over my lips.

"Later, Max. Let me just say that your outburst worked and made me more believable to the minister."

Marcel Jouvet, now in my clothes, seemed to be smiling, as if enjoying this last piece of deception. He was stretched out and the shroud was loosely drawn around him.

"What a loss," La Salle said to the dead justice minister, "France will miss you, Marcel. But do not worry about your replacement. You may rest easy. The French Republic will find you a worthy successor."

"Right on time!" La Salle said. "You are the spitting image of the deputy minister, Max. I am pleased."

He turned to the priest. "Michel. We need your makeup skills."

I looked up.

"You're Nicole's son, the actor," I said.

The priest grinned.

"Yes, Max. I always wanted to meet my father and the man my mother never forgot. Now I have."

Michel took cosmetic cream and powder from his pockets and worked his magic on my face.

"And I am glad I did," he continued. "You are everything my mother said you would be."

"Are you disappointed?"

"I am saving your life, am I not?"

Pierre checked his watch again.

"We are now going to walk out into the compound. A replacement crew is on shift so you will not be recognized in the semi-darkness. You keep shut and pretend to have a sore throat. I will do the talking. The soldier who was going to act as your executioner took ill and is away. Your friend Tom Lyons will cut the cord to the guillotine with George Lerman's assistance at your signal."

"George is here?"

"Yes. We will his pilot's license and his experience flying jets."

"Who is being guillotined?"

"It is Ed Houston's corpse. He will serve us one more time." One of the guards nodded his hooded head in my direction.

"Listen carefully, Max," said Pierre. "The cord will be cut while the band strikes up our national anthem. When the job is done, we return with the body to the cell. Everyone will disappear except for us. We will walk to a limo in the ministry's main courtyard and drive away like two honored dignitaries."

"How will they disappear?" I asked.

La Salle pointed to the floor.

"The sewers, mon ami. I told you before. You are not alone. We too know how to run like rats."

We left the cell slowly. Outside on the ground was an open hole partially covered by an iron lid. So that was the noise I heard during the night. While I was trying to sleep, the lid was being pried loose.

32

Exodus

Leaving Jouvet's body in the cell, we began the solemn procession. We entered the courtyard in the half light and marched to the beat of a martial tune and a call to colors played by a band flanked by a squad of military police standing at attention.

"National police," Pierre motioned.

"They shoot first and listen later. But most are on vacation. The rest belong to us. Ed Houston's body is already in place."

In front of them stood the guillotine, towering over us against the thick gray clouds in the dawn sky. An empty wheeled stretcher waited patiently next to the silent killing machine. Ed's body lay with its head in the cutting slot, facing the wicker basket on the ground.

Not a single word was exchanged. Two soldiers in front of the guillotine smartly presented arms. La Salle saluted. I followed suit and they returned to attention.

No cues were missed. An attendant nearby held a string bag, opened it wide and placed it carefully into the basket.

I noticed that the band's conductor had his eye on me. La Salle nudged me and I raised my arm.

He poked me again and my arm went up again. The guard who was nearest to the guillotine cut the restraining rope and the massive blade thundered down and lopped off the body's head to a fast drum role cadence. It dropped neatly into the string bag inside the wicker basket with a dull thud.

The bag was quickly removed while Ed's headless body was placed on the stretcher that two guards began wheeling back to the prison with the rest of us marching slowly behind.

We returned to the cell where everyone removed their disguises.

"Allow me to introduce myself properly," said the priest.

"I am Michel Darcy, your son. And here are your friends and some of mine."

The other guards and some of the national police troops gathered around me in the cell.

"We are actors in Michel's theater group," one of them explained.

"We did some fast rehearsing for this occasion. We hope you appreciate it."

"I do. I do!" I exclaimed. "How can I ever repay my friends?"

"You will, Max. You will."

It was Tom Lyons, now in his usual blazer and tan slacks.

"Tom! How did you get here?"

The New Jersey detective grinned and pointed to Jake Santana and Stanley Short.

"They talked me into this, Max. It was a last minute and last ditch decision. Stan arranged for a charter jet. And let me tell you. This is costing us plenty. Old Stan here always collects."

"That's right," said Stan. "I have an investment to protect. I'm paying for this trip out of your fee."

"But the Blue Danube is a fake, Stan."

Stan Short held a finger to his lips.

"Yes. That's what I understand. But let's not tell the world that just yet, Max."

La Salle held up his hands.

"Gentlemen, we must go."

Jouvet's head and all the uniforms were thrown into the body bag with his body. Within seconds, every last man had disappeared through the hole outside the cell which La Salle and I covered with the heavy lid, spreading dirt and dust over it to make it appear untouched.

"What now?" I asked.

"Everyone will follow Michel. He knows the way to an incinerator not far from the Opera. They will dispose of everything there before dispersing. Michel will catch a commercial flight to the islands. All the others will take separate flights to different destinations. As far as you and I are concerned, my friend, we leave here together. George Lerman is waiting for us with a private jet at the airport."

"There is no Blue Danube, Pierre. And soon questions will flow like wine. Have you a plan?"

Pierre La Salle smiled mysteriously. He placed an arm under mine and we walked casually to the waiting limousine.

"It is a fake, but what a fabulous fake it is. It has created fortunes. It can do so again."

"So, what do we do?"

"Our candles here are spent, Max, and it is time to extinguish the flames. I have been speaking with Lyons, Santana and Stanley Short. They are in the same boat I am. Their careers are over. We thought that you might want to join us in a new business venture."

"What and where?"

"A chain of fine jewelry stores in the Caribbean. Perhaps, this new enterprise can be based in the French West Indies where Christine and Nicole are waiting for us, as is your daughter and family. You know, old friend, you too should think of retiring to the West Indies. The climate is glorious, the cuisine is superb and our women are beautiful."

What a crazy idea.

"Moreover, the laws are lax and the people are friendly. What do you think, Max?"

"What do we do for money?"

We stepped into the limo.

"We have several good cards to play. A vacancy exists for the position of deputy minister. By law, the interim position goes to me and I propose to take it. It will help us to protect our interests. Then, when this mess finally blows away, you should enforce your claim to the Basse Terre estate that rightfully belongs to you. And after a permanent minister is selected, I too will retire to the islands and join you in this venture.

And, as a final inducement for you, Max, I have the winning lottery number."

"What is that?"

"That special airway bill, number One Zero Seven. It is our claim check for all those wonderful conflict diamonds waiting in Belgium. Indeed. I propose that we make Belgium our first stop. I understand the cuisine in Brussels is wonderful."

"I guess life is good after all, Pierre," I said.

Pierre La Salle smiled.

"It is, Max. It is."

A guard at the gate gave the Interpol director a smart salute.

La Salle returned the salute with a hand flourish and we drove out of the justice ministry into Vendome where the holiday crowd was beginning to assemble under a bright blue sky. It was Bastille Day, and the day of glory had arrived.

*   *   *

The recorder stopped running and the young FBI agent sat silently for a long time, pondering the story he had just listened to on the tape. The shadows were longer and the sun, which had been high in the sky, was falling on the horizon beyond the lagoon with a fiery glow.

"I heard bits and pieces about the Blue Danube diamond," the young man said. "But this thing about the justice minister throws me. I thought that this Marcel Jouvet was a hero of the French Republic since he was just given a state funeral with full honors."

"Yes," Stan Short murmured. "Full honors right after Bastille Day. France could have done no less."

"And this Emile Barco. I heard he died by accidentally falling into a water treatment tank on one of his tours. Are you sure Max was not hallucinating or living in some sort of fantasy world?"

"My father was known to exaggerate things sometimes," Janine replied, smiling sadly.

"That's right," Jake Santana agreed. "Max did slant the truth on occasion. Both men certainly did great things for France and we truly don't want to soil their reputations. What do you think, Tom?"

Tom Lyons got up to stretch his legs.

"Janine and Jake are right. Much of what you heard on the tape should probably be discounted."

The FBI agent scratched his head.

"I understand that some guy named Simon Perez was just appointed to be an acting Interpol director in Pierre La Salle's temporary absence. Do any of you guys know him?"

Tom sat back down and they all shook their heads.

"I didn't think so. Now, what about Rajeesh Kumari? What happened to him?"

"Nothing," Stan Short replied. "I would imagine that he'll acquire Maison Dore and merge it with his business. He should be very happy. He always was."

"What about Sol Weinberg, the one with the cigar?"

Tom laughed.

"The schmegegi, as Max always called him? He'll do well no matter what. He now owns two insurance companies."

"And I suppose you all came here to meet the plane and join up with Max Gordon and Pierre La Salle who presumably have the Blue Danube and another bunch of diamonds with them?"

Janine started to cry again and Jake tried to calm her down.

"Now, see what you've done. That's an indelicate question, man," he said angrily. "So what if you're right? Does it matter now? Does anything matter now? Why don't you just take this tape and go back home and keep investigating?"

The FBI seemed puzzled by the sudden outburst.

"I don't think there's much to investigate unless some evidence materializes. You can keep the tape. My guess is that the Blue Danube and the conflict diamonds are somewhere at the bottom of the sea and will never be found. I therefore have nothing to report."

There was a noise outside the breakwater at that moment and a small trawler could be seen making its way into the lagoon. A salvage flag blew in the breeze from the top of one of its outriggers as it made its way to the dock near the house. A crew member jumped off and tied down the vessel.

Janine rose to her feet, followed by the others. They watched Barry Benson come out of the trawler's wheelhouse in his scuba diving outfit and walk to the bow where he stood silently and slowly shook his head. It was over.

The End

0-595-30471-0